A NEW LEASE OF LIFE

CELIA ANDERSON

B
Boldwood

First published in 2025 as *Onwards and Upwards*. This edition published in Great Britain in 2025 by Boldwood Books Ltd.

Copyright © Celia Anderson, 2025

Cover Design by Rachel Lawston

Cover Images: Rachel Lawston

The moral right of Celia Anderson to be identified as the author of this work has been asserted in accordance with the Copyright, Designs and Patents Act 1988.

All rights reserved. No part of this book may be reproduced in any form or by any electronic or mechanical means, including information storage and retrieval systems, without written permission from the author, except for the use of brief quotations in a book review. This book is a work of fiction and, except in the case of historical fact, any resemblance to actual persons, living or dead, is purely coincidental.

Every effort has been made to obtain the necessary permissions with reference to copyright material, both illustrative and quoted. We apologise for any omissions in this respect and will be pleased to make the appropriate acknowledgements in any future edition.

A CIP catalogue record for this book is available from the British Library.

Paperback ISBN 978-1-83617-145-4

Large Print ISBN 978-1-83617-146-1

Hardback ISBN 978-1-83617-144-7

Ebook ISBN 978-1-83617-147-8

Kindle ISBN 978-1-83617-148-5

Audio CD ISBN 978-1-83617-139-3

MP3 CD ISBN 978-1-83617-140-9

Digital audio download ISBN 978-1-83617-142-3

This book is printed on certified sustainable paper. Boldwood Books is dedicated to putting sustainability at the heart of our business. For more information please visit https://www.boldwoodbooks.com/about-us/sustainability/

Boldwood Books Ltd, 23 Bowerdean Street, London, SW6 3TN

www.boldwoodbooks.com

This one's for Ray

A thing of beauty is a joy forever.

— JOHN KEATS

On the other hand:

We all have a million things vying for our attention. If you tell yourself that you don't have enough time to clear out your junk, you might be delaying the wellbeing and relief you could experience by tackling it. If not now, when?

— LISA J. SHULTZ, *LIGHTER LIVING: DECLUTTER. ORGANIZE. SIMPLIFY*

PROLOGUE

The three ladies stood in a semi-circle on the pavement outside the deserted shop. They were in the autumn of their years, so to speak, but none of them looked as if they were ready to accept that fact. The smaller one pulled her camel coat around her ample bosom more firmly, glanced both ways along the empty street and then leaned forward to peer through the shop window.

'I can't see much,' she said in disgust. 'They've done that thing with the pink window-cleaning stuff so nobody can get a proper look in. I think it's empty.'

'Of course it's empty, you numpty,' said her friend, who was dressed as if for a jog, in a white shell suit and pink trainers. 'Sylvia Nightingale moved out months ago and she's not daft enough to leave anything behind for burglars, is she, Anthea?'

The third one of the group laughed. 'Not likely, darling. Sylvia never gave anything away when she had the shop up and running, so there's no way she'd let anyone come along and scoop up her leftovers, even if she didn't want them herself.

Come on, Beryl, we're not going to find out anything interesting here.'

Beryl sighed and stepped back. 'You're right. I just wanted to know what's going to happen to the building now, that's all. There's a decent flat upstairs with three good-sized bedrooms. It's a waste to have it all closed up and we really need a general store this end of the village. I was hoping someone would take the business on and liven it up a bit. You can't get a decent bottle of prosecco from that other place and anyway it's nearly a mile up the road. No good at all for our film nights.'

The three women turned their backs on the shop and, arm in arm, began to take a steady stroll across the green towards the pub. It was an idyllic scene, but they were all too used to it to take much notice, having been born and bred in Willowbrook. Although the day had been chilly, a brisk wind had blown the storm clouds away and the residents of Willowbrook were at last beginning to think that spring was really here. Now the evening sunshine illuminated the gang of children playing by the stream under the willow trees that gave the place its name and their yells and whoops filled the air. It was like a perfectly arranged film set. Winnie sniffed.

'Time that lot were in bed,' she said. 'My lads would have been tucked up by now at their age. How are their parents meant to have their own space, for... well... you know what I'm saying...' She waggled her eyebrows.

The other two chortled. It was clear they did indeed know.

'Maybe the old place is going to be one of those adult emporiums,' said Beryl, hopefully. 'We could do with a bit of oomph around here.'

'A sex shop, you mean?' Anthea pulled a face. 'We're all a bit broad in the beam to be squeezing ourselves into slinky undies.'

'You speak for yourself. A lot of men prefer something to hang on to,' said Winnie, giving the sort of laugh that belonged in a *Carry On* film.

'Chance'd be a fine thing. It's not so bad in some ways, having your freedom when you find yourself on your own again after years of being a couple,' said Beryl. 'But I don't half miss the hanky panky, don't you, girls?'

The other two nodded. 'We've not given up yet though, have we? Look at Anthea and her Maurice. I bet he wouldn't mind seeing you in some skimpies, would he?' said Winnie, with a sidelong glance that held more than a touch of envy.

Anthea pulled a face. 'No way. By the time I'd wriggled myself into anything like that, he'd probably have gone off the boil. No staying power, these older guys. I'm thinking of giving him the boot.'

They'd reached the far edge of the green by this time and paused to contemplate Beryl's suggestion further.

'Nah,' said Winnie eventually. 'A sex shop's out of the question. Sylvia would never allow that to happen. It'll probably be a cycle store or a discount place selling end-of-line stuff that nobody wants, or a greetings card shop or...'

'Enough of the gloom, you've made your point,' said Beryl, holding up a hand. 'No sex toys here. Mind you, all this talk about frisky business has made me thirsty. We're wasting time. It's your round, I think, Anthea. Let's get some fizz in the glasses. Those drinks won't pour themselves. Whatever the old shop turns out to be, I'm sure we'll soon find out.'

And as it happened, the three ladies didn't have very long to wait.

1

'Well, there you are, dear. The shop's all yours for the next few months. A year at the very most. That should be plenty long enough. I don't envy you, I'll tell you that for nothing.' Sylvia Nightingale gave one of her trademark sniffs and pursed her lips.

Ingrid took a deep breath of the dusty air, undisturbed for the last few weeks. It had lost most of the scents she remembered from the childhood visits to her aunt's general store, but it was just possible to catch a hint of lavender from the bunches that still hung over the door, dry and withered now. The shelves were bare apart from a trail of red lentils, a mouldy apple and one black school plimsoll lying on its side. She wondered what on earth had possessed her to come up with the idea of moving to Willowbrook. It would have been better to go with her original plan of buying a second-hand camper van and setting off on a real adventure.

'Oh, there's no need to look like that, I know it's a bit grim in here at the moment,' said Sylvia, sensing Ingrid's shudder. 'The cleaners will be here this afternoon and they'll leave everywhere spotless, or there'll be trouble. Useless lot. They were meant to come yesterday and do a full sweep of the place, but Dot was having trouble with her Willy.'

'Her... willie?'

Ingrid's mind began to conjure up pictures that she didn't want to see, but luckily Sylvia hadn't finished her explanation. 'Yes, you remember I told you that Dot and Willy run the local cleaning company? Well, the silly man only went and fell downstairs yesterday. Dot's had to call in some temporary help. So annoying.'

'Yes, I can see it would be, for him.'

'For all of us, not just for him. I said to her, I said, "Dot, has he been overdoing the brown ale again?" and she got quite huffy but apparently it was because he's recently had new glasses. Varifocals. Willy's not so agile these days. His legs play him up sometimes. He's just turned sixty.'

Sylvia stopped, as if this was quite enough of a reason to fall downstairs. Ingrid frowned. At fifty-two, her own eyesight was still spot on, and all her limbs were in excellent working order. She couldn't imagine going so far downhill in a handful of years, but she supposed the unfortunate Willy might not be in such great shape.

Seeming to follow her niece's train of thought, Sylvia looked Ingrid up and down. 'Of course, you've always looked after yourself, haven't you, dear? I suppose not having children, you had the spare hours to do the pampering. Face packs and the like. Willy and Dot have got six kiddies and a couple of grandchildren to keep them busy.'

Ingrid resisted pointing out that until fairly recently she'd worked full time, running a very successful chain of hotels and keeping house for a man whose larger-than-life character meant he loved to entertain and insisted on his wife accompanying him to various dinners and fund-raising events. Sylvia wouldn't be impressed by talk of high-powered careers. She'd kept this village shop and her family ticking over for years, with minimal help.

The two women made their way through the deserted shop and into a room at the back, Ingrid matching her pace to her aunt's ponderous progress. She thought about offering an arm for support, but Sylvia was managing quite well with her new walking stick now she'd at last given in to using it. They both paused to look around the storeroom, which was festooned with more dust and debris. Another door stood open to reveal a rudimentary kitchen and small cloakroom that finished off the downstairs space. Ingrid suppressed another shudder. She'd not thought this far ahead when she'd come up with the plan of taking over Sylvia's business premises for a short while. The draught blowing through the empty rooms was getting right into her bones, even though outside the shop, the late-March sunshine was doing its best to warm up the village.

'The upstairs flat is better than this,' said Sylvia encouragingly. 'I've left you most of my furniture and kitchen paraphernalia. I only really needed my favourite easy chair. Everything else is provided for us at Cedar Grove. I've got a view of the gardens and my own shower. They call it a wet room, which seems ridiculous, if you ask me. I mean, we all know you get wet in a shower. Anyway, it's very comfy, and the meals aren't bad at all.'

This was high praise from a woman who refused to countenance eating anything spicy, sloppy or too chewy. Breaking her hip had changed Sylvia's life entirely and she looked as if she was thriving on the new regime.

'Was it hard to leave this place, or had you had enough of shop life in the end?' Ingrid asked tentatively. Sylvia was notoriously easy to offend, although to be fair, she'd lost some of her spiky edge since the move.

'Oh, I'd definitely had enough, although I didn't realise how bored I was until I had that ridiculous fall. I suppose I've been lucky really. I've had part-time staff and Christopher and his family have popped in and out over the years when they weren't busy, but his wife wasn't keen to take it on permanently. And of course, our Lennie was never interested in the business. He's got bigger fish to fry.'

Sylvia sniffed loudly again and added an eyeroll for effect. 'Anyway, they all like living in the hustle and bustle of Meadowthorpe and they don't fancy village life. According to Christopher, everyone knows each other's business here in Willowbrook.'

'And do they?' Ingrid experienced a momentary wave of claustrophobia. Had she done the right thing coming here?

'Well, yes, I suppose they do but that's never bothered me. I like a good gossip as much as the next person and I'm not ashamed to admit it. While I think about it, Christopher and Veronica are in Marbella for a fortnight and then they're moving on to Cyprus, but Lennie said to tell you that he'd be glad to help you settle in if you need him. He said cousins should stick together and he'd drop in and see you tomorrow. I must admit that surprised me.'

Ingrid didn't answer. It surprised her too. Sylvia didn't seem to notice the lack of response.

'Of course, I love both my boys, you know I do, but Lennie hasn't been near the shop for months. Oh well, take help where you can get it, that's my advice.'

Ingrid felt a cold prickle of apprehension run down her spine at the thought of seeing Lennie Nightingale again after all this time. As children and teenagers, Lennie had spent most of their brief time together either pulling her blonde pigtails or trying to look up her skirt. He was two years her junior but had matured quickly, in some ways. It had soon been advisable to wear jeans for family gatherings and to avoid being anywhere alone with him. What happened at Christopher's eighteenth birthday party was best forgotten. Ingrid had been avoiding that memory ever since.

'I'm sure I'll be fine,' she said. 'The removal van's arriving later today, and the men will unload everything for me. It was good of you to recommend Joel and Sam. I'd much rather give the work to local people if I can. After that, it's just going to be a case of getting the shop ready and then everything needs to be sorted and labelled. I packed up my house in a hurry because the new people were keen to move in as soon as possible.'

Ingrid saw Sylvia hesitate at the foot of the staircase and decided to risk a rebuke rather than a tumble. She held out an arm and, relieved Sylvia was being sensible, helped her aunt up the stairs to the flat. They made their steady progress in silence, and for a brief time, Ingrid was at last able to concentrate on the matter in hand.

From the moment when she'd opened her eyes that morning, Ingrid's mind had been going back over the previous nightmare week. Since Tommy's death six months ago, her main aim had been to move out of their vast house on the swanky gated estate and find somewhere that was just the right size for one woman. Or more to the point, one woman with very few possessions. Her marriage was over, through no fault of her own, and she had no choice about moving, even if she'd wanted to stay. Several painful meetings with their solicitor and Tommy's financial advisor had made that clear. Ingrid wasn't sure how anyone could give out financial advice that resulted in such devastation, but maybe her husband had overruled the poor man, who wasn't the most dynamic of characters.

Thomas Winston Archibald Copperfield had been charming, witty and handsome in a rather bear-like way, and their marriage had worked. He'd not interfered with Ingrid's life so long as she agreed to dress up and be on his arm whenever he needed a trophy wife. Better than that, he'd given her endless encouragement to spread her wings and follow a career that had satisfied her completely. Until now. With the take-over of her beloved hotels and the loss of the man who cheered her on, not to mention the fact that he'd secretly managed to run up a staggeringly large amount of debt, Ingrid had wanted out. Out of the house, out of her job and right out of Yorkshire.

Pushing the memories away as they tried to slither back in, Ingrid negotiated the last few steps and let go of her aunt's arm. Sylvia was panting slightly from the effort of the stairs, but otherwise undaunted she opened the door to the apartment over the shop and ushered Ingrid in. Here, Ingrid could see that a few changes had been made in recent years. The main improvement was the removal of the swirly green and brown carpet that had covered the floors in the living room and bedrooms. In its place was smooth, ash-coloured laminate.

'So much easier to keep clean,' said Sylvia, seeing Ingrid glance around with obvious approval. 'Give the lad his due, Lennie did do that for me a couple of years ago. He's a good boy sometimes.'

Ingrid didn't reply. She wondered if she could arrange to be out when her cousin called. Her aunt had lowered herself onto the sofa now and was patting the cushion beside her.

'Come and sit here and tell me about your plans, dear,' she said. 'I still don't really understand why you only wanted the place for a short while. Mind you, that suits me down to the ground. It gives me a breathing space to decide whether to sell up or rent it out. There's always a chance that one of the boys will change their minds about taking the shop on.'

The plum-coloured sofa was more comfortable than it looked, and Ingrid settled into its softness with a sigh. She felt as if she hadn't had a proper rest for weeks.

'I'll be honest, I've been worried about you lately,' Sylvia said. 'You've had a strained look about you ever since your poor Tommy passed over. It's only natural, after all those years together.'

Ingrid considered the phrase *passed over*. It was one her own mother had always used to describe the end of life, but she couldn't really imagine her husband passing over anything. It sounded far too ethereal. He'd be more likely to blast his way through to the next world, singing lustily in his deep baritone voice and brandishing a whisky glass. That was the way he'd died, of course, in the middle of an impromptu karaoke session at their local diner. A massive stroke, as it turned out. It had caused quite a sensation when he demolished the salad bar on his way down.

'I guess I should have explained in more detail what I was going to do with the shop before this, but it's been a crazy few weeks. I've decided to use this place to get rid of all Tommy's possessions, and most of mine too,' Ingrid said.

'Really? Why on earth would you want to do that?'

Ingrid tried to come up with a simple way to explain the panic she felt when she'd looked around the crowded rooms of her old home and accepted that this was just the tip of the iceberg and there were so many more of Tommy's treasures boxed up in the garage and the loft.

'I just want a fresh start,' she said. 'Tommy was a compulsive hoarder, and he could never see how much I hated being surrounded by so much random... stuff. I need to make a clean sweep.'

Sylvia nodded thoughtfully. 'I can understand where you're coming from in a way because I've done exactly the same thing, but my bits and bobs were a lot less interesting than yours. The furniture's decent stuff but I didn't think you'd want the rest of it.'

Ingrid looked around at the few items that had escaped Sylvia's brutal cull. She could see a brass jug full of dried grasses, a large wall mirror that reflected the swaying willow trees on the village green opposite and a footstool embroidered with poppies. Gone were the two ornate pottery dogs that had graced the mantelpiece, and the pale porcelain Lladro figurines that had been such dust-gatherers. The plates that had hung on the wall had disappeared too, leaving ghostly marks, and the shelves that held her aunt's collection of much-loved romance novels were bare. Sylvia really had made a clean sweep.

'They weren't special to me, the things Tommy left behind. He never could resist bringing home auction lots that caught his eye,' said Ingrid.

'Ah yes, he was wedded to his work, that man of yours, wasn't he? A character, if ever I saw one. What a lovely man he was. Well-liked and very generous too. I'll always remember how he used to bring me the most magnificent boxes of chocolates from that fancy shop near his workplace on the odd times when you both visited.'

Ingrid nodded, unsure how to answer this without bad-mouthing Tommy. It was true that he'd been a great one for lavish gifts and also had the ability to chat at length to anyone and everyone he met. In addition to being a great raconteur and lover of fine food and wine, Tommy Copperfield was a natural-born auctioneer, and his work brought him huge satisfaction. Six feet five inches tall and built like an ox, his bushy red beard, bristling eyebrows and shiny bald head had all helped to make him a well-known figure in their hometown. Add in a beaming smile, and it was no wonder everybody loved him.

'There'd usually be a couple of interesting items in the crates, but the rest was tat,' Ingrid continued. 'The house and the garage were stuffed full of Tommy's junk, not to mention the boxes he'd squirrelled away in the loft without telling me. I want to sell it all off as soon as I can. It's time for big changes.'

'But where will you go after that? You loved that house and your life in it with Tommy... didn't you?'

Sylvia's words gave Ingrid the sudden, horrible shock that happened every time she let herself forget for a moment that Tommy had gone for good. He may have left her in a mess, but life still felt very strange and sad without him. She swallowed hard.

'Not as much as you'd think. This has been like one of those life-laundry programmes on TV. When I got down to the important stuff, I knew I wouldn't need to hang onto much. I'm going to buy an old caravan out in the wilds, or a narrowboat that needs doing up, or maybe a log cabin deep in the woods somewhere. I don't need people around me.'

Ingrid looked across at Sylvia, who was regarding her niece with her head on one side. 'We all need people, dear,' she said quietly.

'Not me. A comfy space to live in, good books to read and a cat to sit on my lap and purr in the evenings. Tommy hated cats. That'll do nicely.'

Sylvia nodded, but her expression was dubious. Ingrid sighed. She'd just have to prove to her aunt that she meant what she said. She'd paid off the rest of their mortgage and used most of the remaining money from the sale of the house to settle the debts Tommy had left behind. A simple life was what Ingrid craved now. She wanted... no, desperately *needed* to get rid of Tommy's accumulated 'treasures' and at the same time do her best to avoid getting embroiled in village life. Nobody knew about the dire financial part of her situation, and it was best to keep it that way. Tommy's friends would have been horrified to know that the endlessly sociable host of so many festivities had been absolutely useless with money, as had his so-called financial advisor.

Ingrid sighed again, this time with resignation. The gradual revelation of the mess Tommy had left her in had been terrible. Too late, she realised why he had been insistent that they kept their own bank accounts and, as the years had gone by, had also taken sole charge of household expenses. At least that had left her with her savings and just about enough to live on, but the bills had piled up as Tommy got more and more careless with his paperwork. It was as if he'd washed his hands of anything practical and concentrated on living his life out in style.

Maybe Tommy had somehow sensed he was on borrowed time? He'd never looked ill, but Ingrid knew her husband wasn't the kind of man to haunt the doctor's surgery or google symptoms. Perhaps she was overthinking everything and Tommy had just been like his father before him, charismatic but reckless. There was no point in going over and over it all in her mind. She'd only send herself mad. The challenge now was to find a bijou and compact home and settle into her brand-new single life. How hard could that be, after all?

2

As he took the turning for the road that would skirt Meadowthorpe town and point him towards Willowbrook, Joel stretched his tired shoulders and yawned. It had been a long morning and the drive from York had been dogged by roadworks and red lights. He'd thought that making the trip midweek would be straightforward but the crawling Wednesday traffic on the motorway had been as bad as any Friday-afternoon nightmare journey. Thank goodness for his friend Sam, who had agreed to help with the loading and unloading of Ingrid Copperfield's amazing array of goods and chattels.

'Pass us a chocolate biscuit, would you?' Joel said, glancing at the other man's pristine jeans and well-ironed black T-shirt. The younger guy looked as if he'd just stepped out of the shower instead of having spent two hours stacking dusty boxes and crates and then sitting for ages in the cramped cab of Joel's van. Sam was skinny as a whippet and as glossy as a supermodel with his mop of blond curls and designer stubble, but boy, the lad was strong. He'd really stepped up to the mark today.

'It was good of Kate to let you swap shifts at the café. I'll take her some flowers next time I'm passing the park,' said Joel.

'Yeah, she's a star,' Sam said, unwrapping a wafer biscuit and passing it over. 'The best boss in the world. Kate's house is just along the terrace from where we're dropping all this gear off, did you know that? Fiddler's Row's great. And she's even got Beryl next door. The woman cracks me up. Beryl and her cronies liven this place up no end.'

'I've lived in Willowbrook for years, Sam. I think I know the locals by now,' said Joel snappishly. He saw his friend's face fall. 'I'm sorry, ignore me, I'm just a bit knackered today. I was up late every night this week trying to finish a bench. It's been harder to do than my usual furniture commissions. This one's a bit more personal.'

Sam's mind was still on his dream house, and he didn't seem in the least offended. 'I'd buy a place in Fiddler's Row for Elsie and me like a shot if I had the dosh. Kids need a garden. The flat's okay and we were lucky to get one in the village when she was a baby, but I'd like her to have a swing and maybe a sandpit like other kids.'

Joel nodded, his tired mind unable to come up with anything useful to say. He ate his chocolate fix in two bites and wished he'd had time for breakfast. Living alone for so long had made him less than organised when it came to shopping. He usually remembered to stock up with the ingredients for easy lunches and dinners, but things like muesli and yoghurt never looked very appealing when he did his monthly trolley dash.

'We're nearly there, thank goodness,' Joel said, noticing the familiar landmark of the sign for Willowbrook Country Park. The long, tree-lined road was narrower now, and he could see the church spire in the distance. 'I hope she's got a kettle handy.'

'No worries, I made a big flask of coffee before I left. I know how you get if you're starved of caffeine. She didn't seem like a very sociable person, that Mrs Copperfield. A bit... chilly?'

'Yeah. Maybe she was just having a bad day, though. Give the lady a chance, eh? She looked shattered by the time she walked out of her house for the last time.'

Joel thought about Ingrid Copperfield as he indicated left to turn into the village. She'd made him feel uncomfortably like a teenager earlier this morning just before she'd left them to the loading of the van and set off for Willowbrook. Forty-eight years of living, a broken marriage and a volatile daughter had toughened Joel up to the point where he could manage most situations, but confronted by Ingrid's cool gaze and stunning looks, he'd found himself stammering for the first time in years, suddenly awkward and gauche. It was mortifying.

Sam's mind was clearly still on the subject of their temporary employer. 'Would *you* be able to just ditch all your furniture and clear a place out completely though, straight after your partner snuffed it? It seems a bit heartless to me.'

'It's not exactly straight after though, is it?'

'About six months, she said. It's not long.'

Joel had to agree with this. When Trina had left him, he'd grieved for their marriage a lot longer than six months and hung on to the last of her unwanted belongings for over a year before doing a charity shop run. Granted, he'd felt a lot better afterwards, but the empty side of the wardrobe still haunted him.

'Maybe she wasn't that keen on her bloke?' Sam suggested.

It was hard to answer this one, because Joel thought he'd seen sorrow in the woman's eyes when she'd thought nobody was watching her. It had made him want to sweep her up into a big hug and pat her on the back, like he'd done in the old days with his little daughter when she'd tumbled off her skateboard yet again. He'd better get a grip before they reached Ingrid's new place. She didn't look like the kind of person who was asking for sympathy, quite the opposite in fact. Joel firmly turned his attention to the matter in hand, which was getting this job done quickly and efficiently.

The road now ran past a small park and a fine stone church with a square tower, between rows of houses and then eventually around the southern edge of the village green. A lively little brook splashed its way across the middle of the green space, and willow trees trailed their branches over and around its banks. There was even sunshine on tap today, making the ripples in the brook sparkle. It was a peaceful scene. Not for the first time, Joel experienced a wave of gratitude that he lived in such a lovely village. He drove the van slowly along the road to the point where it curved away again towards the local primary school, and finally came to a halt outside the corner shop at the end of Fiddler's Row.

'I hope she's got here okay. I can't see anything through the glass,' said Sam, peering at the large, pink-smeared window that faced the green. 'This place looks as if it's been empty for ages.'

'A few months at least. Sylvia Nightingale's only in her seventies and she's always been really sprightly, but she had a nasty fall, and her hip operation didn't go too well so she decided to call it quits. She's been running this place for donkey's years. It must seem weird to be living over at Cedar Grove after all that time of keeping an eye on everyone.'

'Did you use this shop? Your house isn't far away, is it?'

Joel shook his head. He didn't want to explain that after

Trina left, taking their small daughter with her, he'd felt as if everyone in the village was talking about him. When the locals gathered in the shop, gossip always ran rife. Being parted from his beloved child was the worst thing that had ever happened to Joel, and he still couldn't think of that time without pain. Ten years had passed since then, and he tried to see Olivia – or Leo, as she now called herself for some unfathomable reason – as often as possible. It wasn't easy. His daughter was now fifteen, and she could be... well... a bit volatile. Also, his ex-wife seemed to loathe him more and more as the years went by, which was odd, because she was the one who'd been unfaithful and then decided to leave.

Sam was getting out of the cab now, clearly bored by waiting for Joel to answer. 'Come on,' he said. 'Let's get this show on the road. I've never seen so much crap in my life, and we haven't even had to bring any of her furniture with us. She'd already sold that off, she told me. It's just boxes and boxes of— What's up, Joel? Why are you pulling faces at me?'

It was no use. Even with his extensive eyebrow raising and gurning, Joel hadn't been able to warn Sam that their temporary employer was standing behind him on the doorstep of the shop with her arms folded. *Oh dear.*

'Well, you made it eventually,' Ingrid said. 'I'm sorry to hear you think this is all crap. Never mind, let's get them inside, shall we? I'm paying you by the hour and you're already very late.'

Joel opened his mouth to explain about the various hold-ups en route, but Ingrid had already turned on her heel and was leading the way into the shop. He grimaced at Sam, who was now bright red in the face.

'Sorry, mate,' Sam said under his breath. 'I didn't see her. Told you she was a bit chilly though, didn't I?'

Joel didn't reply. He followed Ingrid inside, sneezing as a wave of dust hit his nose.

'You know my aunt, don't you?' Ingrid said, gesturing to the older lady who was sitting on a folding chair, holding her walking stick like a weapon.

Sylvia nodded. 'Oh, yes, we know each other,' she said, in a tone that suggested Joel was about as important as a small slug that had crept under her door. 'He's Trina's ex. Nice girl, Trina, and a sweet little daughter, she had.'

'*Has*,' corrected Joel, before he could stop himself. 'Olivia's a lovely girl.'

'Don't see her round here much these days. Lives in Meadowthorpe with her mum, doesn't she?'

Ingrid held up a hand. 'Look, we've wasted enough time as it is without hearing this man's personal history, riveting though I'm sure it is.' She turned to face Joel. 'Can we get the van unloaded now, or do you want to fill us in on any more details of your private life?'

This time Joel didn't respond, just gestured to Sam to come back outside. He opened the back of the van and viewed the heaps of boxes and crates without enthusiasm. Hard work had never bothered him, but if it came without appreciation, it wasn't so great.

'What a snotty pair of—' Sam began but Joel shushed him and started to pile some of the nearest boxes on the ground.

'You take these in on the sack truck while I unload a few more, and then I'll help,' he said. 'Let's just get this job done and get out of here. I could murder a pint and I promised I'd treat you to pie and chips at the pub as soon as we've taken the van back to my place, okay? I'm not even going to think about healthy eating today.'

They both looked longingly across the village green, where

The Fox and Fiddle stood, the outdoor tables already beginning to fill up with Friday-afternoon drinkers. Then they squared their shoulders and got to work.

It wasn't long before the entire contents of the van were stacked to Ingrid's satisfaction in the storeroom. Joel noticed that each one was clearly labelled, with tags such as *small ornaments*, *kitchen gadgets* and *decorative flower vases*. He couldn't help but be impressed by such organisation. When Trina moved out, she'd loaded up a hired van with their joint belongings, mostly without consulting him, but they'd been hurled into bin bags and old suitcases without any regard to sorting. He remembered sitting on an upturned beer crate in the front garden, because she'd even taken the picnic bench, watching her drive away with Olivia strapped on a booster seat by her side. His little girl had waved to him, her bewildered face tearing at his heartstrings as they pulled away from the kerb.

Ingrid coughed loudly, bringing him back to the present with a jolt. 'Well done,' she said, with a lot less ice in her voice now. 'You worked very quickly in the end. I'm sorry I was a bit...'

'Grumpy?' suggested Sam, giving her his most winning smile, the one with dimples.

Joel grinned too. He'd seen Sam in action before. With his blond curls and his little-boy-lost air of not having eaten for weeks he could charm anyone he chose to if he put his mind to it, and this woman was no exception. Her gaydar clearly wasn't working if she thought Sam might be flirting but she wouldn't be the first female to make that mistake and no doubt she'd not be the last until Sam was safely married to his equally gorgeous boyfriend. Ingrid Copperfield flushed slightly and smiled at Sam as she handed over an envelope full of cash to Joel.

'Yes, I was grumpy, you're right. It's been a difficult time, trying to decide what to sell, what to bring and what to throw in the skip. I think I told you that my husband died six months ago, and I've managed to get rid of all our furniture now. I'm starting again from scratch, and I don't need much this time.'

Joel's eyes were drawn to the open door that led to the crowded storeroom. He raised his eyebrows.

'Oh, I know what you're thinking,' Ingrid said. 'But I'm not keeping this lot. It's going up for sale in the shop. I've got a maximum of twelve months to shift it all but hopefully it shouldn't take anywhere near that long. Then I'm off.'

'Off where?' Joel was intrigued now, his earlier irritation with her fading away. She was certainly good to look at, especially now she wasn't sending out the evil glares. Tall, elegant and willowy, her blonde hair was scooped back into what he remembered his ex-wife once describing as a French plait. Her jeans and white shirt were simple, but the way she accessorised them gave her a more stylish air than he'd have expected from someone in the process of moving into a grimy residence that urgently needed a good clean. A chestnut-brown leather belt with intricate markings was looped through her waistband and it perfectly matched her loafers. She was wearing twisted gold earrings and a necklace of small wooden beads painted in shades of deep red and russet. Even her lipstick seemed to have been chosen to tone with the necklace.

'I don't know where I'll go next,' Ingrid said vaguely. 'I've got no ties any more. Somewhere small... and cheap. Actually, anywhere that isn't full of tat and bulky furniture.'

Now he'd stopped to take notice, Joel could see that this woman was absolutely exhausted. Violet shadows under her eyes accentuated her pale cheeks, and delicate strands of her hair were starting to work their way out of the neat hairstyle, giving her a much less austere look.

'Right, that sounds like a plan. I'm all for a simple life. We'll get out of your way now. I'm sure you're ready for a rest,' he said.

'Yes, I suppose I am quite tired,' she replied. 'I'm not doing any unpacking tonight. I'll take my aunt back to her new place and then... oh, have a bath or something. Thanks for your help, you've both been great. And I'm sorry again, for... you know...'

Joel turned to leave but Sam's voice halted him in his tracks. 'Look, have you had a chance to get anything in to eat for tonight?' he heard his friend say. 'Only, it's going to be a long evening if you're hungry. We're off to the pub for a pie and a few drinks when we've taken Joel's van back up the road. Why don't you join us?'

There was a short silence. Joel inwardly cursed Sam for dropping them both in it like that. What if she said yes? He'd be stuck making polite conversation and being paranoid about his table manners instead of having a relaxing pint and a game of darts, but when Ingrid shook her head, Joel was surprised at the pang of disappointment he felt.

'I'm too shattered, to be honest,' she said. 'I've brought a good stock of emergency food with me to keep me going. It's a kind offer though. Maybe another time?'

They said their goodbyes and Joel and Sam got into the van. 'You didn't mind me asking her to come with us, did you?' Sam said. 'Only, I thought she looked kind of dejected.'

'Not at all,' Joel lied. 'It was nice of you.'

'We should take her over there and introduce her to some of the guys another day. I'll get a babysitter organised for Elsie. Or I bet Kate would step in for me when it's a good cause like this.'

'We're not a charity, Sam,' Joel said, then mentally kicked himself as his friend looked crestfallen. 'Yes, we'll do that. We really will. I suppose she's not as scary as she first seemed,' he added.

'Not at all. She's cool. Not frosty, like I thought. Just... you know... cool.'

Joel didn't reply. The thought of spending an evening with Ingrid Copperfield was daunting. The Fox and Fiddle was his safe place. Everybody knew him in there and nobody seemed to think he was a sad loser whose wife had got bored with him. On the other hand, maybe now was the time to step out of his comfort zone and try to make some new friends? Or maybe not. There was no point in rocking the boat when he was contented with his life at long last. That would be the worst possible thing he could do.

3

For the first two days in Willowbrook, Ingrid did little more than unpack her clothes and get to grips with the uncertain plumbing in the bathroom and kitchen of the flat. The supply of hot water was unpredictable, and all the taps dripped. At least the fridge worked, and Ingrid soon stocked it with the provisions she'd brought with her.

These were mainly uninspiring but designed to last. She filled the small freezer with basics and the cupboards with dried goods, cartons of long-life milk and fruit juices, tea, coffee, cornflakes and crackers. There was a selection of ready-meals that would keep her going until she could find a handy shop, but even though the solitude was soothing and it was good to familiarise herself with her new home, it wasn't long before Ingrid finished off one of the less-interesting dinners – a pasta dish that had about as much flavour as a plate of sawdust – and decided it was time to venture out into the world again.

On Saturday morning, she woke early, took a tepid shower in Sylvia's very dated bathroom and dressed in her favourite jeans again, pulling on a soft grey sweater that always felt comforting. She brushed her hair hard in lieu of washing it and made a reasonable effort of plaiting it high at the back of her head again before having a good look at herself in the long bathroom mirror, something she hadn't done for a while in the previous house. It had been much too depressing to see that her usual sparkle had totally disappeared and in its place was a kind of flatness, like lemonade left too long with the top off.

Today, the shadows under her eyes were less pronounced, but she still felt every one of her years. Ingrid had always done her best to keep young-looking and for a long time had felt somewhere around thirty in her head. Disguising the greys in her hair with pale blonde streaks had been routine for a while now. Tommy hadn't much liked the idea of an ageing wife, appreciating her being so slim and stylish even though his own girth had spread, and his red hair had long gone.

'You're a stunner, Ingers. You knock the spots off the other wives,' he'd said when she'd occasionally had a mild crisis of confidence before attending yet another of his fund-raising knees-ups. Rotary Club, Lions, random auctioneers' charity dos – they all blurred into one when she looked back. Dressing up, slipping her feet into spindly heels even though they made her tower over most of Tommy's friends, smiling endlessly. It became a chore quite early on, but she had to keep going. It was part of their deal. She'd known what the score was when she went along with his offer of marriage.

'We'll be great together, girl. Go on, make me the happiest man in the world. We'll be a fantastic team,' Tommy had said fifteen years previously, when he'd produced the knuckle-duster of a diamond ring he'd selected before his proposal, down on one knee (obviously), and in front of a crowd of whooping friends at a Christmas party.

Taken by surprise, Ingrid had put both hands over her

mouth, lost for words. He'd taken that as a *yes* and the cheers had redoubled. Before she knew it, Ingrid was engaged, destined to be Mrs Tommy Copperfield, wife of an up-and-coming local legend. It was true, they had indeed made a good team, and he'd provided security and stability at a time when Ingrid had been cast adrift by sadness. Tommy had provided more and more expensive jewellery as his popularity in the auctioneering circuit increased. He'd even picked up several awards in his chosen field along the way too.

Ingrid had sometimes managed to avoid staying too late at the more raucous events. She didn't think that was part of the contract, so long as she put in an appearance for the first part. She protected her own working life carefully and needing to be on duty quite often at weekends she couldn't function without a good night's sleep, no matter how much her husband tried to persuade her to stay to the bitter end so she could drive him home. Even so, she did her duty in that respect more often than not.

It was a very different world to the one she'd inhabited before she met Tommy. Ingrid's single life had been satisfying enough. She'd never wanted children and had avoided this life choice by only ever dating men who felt the same. By her mid-thirties she was living in a comfortable flat in a quiet part of York, happy enough to carry on in the same way for as long as it suited her. She was making a success of hotel management, socialising outside work as and when she felt the need and generally enjoying her independence.

It was at this point that both of Ingrid's parents died, within five agonising months of each other, her father from a particularly rare form of cancer and her mum succumbing to pneumonia after a nasty bout of food poisoning, having neglected her own health and worn herself out looking after him. An only child, Ingrid was left numb and reeling. She knew she hadn't made the effort to see her mum and dad nearly enough due to work pressures, but she did her best to make up for the shortfall before it was too late. The following flurry of appointments, consequent treatments and endless hospital visiting were devastating. Afterwards, Ingrid had muddled through her crippling grief somehow, working longer and longer hours and usually managing to avoid well-meaning colleagues who always seemed to want to *talk it through* with her. It wasn't until she'd met generous, effervescent Tommy Copperfield that life had taken a less gloomy turn.

'I did my bit, Tommy. I didn't let you down,' Ingrid whispered to her reflection now, pinching her cheeks to give herself a bit of natural colour. 'I appreciated you more than you realised, even if you did eventually leave me with a lot of sorting out to do, but now it's my turn.'

Sliding her arms into the black faux-leather jacket that made her feel sassy and confident, Ingrid added a slick of pearly lipstick, turned her back on the piles of boxes waiting in the storeroom and headed for the great outdoors. There had been a shower of rain in the night and the morning breeze was cool, but the weather forecast on her phone predicted that this was going to be a near-perfect spring day and the lane was illuminated by rays of early sunshine. The green stretched out in front of her, invitingly. Ingrid breathed in the heady scents of wet grass and leaf mould and was soon striding along the winding path that followed the brook, taking her towards The Fox and Fiddle.

She glanced up at the pub sign as she passed the attractively thatched hostelry. In the picture, a fox was playing a violin and wearing a rakish red hat. The door was firmly closed at this time of day, but through the window Ingrid could see someone mopping the floor and another person following him round taking chairs down from tables. She wondered if she'd been wimpish, refusing the two men's offer of an evening at The Fox and Fiddle on the night she arrived. It might have been fun, but equally, it could have turned out to be a big mistake because she might not have been able to escape before her bone-weariness became a problem and she face-planted the table.

'Morning!' called a voice from an upstairs window. 'You must be Sylvia's niece, yeah?'

Startled, Ingrid looked up. A black-bearded man was leaning over the sill, shaking out a duster. 'Hello, I'm Ned,' he said. 'This is my boozer. I know who you are because I don't know you, if you know what I mean? And anyway, I saw you outside the shop with Sylvia the day you moved in. How's it all going?'

'Oh, erm...' Ingrid, completely thrown by this unexpected interruption of her peaceful walk, struggled to find a reply.

'I get it. You're still settling in. Joel and Sam said they'd brought your gear down from the frozen north, but they couldn't lure you in here for pie and chips. It's burger night tonight, do you fancy that? All home-made, with a veggie option and a bonus 20 per cent off for locals if they provide proof that they live within five miles of us, but you're okay, I can see your gaff from here.'

He laughed and withdrew into the room, leaving Ingrid with mixed emotions as she walked on. This must be how village life was going to be, much like sitting under a microscope while the rest of the locals checked her out. On the other hand, the landlord's words had felt strangely warming. Joel and Sam probably wouldn't invite her again after she'd shown them her worst side. If only she hadn't felt so lost on moving day.

Grief and exhaustion had made Ingrid stroppy, and the loss of Tommy was finally sinking in properly, bringing with it all sorts of buried regrets from their past and beyond. Words unspoken, thoughts not shared. The middle-of-the-night demons were hard to handle.

Crossing the lane behind the pub, Ingrid saw the sign for a footpath to Willowbrook Country Park and, on impulse, decided to explore in that direction rather than wander through the main part of the village, making herself prey to even more curious stares. The track was uneven in places but wide enough for her to avoid getting snagged on the overhanging hedges, and every now and then a gap in the thick foliage gave Ingrid a tantalising glimpse of the blue waters of a nearby lake. The further she got from the pub, the louder the birdsong seemed. Avoiding the worst of the ruts, Ingrid made good progress, glad she'd remembered to leave her walking boots handy when she packed. The morning air was still on the cool side, but her cheeks were soon glowing as she trudged along, breathing in lungful after lungful of the earthy scents of fast-approaching autumn mingling with the greener echoes of the summer just past.

Soon, Ingrid came to a fork in the path and stopped to look around. In one direction lay the lake she'd glimpsed, stretching away into the distance. A few windsurfers were already out there, flitting back and forth as the breeze gained strength. Gulls wheeled and called to each other over the water and a family of ducks chugged their way around the nearest bank, scouting for food.

Turning to face the other direction, Ingrid's attention was caught by sunlight reflecting off a row of parked cars. She could see a cluster of weathered roofs above the trees and, intrigued, she set off towards what looked like civilisation. She followed the path around another smaller lake, keen to find out what was bringing in the gaggle of visitors to this otherwise peaceful place.

When she was close enough to see what was going on, Ingrid quickened her pace. A farmers' market was already in full swing, with people browsing between the stalls, sipping coffee from takeaway cups and peering at the goods on display. Tempting though this was, the prospect of a hot drink and a sit down won the day, and Ingrid headed for the café that was sited in one of the buildings clustered around what looked like an old stable yard.

A bell pinged as she pushed open the café door, and several heads swivelled to see who the newcomer might be. Most of the tables were full but the sound level of chatter only dropped for a second or two before the other customers went back to their own business. With a jolt, Ingrid saw that the man behind the counter, half facing away as he operated a very fancy coffee machine, was a dead ringer for Sam, the driver's mate from yesterday. Ingrid was overcome by a weird *Midwich Cuckoos* moment. Maybe all the males in Willowbrook were made from an identical mould, either slim and blond like Sam or wiry and dark and slightly haunted looking, like the enigmatic Joel Dean, who'd obviously been the one in charge of her move. Then the man turned towards her, and his eyes lit up.

'Mrs Copperfield,' he exclaimed, beaming at her. 'Or should it be Ms? I can never get the hang of formal titles. I was wondering how your first few days in the shop were going. Have you had breakfast yet?'

Ingrid gave herself a mental shake and smiled back. 'Just *Ingrid* is fine. I wasn't expecting to see you here, Sam,' she said. 'I haven't been shopping for fresh bread yet. The toast smells wonderful, and I'd love a large latte.'

'No sooner said than done,' Sam said. He passed across two brimming mugs of coffee to an elderly man who was now on his feet eagerly awaiting them and busied himself with the machine again.

'Is there a market here every weekend?' Ingrid asked, trying to ignore the renewed curiosity that Sam's greeting had inspired within the café.

'No, just once a month. It's very popular. We'll be serving lunches later and it'll be packed in here, but I can reserve you a table if you'd like?'

He glanced down at a list on the counter and frowned. 'Scratch that, I can see Kate must have added a few more bookings while I was on my break. Sorry to disappoint.'

The sound of someone clearing their throat loudly behind her caused Ingrid to turn around. A sprightly looking older lady stood there, eyes bright with interest. She was wearing a camel coat over a cornflower-blue cardigan and the sort of comfortable trousers that Ingrid's mother had called slacks. Her eye shadow exactly matched her cardigan and her low-heeled court shoes were the same shade of navy as her trousers. Although the general impression was traditional, there was something about her that said this wasn't your average octogenarian. Maybe it was the purple-patterned silk scarf draped artfully around her neck that made her look like someone to be reckoned with, thought Ingrid, or perhaps it was the bright red lipstick and the diamante clip nestling in her hair.

'I couldn't help hearing Sam telling you there was no room at the inn,' the lady said, smiling up at Ingrid. 'I've got a table booked for half past twelve and you'd be welcome to join us – Anthea and Winnie and me, that is. We always have a nose around the market first and then have an early lunch because we like a good sit down in the afternoon before *Pointless* starts. I'm Beryl, and I know who you are.'

'You know who everyone is,' said Sam. 'And I'm not sure if Mrs Copperfield... I mean, Ingrid... is ready for lunch with the Saga Louts yet.'

'The... what?' Ingrid stared at Beryl, who looked nothing like any kind of lout with her coordinated outfit and air of confidence.

'Oh, it's just what they call us,' Beryl said. '*Saga* because we love our holidays, and we tend to go on the ones where the average age is pushing eighty. You know what you're getting then.'

'And *louts* as in Lager Louts, although these three are more likely to be seen in the pub chatting up defenceless old men and downing prosecco rather than beer,' added Sam to Ingrid.

'*Old* men? Get away, I've got my standards,' Beryl said. 'We like a laugh, that's all. Some of the men are quite young. Comparatively,' she added, under her breath.

Ingrid blinked. She was beginning to feel like Alice suddenly plummeting into the alien landscape of Wonderland. 'I... see. Oh, and I've just told Sam to drop the formalities. Mrs Copperfield makes me sound like his teacher. I'm Ingrid.'

Beryl nodded approvingly. 'So, will you have lunch with the gang later, Ingrid? I've been wondering who was taking over Sylvia's shop. My house is number five, just along the row. I saw the van go by yesterday, but Sylvia's been keeping her cards close to her chest, as usual.'

Ingrid bit her lip. This was all going too fast for her liking. She'd only come out to explore for an hour and now here she was being sucked into some sort of ready-made social circle. Beryl and her friends would be bound to want to ask her questions. The other two were both waiting for an answer though, and their faces showed identical expressions of kind interest, so she swallowed her misgivings and nodded.

'I'd like that,' she said untruthfully, pasting on a smile. 'I'll have my breakfast and then a wander around the market first, too. It's lovely of you to invite me.'

Was it lovely? Ingrid moved over to sit at the only free table, a small one in a corner. She drank her coffee and gradually began to acclimatise. The warmth of the café seeped into her tired bones and the yellow and white checked cloths and small vases of flowers on each table were cheery. By the time Sam carried over a plate containing two slices of wholemeal toast, flanked with tiny pots of butter and cherry jam, she was beginning to feel her tense shoulders relaxing.

'This is a very welcoming place,' she told him.

'I can't really take credit for that, but it's a good café to work in. My boss is called Kate. She runs it, and her partner helps. He's Milo and he lives in the flat upstairs. They haven't been in charge for long, but they've already made a few changes.'

'You're not usually a delivery driver then?'

He laughed. 'No, Joel just rings me when he needs a bit of extra brawn. I'm stronger than I look. He's a carpenter, and a very good one. He often makes large items of furniture, and they tend to be too heavy for one man to shift.'

Sam glanced around, and when no customers appeared to be waiting, he perched on the chair next to Ingrid. 'It's thinning out now, so we'll have a lull until elevenses time. Look, I hope you don't mind me suggesting something, but it's burger night at the pub tonight.'

'I know, I met the landlord earlier and he told me.'

'Wow, Ned didn't waste much time doing his sales pitch!' said Sam. 'Anyway, I'm going in there early doors with my daughter, Elsie. She's only seven years old so we need to eat before her bedtime. Why don't you join us?'

Ingrid's mind was whirling now at the prospect of all this unaccustomed socialising. She'd planned a quiet weekend, unpacking boxes and deciding how best to tackle her sales pitch. The idea of someone providing food for her was enticing, and Sam looked so eager, but Ingrid felt that this was all getting too much. Was everyone in the village going to be interested in making sure she got fed? She decided it was time to make it clear that she needed some space, at least for now.

'It'd be great to do that when I've settled in a bit more, but could we put it on hold for a little while, Sam?'

'Oh... sure.' He looked crestfallen, but soon rallied. 'Anyway, you've already got a lunch date. You're going to love the Saga Louts. They know everything there is to know about this place. They'll soon make you feel at home.'

Ingrid smiled, but doubts were rearing their ugly heads again. She didn't in the least bit want to feel at home in Willowbrook. It was meant to be a temporary stopgap while she got ready for her new life of solitude and peace. Her marriage had come to an abrupt, if natural end, her management role had ceased to exist due to the hotel chain being taken over by a consortium, her house was sold and here she was being dragged into a social life that she hadn't asked for or needed.

'Don't look so worried,' Sam said, patting Ingrid's hand and getting up to go back behind the counter. 'I don't want you to feel swamped by us locals, but we're very friendly around here and we like to make everyone welcome. You'll enjoy lunch with the old girls today and you can have dinner with me and the offspring whenever you're ready, okay?'

'Thanks, Sam. You're very kind,' Ingrid said, thinking that after today's lunch she'd be more forceful and pull up the drawbridge so she could get on with the work in hand. He moved away to clear some tables and Ingrid breathed a sigh of relief.

'Sell up, move on,' she murmured to herself, like a mantra. That was the goal. The next chapter was tantalisingly close, almost within her grasp. Nothing and nobody must be allowed to stand in her way.

4

The market was buzzing when Ingrid returned to have a proper look around. It was easier to blend into the background now it was busier, and she browsed happily for half an hour before buying herself a woven shopping basket and loading it with a mouth-watering selection of local cheeses, a rustic loaf, some butter from a nearby farm and a bag of apples. She added another of tomatoes that smelt so good she had trouble resisting biting into one of each as she picked them from the glossy heap.

'You can test out a tomato, you know,' said the stallholder. 'We often let our customers try before they buy.'

'It's okay, I'm going into the café for lunch now,' Ingrid said, packing her purchases away and digging out her purse. 'I'll save myself for that.'

'Make sure you go for the soup if there's any left,' said the man. 'Kate fetched the veg for it from us before we opened up. Everything's fresh and local. Just like me,' he added, winking at her.

Ingrid had never been keen on being winked at, but today it

all seemed part of the day's friendliness. She spotted Beryl and two other ladies heading for the café, so she hooked the basket over her arm and followed them in. The noise level had risen to a louder hum now, and every table but one was taken. Beryl waved enthusiastically when she saw Ingrid.

'Here she is, my classy new neighbour,' she shouted, making all heads turn again. 'This is Ingrid. Come on over, love, you've got the last seat in the house. Budge up, Winnie. If you take that ridiculous body warmer off, we might have enough room and poor Ingrid won't need sunglasses.'

The larger of the three ladies flung a dirty look at Beryl and took off the offending item of clothing. It was fluorescent green and very puffy, but the tracksuit underneath was no less dazzling, being a combination of bright pink and purple. The whole ensemble was finished off with a pair of brilliant white trainers with glittery laces and a striped pink and purple head wrap.

'Hello, I'm Winnie,' the lady said, pulling out a chair and patting the seat. 'Don't look so anxious, I expect she'll let *you* keep your jacket on. It's a bit smaller than mine.'

'And her jacket's not at all hideous. In fact, you look amazing, Ingrid,' said the third member of the group, who was much more elegantly dressed in a collection of draped linen garments. 'I'm Anthea.'

Ingrid slipped her own jacket off and sat down. The warmth inside the room and the not-so-furtive glances they were all getting were making her feel flushed. It was like being one quarter of a stage act about to burst into song.

'I love your sweater. Is it cashmere?' asked Anthea.

Ingrid nodded. Tommy had always encouraged her to buy the best. A lot of her more elaborate clothes had gone into bags along with a collection of Tommy's designer outfits soon after his death, destined to be sold at a very trendy second-hand shop in York, but she'd kept a few old favourites. The luxurious softness of the pale grey jumper always felt comforting. She found herself clutching her silver pendant, something she tended to do when she was nervous. *Sort yourself out, for goodness' sake*, she told herself. *You've managed busy hotels for years and met all sorts of important people. This is a village café. What's got into you?*

The ladies were focusing on the menu now. 'Is there any soup left, Kate?' Beryl called to the woman behind the counter.

'I think I can just about stretch it to four portions if you all want some,' she answered. 'And the rolls are lovely and fluffy today. Don't want you breaking your dentures, Beryl. Not when they're still so new and shiny.'

'Cheek,' said Beryl, laughing. 'Soup all round, is it? And a large pot of tea? We can choose our cake later.'

Ingrid nodded again. She seemed to have temporarily lost the use of her voice.

Her three companions settled back into their seats now the serious business was done.

'So, how's it going in your new place?' asked Anthea. 'We've all been intrigued. What exactly are you selling? You don't look much like a shopkeeper, I must say.'

'That's a snobby thing to say,' said Winnie with a loud sniff. 'Ingrid will think we're all as stuck up as you are!'

'How rude,' said Anthea. 'I'm not a snob. Well, not in this instance, anyway,' she added when her friends snorted. 'But you've got to admit our new resident has got more style than Sylvia Nightingale ever had.'

Beryl and Winnie were exchanging furtive looks now. 'Sylvia's Ingrid's aunty!' hissed Beryl. 'Mind your tongue.'

Ingrid laughed, beginning to relax at last. 'It's okay,' she said. 'I don't think Sylvia's ever held herself up as a fashion icon. And I'd love to tell you about my plans for the shop, if you're interested?'

The three others waited impatiently as the soup and rolls were delivered to their table and a huge pot of tea was deposited in the centre by Sam, who gave Ingrid a reassuring grin.

'Go on then, dear. That's if you don't mind talking and eating at the same time?' said Beryl. 'We're dying to hear what you're up to, so long as you don't give yourself indigestion.'

'Ooh, no, don't do that,' said Winnie. 'I get terrible trapped wind if I eat and talk.'

'I think that comes under the heading of TMI,' called Sam, as he passed their table with two plates of scones. 'Don't get them on the subject of wind, Ingrid. It's their favourite topic.'

'Less of your cheek, young 'un,' said Winnie. 'Go on, give us the gen, Ingrid. We're all ears.'

'All ears and wind,' Sam said under his breath.

Beryl shot him a look that said *don't mess with us, sonny*, and gestured for Ingrid to speak. It was surprisingly good to find people who were so interested in her affairs. Ingrid hadn't been used to sharing her innermost thoughts with anyone since her parents had died. Tommy had once remarked that she'd have made a great secret agent, because she would never cave under interrogation. Ingrid told herself that there was nothing wrong with being a private kind of person. She was just reticent, not cagey. She ate a spoonful of the delicious vegetable soup and broke a roll in half while she tried to think where to begin. The yeasty aroma of the bread made her stomach rumble.

'I guess I need to give you a bit of back story to set the scene,' she said. 'Let's have our lunch first though. This is too good to be sidelined.'

They all got on with their soup, but soon it was time for Ingrid to explain why she was here in Willowbrook taking on a project which, to all intents and purposes, was a shot in the dark. Her idea had seemed completely logical when she'd come up with it during one of many sleepless nights after Tommy's death. The king-sized bed seemed way too big without him. She missed his warm body beside her and even his snoring, which in any case had never kept her awake much. The bedroom seemed eerily quiet now.

Eventually, Ingrid pushed her empty bowl away and reached for her cup. She took a restorative sip. The tea was strong and aromatic, and along with the soup, it did the trick. She was ready for anything now.

'Right, here goes. I was married to Tommy Copperfield for the best part of fifteen years. He was an auctioneer – a big man in every way.'

'Ooh, nice,' giggled Beryl, nudging Winnie.

'Ignore them, darling,' said Anthea. 'They can sometimes be a little... earthy.'

Ingrid pulled a face. 'I just meant he was the sort of person people tend to describe as larger than life.' She pretended not to notice Beryl and Winnie's titters this time. 'He was very sociable and loved to party. Unfortunately, I think that's what finished him off. He died with a glass in his hand, having a good old singsong.'

'A great way to go,' Beryl said. 'I'd definitely choose that method of shuffling off this mortal coil rather than sitting in a wipe-clean chair with a crocheted blanket over my knees for years.'

'You've got a point. Anyway, he left me with a large house where I rattled around sadly for a while, and countless boxes and crates of...'

Ingrid paused, unsure how to describe the unwanted legacy. It seemed ungrateful to lump it all together as junk. There were undoubtably treasures amongst the heaps.

'Go on,' said Winnie, pouring them all a cup of tea. 'We'll wait till you've finished to order cake.'

'Okay... well... Tommy used to bring home unsold lots from the auctions. He'd maybe have spotted one thing in them that he wanted, and the rest had to come too. He did this for years. They mounted up. When I heard the village shop was going to be empty while Aunty Sylvia decided what to do with the premises, I asked her if I could borrow it for a while and try to sell it all.'

'Hmm. Why didn't you just bin the worst and send the rest to a charity shop?' asked Anthea, looking at Ingrid over her gold-rimmed spectacles. 'It all sounds like a lot of hard work to me.'

'I was going to do that,' said Ingrid. 'But then I thought the money would be... useful and I could get more for the stuff if I sold it myself. I'm not going to be greedy, the prices will be reasonable. Afterwards I'm going to just keep my very favourite few things and buy somewhere small to live.'

'You could do worse than getting something like mine and Kate's,' said Beryl. 'The terraced houses in Fiddler's Row are just big enough for us.'

'Oh no, I couldn't afford one of those and anyway, I'm thinking much smaller than that,' said Ingrid. 'A caravan, maybe, or a narrowboat. I want a less complicated life.'

'Quite frankly, it sounds hellish, darling,' said Anthea. 'All that work and then hiding yourself away in a hovel with no space to breathe.'

'Anthea!' Beryl burst in, eyes blazing. 'You really need to think before you speak. Sorry, dear. She's got absolutely no filter,' she said to Ingrid. 'Not everyone wants to live like you, Anthea, in a big flash house with a cleaner and walk-in wardrobes and so on. This sounds like a great idea to me. What do you think, Winnie?'

Winnie's eyes were shining. 'I love it!' she said. 'And I'd like to help, if you need a hand sorting the boxes. I'm thinking your window dressing is going to be the key to getting people in. I used to work for a jeweller, and I've got lots of experience in making a tempting display.'

'You should take her up on that. She's really got the knack,' said Beryl. 'And while we're at it, why don't you join us one Wednesday evening at mine? It's our weekly film night and we have prosecco and nice things to eat. Seven p.m. I'm at number five, Fiddler's Row. Oh, but I already told you that, didn't I? No need to knock, just walk in. Bring your slippers if you like.'

Ingrid didn't know how to reply. This was getting out of hand. She'd hoped for a quiet life in Willowbrook pottering around and selling her collection of tat at a gentle pace. Already she was in danger of landing herself with an assistant in the shop when all she wanted was time to herself to regroup. She looked around at the trio of smiling faces and her heart melted slightly. Window dressing was never going to be one of Ingrid's talents if she was brutally honest, and accepting help wasn't a weakness, especially when the offer was given so generously.

'Thank you, Winnie, I'd appreciate that,' she said. 'And a film night sounds lovely, when I'm a bit more settled.'

Ingrid looked up to see Sam smirking at her from behind the counter. He gave her a thumbs-up sign. She sighed. Living in the village goldfish bowl looked as if it was going to involve her climbing a very steep learning curve, and she was starting right now.

5

Tucked away in the workshop at the side of his house on the other side of the village, Joel Dean turned up the radio and continued to sand his latest bench. Over the years since Trina and Olivia had left him, his lifestyle had changed considerably. The trigger had been the removal of the first garden bench, the one he'd created for his family. He'd been intending to make a matching one and a table to go with it, hoping that the three Deans might one day become four or even five, but Trina had put paid to that. Finding her in bed with the window cleaner had been something of a shock.

Joel gave a shudder as he remembered that fateful day. Olivia had been at school, and he'd had a booking to fit a kitchen fifty miles away, but at the last minute the job was cancelled, and he'd driven home anticipating making a bacon sandwich and having a crafty read of his latest library book. His car at the time had been much quieter than the van he now owned, and it wasn't until he opened the front door and shouted hello to his wife that he alerted her to the disaster that was about to unfold.

'Joel? Hello?' she'd shouted from upstairs. 'Hang on, I'll come down! I was just... er... sorting the laundry.'

'I'm coming up!' he'd yelled back. 'I need to get changed. I've got an unexpected day off.'

He was about to enter the bedroom when at the last moment he registered the alarming sight of his wife clutching her dressing gown to her naked chest and a man who looked vaguely familiar struggling into a pair of trousers. Joel stopped dead in the doorway, his mouth hanging open. The penny dropped. It was their window cleaner, Trevor, but he was clearly giving a different kind of service today.

'You said you were going to be out all day!' Trina cried accusingly. 'I... I...'

'Sorry, mate,' the other man said, crimson in the face. 'I'll just—'

'You'll just nothing,' said Joel, grabbing the interloper by the shoulders and flinging him down on the bed. The other man bounced off the pillows, hitting his head on the bedside lamp which fell to the floor with a crash.

'What the f*** is going on?' Joel bellowed. 'Is this some sort of new offer you're trialling? Twelve windows, full conservatory and a quick shag?'

Looking down at the man, Joel realised what pointless questions these were, and the rage left him as suddenly as it had arrived. Only a sense of desolation remained. Trina started to gibber an excuse, but he turned and left the bedroom, rushed out of the house and climbed into his car, his hands starting to shake almost uncontrollably as he drove away.

It was two whole days before Joel returned. He stayed with a friend, licking his wounds and talking the incident through over way too many beers. Eventually he decided to go home and have it out with Trina. Joel had been uncomfortably aware for a while that their marriage was by no means perfect, but surely it was worth saving? It was much too late for talking though. By the time Joel reached the house with the cleanest windows in the street, his wife and child were already on the point of leaving. The van Trina had hired was almost full and Olivia was strapped in, clutching her favourite teddy and looking completely lost.

It was a horribly painful time, but once the dust had settled and he'd vented some of his fury and sadness in a cathartic way by clearing out the garage and making countless trips to the tip, Joel resolved to start again. He'd hated fitting kitchens for a company who cared nothing for the welfare of their customers and cut corners wherever possible. It was time to take stock of his life. For some months he'd been making furniture in his spare time, selling it to friends and through word of mouth, but his job had never left him enough hours spare to take more than a few orders. When Trina next rang to talk about access to Olivia, and of course, money, Joel told her about his plan.

'I'm going to make the garage into a proper workshop,' he said, unable to dumb down his excitement at the prospect of finding actual job satisfaction every single day. 'I'll go into business properly. It won't be long before we can make a firm arrangement for maintenance, so you don't need to worry about that.'

'Ha! You're actually delighted we're out of your hair, aren't you? You can live the dream at last!' Trina had shrieked. Her shrill voice had ranted on for several minutes about what a terrible husband and father he'd been, out of the house for hours with no thought for her sanity and no desire to cook or help with the cleaning or childcare.

Joel was left speechless for a few moments. Yes, he'd worked long shifts, but the pay was no good unless overtime was added on. He'd tried his best to give Olivia as much attention as he could when he was home. As for cleaning and cooking, Trina was a control freak, and had very specific rules about how these things should be carried out. Whenever he'd volunteered to take on some of the housework or cooking, she'd laughed scornfully and told him he'd only make a pig's ear of it.

'I think we need to talk calmly about this,' he'd managed to say in the end. 'Shall I come round to yours tomorrow?'

'That's not a good idea. Trev doesn't want you in the house. You *attacked* him, Joel. He's not feeling like inviting you into his... I mean *our* home. I'll meet you at the pub, okay?'

Since then, Joel had avoided the loathsome weasel of a man he thought of as Trevor the Tosser and concentrated on forging a stronger relationship with his daughter whenever he was allowed to take her out or back to his house at weekends. His business gradually grew more successful, and he bought an elderly but spacious van to deliver orders, which gave him a useful sideline in extra man-with-a-van jobs. Weirdly, the harder he tried to be a good dad and to provide a steady stream of maintenance cash, the more Trina seemed to dislike him. Their relationship was now just short of frigid, but Olivia was always happy to be with her dad, and so he took that as a win.

Joel was singing along tunefully to an old Robert Palmer hit about being addicted to love and thinking vaguely about Ingrid and her intriguing Ice Maiden image when he heard the door rattle and a familiar voice calling, 'Dad? Are you there?'

For a moment Joel panicked. Had he forgotten to pick Olivia up from somewhere or other? Trina would be livid if he had. But almost instantly he remembered that although it was his turn to fetch Olivia today, she was meant to be going on holiday for a couple of nights with Trina, Trevor and his teenage son, Marcus, to a Center Parcs somewhere in the Midlands.

'Olivia? Are you okay?' he said, as she came into view from behind a large Welsh dresser that he'd been renovating whenever he had a spare hour or two.

'I'm Leo now,' she corrected. 'You never remember to call me that, do you? It's like you don't listen to me. But then nobody ever does. I'm just in the way. Everybody hates me.'

At this, his daughter began to wail, wrapping her arms around her thin shoulders and rocking to and fro. Joel leapt to his feet and took two strides towards her, pulling her to him. At first she resisted but then flung herself onto his chest, howling and keening as if her world had ended.

'I'm sorry, love. I do know you want to be called Leo, but it slipped my mind,' Joel murmured as she sobbed. Surely just getting her name wrong wouldn't have caused this outburst? There must be something else upsetting her. He'd need to find out, but subtly. Going back to his earlier mistake, Joel racked his brains to try and recall why his daughter had told him she'd decided to change her name. He'd chosen the original one himself the week before she was born after Trina had rejected all his other suggestions. And why Leo? His daughter had certainly been going for an androgenous kind of look lately with her short, spiky hair dyed an even more dense black than Joel's own. With his arms around her, Joel could feel Leo's ribs, sharp and uncomfortable against his chest. In his opinion his daughter had lost far too much weight lately. Was there a sinister reason for this? Maybe she was going to share some awful, earth-shattering news with him today. Joel's stomach churned in readiness, and he hoped fervently that whatever was the matter, he'd be able to find the right response.

Gradually the sobbing ebbed, and Leo pulled away from

Joel, digging in her pocket for a tissue. She hiccupped a few times and then looked him straight in the eye.

'I've had enough of them all, Dad,' she said, her voice only quavering slightly. 'I can't stand Trevor, he smells of cleaning fluid and chip fat, and Marcus is just a complete dickhead. He wees on the toilet seat and the floor round it *every single day*. Mum doesn't even like me now and Marcus creeps around them being sooooo perfect all the time, unless they're not looking. He's been given a stupidly expensive new bike so he can go cycling with them this weekend. They wanted to get me one, but you know how crap I am at that kind of thing. I'd just fall off. I asked them to give me the money instead.'

'And I'm guessing they said no?'

'You got it. They said I'd only spend it on... on...' She was crying again, but more quietly now.

'What did your mum think you'd spend the money on, love?' prompted Joel as gently as he could. Was the answer going to be terrifying? Drugs? He dreaded Leo going anywhere near that pathway. Her moods tended to fluctuate at the best of times. Heaven only knew what she'd be like if she started with that kind of caper.

'On... Baz.'

Joel was hopelessly lost now. Was that the cool name for a new kind of weed, or worse? He waited to see if his daughter was going to elaborate. She did.

'I'm guessing Mum hasn't told you about Baz?'

Joel shook his head and waited again. His daughter scrubbed at her eyes just as she'd done when she'd fallen off her bike when she was small.

'He's my boyfriend and he's amazing,' she said eventually.

'Right.' So, his first guess had been way off the mark. Leo wasn't going to tell him she was gay. Maybe she was one of those other things the teens were these days, though. Bi? Non-binary? Joel felt ridiculously out of his depth. 'Tell me about Baz,' he suggested.

He sat down on the bench he'd been sanding, and Leo came to sit beside him. He considered putting an arm around her, but she wasn't close enough.

'You'll like him, Dad. He's kind of a free spirit. Nobody tells Baz what to do. He's seventeen. He does his own thing.'

'That sounds... impressive. And at the risk of sounding like a boring old geezer, what does he do when he's resisting being told what to do?'

'Do? You mean does he have a stupid dead-end job or go to college or something?'

Joel supposed that's what he had meant. He didn't think it was an unreasonable question for a father to ask. Leo hadn't finished.

'Baz hasn't decided which direction he's going in yet, but everyone keeps judging him all the time. Trevor says he's a waste of space. The git. Anyway, we had a... bit of a row and I told them to go on holiday without me. I said I was going to stay at yours this weekend. Mum didn't like it but said she was going to message you to say I was on my way.'

Joel patted his pockets to see if this was true, then realised he'd left his phone in the house. Leo was looking at the floor now. She seemed to be fascinated by a spider that was making its way into a corner of the workshop.

'Actually, I don't just want to stay for the weekend, I want to be here all the time,' she said, glancing sideways at Joel. 'Mum and Trev just don't get me, and I can't stand them any longer. Is that okay, Dad? Can I come home?'

6

Oddly enough, even with the turmoil of thoughts that had been battling for pole position since Tommy's death, Ingrid was sleeping more peacefully in her new home than she had done for weeks. Accustomed to traffic noise, although previously it had been muffled by the high hedges around her old property, it was lovely to be able to open the window when she went to bed and hear nothing but owls hooting in the willow trees and the faint ripple of the brook. Once or twice, distant sounds of a few late revellers coming out of the pub drifted across the green, but nothing got in the way of her ability to switch off her thoughts when she woke briefly in the night.

Unfortunately, this wasn't so easy in the daytime. With the best will in the world, Ingrid couldn't seem to shake off the torpor that overcame her whenever she tried to tackle the mammoth task of unpacking Tommy's belongings and making sense of her shop idea. It all seemed like too much. She spent a great deal of the next few days either lying on the sofa or sitting in the small courtyard behind the shop wrapped in a fleecy blanket. Her mind travelled in circles, remembering both good and bad times with Tommy and agonising over whether she could have somehow prevented his death by insisting he took better care of himself. It was like having a series of short, painfully realistic video clips running constantly in her head, each one more disturbing than the last.

A week passed with nothing useful accomplished and with Ingrid's mood getting ever lower. She was beginning to think she'd made the biggest mistake of her life in coming to Willowbrook when a phone call from an unfamiliar number disturbed her morning routine of doing nothing much. She debated ignoring it, but at the last moment decided to answer.

'Hi, Mrs Copperfield... I mean, Ingrid... it's Sam. Removal and café man?' he added when Ingrid didn't immediately respond.

'Oh, of course... Hello Sam.' Ingrid couldn't think of a reason why he would call but it was a welcome distraction in any case. She found herself smiling into the phone.

'Right, tell me to leave you alone if you want to, but I was wondering if you'd like to come over to the pub later for dinner with me and Elsie? It's curry tonight, and we're eating early. You could meet us at six, maybe? Ned makes a mean tikka masala, and his Peshwari naans are out of this world.'

Ingrid debated making her excuses but the thought of something different to eat and a change of scene was suddenly very appealing.

'I'd love to,' she said, surprising herself with the enthusiasm in her voice. 'See you at six. And Sam...?'

'Yeah?'

'Thanks so much for thinking of me. It's been a long week. Bye.'

Ingrid rang off before she could embarrass herself by

getting emotional and went to rummage in her wardrobe for something to wear that wasn't jeans.

* * *

The Fox and Fiddle was still quiet when Ingrid walked in at five to six, so it was easy to spot Sam and his daughter Elsie. They'd chosen a table overlooking the village green and were watching a group of older children playing rounders. Ingrid had skirted round the fielders to reach the pub and had suddenly wished she was that age again, with nothing to think about but winning a game on a Saturday evening and then maybe going home for a barbecue or a pizza with the family.

'We saw you coming,' said Sam, standing up as Ingrid approached their table. 'Elsie says you look *well cool*.'

The little girl smiled up at Ingrid. She had curly auburn hair in two bunches and a sprinkle of freckles over her nose. Her eyes were brown, and even in Ingrid's unpractised opinion, unusually shrewd for a child. 'I like your dungarees,' she said, looking Ingrid up and down with the air of a fashion expert. 'And you've got the new Converse. Even my teacher hasn't got any of those yet and she's super-cool.'

Ingrid felt unreasonably pleased with this comment. She'd taken a long time to decide what to wear for an early-evening dinner in a country pub with one person she didn't know anything about and another she'd never even met.

'Thank you, Elsie. They're my favourite dungarees,' she said. 'I bought them when I was on holiday in Italy ages ago. There was a lady selling them on a market and she said she designed them herself and then added all the embroidery and tiny mirrors. My husband said they made me look like an ageing hippy. I like them though.'

'Where's your husband?' asked Elsie, abandoning the subject of the dungarees for a more interesting one.

'Oh... er...' Ingrid looked at Sam for guidance. How much did Elsie, at seven years old, understand about death? Her own experience of children was almost non-existent. The ones she'd encountered in the hotels were usually well-supervised and certainly not about to chat to a member of staff, especially one whose work persona verged on stern.

'Ingrid's husband died a little while ago, love,' said Sam gently. 'I'll get Ingrid a drink before you interrogate her any more, shall I?'

Elsie ignored this remark. 'Have you got any pets?' she asked Ingrid.

'No. I used to have two cats when I was much younger but...' Oh dear. The conversation wasn't going well so far.

'Both dead too, I s'pose,' Elsie said sympathetically. 'Our cat got squashed on the road. His name was Scarface. We were sad, weren't we, Dad? Now I've got a guinea pig and he's called Bill, but he's not allowed outside. Were your cats squashed on the road?'

'That's enough, Elsie. What would you like to drink, Ingrid?' said Sam. 'I expect you need one by now.'

Ingrid certainly did. She said she'd like to try the local bitter if they were going to eat curry, and Sam departed, giving his daughter a warning look.

'I think Dad wants me to stop talking for a bit,' Elsie said, leaning towards Ingrid confidingly. 'But *you* don't, do you? I want to know stuff, that's all.'

'And I do too,' said Ingrid, hoping to deflect any more questions. 'Why don't we swap places, and you tell me about yourself next?'

She thought she might need to add a few prompts to get the

ball rolling, but Elsie needed no more encouragement. 'I'm seven and I live with my dad. I haven't got a mum... well, actually I have, but she didn't like me much, so she went away. We live in a flat with Bill. My favourite colour is pink, but I also like yellow. My dad works at the café with Kate, and she's one of my best friends. I have sleepovers with her sometimes. Her sofa is purple.'

Elsie took a deep breath to continue her monologue, but Sam was back now, carrying a brimming pint of golden beer for Ingrid and a menu. He put both down on the table. 'Time to take a break from your life story, love. Let's order our dinner before Ned gets too busy.'

Elsie didn't bother to look at the menu. 'I'll have chicken korma and a naan bread please,' she said. 'I always have that,' she explained to Ingrid. 'Dad will prob'ly get chips for us to share so don't bother choosing them. He'll have a chicken tikka masala with rice.'

Sam grinned at Ingrid as she tried to make up her mind what to order. 'Just be aware that if you join us again for a curry, whatever you pick now will be your usual, forever.'

Ingrid laughed and took a large swig of beer while she decided. She glanced up at that moment and started to splutter when she saw who'd entered the pub. Sam patted her on the back and looked across to see what had caused Ingrid to choke on her drink.

'Hey, there's Uncle Joel!' said Elsie. 'And he's got my friend Olivia with him. She wants to be called Leo now though. I keep forgetting. It's because she hated her name. I don't know why. It's quite a nice name really.'

By this time Joel had seen them and waved. Sam got up again. 'Are you ready to order, Ingrid? I'll go and see if Joel wants to join us. I didn't know he was coming.'

Ingrid chose quickly and Sam went over to the bar. She watched the exchange, feeling her heart rate go back to almost normal as Joel turned to speak to him. There was something unsettling about this man, with his high cheekbones and dark eyes. He carried with him a faint hint of tragedy. She had a feeling his stubble was because he'd not had time to shave rather than being Sam's designer kind, and his clothes looked as if he'd just put on what he'd found on the bedroom floor. Her cheeks burned as she remembered how shirty she'd been with Joel on moving day just because he was a bit late. This was obviously a busy man, especially if he had a teenager to care for too.

The girl was now coming over to their table. 'Hi, Elsie,' she said. 'I was hoping you'd be here.'

'Were you?' Elsie's eyes sparkled at this. 'I didn't think you were coming to see your daddy this weekend. You said you were going on holiday to an amazing place with water slides and stuff.'

'Well, I didn't, as it happens.'

Ingrid smiled at the girl. As with younger children, she had no knowledge of teenagers apart from having been one herself, but here was someone who looked as if she was having a bad day. Her hair, standing on end in oily spikes, could probably have done with a wash, and she had an angry spot appearing on her chin. Ingrid could feel the waves of stress coming off the girl. She'd just have to do her best to be friendly and not sound like a grown-up making cheesy conversation.

'I'm Ingrid, and I've heard your name's Leo,' she said. 'That's my birth sign. It's a good choice. We should all pick our own names when we're old enough, I reckon.'

Elsie pounced on this idea straight away. 'I want to be called my birth sign too,' she said. 'I don't know what it is though.'

'When's your birthday?' Leo asked. 'Oh, hang on, I know that already because I was here for your party last year. It's 10 May, isn't it? That makes you...?' She looked at Ingrid for help.

'Taurus,' said Ingrid. She'd occasionally shared an office at their flagship hotel with a lady called Sandra who read her horoscope obsessively every day, so the information popped into her head automatically now.

'Taurus,' repeated Elsie. 'It's not as nice as Leo. I might change my name to Anton instead. He's my favourite on *Strictly*. What would your name be if you could choose, Ingrid?'

'Oh... erm... I've never given that question any thought. Why didn't you like your original name, Leo?' said Ingrid, keen to move the focus away from herself before she said the wrong thing.

'I used to think it was okay and then I didn't. It was because of that dork Trevor. He kept calling me *Livvie*. It was gross. It rhymes with Divvy. Don't you just think Livvie is the worst name ever?'

Ingrid was saved from replying by the arrival of the two men. Joel pulled up more chairs and they rearranged themselves so the girls could sit next to each other. Leo immediately got out her phone, gave Elsie one of her earpieces and they began playing a game. Sam sat down and visibly relaxed.

'Phew, that's a relief,' he said quietly. 'I usually love hearing Elsie prattle, but I could do with a break tonight. The café was full-on. It always is, on market days.' He lowered his voice even more and leaned towards Joel. 'So, you're saying Olivia... I mean, Leo... just turned up and said she wanted to move in? And Trina agreed?'

Joel looked across at Ingrid, who was intrigued but trying not to look nosy. 'Leo usually lives with her mum but now she's going to stay with me for a while,' he explained. 'Big problems,' he mouthed silently, after checking Leo was safely occupied.

Once again, Ingrid experienced that Alice in Wonderland feeling. A short while ago she'd been in the depths of a lonely, rather dull existence with the only excitement being the prospect of moving. Now she'd accidentally dived into this complicated world of single dads, a troubled teen, an apparently motherless child and three energetic older ladies who seemed to be totally absorbed in living their best lives. Her temples began to throb. Perhaps she was just hungry. She really hoped that was the only problem. At least it looked as if the food was on the way. Thank goodness for that.

7

It was the landlord himself who approached their table, carrying a loaded tray and beaming at them all.

'It's good to see the new local supporting my gaff,' he said, grinning at Ingrid. 'You're going to love this. You won't get grub like mine in any old boozer, you know?'

The men shuffled the drinks around and made room for everything while Ingrid breathed in the enticing aromas. Fluffy naans jostled with a large dish of rice, a bowl of golden, crispy chips and several curries.

'Cheers, Ned. Dig in, kids,' Sam boomed, and they looked up from their game, startled. Soon, silence reigned as everyone filled their own dishes and began to eat. Ingrid was in curry heaven. This was the best tikka masala she'd tasted for years. Her main meal had often been taken at the hotel because Tommy ate out most days with his staff. Curry hadn't been the chef's strong point, so she'd rarely risked it. Now, breathing in the mingled fragrances of spices, coconut and fries, Ingrid decided she'd need to go shopping soon and find somewhere to buy salads and vegetables. If she carried on eating out like this, she'd soon need new jeans. Luckily, her dungarees were roomy, and today nothing mattered except beginning to find her feet in this village and then getting another early night.

They finished eating and were just contemplating another drink when Ingrid's attention was caught by the sound of loud laughter. The small, slight man standing at the bar must have told a joke because he was guffawing, although the landlord looked dubious and the two other men with him were only managing polite chortles. An icy shiver ran down Ingrid's spine. Joel turned to face her.

'Are you okay? To use a cliché, you look as if you've seen a ghost.'

He followed her gaze. 'Oh, there's Lennie Nightingale.'

'That's all we need,' said Sam.

'I should have guessed where all the noise was coming from. Do you know him?' Joel slapped his forehead. 'Of course you do, I'm being stupid. He's Sylvia's youngest, so he must be your cousin. Is there a problem?'

Joel sounded so concerned that a lump came into Ingrid's throat. She willed Lennie not to notice her, but just at that moment, some sixth sense seemed to tell him he was being watched. He wheeled around and his eyes raked the bar which was now starting to get busier.

'Aha, so that's where you're hiding,' he said, loudly enough for everyone around him to hear. 'I've just been over to the shop and left you a note. Long time no see, lovely Cuz.'

Lennie put his pint down on the bar and moved towards their table and Ingrid had the distinct impression that her two male companions were watching him with a lack of enthusiasm. As he reached them, Joel said, 'Hello, Lennie. We haven't seen you around here for a while.'

'Maybe I've got a better motive for visiting Dullsville now. Talk about the land that time forgot.'

'Wasn't your mum a good enough reason?' Sam's voice cut in sharply and Ingrid turned to look at him, but he avoided her gaze. 'I heard you didn't give her any help with the move. Too busy, were you?'

'I don't think that's any of your business, is it? And you shouldn't listen to old wives' tittle tattle. Mind you, that kind of sums you up, doesn't it?'

Sam was on his feet now, and Joel reached out a hand to grab his arm, but Lennie was already retreating. 'I'll call in on you again tomorrow,' he said to Ingrid. 'This pub's too full of old women tonight.'

'Leave it, Sam,' said Joel under his breath, gesturing to the two girls who were watching with keen interest.

Sam sat down again, but his eyes followed the older man until he'd left the bar.

'Daddy doesn't like that person,' said Elsie. 'He's rude. He did our living-room floor for us and then asked us for too much money. Is he your relation, Ingrid? That's not very nice if he is.'

'Elsie, zip it,' said Sam.

His daughter made a big show of fastening up her mouth with a zip and Leo giggled.

'Sorry, Ingrid,' Sam said. 'That man always makes me lose my cool. He's one of your family though, and we won't say any more, okay, Elsie?'

Elsie nodded mutely, pointing to her tightly closed mouth and Leo laughed again. Ingrid thought how much more relaxed she looked now. Her cheeks were pink, and she'd lost some of the pinched look.

'No problem. You can't choose your family,' said Ingrid. 'There's no love lost between Lennie and me. Anyway, it's time I went home, my eyes won't stay open much longer. I'll settle the bill on my way out.'

'You *so* won't,' said Joel, and both he and Sam started to rummage in their pockets for their wallets, but Ingrid held up a hand.

'Look, I know I was very antisocial towards you two when I arrived and I'm sure you didn't charge me enough for all that packing and unpacking. Let me at least do this and then I'll feel as if we can start again.'

Joel and Sam looked at each other and then both reluctantly agreed. 'But only if it's our shout next time,' Joel said.

'There's going to be a next time?' Ingrid felt anxiety mingled with pleasure at this assumption that she was already one of the gang.

'Yes, there is,' said Elsie, before the others could answer. 'And Leo and me, we want to come and see your shop. It's Sunday tomorrow. Can we come and have a look?'

Lost for words, Ingrid bit her lip. This was all going too fast.

'We're not going to get in Ingrid's way until she's ready,' said Joel, saving her from replying. 'She's going to have a lot to do.'

'And with that in mind, I'd better go home and have an early night. I've done nothing useful yet but tomorrow might actually be the day when I get my act together,' said Ingrid, with more confidence than she felt.

She said goodbye and made her way to the bar, stopping to pay the bill, which to her city brain seemed ridiculously small for all the food they'd eaten. As she passed by the window on her way home, Ingrid could see all four of the others waving to her, smiling broadly. Joel raised his glass and their eyes met.

An unexpected surge of pleasure took Ingrid's breath away for a moment. She upped her pace and strode away across the green, now empty of rounders players. She didn't need this complication. Men, especially those with baggage, should be avoided. This one had what sounded like a tricky ex and a troublesome teenage daughter and Ingrid wasn't going to let him make her heart flutter, even if he was gorgeous and looked as if he was in dire need of some love.

It was time to start her new life, and it was going to be a straightforward one, with nothing in it to give her restless nights. Losing Tommy and the whirlwind of her life with him had been devastating. Ingrid still felt bruised all over. Tommy might not have been the romantic hero she'd wanted when she was a young girl, but he'd been her man, for better or for worse. The nights were often punctuated by dark dreams, and she'd wake to find she'd been crying. The house in York, beautiful and luxurious though it was, had begun to feel like a morgue. All that was behind her now though. This fresh chapter must have no curve balls and no torrid emotions. A small voice inside her head whispered *and no fun?* but she ignored it and carried on towards home. Granted it was a temporary home, but it was her own nest all the same. A hot bath, a warm bed and a complete lack of worrying about the future was what she needed. The first two she decided would be easy to achieve, but the third – not so much. Especially with Lennie Nightingale on the scene.

8

On the following morning, after a surprisingly dreamless sleep, Ingrid at last felt ready to tackle the mountain of boxes that were lying in wait. For the first time since the move and for no discernible reason apart from last night's socialising, she awoke full of energy and with a sense of purpose that had been lacking up to now. Even trying to get the conditioner out of her hair in the less than impressive shower didn't dampen her spirits, and she dressed quickly before running downstairs to the storeroom with the aim of taking a proper, calm look around.

It was worse than she'd thought. Joel and Sam had made a wonderful job of stacking the boxes but there were rows and rows of crates in there, standing at least four high and completely filling the room. Ingrid's stomach rumbled. Maybe she'd feel better if she ate something before tackling all this. The provisions from the farmers' market were long gone and the last few cornflakes in the packet were uninspiring, but when she'd defrosted and toasted a bagel and used the last of the cream cheese to liven it up, the job in hand felt a little less daunting.

As soon as she'd cleared away the crumbs and crockery, Ingrid settled down with a sheet of paper and tried to organise herself into making a plan for the next few days. It was very hard to know where to begin. She was just biting the end of her pen and wondering if she'd taken on a ridiculously complicated mission when she heard a rap on the front door. Her heart gave an uncomfortable leap. Jumping to her feet, she peered out of the upstairs window of the flat, but instead of the dreaded sight of her cousin Lennie, three smiling faces looked back up at her.

'Well, aren't you going to let us in?' Beryl shouted, waving a duster.

Ingrid hurried downstairs to open the door, and the ladies jostled to get inside.

'Can I nip up to the flat? I'm dying for a wee,' said Winnie. 'Beryl made me a pot of tea while I was waiting for her to sort out her stuff. I should never have had three cups.'

'It's lovely of you to come, and so early on a Sunday morning too, but I'm not sure why you're here because the cleaning's already been done,' Ingrid said, as Winnie bustled away. 'Aunty Sylvia organised it. That's the least of my problems. There are just so many boxes and I just don't know where to begin. I'm not normally indecisive, honestly I'm not.' She could hear the unfamiliar wobble in her voice but there was no stopping it as her memories took over. The sudden image of Tommy grinning at her was almost unbearable. He'd think she was unhinged doing all this.

'Well, that's where we come in,' said Anthea. 'We can help you to unpack, can't we? I hate cleaning anyway. I've got a woman that comes round once a week while I'm going for a swim. It's much better.'

Beryl snorted. 'All right for some,' she said. 'So, do you need us or not? I thought you might prefer to do it all yourself, but we wanted to at least offer to help. We won't be offended if you'd rather we went away. This was one of our snap decisions. When we turned seventy, which was a good while ago now, although you probably wouldn't believe it to look at us—'

'Stop waffling and fishing for compliments, Beryl,' said Anthea. 'What she's trying to say is we've promised ourselves to be more impulsive, so we came anyway. We gave it a few days so that you'd have time to feel a bit more at home, but now...' She did a graceful twirl. 'Here we are, the Saga Louts at your service.'

Ingrid tried to speak but the lump in her throat was threatening to choke her. Anthea reached out and patted her arm. 'I'm sorry, darling,' she said quietly. 'You're not used to us yet. Beryl tends to operate like a steamroller and Winnie's as bad. It's a good job they've got me to keep them in check.'

Beryl opened her mouth to say something, eyes flashing, but Anthea held up a hand. 'I didn't bring spray polish and rubber gloves, but I've got something much more useful.' She held up her basket, which Ingrid recognised as one of the more stylish designs from the farmers' market. 'Almond croissants.'

Winnie was back by this time and caught the tail end of the conversation. 'Now you're talking,' she said, raising her eyebrows as she looked across at Ingrid for permission.

Ingrid had managed to get her emotions in some sort of control now. She took a deep breath. 'This is so good of you,' she said, leading the way upstairs. 'I don't even know where to start with the unpacking. I must have been mad even thinking about opening a shop, even if it was only going to be temporary.'

'Not mad, just enthusiastic. That's always good,' said

Winnie. She settled herself on the sofa and watched Anthea familiarising herself with Sylvia's unsophisticated kitchen. 'I must say, this place hasn't had much done to it for ages. Christopher and his missus helped in the shop occasionally, I'll give them that, and Lennie provided the laminate floor, but the blokes who work for him mostly did that and he's not lifted a finger otherwise.'

Beryl nodded. 'That Lennie – he's no better than he should be. Don't let him winkle his way in here, dear. He'll be wanting to see how the land lies. He wants his mum to sell up and release some cash.'

Ingrid, once again lost in her worries about having taken on an impossible task, registered her cousin's name. She shuddered, pushing the thought of him away. There would be time to deal with Lennie Nightingale later. By now Anthea had boiled the kettle and found a coffee pot, then took a small grinder and a tin of coffee beans out of her bag. She was beginning to remind Ingrid of Mary Poppins. Would she pull a standard lamp and a wall mirror out of there next and pronounce herself 'practically perfect in every way'? The comforting aroma of freshly ground coffee soon filled the room and Beryl got up to fetch the plate of pastries. Anthea had even provided linen napkins.

Ingrid reached for the mug that Anthea had given her, refusing milk and sipping slowly. The intense darkness of the coffee seemed to clear her head slightly. The ladies were silent for a while, concentration on eating every crumb of the buttery croissants. Eventually Beryl finished her coffee and sat back with a happy sigh.

'That was a great idea, Anthea, even if we are all covered in pastry flakes now,' she said. 'You're not just a pretty face even if you've never been keen to roll up your sleeves and spoil your French manicure.'

Anthea laughed. 'I have my uses, darling,' she said. 'Now it's Winnie's turn. She's bursting to make a list, I can tell.'

Ingrid hadn't noticed Winnie pulling out a large spiral-bound notebook and pen, but it was obvious that this was going to be a proper meeting, rather than just friends getting together for a chat.

'I'm going to do a bit of plain speaking now,' Winnie said. 'It's best to call a spade a spade, I've found. I hope you're not going to be offended, Ingrid, because you've only known us for a short time, but you haven't really thought this thing through, have you?'

'You'll have to excuse Winnie,' said Anthea. 'Tact isn't her strong point. Neither is fashion sense,' she added.

'I'll have you know these trousers have got a designer label,' said Winnie. 'They were a snip from the charity shop. I don't know why nobody else had snapped them up.'

Beryl raised her eyebrows and looked Winnie up and down. 'Lemon yellow isn't everyone's colour, dear,' she said. 'Anyway, they're very cheerful. Carry on with what you were saying. I'm sure Ingrid is strong enough to take it.'

Speechless, Ingrid nodded. Being with the Saga Louts felt a lot like dropping in on the film set of *Dinner Ladies*, with Victoria Wood and the rest of the cast running rings around each other.

'Right,' Winnie said, writing the date at the top of the page and underlining it. 'In my opinion, what you need more than anything at this point is a working party to get your shop up and running. This job is too much for one person to tackle.'

'But... *I* made the decision to take it on,' said Ingrid, feeling herself beginning to come back to life properly at last as the caffeine worked its magic. 'It's nobody else's responsibility. Anyway, where would I get the people to help?'

There was a silence. Ingrid looked around the room and saw that all three ladies were waiting. Beryl was leaning forward, eyes bright as a robin's. Winnie's pen was raised, as if it was wanting to set off without her, and Anthea had crossed one elegant leg over the other, smoothed down her linen tunic and leaned back in her seat, completely relaxed.

'Have I got this right? Are you all offering to be my... team?' asked Ingrid, swallowing hard. The painful ache in her throat had been a regular visitor in the agonising days and weeks after Tommy died but lately, not so much. Now it was back.

'Not just us, darling. We need a full skill set for this,' said Anthea. 'Winnie's fabulous at designing window displays, as she told you. We call Beryl "Mrs Method" because she organises us so well, so she'll plan what order we need to do everything in. I'm the overseer.'

'Which means you do very little work and swan about looking glamorous,' said Beryl.

Anthea ignored the interruption. 'And that's good so far, but we should add some muscle power for humping boxes around and changing the shelving arrangement and so on. We could also do with someone artistic who can paint you a new sign to go over the window.'

As she spoke, they heard a loud knock at the door. 'That'll be Wave Two of the team,' said Winnie, going towards the stairs. She paused by the door. 'That's if you don't mind Joel and his girl joining us?'

Ingrid got to her feet and went across to the window. 'Is that Joel and Leo outside? What are they doing here?'

Anthea sighed. 'Keep up, darling. That's our muscle man.'

Ingrid nodded to Winnie. 'You'd better let him in then. But I can't see why you're all willing to do this. It's going to be hard work, and you don't even know me properly yet.'

'Oh, but we will, we certainly will,' said Beryl. 'Before long you'll feel as if you've known us all your life.'

Ingrid couldn't decide if this sounded like a promise or a threat. She turned to face the door as the newcomers entered the room. Her eyes met Joel's and they both looked away quickly. This was turning into a very interesting day.

Leo followed him in, looking as if she wished she was somewhere else. The Saga Louts gathered around her, taking turns to give her a hug, which she bore with fairly good grace, only rolling her eyes once.

'And Joel's lovely daughter is someone else we could do with enlisting to help,' said Winnie. 'This girl's a budding artist. She painted some pictures to put in the exhibition at the last village show and she sold nearly all of them. I bought one myself. She might do your shop sign for you if you play your cards right.'

Joel smiled. 'Do you really think Leo is up to that kind of thing, Winnie?'

'Rude,' said Leo. 'You've never had any faith in me, Dad.'

'I absolutely have, it's just...'

Winnie stepped in to prevent any further ruffling of Leo's feathers. 'Damn right she's up to the job. That's if Ingrid's willing to give her a chance?'

Ingrid smiled at Leo, who was doing her best to look invisible now she'd disentangled herself from the ladies. 'If you're willing to have a go at designing me a sign, I'd love to have some original artwork over the shop. Go for it, Leo. Let's make this place stand out from the crowd. Willowbrook will never have seen anything like it.'

'That's for sure,' muttered Leo, but she couldn't hide her delight at the idea.

Ingrid felt a surge of optimism. 'This is going to be one hell of a team,' she said happily.

9

The next couple of hours passed by in a blur of frantic activity, once Winnie had started her list and Leo had made short work of the last croissant.

'Are you sure you want me to paint your sign?' she said to Ingrid, brushing crumbs off her hoodie. 'I've never done anything that big before. It's freaking me out a bit.'

'Well, Anthea's given you a glowing reference,' said Ingrid. 'I can provide all the paint and so on if you let me know what you need. Let's give it a go, if you're happy to spare the time.'

'I've got plenty of time now I'm living at my dad's house,' Leo said, grinning at Joel. 'Although he does keep going on about some stuff he likes to call "housework".'

Joel pulled a face. 'No sign yet of you doing any of that. It's a work in progress. But it'd be great if you could make a go of a project like the shop sign. I bet the school would count it as coursework towards your art exam. You haven't got nearly enough done yet.'

'It's not my fault!' The words came out as a shout and the others all flinched. 'Mum hates me making a mess in Trevor's *beeeoootiful home*. How am I supposed to get any painting done?'

Ingrid was about to step in with some much needed peace-making when an unfamiliar sound made her stop and listen. She'd almost forgotten it was Sunday. 'Is that church bells I can hear?' she asked.

Beryl nodded. 'Yes, it's St Stephen's over yonder.' She glanced at Leo, who had folded her arms and was glaring at her father. 'Are you thinking of going to church when you get settled, Ingrid?' she asked, clearly glad of the distraction. 'Not today, obviously, we've got too much work to do, but later, maybe? We've got a lovely vicar. The Rev Bev does a great funeral.'

'Err... No, I don't think so. I'm not much of a one for religion,' Ingrid said. Once again, Joel's eyes met hers and she had the sudden lurching feeling that he could see right inside her soul. The trigger word had taken her straight back to Tommy's send-off. His funeral had been a well-attended affair at an Anglican church in the centre of York, with part two leading to the awful moment when his coffin disappeared behind the heavy velvet curtains at the crematorium. This was followed by a wake full of slightly dodgy anecdotes, champagne and endless platitudes. Just the word *funeral* was enough to give Ingrid goosebumps.

'Come on, gang. It's action time,' said Joel, coming to her rescue just as the tears threatened to start. He stood up and rubbed his hands together. 'Otherwise the day's going to be half gone before we begin. Read out the first bit of your list, Winnie, and we'll get going.'

Winnie got up, too, and cleared her throat. 'Leo, you should start mapping out the sign. Have you got some paper and a pencil?'

'I always carry my sketchpad in case I get an idea,' Leo said, already rummaging in her backpack. 'What's the shop going to be called?'

'The Treasure Trove,' said Ingrid, with a thrill of excitement. It was going to happen. It was actually going to happen.

Winnie's eyes were sparkling now. 'Okay then, give me a very brief overview of how you'd like the shop window to look. Do you like my idea of having just one beautiful thing at a time in there? If you do, I can get started on that.'

Ingrid clapped her hands. 'Yes, that sounds just right. Carry on with the list, I'm starting to see it in my mind's eye now.'

'Good. You and Joel should go into the shop next and decide if the shelves and till desk and so on need moving around, and Beryl and Anthea can start unpacking the first few boxes.'

Anthea looked as if she was going to comment on this part of the plan, but Winnie fixed her with a steely gaze, and she gestured resignedly to Beryl for them both to make a move downstairs.

Soon everyone was in their places. Winnie climbed into the window and began to set up a collapsible wallpapering table she'd found in the back room to be the base of her display. Beryl and Anthea pulled out overalls from their bags and headed for the storeroom, Leo stretched out on the floor of the flat and began to sketch out her ideas and Ingrid and Joel found themselves standing in the centre of the shop.

'We've railroaded you today,' he said apologetically. 'Are you okay with all this?'

'It's wonderful,' said Ingrid, looking around at the empty shelves. 'I'm not sure how to make the place seem more welcoming though. It still looks too much like a mini supermarket.'

A New Lease of Life

Joel scratched his head and walked around the edge of the shop. 'I think it's mainly that there are too many shelves. I get the impression that you want the goods to look tempting and desirable, rather than all crammed together to get as many as possible in at once, is that right?'

'Absolutely. Would it be a big job to get rid of some of these units and make the rest into a kind of informal arrangement? Maybe have just one or two around the edges?'

'That'd be possible. They're quite substantial but I think they're all free-standing. Tell you what, I'll load the ones you don't want straight into my van. I brought it just in case.'

Leo wandered in at this point. 'I can't do any more designing till I've talked to you,' she said to Ingrid. 'Can I help move stuff? And what about a sofa? You could have somewhere for people to sit down while they have a think about what they want to buy. We might bring that navy blue one out of the spare room, Dad? The sofa bed? It's a naff colour but we could jazz it up with cushions. You never have guests... and that'd make enough space for me to have the room as a studio.'

Joel grinned at her. 'How long have you been planning that?'

'Oh, only since you said I could definitely stay.'

They looked at each other, and Ingrid could see that Joel was touched. 'Can we donate a sofa?' he asked her. 'It's in good nick, and it's not too big for the space.'

'Perfect,' Ingrid said. The three of them got to work shunting out several of the bulkier shelving units and the shop was soon feeling much airier. Now, customers entering the space would be greeted by a much less austere arrangement. There was room for the sofa at one side, and the till counter had been re-sited at the back. By this time, Beryl and Anthea had, with various cries of delight and some of horror, unearthed a few objects ready for the initial set-up.

'We all need a break,' said Ingrid. 'You've been amazing, but you should feel free to go home now. I can carry on by myself after this, I'm sure.'

'Do you really want to manage on your own though?' Beryl asked, head on one side. 'We're having a great time. I love a project to get my teeth into, and Anthea has got herself quite grubby for once this morning.'

'I'd like to work on this window with some of my drapes and accessories now,' said Winnie. 'I'll need to go home and fetch some. I inherited the ones from the jeweller's shop when it closed down. Hoped they'd come in handy one day.'

'You haven't even had time to look at my sketch,' said Leo. 'And we've still got to fetch the sofa.'

Joel didn't say anything, but Ingrid could somehow tell he was willing her to let them carry on with the job. He smiled at her, and her heart lifted. They were all being so kind.

'Well, in that case, I'm not going to argue. I'd love to have you all working with me,' she said.

There was a unanimous cheer and Leo did a strange little dance on the spot. 'We can ask Sam to help sometimes too, when he's not working,' she said. 'I'd keep an eye on Elsie. She's a good kid.'

'Is it warm enough for a picnic?' Beryl asked hopefully. 'I could nip along home and make some sandwiches if you like, and we can sit on the green and eat them?'

'Great idea,' said Joel. 'If Sam's free later we can ask him to come and help with the sofa and I'll take these spare shelves to my workshop for now, in case you need more when you're up and running, okay? Come on, Leo, you can give me a hand. We can fetch some crisps and juice from our house and bring blankets to sit on.'

Half an hour later, Ingrid was sitting on a rug eating the best egg and cress sandwich of her life and drinking ice-cold apple juice from a plastic mug. How had this happened? One minute she was panic-stricken as to how she could make her mad idea work and the next there was a competent team in place, each of whom had their own inspirational thoughts about how the dream could be a reality. Joel raised his mug to her in a silent acknowledgement of the work done so far and Ingrid was about to respond when she saw a familiar figure on the far side of the green. The man lifted a hand and nodded his head. Even at this distance it was clear that Lennie Nightingale was smiling. It wasn't a pleasant smile.

10

'Is the new shop going to be open tomorrow?' Elsie asked, hopping up and down as she surveyed the open boxes and stacks of random goods on the floor.

Ingrid laughed. 'No, there's still a lot to do, but we've got on really well today, thanks to...' She glanced around the room, lost for words. Beryl, Anthea and Winnie were packing away their various belongings, Leo and Joel had just helped Sam to manoeuvre the sofa into place and as she watched, Elsie leapt onto it and lay down flat.

'Thanks to...?' Beryl said. 'Were you going to give us a name? You can't all be Saga Louts, you know. We're unique.'

'How about "The Treasure Team"?' suggested Sam. 'It looks as if you've unearthed a fair few of those already.'

'Well, a mixture of treasure and tat, but I like it,' said Joel. 'Can we be your Treasure Team, Ingrid?'

'That'd be great. More than great, actually.' Ingrid's voice was husky as she waved them on their way. Soon only Joel was left, still busy sweeping around the shelves.

'You don't have to do that,' Ingrid said. 'It's Sunday evening.

Haven't you and Leo got somewhere to be? Dinner to cook? I've already hijacked your day off.'

'I'm my own boss these days, and Leo's gone to see one of her mates. Ten o'clock curfew. We need a break from each other sometimes, to be honest. I'm glad she's back home at last but living with a teen isn't a bed of roses all the time, and she must feel the same about me.'

Ingrid took the brush away from him. 'Stop sweeping, Joel, for goodness' sake. I'm not doing any more now.'

'Really?'

'Yes, I've had enough for one day. Look, it's good of you to do all this, but I never meant the shop to be anything but my own project. Do you think the ladies and Sam and Elsie and Leo actually want to be part of my team? I feel as if they've been press-ganged into helping.'

Joel shrugged. 'When you get to know them all better, you'll realise none of that lot ever get pushed into doing what they don't want to do. They haven't had this much fun in ages. Right, I'll get off home, if you're sure you don't need me?'

Worried she might have hurt his feelings, Ingrid made the mistake of looking straight into Joel's eyes and then somehow couldn't tear her gaze away. His hair was tousled and decorated with a few cobwebs after crawling around his workshop to stash away the spare shelves, and he had a smudge of dirt all down one cheek. She had a random thought that he looked as if he didn't eat enough. The slightly hollow cheekbones made him appear gaunt and there were shadows under the dark blue eyes. They were kind eyes that made her want to change her mind and ask him to hang around for longer, but that would make her seem needy. Ingrid was an independent woman now, and she had to stay that way.

'No, it's fine. I'll see you whenever you want to drop in,' she said, breaking eye contact with difficulty. 'Leo says she's coming round again after school tomorrow to finish her design for the sign. I hope that's okay?'

'Sure. Maybe you can get her to do some homework while she's here. I just get filthy looks when I mention the subject.' He grinned and turned to go. 'Lock the door behind me,' he said. 'I know this is a quiet backwater but better to be safe.'

Ingrid stood on the step and watched Joel drive away with mixed feelings. She definitely didn't need the complication of a disturbingly attractive single man around when she was in the place alone, even if he would probably never be interested in a woman like herself, with baggage and worries and an aching heart. How old must he be? Surely no more than late forties – younger than her. Why was she even thinking about Joel on those terms anyway? The long look they'd just exchanged meant nothing. He was just a friendly soul who liked to help. She shivered. The evening was growing chilly, and she was about to take Joel's advice and lock up for the night when she heard the purr of an engine, and a bright red sports car pulled up on the pavement outside the shop.

Ingrid peered into the driver's window, hesitated for just one moment too long and stepped back a pace. She tried to close the door, but it was too late. The driver was out of his car and on the step of the shop in a flash, with his foot preventing her from shutting him on the other side.

'Now, now Ingrid, my love,' said Lennie Nightingale. 'Don't be unfriendly to your poor relation. Aren't you going to ask me in for a coffee... or something stronger? For old times' sake?'

'I'm absolutely not your love, and the old times we've got aren't anything to celebrate, are they?' said Ingrid, holding tight to the door. 'Why would I want to get nostalgic with you?'

'That's not very nice,' said Lennie. 'I'm sure if we try, we can

A New Lease of Life

come up with some good memories to share. If you don't want to let me in, how about a drink at the pub? Neutral ground?'

Ingrid took a deep breath, furious with herself to find her stomach churning, just as it always had whenever she thought about the birthday party she'd tried so hard to forget. 'I'm going to close the door now, Lennie,' she said. 'You'd better move your foot before it gets crushed. And if you try to stop me, I promise you I'll yell so loudly that someone somewhere is bound to hear me. Nobody takes much notice when girls and women scream, if you remember. They tend to assume it's a game. But a good old yell usually gets attention, I've found since then.'

Lennie stared at Ingrid, his face impassive. 'Boy, you really do know how to bear a grudge, don't you?' he said eventually. 'All I wanted to do was to talk to you about the future of the shop. You're wasting our time with this stupid idea of yours to sell Tommy's leftovers. We need to get the place sold and put Mum's mind at rest. It's cruel letting it drag on, can't you see that?'

Sounds of gentle revelry drifted over from The Fox and Fiddle in the still evening air. Ingrid wished more than anything that she was safely in there with a glass of wine in her hand and the Saga Louts nearby to make her laugh. She could smell the fresh scent of grass cuttings from an earlier mowing of the green. Birds were calling to each other as they prepared to roost. The village was settling down for a peaceful Sunday evening.

'Go away, Lennie,' Ingrid said, trying to muster up a level of fierceness that would send him on his way, even though exhaustion from the day's work was making her shoulders ache and her eyes want to close. 'You're only interested in releasing the cash from the sale. Don't make out you're looking out for your mum's mental health. I know you better than that, remember?'

Lennie folded his arms and regarded Ingrid with a smile. She couldn't help thinking that he'd improved with age. His slim, dark good looks were a little saturnine but that only added to an undoubted air of danger that some women probably found appealing. As a rather solid teenager who hated energetic sports and fresh air, Lennie's waxy complexion had looked sickly, and his hair had been greasy. Now, he was still pale, but the intense green of his eyes and a very sharp haircut, not to mention the black trousers and white linen shirt, made him look as if he was advertising a very expensive aftershave or auditioning for the next *Bond* movie.

'I'll go now, but this isn't the last time you'll see me, by any means,' Lennie warned her, smoothing back his hair. 'You'll soon get tired of playing shops. And then we'll talk properly.' He turned to leave but swivelled back at the last moment. 'You're a bit dusty and crumpled at the moment. It's from all that horrible unpacking I guess, but I have to say you're looking very tasty, Cuz. That *frozen virgin* image always did it for me. I don't think you'll be single for long.'

With that, he got back into his car, leaving Ingrid staring after him with her mouth hanging open. Tasty? Was she being compared to a lump of Stilton or some kind of intriguing canapé now? The nerve of the man. How dare he come around here insinuating that she was on the lookout for another husband? And *playing shops*? She hoped fervently that nobody else thought she was doing that. Ingrid was furious with herself to find she was trembling as she closed the door. She needed to hold on to the banister as she went upstairs to the flat.

The sofa welcomed her as she flopped down, close to tears now she was finally alone, and realising with a pang that she was also very hungry. There was nothing much in the fridge and cooking seemed too much effort at this point anyway. As she wavered between cheese on toast or going to bed early to distract herself from her rumbling tummy, there was a knock at the front door. Was this Lennie back? Surely he'd have got the message. Ingrid went over to the window and saw to her relief that it was Joel's van parked outside this time. He must have forgotten something. She ran downstairs and opened the door, unable to stop herself beaming at him in a most uncool way.

'Sorry to bother you again, but I had a sudden idea that you might not feel like rustling anything up to eat after that busy day,' he said. 'I haven't even thought what to have for dinner yet, have you?'

'You must be a mind reader. I was just wondering the same thing,' Ingrid said. 'Is anywhere open for a takeaway at this time on a Sunday? I'll treat you if there is, you've earned it, and we've both got to eat.'

'Not a chance. The nearest one open tonight is miles away and they don't like delivering this far out. I can knock up a decent pasta and tomato sauce though if you want to come over to mine? I'll even throw in a few olives and some anchovies.'

She hesitated, and he blushed. 'That's if you can stand having dinner with me for two nights running. I... I mean I expect you'd rather have some time to yourself, and you don't really know if I'm an axe murderer or something...'

'And are you?'

'Not so's I've noticed. And I've got fresh parmesan.'

'I'll get my coat.'

Driving through the village in Joel's van, Ingrid felt deliciously reckless. It had been a long time since she'd acted on impulse. The last six months had been a mixture of grief and confusion. Her life had felt as if it was on hold until she'd made the deal with Sylvia to take the shop for a year. Since that conversation, there had been a blur of packing, house selling and financial tangles. Now, with the evening light illuminating the church tower and the cottages lining the narrow streets, a feeling of adventure was afoot. It was the last day of March, Ingrid realised, having lost track of time since her move. The evening air smelt exciting, with the tantalising aroma of Sunday barbecues wafting through the open van window. Clearly, the Willowbrook residents weren't tied to the traditional roast at the weekend and must be hardy enough to start the barbecue season early. Relaxing at last, Ingrid yawned so widely that her jaws cracked. She covered her mouth with a hand and glanced apologetically at Joel.

'Stick with it, we're nearly there and I've got a bottle of quite decent red wine that's asking to be opened,' said Joel. 'I promise I'll walk you home as soon as you're ready to call it a night. It's only ten minutes' stroll if you take all the shortcuts, but you're not doing it on your own.'

Ingrid didn't answer because she was concentrating on trying not to let her eyes close, overcome with tiredness and the relief of not being alone in her quest. This embryonic friendship with Joel seemed to be developing at an unusually fast pace. She wondered, sleepiness forgotten for the moment, if the electricity she'd been feeling between them was one-sided and just due to her vulnerable state, or if it might be that he felt a similar bond growing between the two of them. In that case, was this dinner invitation... an actual date? The thought was unnerving. A shiver of excitement ran down Ingrid's spine. She sat up straighter and rubbed her eyes as the van slowed down. She'd need to be fully alert for this, whatever it turned out to be.

Joel pulled onto the drive of a compact semi-detached

house that looked as if it might date back to the 1930s. It was bay-windowed, edged by a tiny walled garden with a large opening onto a paved driveway. The front door was painted buttercup yellow and there were hanging baskets either side of it that were filled with pansies. As Joel turned off the engine, two small cats appeared, miaowing plaintively. The white one wove around Joel's legs as he came round to open the van door for Ingrid, but the black one was timid and watched them from a safe distance.

Charmed, Ingrid bent to stroke the white cat. 'What are their names?' she asked.

'I have no idea. They're not mine but they visit most days. I call them Randall and Hopkirk.'

Ingrid laughed. 'And I suppose you never, ever feed them scraps of cheese, or ham, or suchlike?'

'You sound as if you know the score. Has this happened to you?'

'Oh yes, but my visitors were posh Persians with squashed faces. They were meant to live next door, but their owner was often away, so I stepped in. They sneezed a lot, but they were otherwise quite cute. I haven't had a cat of my own since I was a child. Tommy wasn't a big fan. He wanted us to adopt a dog but we both worked long hours so it would have been cruel.'

Ingrid forced herself to stop thinking about Tommy, at least for now. There had been enough memories flowing around for one night already. She knew once she got into bed, Tommy's confident, smiling face would haunt her thoughts again but for this one evening at least, she was going to make a big effort to live in the moment. She followed Joel through the back door into the kitchen, firmly pushed all the sad and worrying thoughts to the back of her mind and slammed the door on them.

11

Joel settled his guest in a comfortable armchair in the corner of the kitchen and wondered why on earth he'd been so keen to get her here. Ingrid was obviously knackered, and he hadn't even given her the chance to change out of her grubby clothes. Joel wasn't used to low-maintenance women. In his previous and only long-term relationship, Trina would never have left the house without a shower, several outfit appraisals and full make-up, but Ingrid had just grabbed her jacket and bag and jumped into the van without a murmur. It was refreshing, but now she was here, he felt awkward and clumsy. Nobody had ever watched him cook. He'd taught himself several failsafe recipes when he realised that if he didn't learn a few basics, he'd be living on beans on toast or takeaway fish and chips, but he was still no expert.

'Right, time for a glass of wine,' Joel said, making his tone breezy, as if he was well used to unexpected visitors popping in for dinner. He opened the bottle, luckily a screw top, one less thing to bungle, and poured them both a generous glass.

A New Lease of Life

'Cheers, and all the best with your project,' he said, clinking glasses with Ingrid. She smiled at him and took a sip.

'Mmm, good choice. Are you a wine buff as well as a rescuer?'

'Nah. I usually just wander around Aldi's booze aisle and copy what the smartest person I can see is buying,' he admitted. 'I've liked most of the ones I've picked so far but then I'm not choosy. In wine, that is...'

The sentence petered out as Joel realised how that sounded. He reached to switch on the radio on the kitchen counter and the gentle sound of piano music filled the room. 'Okay, I'm going to chop some onions and garlic. You need to sit back and recover from the last few days, I imagine?'

'But I can help if you want me to.'

Joel could see that getting up out of her chair was the very last thing Ingrid wanted to do. 'No, stay put. Close your eyes for a little while if you like. I'll be less likely to chop a finger off if you're not watching me. Maybe put your glass down first though.'

Ingrid did as she was told and yawned again. She stretched out her legs, crossed them at the ankles and leaned back into the cushions with a sigh of relief. In seconds she was fast asleep, looking so at home that Joel's heart melted. He wondered how long it had been since someone took the pressure off her. Ingrid's husband's death must have taken an awful toll, and then she'd made the brave decision to make a brand-new start, with all the sorting and packing and upheavals involved in that.

Joel dragged his thoughts away from curiosity about Ingrid's previous life and assembled his ingredients. A bowl full of tomatoes from the farmers' market meant he could make the sauce from scratch, and he flicked the switch on the kettle ready to put them in boiling water for skinning. Soon, he was humming along to the music, lost in the pleasure of creating a meal for someone other than himself. He always cooked for Leo when it was his turn to be the parent, but she was more of a pizza and salad girl, with a few oven chips on the side.

The tantalising aroma of garlic and onions frying in olive oil reminded Joel how hungry he was, and he deftly skinned and chopped the tomatoes, adding fresh basil from a pot on the windowsill and a good twist of black pepper. He opened a tin of anchovies and rummaged in the fridge for black olives. Soon, the sauce was bubbling away merrily. Joel refilled his glass.

Once the pasta was ready, Joel set the kitchen table, put the bottle in the middle and touched Ingrid lightly on the shoulder. She stirred, and mumbled something incoherent about a party but didn't wake up.

Joel tried again. 'Ingrid, dinner's ready,' he said, a touch too loudly, and she woke with a start, sitting up straight and looking around her in alarm. She saw Joel watching her and rubbed her eyes.

'I can't believe you scooped me up and brought me round here and all I did was fall asleep!' she said, mortified that she'd finally given in to the torpor that had threatened in the van. 'That's so rude.'

'Don't be daft. You're exhausted, and it's understandable. You've had a power nap so now you can eat without nodding off in your dinner. Leo used to do that, I remember. Back when she was still Olivia. She once went face first into a dish of casserole. Getting the gravy out of her hair took ages.'

Joel rambled on about more of Leo's childhood quirks as he drained the spaghetti and dished it up, topped with the sauce.

A New Lease of Life

Ingrid was gradually coming back to life now, and he poured her a glass of iced water from the jug he'd placed on the table. She drained it gratefully and then reached for her wine.

'This is absolute bliss,' she said. Joel could see that her eyes were full of tears.

'It's nothing much. Come on, eat while it's hot,' he said. 'I'm no Jamie Oliver but this is going to do you good. Lots of vitamin C and some carbs to get your energy levels going again. You're running on empty.'

Ingrid picked up her fork without another word and began to expertly twirl spaghetti around it. Joel watched, impressed. 'And I bet you're not even going to spill tomato sauce on yourself,' he said. 'I always end up putting my T-shirt in the wash after this kind of food.'

Joel had retuned the radio to a channel featuring eighties hits and they were now listening to songs that took Joel right back to his teens, when mix tapes were still a thing and he'd spent hours trying to impress mates with his choices of tracks.

'What kind of music do you like?' he asked Ingrid, as she put down her fork and sighed with satisfaction.

'That was the best thing I've eaten in months,' she said. 'Oh, and I don't really have a favourite type of music these days. Tommy liked heavy metal. He had a sound-proofed study where he'd blast it out late into the night. He never slept well so he was often up till the small hours. We never went to bed at the same time. I used to listen to podcasts in bed to send me to sleep.' She stopped abruptly, as if suddenly realising she was giving too much away.

'It's okay to talk about him, if you want to,' Joel said. This felt like thin ice. He hadn't known Ingrid for long, but he was already aware that he really wanted her to be his friend. She was beautiful and elegant, but that wasn't the pull. Well, not just that anyway. He'd watched her make an effort to socialise with Beryl and the rest of the gang and had seen how hard she'd worked today. Nothing had daunted her, and she'd been incredibly grateful for their help, even though he thought she was probably disappointed with herself for not managing it all alone. The earlier frostiness that had irritated Sam was not in evidence now, but Joel sensed that it wouldn't take much for Ingrid to retreat into her shell.

'I haven't really felt like talking about Tommy up to now,' Ingrid said after a moment. 'Well, I haven't had anyone to discuss him with really, I suppose.'

'Why not? You must have lots of friends.'

'What makes you think that?'

'You're such a friendly person,' he said, wondering if that was an exaggeration, given their earlier bad start. 'The Saga Louts have taken to you straight away and they don't let just anyone into their exclusive group, you know.'

Ingrid smiled. She picked up her wine glass and realised it was empty. Joel refilled it, and waited, willing himself not to jump in and say the wrong thing. He hoped the atmosphere of the kitchen was soothing. The hum of the fridge, the radio, the gentle tick of the clock on the wall and the muted wail of the baby being put to bed in the house next door were the only sounds. Ingrid seemed miles away. Still Joel waited.

He glanced around, wondering if this surprise visitor thought his home was shabby. He'd concentrated all his efforts on getting the business going and the workshop organised after Trina had left and the rest of the house had had to fend for itself. Luckily, Trina hadn't wanted the table and chairs or the contents of the cupboards, as apparently Trevor had much better taste in kitchenware. This room could certainly do with a lick of paint, but the various terracotta and bronze shades of the tiles were warm and friendly and the rug on the floor was a cosy weave of red, brown and cream.

Joel remembered taking Leo with him to buy it as a surprise present for Trina because she said the floor tiles made her feet cold. She'd hated it. It wasn't long after that she had left. He couldn't blame her departure on the rug, or even totally on Trevor. Their marriage had been hanging on by a thread ever since small Olivia had deprived Trina of the sleep she said she couldn't manage without. Joel had taken over as much of the night-wakings as possible, but he'd been working long hours at the time and was also finding it hard to function with a baby and then a toddler who seemed to wake on the hour, every hour. It was mind-numbingly tiring for them both.

Ingrid broke the silence quite suddenly by putting her glass down and clearing her throat. Joel dragged his thoughts away from the train crash of his marriage and gave her his full attention as she began to speak.

'I hardly know you, Joel, but I've had two glasses of wine and a nap and now I feel as if I want to tell you a bit about my marriage. Is that too much? Would you be bored?'

Joel shook his head and poured the last of the wine into her glass. He debated opening another bottle but then remembered that had been the last one in the cupboard, so he contented himself with water. 'Go ahead. I'm happy to listen.' He grinned. 'I might even return the favour sometime if you play your cards right.'

He moved the dirty dishes onto the worktop and waved away Ingrid's offers to wash up. 'I'll load the dishwasher later, but I'll just turn the radio down. Make a start, I'm all ears.'

She took a deep breath. 'Well, I'm not going to go into detail about all the years we had together, but I just wanted you to know that I'm not trying to airbrush Tommy out of my life by getting rid of his stuff. He was the life and soul of any party and the most generous, open-handed person I've ever met, but he was a magpie. He always knew I hated all his clutter, so he stashed most of it away in the garage and the loft. Even so, there were still rooms in the house that had loads of boxes stacked in them. The trouble was he couldn't resist bringing home random lots from the auction house, even if there was only one object in them that had caught his eye. It was a sort of weird compulsion.'

'He loved his work though?' Joel asked, thinking privately that the man must have been a pretty selfish git to have ignored his wife's feelings on the matter in such a big way.

'Yes, he did. And everyone there loved him too. They encouraged him, as if it was an endearing little hobby to stockpile junk. Then, he opted out. He died so suddenly that I didn't even know how I felt myself, and then there was this huge outpouring of grief from his workmates and all his dozens of friends. He had no family. His parents were dead, and he was an only child but the rest of the people who knew him made up for that.'

Ingrid stopped talking. Her jaw was set now and her eyes flashed fire. Joel reached out and took her hands in his. 'This all sounds so very sad. Can you carry on with the story? Best to get it all out, I think.'

'Okay. You're probably right. It was as if I had nothing to do with what happened next. Tommy's colleagues wanted to be part of the funeral arrangements but soon they'd completely taken over, and I couldn't seem to stop them. I didn't want to, if I'm honest. I felt numb, and I couldn't seem to get a grip. They chose the music, wrote eulogies and invited scores of people who'd known Tommy. It turned into a huge affair. Caterers, a live band at the wake... and I just sat back and let them do it, as if he was nothing to do with me at all.'

'But that's not a bad thing, Ingrid. From how you've described Tommy it sounds as if that's the sort of send-off he'd have appreciated, and you really weren't up to sorting out the details of a big wake yourself, so letting his friends do the donkey work probably helped them to cope too. Double whammy.'

Ingrid considered this point. 'I guess so. They did seem to enjoy doing it. Afterwards they kind of melted away. Either that or I froze them off. Most of them were very full-on. I couldn't handle them, but I can't help feeling as if I let Tommy down by losing touch with his friends and workmates.'

'I don't suppose they've lost touch with each other though, have they? They're not likely to need you to keep them together if they're all so... sociable.'

The new idea looked as if it was filtering into Ingrid's mind now. 'So, you don't think I'm a bad person for backing off from them all and then planning to get rid of everything he loved? I feel like a deserter sometimes.' She rubbed her eyes again and the biggest yawn yet escaped her.

Joel let go of Ingrid's hands and got up. 'Come on, I'm walking you home before you slide off your chair and go to sleep under the table. You're definitely not a bad person but you are a tired one.'

Ingrid slipped on her coat and slung her bag over her shoulder. She followed Joel out of the kitchen. As they walked through the quiet village, Joel reflected that this had been a very interesting evening, although looking back, Ingrid had told him about her feelings towards Tommy's friends and his habit of accumulating junk, but she hadn't actually filled him in on anything very personal about their marriage. Even so, two things were now clear in his mind. The first was that he was glad he and Ingrid appeared to have skipped some of the early stages of friendship and were now on a much better footing. The second was that if he'd ever had the misfortune to meet the party animal that was Tommy Copperfield, he wouldn't have liked him. Not one bit.

12

On Monday morning, Ingrid woke with a start just before six o'clock, jittery with energy and ready to tackle more sorting. Her evening with Joel had been a peaceful interlude, although she couldn't help thinking that she'd said far too much about Tommy. Joel had egged her on, for sure, but she cringed when she remembered how forthcoming she'd been about his annoying friends and his hoarding tendencies. She wondered why she'd let herself go so much. Her usual reticence had disappeared last night. It could have been the wine, or her tiredness or just Joel's easy, sympathetic manner that had edged her further and further towards opening up. Probably a mixture of all three, she reflected. Still, there were plenty of other more personal things that she'd held back from sharing.

Ingrid promised herself to put such niggles out of her mind, at least while she worked, otherwise nothing would get done. There was no point in beating herself up about letting out some of the angst. Her marriage had been by no means perfect, but she'd loved Tommy and still felt a strong sense of loyalty to his memory. The last six months had seemed like a rollercoaster of emotions, and she was still nowhere near doing what people who'd never experienced grief described as *moving on*. In her opinion, you didn't move on from loss and the often-overwhelming sadness that went with it, you just kind of worked around the pain and shock, weaving it into your daily life until it became a bit more manageable. And to do that, she needed to start by having breakfast and a shower.

Not long afterwards and wrapped up warmly in her dressing gown, Ingrid towelled her hair as dry as possible and then went into the kitchen. She glanced at the calendar on the wall, left behind by Sylvia, which boasted a collection of inspirational sayings. Today was 1 April, and Ingrid happily tore off March's message telling her that tomorrow was the first day of the rest of her life. True or not, it had been annoying her ever since she arrived. April's text was marginally better. It proudly declaimed:

The best is yet to come.

Ingrid fervently hoped so.

The laminated flooring felt sticky under her bare feet as she pottered around. So much for Dot and Willy's cleaning skills. She mentally put floor cleaner and a new mop on her list of things to buy as she fished the last two crumpets out of the freezer, luxuriating in the comforting, homely aroma as they browned in the toaster. There was no dodging the fact that she was going to have to go shopping later today and that meant getting the car out. Since the nerve-racking journey down from York, it was time to face up to the fact that Ingrid hated driving with a passion. The car had been Tommy's pride and joy; a classy Range Rover with every additional feature he could lay his hands on. He'd enjoyed taking her out in it, on the rare occasions when they'd both been off work at the same time.

The Range Rover was a dream to be chauffeured in, especially through the beautiful Yorkshire Dales, stopping off for a pub lunch and then having a gentle stroll around a village or two. They'd both loved the rolling countryside, although Tommy was no hiker. He preferred to see the scenery from the vantage point of the car with his window wound down and one elbow propped on the sill. 'Breathe in all that lovely fresh air,' he'd said, taking a great lungful of it himself. 'This is the life, eh? I don't know why we don't do this more often, love.' Ingrid hadn't replied. She was well aware that their working lives took precedence over everything else, and that was the way they both liked it.

The problem was that Ingrid had never needed a car for work. The nearest of the hotels she managed was in walking distance of home and if she'd needed to travel to the others, she'd only had to ask and one of her staff would be glad to have the excuse of a jaunt. When Ingrid had finally arrived in Willowbrook, she'd inched her way into the only parking space left in a tight corner of the paved area shared with the nearby flats. Looking out of the back window this morning it was hard to see how she'd avoided scraping the wall or hitting the car right next to hers. To reverse out of there and then set off to find the nearest big store would need steady nerves and a lot more willpower than she had in reserve at the moment.

Spreading the final chunk of the creamy farm-produced butter on her toast, Ingrid decided that she'd be best to shelve the supermarket trip until later and concentrate on the job in hand. With that in mind, and relieved to have postponed the dreaded task, she finished her breakfast and dressed in her oldest black jeans and baggy sweatshirt. At least they wouldn't show the dirt. She twisted her damp hair on top of her head, secured it with a scrunchy and rolled up her sleeves.

With the radio tuned to a local station playing cheerful morning-type tunes, the day in the shop started well. For one thing, the more boxes Ingrid emptied, the better she became at sorting out the beautiful, useful and saleable from the absolute dross. The dust and grime that had accumulated in some of the crates made her sneeze but the delight she felt on unearthing something unusual kept her going. She arranged all her best finds along the counter in the back kitchen of the shop, re-boxed again anything that she considered not worth trying to sell or suitable for a bargain table and interspersed her unpacking with brief coffee breaks sitting on a bench in the tiny, paved courtyard behind the storeroom, drinking in the sunshine along with the aromatic black brew. This didn't feel like a day to be cutting back on caffeine.

The weather had become unseasonably warm again today. Even the slight chill in the air had disappeared for the time being, and it was tempting to be outdoors when the task of opening any more boxes got too daunting. Ingrid washed her hands, redid her hair and unearthed her walking boots when she'd done as much as she could face. She'd been too busy to think any more about Joel and what had felt almost like a dinner date the night before but now her face burned again when she remembered how she'd poured out all her feelings of guilt about the funeral and what happened afterwards. Joel texted to see if she was okay around 7 a.m. and Ingrid had answered briefly, but the more she mulled over the previous evening's conversation, the more she felt as if she'd drastically over-shared.

With this in mind, Ingrid once again opted to avoid walking around the village in case she bumped into Joel, and also intense pangs of hunger were making her think longingly of the café in the country park. It wasn't quite lunchtime and Mondays should be reasonably quiet there, she imagined, so it wouldn't matter if she wasn't feeling as neat and tidy as usual. A squirt of perfume and a lick of lip gloss were all she needed to get her out of the shop and over the green, with nothing more than her bank card and the shop key in her pocket.

The track that wound its way towards the biggest lake was deserted, and the sound of birdsong soothed Ingrid's troubled soul. She resolved to try and put Joel out of her mind. He hadn't seemed to mind her unburdening herself and there was an air of sadness about him that suggested he was no stranger to loss, even if his own was of a different kind.

Concentrating on enjoying the day rather than soul-searching, Ingrid followed the row of memorial benches spaced out along the lakeside path. Each one had its own plaque, most of them making reference to a person, or sometimes a couple who had loved to sit there. Ingrid glanced at a few as she passed but couldn't bear to stop and look at them properly today. Coping with her own confused feelings was hard enough at the moment without reading memorials to other people's suffering. Nevertheless, one of them caught her eye even as she hurried past. She paused, and almost against her will, read the words on the brass plate.

In memory of Frances (Frankie) Clifford, our sunshine girl
10 February 1987 – 1 December 2022
Four Seasons in One Day

Intriguing. Frankie sounded like an interesting character. So young too. Ingrid thought about the last line, which had immediately triggered one of her favourite songs in her head. It reminded her of Tommy, who'd once taken her to a gig where the band played this as a finale. 'I bloody love Crowded House, don't you?' he'd bellowed, on his feet and singing along. Ingrid had found the words painfully moving. Tommy was a *four seasons in one day* kind of person too. Sometimes sunny in temperament, then thunderous, followed by dark gloom and afterwards as mellow as an autumn day, but not necessarily in that order. He was a maverick. Not in the least bit relaxing to live with but certainly never predictable.

A wave of rage came over Ingrid, and she moved on, walking quickly. Tommy had left her in the lurch, the bastard. Ingrid rarely swore out loud and not even very often in her head for that matter, but today all the foulest words she knew started to fight to escape. She wanted to stand on the bank of the lake and yell out her fury; to cry out to the heavens that Tommy had deserted her without a word. No time for goodbyes, just a drunken song broken off part way through and then a dramatic crash to the floor. Not his fault, granted, but all the same, in her tired and emotional state this new life felt bleak and pointless. At this moment, if she could have chosen a plaque on a bench in Tommy's memory, it would have said:

> You faithless piece of shit. You buggered off and left me. What price your promise to love and to cherish now?

Ingrid stomped along in a state of turmoil, her boots making satisfying clunks on the tarmacked path. As she drew nearer to the far side of the lake, the calm of the water and the gentle quacking of the wildfowl gradually began to soothe her soul. The urge to scream died away and was replaced by a desperate need for more coffee. Hot and somewhat dishevelled,

A New Lease of Life

she entered the café without even thinking to check if it was busy and was confronted by three familiar smiling faces.

'Look who the cat dragged in,' said Beryl brightly. 'We were just talking about you, ducky.'

Winnie nodded, her brightly coloured head wrap bobbing. She'd ditched her tracksuit and trainers today and was dressed in a robe of flowing tropical print which looked incongruous against Beryl's neat trousers and jumper and Anthea's usual collection of flowing linen.

'Talking about me?' Ingrid echoed, glancing towards the counter in the hope that caffeine would soon be forthcoming.

'Yes, get your drink and come and sit with us. I'll explain.'

The woman behind the counter smiled at Ingrid. 'We haven't been introduced properly but I'm Kate and I run this place. Sam's off today because his daughter's not well but my partner's helping me out and he makes a mean lemon drizzle cake. Can I tempt you? With a cappuccino maybe?'

Ingrid thought that sounded like the best idea ever. Kate began to bustle around, fixing the boiling milk and shouting her cake order into the kitchen. A large, broad-shouldered man joined her. He was holding a china plate with a golden, sugar-encrusted lemon cake on a doily. 'Just baked, you're in luck,' he said. 'I'm Milo, and of course I know who you are.'

'You do?'

'Yes, a newcomer in the village is always spotted, especially one with big ideas to zap up Sylvia's shop. We've been looking forward to meeting you.'

Ingrid watched the two of them as they worked around each other in the small area behind the counter. Kate had an open, friendly face, a smooth bob of brown hair and wide green eyes. Milo towered over her, and as he passed, he bent to kiss the top of her head. A pang of envy shot through Ingrid.

These two looked so happy together and it was unbearably sad to think Tommy would never kiss her again. To be fair though, he hadn't been much of a fan of kissing. Ingrid had often wished he was. It would have been nice if he'd gone in for small, spontaneous gestures like the one she'd just witnessed. You couldn't really ask your husband to kiss you. If he didn't want to, he'd just be paying lip service to the idea. Literally.

'Go and sit down with those vagabonds over there,' Milo said. 'I'll bring the tray over in a minute.'

Ingrid smiled her gratitude. Sinking into the chair next to Beryl, she leaned back with a sigh. The ladies regarded her with interest.

'You've done too much today already, haven't you?' said Anthea. 'You should have waited for your team.'

'I didn't know when you'd be free,' said Ingrid. 'And I'm fine. It's just a bit...'

'Overwhelming,' finished Winnie. 'Well, we've just been saying that if you can hang on a couple of days, we'll all come round and lend a hand on Wednesday.'

'And then later on, you can join us for film night at mine,' Beryl added. 'We've decided on a new dress code this week. Winnie's put us to shame with her lovely outfit today so we're going to make it a rule that we all wear a decent frock and a dab or two of make-up when we get together on Wednesday evenings. It's easy to let yourself go if you're not careful.'

'Speak for yourself, darling,' said Anthea. 'You can't go wrong with linen, I always say. I channel Dame Judi Dench when I select my clothes every morning. She knows how to dress in style.'

'Whereas I'm more like Dame Edna Everage when I get tarted up.' Beryl let out a loud chuckle. 'I might get some of those pointed spectacles next with sparkles round the edge. That'd give film night a bit more glitz.'

Milo came over with Ingrid's order and caught the end of this. 'You three are all magnificent dames,' he said. 'I heard Winnie telling some poor unsuspecting man in here the other day that she's proud to go with the 4B model and her motto is *if you've got it, flaunt it*. He looked flabbergasted, poor chap!'

'What's 4B?' asked Ingrid, wondering what pencils had to do with anything.

'Big, bold, black and beautiful,' explained Winnie, speaking slowly as if Ingrid was a three-year-old, which to think of it, was exactly how she felt as the women began chatting again, sometimes talking all at once.

Ingrid sipped her cappuccino and ate the delicious, melt-in-the-mouth lemon drizzle cake, letting their conversation flow over her. It was like being in a warm bath. She tuned in again with some difficulty when she realised Beryl was speaking directly to her.

'So, Ingrid, that's settled. We're all coming over to yours on Wednesday morning at 9 a.m. We'll bring a picnic for lunch again and then we three will go back to mine and smarten ourselves up and let you have a shower, or whatever. Then you can join us at seven for some of Winnie's soul food and a glass or two of prosecco while we watch the film.'

'Erm... great,' said Ingrid, blinking. 'What's the film, Beryl? Not that it matters,' she added hastily. 'It's really kind of you to invite me.'

'*Four Weddings and a Funeral*. We've just discovered that Anthea's never seen it. Can you imagine? We've gradually been educating her, but we missed that one. She tends to go for those black and white films that are usually all in French with subtitles. I can't see the point of them. If you take your eyes off the TV for a minute or go and make a cuppa, you're totally lost.'

Milo was now working his way around the café with a tray, clearing used crockery. He paused by their table as he overheard Beryl's remark. 'I don't blame you, Anthea,' he said. 'A bit of class for a change. I love 'em too.'

Anthea batted her eyelashes at him. 'There you go, ladies, here we have exhibit A: a gentleman with taste. Kate's a lucky woman.'

Sadness mingled with envy engulfed Ingrid again. She swallowed hard. At the time, marrying Tommy had felt like the biggest piece of luck ever, and although theirs had been an unusual relationship in many ways and they'd spent a lot of time in their separate workplaces, she suddenly missed him so much that she couldn't see for tears. The Saga Louts had moved on from films in general now and were discussing the merits or otherwise of Hugh Grant, giving Ingrid time to get herself under control, but when she looked up again, she saw Kate was watching her. The look they exchanged was one of deep understanding. How did Kate seem to know how Ingrid was feeling, when she was so obviously loved up and happy herself? Ingrid decided that one of these days she would really like to find out.

13

By the time Ingrid had strolled back home, it was mid-afternoon. This would probably be a very bad time to drive into Meadowthorpe to one of the big shops, she told herself. The schools would soon be turning their charges out into the world and the roads would be full of fraught parents in people-carriers, vying for parking spaces and then calling at the supermarkets for pizzas and so on. It would be much easier to make a plan to go tomorrow instead. Temporarily relieved, Ingrid headed through the shop to the back rooms and surveyed the chaos.

Empty boxes were heaped everywhere, even overspilling into the back yard. The crates of less-desirable items were taking up far too much room, so perhaps she should deliver a few to charity shops while she was out in the car. Her heart sank at the thought of finding yet more places to park. The Range Rover felt ridiculously bulky and over-sized for one person. Sighing, Ingrid abandoned the idea of doing any more sorting today. She'd spend the time unpacking her suitcases properly instead of just rummaging in them for things to wear.

Upstairs, the flat was overwhelmingly silent. The air felt stale, and everything was just as she'd left it earlier. That should have been a bonus, because living with Tommy had meant that if he returned from work first, the house soon looked as if a tornado had swept through it. Even so, the static feeling of being the sole resident of her new home was depressing. The only way round it was to make the place feel more inspiring. Ingrid opened all the windows, intending to carry on and freshen everywhere up but then made the mistake of sitting down on the sofa and closing her eyes for a moment while she considered how to tackle the problem. Before she'd had the chance to muster her thoughts, tiredness and sleep overcame her.

After what seemed like only seconds, Ingrid was woken by a frantic banging on the front door. She leapt to her feet, unable to think where she was for a moment. Through the open window she could hear someone calling her name.

'Ingrid! It's Leo, are you in there?'

Ingrid hurried downstairs to find her young visitor on the step clutching a bunch of chrysanthemums and looking worried.

'Phew. I was beginning to think you were out,' Leo said. 'Can I come in? I brought you these as a housewarming present. Have you got any bread? I'm starving; I need toast before I start work on the sign.'

'Of course you can come in,' Ingrid said, yawning. 'I must have nodded off, sorry you had to wait. Thank you for the flowers. Let's go and find something for them to go in from all the junk in the storeroom.'

With a tall earthenware vase under her arm, Ingrid led the way up to the flat. 'I've got no food to speak of though,' she said.

'I should have gone shopping today but I... I didn't... and now I've left it too late.'

'What do you mean? The supermarkets are open really late. There's even a twenty-four-hour one in Meadowthorpe.'

Ingrid went into the kitchen and began to trim the flowers. She didn't want to admit to this confident young person that the very idea of driving to Meadowthorpe terrified her. Leo followed her, leaning against the worktop and folding her arms. 'Are you worried you'll get lost?' she asked. 'I could come with you if you like. I know where all the best shops are.'

The offer hung in the air. Ingrid desperately tried to think of a way to refuse without offending Leo. 'Erm... I don't think your dad would want you to just go off with me in my car. You hardly know me, and I might drive like a Formula One racer or... or be a road hog... or something.'

She caught Leo's eye and saw that the girl was trying not to giggle. 'Road hog? Seriously? Come off it. You're bottling out of going for some reason, aren't you?' she said. 'What are you scared of? You can tell me; I'm scared of loads of stuff.'

'Like what?'

'Oh... spiders, maths homework, having sex with my boyfriend.' Leo put a hand over her mouth and her cheeks turned an interesting shade of puce. 'Look, forget I said that. It just came out. My dad would kill me if he heard me even mention sex!'

Ingrid had absolutely no idea where to go with this conversation. She bit her lip. The silence lengthened. Eventually she blurted out, 'Leo, are you sleeping with your boyfriend?'

The girl looked horrified. 'No! That's the problem. He wants to, but I'm scared. That's what I was saying. Everyone else seems to be doing it but...'

'You don't want to. And that's absolutely fine.' The words

came to Ingrid in a rush. She'd been a troubled teen too, a good while ago. 'Anybody who pressures you into going to bed with them isn't worth knowing.'

'It's not even a bed, it's the back of his manky van,' Leo said. 'He's put an old mattress in. I'd rather do my maths homework in a room full of spiders, to be honest. The van stinks of socks. Is that your idea of sexy, Ingrid? Because it ain't mine, that's for sure.'

'Mmm, tempting,' said Ingrid, deciding her best bet was to keep this conversation light, at least for now. 'I think this guy needs to go back to charm school for a follow-up course. I'd at least insist on a garden shed.'

They both started to giggle at the same time, and some of the tension ebbed away. Soon they were rocking helplessly, tears rolling down their faces. Ingrid was the first to get control of herself. 'I don't know why we're laughing, this is a big thing,' she said.

'If it *is* a big thing. I'll never find out at this rate,' Leo said.

Ingrid opened her eyes wide and tried to look stern. 'You're awful. Stop right there. I'm not used to this kind of talk. I thought the Saga Louts were bad enough.'

'Oh shit, I'm sorry, I didn't mean to say that. Hang on though, you still didn't tell me what you're actually scared of.'

Ingrid fiddled with the flowers in the vase, playing for time. She snipped off a leaf, and then another. Leo folded her arms and regarded her with the look of someone who had all the time in the world to wait for a satisfactory answer. There was no getting out of this one.

'I hardly ever drove in the daytime when I lived in York, because there was no need,' Ingrid said eventually. 'Doing a run in the evening to the pub and back was bad enough. I never faced up to how much I don't enjoy driving until I had to make the journey down here. Motorways and even ordinary busy roads terrify me. There. I've said it. You must think I'm such a wuss.'

Leo shrugged. 'Not really. There are way too many cars on the roads, and they mostly go too fast, I reckon. It's not a silly thing to be scared of.' She checked the time on her phone. 'Hey, come on, it's still early. Let's go shopping together. I can take you the back way into town to avoid the traffic and the car park's huge at the Tesco superstore. Even a road hog wouldn't hit anything in there.'

The mission was becoming inevitable, and Ingrid's shopping list wouldn't wait much longer. Should she just take this offer and run with it? She squared her shoulders. 'Okay then, but only if you clear it with your dad first. I'm not going to take you in the car unless he says it's fine.'

Leo quickly texted Joel, the smile on her face suggesting she didn't expect to be disappointed. Ingrid waited, crossing her fingers. Maybe he'd be busy and wouldn't see the message, or perhaps he'd just think the whole thing was too risky. Her hopes were soon dashed when seconds later an answering beep told her that Joel was available. Leo's grin became even wider as she read his reply.

'Dad says I can go if you're sure you can stand me jabbering at you all the way to town and back, and I'm not to let you buy any more junk. Let's go. Road trip!'

There was no escape. Five minutes later, Ingrid eased the Range Rover out of its parking space inch by inch and joined the lane that led to what she thought of as the great metropolis. However, Leo soon directed her away from the main sign that pointed to Meadowthorpe and onto a back road that twisted and turned until they came to an avenue of trees that were beginning to show new lime-green leaves. From there they bowled along past fields of cattle, sheep and various crops and then through an ancient oak wood, where the afternoon sunshine dappled the tarmac and the birdsong stilled.

By now Ingrid was starting to gain in confidence, and Leo kept up a steady stream of chatter, fortunately not relating to her relationship with the boy with the van who had caused her dilemma. 'We're nearly there,' she said as rows of terraced houses began to appear. 'It takes longer this way, but I guessed you wouldn't mind the extra mile or two if it was quieter.'

Soon, they were snaking their way through a large industrial estate and into the back entrance of a huge car park. 'Now, wasn't that easy?' Leo asked, and she sounded so much like a patient driving teacher with a nervous pupil that Ingrid had to laugh. First Winnie explaining things slowly to her and now a teenager giving her therapy. What next? Maybe Sam would pop round to give her some childcare tips in case she wanted to babysit Elsie, or Joel might offer advice on sanding down a bench.

Leo had the bit between her teeth now and grabbed one of the larger trolleys, leading the way into the store as Ingrid trailed behind her, bleating, 'I don't really need that much.'

'You don't think you do, but let's just see. I know you think you only want to stock up on food but this shop sells clothes and soft furnishings and all sorts of stuff. Your flat needs a few little changes. I can help. I'm good at makeovers. Trust me.'

She glanced over her shoulder at Ingrid, who in that moment decided to throw caution to the wind. This was going to be fun.

14

Driving back to Willowbrook, Ingrid couldn't believe she'd let Leo steamroller her into making so many unplanned purchases. A simple stocking-up trip had turned into something completely different.

'I bet you're wishing you hadn't brought me with you now, aren't you?' said Leo, flashing Ingrid a wicked grin.

'Well...'

'Look, you're going to be living in that flat for a while, and it's depressing. All we've done is buy a few great things to brighten it up. You can always take them with you when you go, they won't be wasted.'

'But I might be living somewhere really small next. I don't know where I'll be.'

Leo shrugged. It was getting to be her default mode. 'If you don't want them when you move on, you can give them to me. I haven't told Dad yet, but I'm going to be leaving school as soon as I can, even if it's not just yet because of the stupid rules. I'm sick of it. I'm going to get a job and then I'll probably move in with Baz.'

Ingrid didn't answer for a few moments. She concentrated on avoiding a tractor coming towards her on the narrow road. When the danger had passed, she said, 'The one with the smelly van?'

Another shrug. 'Yeah, but there's more to him than that. We've got plans. He's nearly eighteen and he's fed up with living with his skanky family. His mum's always nagging him to tidy his room, like he's a kid or something.'

Ingrid couldn't help feeling sympathy for the unknown mother. If the mysterious Baz's room was as stinky as his van, it must be hard not to nag. They'd reached the village now and full attention was needed if she was going to slide into her parking space with the car unscathed. It suddenly occurred to her that if she did accidentally scratch its paintwork, there was nobody to moan at her. The Range Rover was hers now. She could get rid of the bulky contraption and buy something small and easy to park. Better still, sell it and not even own a car. Luckily, the driver of the vehicle that had previously been parked next to Ingrid had gone out while they'd been away, and it was easy to slot back in next to the wall. Leo helped to unload the many parcels and bags, and they staggered up the stairs to check their spoils.

'Now I really am starving, so can we eat something before I faint?' Leo said. 'I can cook, you know. I could make us dinner if you like.'

Ingrid regarded the girl doubtfully. She found it strange, if flattering, that a fifteen-year-old would choose to hang out with a person so much older than herself. Was this natural? She clearly remembered trying to avoid her mother's friends when she was a teenager herself, dreading the way they always seemed to want to ask her about school, or discover her plans for a future career. Leo was looking at Ingrid with such a

A New Lease of Life   113

hopeful expression that it was clear she wanted to stay, but would Joel think this was odd?

'Won't your dad be expecting you?' Ingrid asked, playing for time.

'We could message him and tell him to come over too? He loves chilli and we bought all the ingredients. It's the only thing I eat at his house, apart from pizza. He taught me how to make it. Go on, Ingrid, let's do it. I promise I'll clean the kitchen up afterwards. It's cool being here for a change. You don't nag me like my mum and dad do.'

This was vaguely reassuring and if Ingrid was honest with herself, it sounded like a very good plan. She was still flagging from her previous unpacking exertions, and the shopping trip in the car, although much less stressful than she'd expected, had exhausted her. It was strange how this new life was turning out to be much more tiring than her highly demanding career in hotel management had been.

'Go on then. He might say no,' she said hopefully. Socialising with Joel three nights in a row seemed like a step too far when all Ingrid really wanted to do was to have a quick snack, a deep bubbly bath and an early night, but Leo's face was shining as she texted him, and letting her new friend down didn't seem like an option.

'Dad says that'd be fantastic, he was just going to make himself a cheese sandwich and carry on working but my idea is much better. He's going to have a shower and come over at around seven o'clock, is that okay? We can quickly tart up the flat while the chilli is cooking. Can I open some of these crisps?'

Ingrid agreed and set to work unpacking the shopping. She felt an unexpected burst of exhilaration as she opened the bags. Leo was right, it *was* important to make her home more comfortable, even if she wasn't going to be here long. In addition to a substantial array of food, Leo had chosen a large jade-green table lamp with a silvery shade, a soft bottle-green throw and a couple of squishy cushions for the sofa, several chunky candles and a small rug to put in front of the fireplace.

'We can't do anything about the horrible gas fire,' Leo said, as Ingrid surveyed her new treasures. 'But if I shift everything off the mantelpiece we can make it look more like your place, yeah?'

While Leo chopped, fried and stirred the ingredients for her chilli, Ingrid surveyed the living space with a critical eye. She began to rearrange the furniture, trying different layouts until she was happy with the result. When Leo joined her, the two of them got to work making the place more welcoming. The colourful woven rug, the cushions and the throw added comfort, and soon the soft light from the table lamp had replaced the harsh glare from the overhead bulb. Three candles arranged along the mantelpiece added to the warm glow, and the cheerful colours of the chrysanthemums in their tall vase gave the finishing touch.

'You're good at this sort of thing, aren't you?' Ingrid said, as they stood back to admire their work. 'I'd never have been able to choose the right things so quickly and put them together to make an effect like this. It's like a stage set.'

'I know. That's what I want to do when I leave school.'

'What, design stage scenery? Won't you need to stay at school and do A levels or more training for that? Even an art degree?'

'Oh, you sound just like my dad. I can get in somewhere without all that stuff. It's boring. I don't mind just making the tea and being a runner to start with. I'll do a couple of years at the tech to get up to speed with the graphics side and then work my way up from the bottom. It'll be easy.'

Ingrid doubted this, but it wasn't her business to argue. Joel would need to take that job on. The thought that he'd soon be here gave her a sudden attack of butterflies in her tummy. She gave herself a mental shake. It was just that she hadn't had any significant male company since Tommy died, and if she was honest, not much even before that, apart from the go-getting, career-driven members of her staff. Joel was the first man, attractive or otherwise, that she'd had chance to get to know for a long time, and she needed to get a grip. He was shaping up to be a good friend and that was absolutely all.

Leo bustled back to the kitchen area to finish her dinner preparations and Ingrid decided to see what she could find to make the table look more appealing. It was a square Formica affair, tucked into the corner of the open-plan room, and looked as if it had seen many years of use. Maybe Sylvia had left a tablecloth tucked away somewhere. She glanced around and spied a set of drawers in a corner. Investigating, Ingrid let out a whoop of delight as she unearthed a cloth brightly patterned in blue and green, and several raffia placemats. There was even an unopened packet of pretty paper napkins. Sylvia must have reflected that her days of entertaining the family for meals were long gone. The apartment in her new home was probably too small for that kind of thing even if she'd wanted to do it.

Soon, the table looked fit for a party. Ingrid fetched cutlery and glasses and stood back to admire the effect, just as Joel knocked at the door. She went downstairs to let him in. She'd made time for a very quick change of clothes but she wished she'd chosen something that wasn't jeans and a faded checked shirt. When she saw him standing there with a bottle of wine in his hand, she had to smile. Joel was dressed almost identically.

'You got the memo to come as a cowboy then?' she said, smiling at him.

'Yes, I love these theme nights. I'm hoping there'll be line dancing later,' he said, following her up the stairs. When he entered the living room, he gasped and stood quite still.

'How did you make it look like this so quickly?' he said. 'It looks cosy. I remember the place in Sylvia's day. It was a bit...'

'Dated?' finished Leo, turning from the cooker to greet her dad. 'I took Ingrid to the big Tesco and she bought a few things. We did a makeover.'

'Your daughter's definitely got a talent for seeing how to get the best out of a space,' said Ingrid, earning herself a grateful look from Leo. 'I'd have had no idea where to start. It's great, isn't it? And she's even made our dinner, which I've got to say, smells amazing.'

'It's ready, and I'm still starving. Even though I've already eaten most of the crisps we bought. Sit down, Dad. I'll find you a corkscrew. That's two nights you've had wine though. I saw the empty bottle this morning. I'm going to need to monitor your intake,' Leo said, with mock gravity.

Joel pulled a face at his daughter. 'A client gave me this one as a thank you today,' he said. 'It'd be rude not to drink it.' He waited for Ingrid to sit down before he joined her. Leo brought in the steaming plates of rice topped with chilli.

'I like going shopping with Ingrid,' Leo said. 'She let me choose the food for tonight and she didn't make me get the cheapest of everything or the discounted meat.'

Joel looked embarrassed at this, and Ingrid mentally cursed Leo for making her dad uncomfortable. 'I usually shop for the bargains too,' she said hastily. 'It was just that today we wanted to get on with the grocery part so we could look at the fun things.'

They were soon making inroads into their food, and the conversation petered out as they ate hungrily. It wasn't long before all three plates were empty.

'That was absolutely delicious,' said Ingrid. 'It's going to be hard to think how to top it when I'm back to cooking for myself tomorrow.'

Leo sat back in her chair. 'While we're on that subject, I've been thinking...' she said.

15

Joel exchanged glances with Ingrid. 'Do those words fill you with the same dread they give me?' he asked her.

Ingrid laughed. 'Not unless she wants me to take her out in the car again. What have you been thinking, Leo?'

'I was wondering...' Leo stopped, looking unusually nervous.

'Go on,' said Joel. 'The creeping feeling of doom is increasing with every pause.'

'I thought... well, I know you didn't really want me to move in with you permanently, Dad...'

'I never said that.'

'No, but you know Mum hates it. She's jealous of you and me being together. Don't look at me like that, you know she is. She's got this weird idea that we gang up together against her. So, I wondered... what if I moved in with Baz for a little while? He says I could share his room, or we can get a flat together.'

Joel was on his feet in seconds, red in the face. 'You must be joking! You're fifteen, Leo. This is crazy. And where do you think the money would be coming from to do all this? He hasn't got a job and you're still at school. I thought you wanted to stay with me for a while?'

Ingrid could see the hurt in Joel's eyes, which the anger and outrage couldn't fully mask. Her heart bled for them both. Living with parents when you wanted to spread your wings could be intensely frustrating. She remembered it well, but had never been brave enough to push the boundaries like this.

'It's not crazy! I like cooking and making a place homely. Baz has got no idea about that kind of stuff. Why shouldn't we live together? It'd be...'

Leo's voice tailed away when she realised she was getting no response from the other two apart from astonished looks. Ingrid thought the girl looked close to tears.

'Whatever made you come up with this scheme?' Joel sounded as horrified as Ingrid felt. 'You're much too young to be thinking about moving in with some... some... boy. You need to settle down with either me or your mum and stop making daft plans. This is ridiculous.'

'Ridiculous, is it? Dad, I mean it! I can't stay at yours long-term because Mum'll kick off. She's already sending me angry texts. What I really want is to live with Baz. You can't stop me.'

Ingrid got up to clear the plates away, her mind in a whirl. How had she managed to drop into the middle of what felt like an incredibly delicate family situation? When she turned back to the table, Joel was pacing the floor, eyes blazing, and the sound of footsteps clumping down the stairs told her that Leo was already on her way out. She made as if to follow the girl, but Joel held up a hand.

'Let her go,' he said, sitting down again with a sigh.

'But...'

'But nothing. She's having a tantrum, and she needs to get it out of her system. I've been here before. We won't get anywhere trying to talk to her now.'

The use of the word *we* gave Ingrid mixed feelings. On the one hand, Leo's behaviour was nothing to do with her. It felt like a minefield. Joel was very distressed, naturally enough, and in need of someone to help. It warmed her heart to think he was able to share all this angst with her so soon in their friendship but equally it was alarming. Because this was clearly a very big problem, and about to get worse.

Ingrid filled the kettle and switched it on, and to give herself time to think, began to set out a tray with teapot, mugs and one of the many milk jugs that had already turned up in the boxes. This one was Cornishware, pleasingly chunky with blue and white stripes. When everything was ready, she added a plate of chocolate digestives, chosen by Leo, and motioned for Joel to come and sit more comfortably on the sofa. He settled into one corner and accepted his mug with a grateful nod, putting it down on the coffee table.

'So... have you met this Baz?' Ingrid asked. She sat down in the other corner of the sofa, suddenly anxious not to be too close to Joel and make him uncomfortable. He shook his head. Memories of Leo divulging something of the pressure Baz was putting on her to move their relationship forward made her think she should let Joel know about it, but surely Leo had told her in confidence? Leo's safety must come first, though.

'No, we haven't met. I've heard a lot about him,' Joel said. 'He's nearly eighteen, and Leo seems to think the sun shines out of his— I mean out of him in general, but he's a close neighbour of Sam's in the flats near the school. Sam knows him by sight and thinks he's bad news. He's always having very loud slanging matches with his mum, apparently, and the gist of the rows are usually about him being lazy and workshy. He had an apprenticeship, but he walked out after a month and now he's just hanging around the village all day.'

Ingrid sipped her tea and wondered what to say. She thought back to her own teenage years again. It had been a time of cringing embarrassment about many things. She'd hated being tall, because none of the boys she'd liked had been anywhere near her own height and had always chosen the dainty, smaller girls. Ingrid had worn glasses too, which she later swapped for contact lenses and even further on opted for laser treatment once she was earning a good wage, but she still remembered the early nicknames. Speccy Four-Eyes, Lanky, Beanpole, and worse. Leo appeared to be much more confident on the surface but maybe the bouncy exterior was hiding a host of anxieties. Joel must feel as if he was walking a tightrope between making her welcome with him and keeping her safe.

'Ingrid.' The sound of Joel saying her name very tentatively brought her back to the present with a jolt. 'I don't understand where I've gone wrong here. Maybe I should just let her cool down. She's bound to go off this Baz character soon. He sounds like a right knob.'

Ingrid doubted this. Her first crush had lasted for months and the boy in question had not only been bone idle but had also a deep aversion to showering or changing his clothes. As they sat in silence, both lost in their own thoughts, a random idea crossed her mind. She tried to push it away, but it just kept nudging. Why shouldn't she offer to have Leo to stay here with her in the flat for a little while, even if it was just to let all this fiery rebellion settle down?

Ingrid pushed the unruly thought firmly away. Surely Joel wouldn't even think about trusting her with his daughter. *But*, a small voice inside Ingrid's head insisted on whispering, *the shopping trip today had been fun. Leo had made herself at home in the flat very quickly too. She'd made the place look much more homely in a matter of minutes and even cooked a lovely meal.*

A vision of herself and Leo settling down with their dinner on trays to watch one of the reality TV shows she assumed all teenagers liked flashed into Ingrid's mind. Although Ingrid and Tommy had often led parallel lives, the hollowness of her world without him in it seemed to be getting worse rather than better. The gap he'd left felt as if it was widening every day. Perhaps it wasn't such a crazy idea to see if Joel would let Leo come and stay. It'd be good to feel useful, even if just for a short while.

'It's just a thought, and tell me if you think I'm out of order here, but... would you consider letting me ask Leo if she'd like to move in with me? Only temporarily while she calms down,' Ingrid said hastily, seeing the look of surprise on Joel's face. 'Maybe you *both* need some space, and I've got plenty of room for a guest,' she added, watching Joel's eyes light up as she continued to speak.

'You couldn't take something like that on... could you? I mean... I'm sure Leo would love to spend some time here with you and away from her annoying parents. But why should you do this for us? We hardly know each other... yet.'

Ingrid's heart skipped a beat at the word *yet*. 'I wouldn't mind trying, if it'd help,' she said. There was a pause that seemed as if it would never end. Then Joel cleared his throat.

'Let me talk to Leo,' Joel said. 'Or... better still, *you* could ask her if she'd really like to be your guest? It might be better coming from you. I never know if she's saying things on a whim or if she's serious these days. I still don't get why she had to change her name. It seems a weird thing to do. I liked her being Olivia. It was the name I chose for her before she was even born.'

'I guess it's all about taking a bit of control back. I can vividly remember feeling as if I had no say in anything when I was Leo's age.'

Ingrid stood up and walked over to the window. She gazed out over the green, watching as several parents of the children playing there came outside to shout them home for bedtime. They gathered their offspring in like a flock of sheep, rounding them up and shepherding them towards their respective houses. Ingrid hadn't been responsible for anyone vulnerable since her mum and dad had died. Her freedom was important to her. Tommy hadn't tied his wife down, rather the opposite. He'd given her the confidence to spread her wings. Taking on a troubled fifteen-year-old as a houseguest was an unexpected suggestion, and somewhat daunting, but the more she thought about it, the more Ingrid felt as if it would be a worthwhile thing to do. That is, if Leo would actually want to come to stay. The idea might fill her with horror. There was only one way to find out. She smiled at Joel in what she hoped was a reassuring way.

'I'll sound Leo out and see what she says. One of the spare bedrooms is reasonably tidy, but I've filled the bigger one with my clothes. I don't suppose she'd mind having the smaller room though, if she likes the idea. Where do you think she's gone?' Ingrid asked. 'There's no sign of her out there.'

'Leave that to me,' Joel said. 'Ingrid, you're amazing. I can't believe you've suggested this. It's going to make a huge difference if she says yes. There's no saying if Leo will easily give up the idea of throwing her lot in with this Baz character, and we'd still have to explain it all to Trina and get her okay but it's definitely the best option we've got right now.'

Ingrid bit her lip and didn't reply. She really hoped Joel was right.

16

By nine o'clock, Joel was sitting at his kitchen table staring at his work diary and trying to make sense of several scribbled entries that were virtually illegible. He'd sent at least a dozen messages to Leo, all unanswered, and had reached the point of deciding to phone Trina to see if Leo had been in touch with her mum. He didn't want to admit that she'd run away from him, and he certainly didn't fancy discussing the Baz situation with his ex-wife but there must come a moment to accept that it was time to take action. Okay, Leo was fifteen years old and normally fairly sensible, but he'd sensed the underlying tension in her ever since she'd asked to stay with him, and now it had boiled over, a dry-mouthed feeling of panic was building inside him.

To distract himself from worrying about his daughter, Joel had already tidied his workshop, done some rudimentary filing of a pile of scruffy invoices and notes and drunk far too much strong black coffee for this time of night. Wired and twitchy, he reached for his mobile, just as he heard the welcome sound of the back door opening.

'Dad?' Leo called. Her voice sounded tentative, with none of its usual breezy confidence.

'In here!' he shouted back, getting to his feet, legs slightly wobbly with the relief of her reappearance. They faced each other across the kitchen. Leo was almost as tall as her father now, with the same dark, sometimes moody eyes. She was hugging herself as if she was chilly, even though the evening was still mild.

'I... I was getting a bit worried,' Joel said, biting back the irrational anger that every anxious parent feels when their worst fears are unfounded, and their chick is safely home at last.

'No need. I was with Baz. We went for a drive.'

This wasn't particularly soothing to hear. Sam had always been wary of anyone else driving his daughter around, and this new world of boyfriends was much scarier than letting her go out with her friends' parents. Now he wished he'd said something to warn Leo about being careful of getting into strange vehicles in case they weren't safe, but at least she was back and in one piece. 'Tea?' he asked, going over to the sink to fill the kettle.

'If you're having one,' she said.

The familiar ritual filled an awkward gap, and Leo reached for the biscuit tin. 'Ingrid has better snacks than you do,' she said. 'She's got those chocolate-covered cookies. I chose them.'

Leo regarded her father steadily as he made the tea. 'You like her, don't you?' she said.

'Who?' Joel realised this was a foolish prevarication because who else but Ingrid could Leo mean? The look on her face confirmed that this was a very silly question.

'Stop fudging. I know you like her. I reckon you fancy her, Dad. Don't deny it, you've gone all red.'

Joel was already aware that his face had given him away. It wasn't the first time that his daughter had accused him of liking a woman, but he'd never minded before. He'd been able to laugh it off because the few dates he'd ventured in the years since the split with Trina had either been non-starters due to lack of interest on both sides, or resulted in unmitigated disasters when Joel had caused offence by backing off before there was any danger of getting properly involved.

'Ingrid's a nice person,' he said. 'She's had a big upheaval in her life, and I don't imagine that she's looking for a man. She's grieving. Anyway, I'm not interested.'

Leo regarded her father, head on one side, then reached for her mug. 'You don't have to tell me how you feel about Mum. I know you still love her,' she said, before taking a sip of her tea.

Joel always tried to avoid going down this road. It was a tricky one to navigate. He didn't want Leo to think he was unfeeling, but his ex-wife had killed any love he'd had for her by taking their obnoxious window cleaner to bed and then moving in with him without so much as a backward glance. However, it seemed important to display a united front as parents and if his daughter knew how much he despised Trina, it would hurt her. Not only that, she might be even more tempted to play them off against each other. Joel decided to change the subject and override his own suggestion that Ingrid should be the one to invite Leo to move in.

'I don't know how you'll feel about this, but I just wanted to tell you that Ingrid wants to invite you to stay at her flat for a while,' he said. 'If you think that's better than being with me. Or Baz,' he added hopefully.

Joel watched his daughter's face change. She could never hide her feelings for long, and now her eyes brimmed over with tears. 'Really?'

'Yes. She seems to like you. Can't think why,' Joel said, grinning at his daughter. 'I don't think you're ready to share a flat with a boy yet, but I can understand why your mum and me might get you down these days.'

For a moment Leo was obviously lost for words. She swallowed hard and rubbed her eyes. Then she took a deep breath. 'I've been thinking about it since... since I walked out on you and Ingrid. It's not great at the flat where Baz lives with his mum, to be honest, and his room's a tip so I don't think he'd be any better as a flatmate if we had our own place. I mean, I don't want to leave you, Dad. I love living here with you, but you know as well as I do how Mum can get about us being together. Are you sure Ingrid means it?'

'Absolutely. If that's what you want. You'll have to pull your weight though. She's not a nursemaid.'

'As if I need that! Should I text her?'

'That might be a plan. Go for it.'

Relief made Joel's legs wobbly as he stood up, and his feelings seemed to be echoed if his daughter's expression was anything to go by. Maybe her talk about moving in with Baz had been just that – all talk. Leo sent a long message to Ingrid and a reply pinged back almost immediately. And just like that, it was all settled. They moved into the small snug at the front of the cottage and the next hour was spent sorting out the details of what Leo would need to take ('...everything, Dad. I want all my stuff...'). There was also the issue of the best way to sell the idea to Trina and to decide how they would manage rent and board. Leo had her back to the window as she began to make notes on her phone of all the belongings that were essential to her well-being, so she didn't notice the battered white van that cruised along their street several times very slowly. But Joel noticed, and his hackles rose. Underage and, for all her chutzpah, kind of unworldly, Leo still needed his protection. By passing her over to Ingrid like a parcel, was he giving this Baz character a clear field?

Then Joel remembered the stern set of Ingrid's jaw when she wasn't feeling sociable. He'd need to warn her properly about Baz but he sensed she'd be more than a match for the lad if necessary and could easily send him packing if he wasn't welcome. A shiver ran down Joel's spine. He hadn't got the full measure of Ingrid yet, but Leo had been right. He *did* like this newcomer to their quiet village. She'd already added spice to the mix, like a sprinkling of ginger and coriander to a bland curry. The more he saw her, the more he wanted to get to know her better.

17

Wednesday dawned, and with it came the Saga Louts, armed and ready for another day's intensive shop sorting. Ingrid was up early in readiness, dressed in faded denim dungarees and a vest top, with her hair tied up in a brightly patterned wrap very like the one Winnie was sporting.

'We sure look the business, honey,' said Winnie, who was wearing a boilersuit liberally splashed with paint of all colours. 'I've brought my decorating gear, because I think we need a feature wall in this shop. I've got some leftover peacock-blue emulsion that I reckon will look a treat on the wall behind the till, but it's your call.'

Ingrid was only too happy to let Winnie have free rein with where to paint but was beginning to feel a little railroaded, generous as this offer was. She'd imagined a warmer colour if the shop was going to have a revamp.

'It's really good of you, Winnie,' Ingrid said, trying to think of a tactful way to say she hated peacock blue. Her home with Tommy had always been professionally designed and decorated because neither of them had had the time (or inclination) to attempt to do it themselves, and the last time had involved an awful lot of blue paint. Tommy had been delighted to leave the very expensive firm to it, paint choices and all, and Ingrid had been too busy at work at the time to argue.

'If you left the job to me, I'd get paint all over the carpets, Ingers, and you don't want to mess up your nails and hair when you're front of house at work, do you? Let's get the experts in again. They know what they're doing,' he'd said, opening a bottle of port and filling his glass. It had been an after-dinner ritual for him. Port, Stilton and a cigar or two. Ingrid had usually stuck to decaf at that point, but Tommy had never been one to hold back. Life was for living, he'd said. Ironic now.

'Do you mind very much if we don't use the blue, Winnie?' Ingrid said. 'I've got a yen for russet or terracotta. I can order some paint for the wall now and it'll come tomorrow, but what'd be great is if you could touch up the white gloss on the window frames and skirting boards in the meantime. They're really scuffed and I know you'd make a much neater job of it than I would. I found some tins that Sylvia left under the stairs.'

The other woman looked crestfallen, so Ingrid continued. 'I wanted to have a more natural range of colours in the shop wall but you're right, that end wall needs a strong colour. I'm glad you mentioned it. My painting skills are pretty much at nursery level.'

Mollified, Winnie wandered off to hunt for the gloss paint and Ingrid breathed a sigh of relief. It was one thing having help but quite another to have that kind of decision taken out of her hands. She was only going to be here for a short time. Even so, the shop had to feel right. Beryl and Anthea were soon in the storeroom again, and cries of excitement as they unearthed more saleable items punctuated the morning.

A New Lease of Life

Ingrid gave the shelves another polish and at last felt ready to start placing some of her treasures on show. Winnie was happily painting skirting boards now but stopped for a moment to appreciate her handiwork and to glance over at Ingrid.

'Be careful now, easy does it. Less is more, remember?' she said. 'Well, it is in this kind of situation... but not in all of 'em!'

'Are you being smutty again?' Beryl asked, coming in from the back room carrying a particularly beautiful vase. 'When is less *not* more?'

'You don't need me to tell you that,' Winnie said, with a fruity chortle. 'My man was never one to hold back, and neither was yours, from what you've told us.'

She noticed Ingrid's agonised expression and laughed again, her whole generous body shaking inside the voluminous boilersuit. 'You wait till we get some prosecco down you at one of our film nights, honey. You'll be telling us all your bedroom secrets. Even our Anthea can't resist the confessional of the sisterhood when she's had a few.'

'Are you taking my name in vain?' Anthea had followed Beryl through from the storeroom and was clutching a box to her chest. Ingrid thought she looked rather pale today but still stylish in a more workmanlike version of her usual linen collection. 'I want to get some of these beauties on show, girls. Otherwise, this shop's never going to get off the ground.'

Sunshine was pouring through the front windows as Ingrid ceremoniously placed the first object on the shelf nearest to the door. She'd chosen a large amber-coloured trinket box with a domed lid, intricately carved from sandalwood and almost glowing in the beams of light. She felt as if there should be some sort of fanfare to mark the event, and Winnie clearly had the same thought, because she immediately launched into a full-throated version of Stevie Wonder's 'Isn't She Lovely'.

Ingrid burst out laughing. 'Are you referring to me or the box?' she said, raising her voice as the others all joined in.

Winnie finished singing and took a bow. 'Mainly you, but the box is pretty awesome too,' she said. 'And kind of like the words of the song, you're makin' this shop from love.'

'Am I?'

Ingrid looked around her at the empty shelves. She hadn't formulated the shop idea with love in her heart, more like a necessity to make a clean sweep, but she was certainly feeling more joyful now, surrounded by these dynamic ladies and with more treasures emerging from their crates by the minute.

Beryl nodded. 'You're celebrating the life you had before, and getting ready for the next part,' she said. 'You haven't told us much about your Tommy but we all three know how hard it is to lose the one you shared your life with, don't we, girls?'

'We do, even though mine all disappeared of their own accord, nothing to do with the Grim Reaper,' Anthea said, pulling a wry face.

Ingrid swallowed the lump in her throat with difficulty. She was suddenly painfully aware that she still hadn't let herself admit how much being Tommy's partner had meant to her. It was far easier to think of their marriage as something that had suited them both but was now in the past. The final image of him flashed before her eyes before she could close her mind. Not the picture of Tommy lustily singing karaoke but the much grimmer one of him lying in a side room of the local hospital when resuscitation had failed. She'd reached out and touched his forehead and then his bushy red beard. He'd felt... different. His eyes were closed, and he looked almost as if he was just having a relaxing moment in his hammock in the garden.

'Oh, Tommy,' she'd heard herself croak, and a gentle nurse had come closer and taken her by the elbow.

'Are you ready to leave him, my lovely?' she'd asked softly. 'I can give you a little bit longer if you like?'

But Ingrid had been keen to escape from that awful place with its overwhelming kindness, too-clean smell and air of doom.

'Shall I ring someone to come and collect you?' said the nurse, as Ingrid swung round and hurried towards the door.

'No, I've got the car,' she'd answered. 'It was my turn to drive tonight.'

The words hung in the air. They shared a look. It always would be Ingrid's turn from now on.

'Are you sure you're safe to be behind the wheel?'

Ingrid wasn't at all sure, if she was honest, but the car had to be taken home. She wanted to tell the nurse that she only ever drove when it involved short distances and if Tommy wanted to drink. The thought of getting behind the wheel now was quite terrifying.

'Are you having a moment?'

The sound of Beryl's voice cut through the depressing flashback, and Ingrid pulled herself together with difficulty. 'What were we saying?'

'I think it was me mentioning the Grim Reaper that set you off on a downer,' said Anthea. 'Sorry about that, darling. Look, why don't you get a few more of these goodies on the shelves, Beryl, and you or Winnie can choose something fabulous for the window when she's finished painting her wall. One beautiful thing in the centre, didn't you say?'

Relieved, Ingrid agreed and headed straight for the stores. Beryl had switched the radio on and taken the box from Anthea. She was absorbed in picking out her favourite ceramics and Winnie was singing about being a natural woman, but Anthea followed Ingrid into the back room and closed the door behind them. The musty, dusty scent of the rest of the boxes prickled Ingrid's nose as she turned to look at the older woman who had sat down rather suddenly on one of the larger packing cases.

'Is everything okay?' Ingrid asked. 'You look… kind of…'

She gasped as Anthea swayed sideways, and only just managed to catch her before she slid off the boxes. The older woman's eyes were closed now, and her face had an unhealthy chalky tinge.

'Anthea, what on earth's the matter?' Ingrid said, sitting down beside her and putting an arm around her shoulders for support. 'What can I do to help? Can I get you some water?'

Anthea shook her head. 'I just need a minute or two to get my breath back. Don't flap, darling.'

The two of them sat in silence for a while and then Anthea moved out of the circle of Ingrid's arm and got shakily to her feet. Ingrid stood up too and tried to take Anthea's arm to steady her, but she was brushed off quite forcibly.

'I'm fine,' Anthea said. 'It happens now and again. No need to mention it to the girls. They'll only worry and fuss.'

Ingrid was unsure where to go from here. Anthea clearly wasn't fine, but she didn't know her well enough to insist on a longer rest. Before she could think of a way to proceed, Anthea took the decision for her and subsided onto the crates again.

'I can see I'm going to have to tell you a bit more,' she said. 'Don't look so anxious, Ingrid. It's fairly simple and very boring. I've got a bit of a problem, and I can't bring myself to tell the others about it yet.'

Ingrid stared at Anthea. Her usual flippant, rather lofty expression had vanished and in its place was sadness and a

A New Lease of Life

kind of resignation. Here was a woman who looked fragile and in need of care. Concern for the normally confident Anthea made Ingrid's mouth dry.

'Go on,' she said. 'I'm listening.'

'I won't beat about the bush. I've more than likely got to have some tests. It looks as if I might have something rather nasty going on inside me. It's no good pretending any longer and I know I should have gone to see the doctor earlier, but I didn't, so there's no use in telling me off.'

The sound of Winnie and Beryl joining forces in a duet of 'You're the One That I Want' drifted through from the shop. Ingrid stared at Anthea. 'But... it might not be what you think,' she said slowly. 'Everybody gets scared and expects the worst when they get sent for tests. It could be something really simple.'

Anthea didn't answer. The silence lengthened. Eventually Ingrid said, 'I'm glad you've told me.'

'I wasn't going to, but I had no choice. I mean, no offence, but I like to be responsible for myself. Always have been.'

Ingrid nodded. 'But now I do know, maybe you can relax that rule for a while. Can I help in any way?'

Anthea thought for a moment. Then she appeared to come to a decision.

'You could, darling, if you really want to. I'd rather not ask, of course, but I wonder if you might consider driving me to the hospital when the appointment comes through. They said they'd either write or phone with the date and time but it'll be soon. I'm the only one of the three of us girls that has a car. The others always rely on me for lifts but I'm... I'm scared, Ingrid. I can't take myself there this time. I just can't.'

'Where's the hospital?' Ingrid cursed herself inwardly for asking the question instead of giving a straightforward *yes*, but she was afraid to promise to do something so daunting without knowing what would be involved.

'Meadowthorpe. It's easy enough to get to, but the parking's hellish. I know I can't do it. I guess I could get a taxi though, if you...'

Ingrid took a deep breath. 'Of course I'll take you. Having somebody with you will be important anyway. I can distract you with seedy anecdotes about life in the hotel trade.'

Anthea blinked back tears. Seeing this usually strong woman at such a low ebb felt almost indecent to Ingrid, but memories of her mother in similar distress made her abandon her usual reticence when it came to giving out hugs. She put both arms around Anthea. At first, she met with stiffness and resistance, but after a few seconds, Anthea leaned into Ingrid's embrace and let herself be held. No more words were exchanged until the older woman moved away slightly.

'I'll let you know the details of the appointment as soon as I know when it is,' she said. 'They asked if I'd be prepared to take a cancellation, and I said yes. The sooner the better. Now, let's get on with the job in hand. I'm not going to let all this hospital malarkey take over my life.'

They both stood up, Anthea letting Ingrid steady her this time.

'And not a word to the girls,' Anthea said. 'I'll let them know what's happening when I get some proper answers. Until then...'

'Business as usual,' finished Ingrid. 'I've got the message. Now, what do you think about this piece? Stunning or hideous?' She pointed to the large gilt-framed mirror which was propped against the wall. Anthea chuckled.

'Do you really need to ask, darling?' she said. 'That awful thing's destined for the charity shop. I wouldn't give it house room or even put it on the bargain table. It's tarnished and battered. Just like me,' she added, grinning.

The two carried on sorting. Ingrid understood that the subject of the tests was firmly closed, at least for now. The thought of a crowded hospital car park with angry drivers hooting at her from every direction would probably keep her awake tonight, and flashbacks of all the hours she'd spent in similar places with her dying parents were crowding into her head, but for now she'd take her lead from the brave lady rootling through a box full of horse brasses and muttering about the length of time it would take to get them clean enough to sell.

For Anthea to share such momentous information with someone she'd only known for a few days, the situation must be weighing very heavily on her mind. It was time for Ingrid to step out of her comfort zone and up to the mark. The Saga Louts had welcomed her wholeheartedly into their lives and were even now helping her to make a success of her plan. The least Ingrid could do was try to give something back. If only the act of giving didn't seem quite so scary.

18

Several productive hours passed but Beryl and Winnie didn't seem keen to leave, even though it was obvious to Ingrid that Anthea was exhausted. Finally, Ingrid managed to convince them that they'd done more than enough and packed them off home with many heartfelt thanks. They promised to come again as soon as they were all free, although their vibrant social lives made it hard to find a clear day, and they had to agree that the next time they were all available would be the following Wednesday.

'But that works well, because we can carry straight on with film night that evening,' said Beryl. 'It'll give you time to do some more of your own sorting in the meantime without us getting under your feet.'

Anthea hung back as they left, whispering that she'd phone Ingrid with her address and the time of her appointment. The other two looked back over their shoulders to see what was holding their friend up but Anthea ignored them. Ingrid felt a pang of guilt at this deception, but she had to accept the older woman's need for privacy, at least for now. There would be time to persuade Anthea to let the others in on what was happening when she had more information to share.

Ingrid was just about to go upstairs to find something for dinner before getting on with making space in the spare bedroom for Leo when a familiar sight in the street outside caught her eye. Standing on the pavement with his hands in his pockets was Lennie Nightingale. Her stomach lurched. Had he seen her? Maybe Ingrid could pretend she was out. But it was too late. Lennie stepped forward, reached for the handle and found the door still unlocked. He pushed it open and stepped inside the shop, closing it behind him and dropping the catch.

'Hello again, lovely Cuz,' he said, grinning at her as if their last exchange had been a friendly one.

'What do you want, Lennie?' Ingrid asked. 'Only I'm in a bit of a hurry.'

'Busy tonight, are you? I was hoping you'd agree to coming out for dinner with me. We've still got things to discuss. Family matters, you might say.'

Ingrid looked past Lennie as he stood framed in the doorway. He was wearing a sharp black suit and a shirt that was so brilliantly white that it must have been brand new, Ingrid thought inconsequentially. He'd clearly assumed she'd agree to go out with him. Had he planned a swanky meal to impress her? As if. The green behind Lennie was unusually deserted, just when she could do with some back-up. If only Sam or Joel would saunter past at this moment and drop in to help her out. But there was no point in hoping for a rescue. This one was down to Ingrid, and it was high time she annihilated the memory of past-Lennie that had been haunting her nightmares for years.

'Aren't you going to ask me to come upstairs?' Lennie said,

still smiling. 'It's not like you to be inhospitable. You used to be so... accommodating when you were younger.'

His words acted like a cold shower. This not-so-subtle bullying of Lennie's had gone on long enough. He'd taunted her at family gatherings when they were growing up, playing on all her worst insecurities. Now it had to stop. Ingrid drew herself up to her full height, which enabled her to look down her nose at her loathsome cousin.

'You all but raped me at that party when you were sixteen,' she said, through gritted teeth. 'I was traumatised for a very long time afterwards, and now you've got the nerve to come here trying to put pressure on me to step aside and leave your way clear to getting your hands on your mother's money.'

'Raped? Is that how you remember it? Don't overreact, Ingrid. I wasn't much more than a kid. I hardly knew what girls had inside their knickers at that time.' He laughed and spread his hands in what was probably meant to be a gesture of incredulity, but in Ingrid's current state of fury just made him look like a penguin in his black and white outfit.

'A kid? I don't think so. You were much stronger than me in any case and I remember exactly what happened that night,' Ingrid said, making an enormous effort to keep her breathing even.

'Go on then, tell me. Let's see how wrong you've got it.'

Ingrid let her mind go back decades, to that warm evening in May. The party invitation had given directions to a large house on the outskirts of Meadowthorpe. Her cousin Christopher and his best friend Mike were turning eighteen in the same week, and Mike's parents had bravely agreed to host the event. The celebrations had already been in full swing when she arrived, because Ingrid had been undecided about whether she was brave enough to face Chris and Mike's cool friends.

She'd sidled in, trying to make herself inconspicuous as usual, and been greeted by a sea of faces, none of which she recognised. Making her way quickly out to the garden, sidestepping several slightly drunken couples in doorways and on the floor, Ingrid had ended up next to an old summerhouse draped in wisteria. The scent had been intoxicating, and she'd at last begun to relax, slipping off her sandals and dropping her cardigan on the grass.

'Oh, you turned up eventually, did you?' A familiar voice from further down the garden caused Ingrid to turn sharply, twisting her neck in the process. She winced and raised a hand to try and ease the stabbing pain, eyes watering. Lennie was soon standing beside her, holding a bag of crisps and a bottle of what looked like cider.

'What's up? Have you hurt yourself? Why don't you come in here and I'll give your neck a rub?' he said, gesturing with the bottle towards the open door of the summerhouse.

Unable to think for the sickening pain, Ingrid hadn't registered what an odd thing that was for her somewhat gauche cousin to say. Desperate to stop her neck hurting and hearing a group of revellers noisily heading their way across the lawn, she followed Lennie inside.

'Sit on that stool and I'll see what I can do,' he'd said. 'My dad's a sports physiotherapist. I've seen him do this lots of times.'

Lennie had put his hands on Ingrid's shoulders and pushed her down onto the low stool. She'd flinched at the clammy chill of his fingers but had been distracted by what he'd just said. 'I thought your dad had left your mum,' she'd said, thoughtlessly. 'He doesn't live with you any more, does he?'

There was a silence. Lennie's hands tightened, beginning to

massage the flesh around Ingrid's throat. He dug his fingers in, and she cried out.

'I don't know where you heard that. My dad's just working away,' he said. 'Now stop being pathetic and let me get you fixed. That's what he does. My dad fixes people. Everyone knows he's on the road with the England team right now. He can sort footballers' injuries out. Quick. As. Anything.'

The last three words were accompanied by sharp stabs. Ingrid put her hands up to his and tried to prise them away. 'Stop it, you're hurting me, Lennie,' she said. 'I don't like it.'

'You've got to be patient. Stop wriggling, I haven't finished.'

As he spoke, Lennie moved closer so that his whole lower body was pressed against Ingrid's back. She could feel a large bulge forcing itself into the hollow of her spine. Still remarkably innocent even at eighteen years old due to a combination of intense shyness and unhappiness with her gawky body, this was the first time Ingrid had been anywhere near a male erection. She froze, unsure what to do next. Did this mean that Lennie found her attractive? He was an unappealing prospect, not to mention being her cousin, which was weird, but even as revulsion flooded through her, Ingrid couldn't help being strangely flattered.

Lennie's stiffness seemed to be growing, and he started to move rhythmically against Ingrid as his fingers worked on her neck, kneading and pummelling. He was moaning quietly to himself, lost in the moment. What should she do?

Lennie released his hold on Ingrid so suddenly that she fell backwards, capsizing the flimsy wooden stool and landing painfully on the floor. In seconds, Lennie was on top of her, his breath coming in harsh bursts as he fumbled under her skirt. Ingrid could smell the noxious wafts of cheese and onion crisps he'd been eating, and the cider fumes were even more

A New Lease of Life

nauseating. The wooden boards of the summerhouse floor were hard and unyielding, splinters beginning to work their way through Ingrid's thin dress. As she writhed, Lennie forced her legs apart and was about to undo his jeans when Ingrid at last came to life, remembering the limited self-defence advice they'd been given at school. Yelling was better than screaming in an emergency. Screams often went unnoticed, as if they were just part of harmless horseplay, but a good loud yell usually did the trick.

Ingrid took a deep breath and bellowed at the top of her voice. 'Help, he's attacking me. Help! I'm in here. Stop him!'

Lennie rolled off Ingrid and scrambled to his feet just as two girls flung the summerhouse door open. They looked down at Ingrid frantically rearranging her clothing, and they started to laugh.

19

Wrenching her mind back to the present, Ingrid stared at Lennie who was still waiting for her reply. He walked over to the wall and leaned against it, arms folded and head on one side, almost as if he was posing for a photo shoot. 'Go on then,' he said. 'You *think* I tried to get it on with you when I was not much more than a kid. What are you going to do about it? You're a big girl now and you were bigger than me even then. Isn't it about time you stopped harping back to the past?'

'Harping back? Is that really how you see it? I didn't have a proper relationship with a man for years after that, Lennie. You messed up my life for ages and it's time you faced what you did instead of making me out to be some kind of drama queen.'

Lennie laughed again. He was really enjoying himself now, so enthralled in the old story that he didn't see the door to the back room opening slightly. Ingrid noticed it though and was torn between relief that someone else was in the building with them and panic as to who might have heard her shameful accusation. She'd never mentioned any of this to her parents or even to friends later on. Even Tommy had never known. He'd have been sure to go searching for Lennie. He was a protective soul when people he cared about were concerned, and he never held back when he was angry. A charge of GBH or worse definitely wasn't what Ingrid had wanted for her husband, however satisfying it would have been to see Lennie get his just desserts.

'So, I'll ask you again, what do you think you can do about it now?' Lennie said, the sneer on his face making Ingrid long to punch him. She had actually taken a step forward, hands clenched so tightly that her nails were biting into her palms, when the storeroom door swung open fully.

'Ingrid doesn't need to do anything about it, because I'm dealing with this one, Lennie,' said Joel, emerging from the back of the shop. 'That was a great story. I think your wife would be even more interested to hear it than I was. Oh, and your boss too. I meet up with Craig in the pub sometimes. Nice bloke.'

Lennie took a pace backwards and then rallied. 'I don't know what *you're* doing nosing around here, but you're joking, I hope,' he said, narrowing his eyes. 'Nobody in their right mind would believe you if you tried to spread filth about me. Janice trusts me and so does Craig. You should try finding a woman of your own instead of stirring things up with mine.'

Ingrid saw the dangerous glint in Joel's eyes as he moved towards the other man. She opened her mouth to try and stop him taking any sort of violent action, but he was holding up his phone rather than his fists. 'It was lucky I recorded the conversation then,' he said. 'That should cut out any doubts.'

'That old chestnut. You've been watching too many detective programmes. You must think I'm a complete mug,' Lennie said, reaching forward to grab the phone, but Joel was too quick for him. He stepped out of range, pressed a button and

Ingrid's voice rang out loud and clear, followed by Lennie's jeering tones.

'It's all here,' Joel said, pocketing his phone. 'And you'd be wrong if you think I won't use it. Leave Ingrid alone and she might not take this any further. Or then again...'

Joel left the sentence dangling, and Lennie turned on his heel, storming out of the shop and letting the door slam behind him so hard that Ingrid feared for the glass. She heard his car roar away, and made her way over to the nearest seat, flopping down suddenly as her legs gave way.

'I don't know how you came to be in exactly the right place at the right time, Joel,' Ingrid said shakily.

'I was just passing on my way to... to the general store and I saw his car parked outside. It rang alarm bells.'

'That was way beyond lucky. If you hadn't done what you did, heaven only knows what I'd have been up against next. Do you think that's really nailed it? Will he try again?'

Joel shook his head. 'He wouldn't dare. I meant what I said about his wife and his boss, and he knows it. We've never been mates, Lennie and me. He's a snake. Look, are you okay? You don't look great, to be honest. I mean...'

Ingrid got to her feet, feeling better by the moment. 'I know what you mean but I'll be fine. It was so good of you to step in like that. I... I don't know how to thank you.'

'No need,' said Joel. 'I'm just glad I was passing. Just give me a call if you need me. I'm usually available for pest removal jobs like that one. See you around.'

Ingrid watched him go, half wishing she'd asked him in for a drink but feeling that her own company would be best tonight. It didn't occur to her until she was safely upstairs in the flat trying to decide between tea and wine that Joel's reply to her question about why he was in the area again so soon was confusing. The general store in the village was surely in the opposite direction. Odd. Ingrid put the mystery out of her mind with an effort. Tonight was for relaxation, with Lennie hopefully out of her hair for good. Any other questions could wait, and now the thorn in her side had been removed, she could get on with opening her shop without any more unexpected visitors. Or so she thought.

20

Joel couldn't get to sleep that night. The toxic interlude with Lennie Nightingale had left him still boiling with anger at the way Ingrid had been treated by the weedy little shit and he was filled with an uncomfortable mixture of pity and frustration that she had clearly never been able to leave her horror of Lennie behind. Ingrid must have endured years of bitterness since the assault, but he'd caught a look of what looked a lot like shame on her face when she'd watched Lennie go. Surely she wasn't blaming herself for what Lennie had done?

The restlessness wasn't helped by the fact that Leo had come back late again, and the rattle of the van as Baz roared swiftly away told him that this young man was in no mood to meet the father of his girlfriend. In his heart of hearts, Joel knew that to antagonise his daughter at this point would be madness, even though his instinct was to build a protective shield around her, like Sleeping Beauty in her palace. As many thorny hedges as possible, and maybe a trench and an electric fence thrown in. That'd stop the slimy bugger. Instead, he'd raised his eyebrows and looked pointedly at the clock on the living-room wall as she'd put her head around the door to say goodnight but had held back from commenting. If their plans went ahead, she'd soon be safely ensconced in Ingrid's flat. It would be madness to rock the boat and have a row tonight.

Joel plumped up his pillows, giving them a hefty thump in lieu of Lennie's face, and tried once again to settle down. The evening had been warm, and through the open window he could hear the familiar sounds of night drawing in. An owl hooted from the thicket of trees at the bottom of the garden, and next door's cat gave an answering yowl. The evocative scent of honeysuckle drifted in, just a hint in the air at this time of night but enough to bring back memories of the day Trina had planted it, when Leo had still been Olivia and their three lives had seemed set to be entwined forever just like the honeysuckle would hopefully be, with the new trellis Joel had constructed. He remembered later that evening resuming his efforts to persuade Trina that they should try for another baby. She'd been adamant that one child was plenty, saying she couldn't face the threat of the crippling postnatal depression that had dogged her early months with baby Olivia.

Deciding that sleep wasn't going to come, or at least not for a while, Joel sat up in bed and made himself a nest of pillows. He was still sleeping with all four of them, even all these years after Trina had gone. At first, it had been comforting to be surrounded by a feathery mountain and soft sheets when he'd been getting used to being alone. Trina had always loved good-quality bedlinen. Joel had been surprised she hadn't stripped the bed along with everything else when she'd left, but he assumed Trevor the Tosser could afford even better quilts and pillows, not to mention sheets of the finest Egyptian cotton.

Now he was more alert, Joel realised that the muffled noises that he'd assumed were coming through the wall from the neighbours' house on his left-hand side were actually closer to home. He listened more carefully, even going so far as to put his ear to the wall between his own room and his daughter's. Yes, someone was definitely talking in there. Was she Face-Timing her mum? It seemed unlikely. Or horrible Baz? It was high time Leo was asleep. Joel slid out of bed and tiptoed out onto the landing, making his way quietly along the corridor. When he reached Leo's bedroom door, he froze in horror at the rumble of a gruff voice which definitely didn't sound like the tinny tones that usually emitted from his daughter's phone. What the hell?

Flinging Leo's door open, Joel marched in. His daughter, eyes wide, was staring at him with her mouth open. Unlike the usual floral scent coming from Leo's limited range of beauty products there was a rank smell in the air, a combination of sweat and nervous energy.

'It... It's not what you think...' Leo stuttered, pushing back the covers.

Joel felt a surge of relief that she was fully dressed, or at least in her most sensible pyjamas that were actually more all-encompassing than the clothes she wore in the daytime, and the other person in the room was sitting on the bed rather than, awful thought, rolling around inside it.

'But I heard you drive away,' Joel said to the giant of a boy who was clearly trying hard to be a man, with his wispy goatee and large clumpy work boots.

'Parked round the corner, didn't I? She let me back in.' The boy smirked. Big mistake. Joel's temper, only recently calming down from the encounter with Lennie, was back on red alert.

'What do you think you're playing at?' Joel demanded of his daughter, fury rising as he trotted out the words that his own father had said to him more than once in his teen years. 'I can't believe you'd go behind my back like this.'

'I wanted to explain to Baz about going to stay at Ingrid's flat, but he went off in a huff. Then he came back and threw stones at my window. It was just like they do in the films. I was worried he'd wake you up, so I went down to open the door,' Leo babbled, coming to stand in front of Joel and simultaneously blocking his view of Baz.

'*You* had better get out of here right this minute,' Joel hissed, leaning round Leo to face the interloper. 'I don't appreciate you being in my daughter's bedroom, and you shouldn't have put her in the position where she felt as if she had to let you in.'

'Oh, chill, man,' said Baz, easing himself up from the bed as if he'd got all the time in the world. 'It's no wonder she doesn't want to live with you when you act like a prison guard. She can't wait to get away from you an' I don't blame her.'

Before Joel could think of a suitably crushing reply, Baz slid round him and took the stairs two at a time, letting the front door slam as he left. The chug of the van clunking away down the road died away as Leo and Joel looked at each other, neither sure where to go from here. The putrid stench of unwashed male still hung in the room.

'How do you even stand the armpit stink of him?' Joel asked, going over to open a window to give himself time to think.

'Baz can't help that. His mum won't let him use the shower unless he chips in with the electric bill, and he's skint.'

Joel opened a window and motioned for her to follow him into his own room, because he was beginning to feel queasy. They both looked at his bed, and then without a word sank down to sit on the floor with their backs against it. After a moment, Joel stirred himself. 'Do you really hate living with me?' he asked sadly. 'I've never thought of myself as a prison guard.'

Leo shrugged. Her face had the mutinous look that she'd often adopted as a sulky toddler. 'You didn't have to throw him out,' she said. 'Baz has had a tough life. He's got no dad and his mum's horrible to him. All he wants to do is paint. She doesn't get it.'

'If he wants to paint, he can make a start on the rendering on the front of our house,' said Joel. 'That should keep him busy.'

'You know that's not what I was getting at. He's an artist. He's got talent. And anyway, even if he did want to paint our house, you wouldn't want him to. Don't say stuff you don't mean. It's... it's hypocritical.'

They both fell silent, lost in their own thoughts. Joel's misery threatened to overwhelm him. He'd hoped so much that Leo living here would bring them closer together again, but now it looked as if her mother might make life difficult for them if she stayed, he'd antagonised her over her boyfriend, and she was moving out to stay with a woman they'd only just met. It was all going badly wrong. Still, at least Ingrid would be a stable influence. At the thought of his new friend, Joel's heart skipped a beat or two. Tall as she was, she'd looked so fragile in the shop earlier, although he was pretty sure she was a lot stronger than he was giving her credit for.

'Am I still going to Ingrid's?' Leo asked. 'Or are you going to warn her off, now you probably think I'm going to get Baz round there as soon as your back's turned?'

Joel looked at her in alarm and she pulled a face. 'See, I know you don't trust me, wherever I stay. You only want me to move in over the shop so you can have an excuse to go round and chat Ingrid up, don't you?'

'I... no, that's not what I...'

'You're going red again, Dad. She's way out of your league anyway. Ingrid's got class. You're just an odd-job man.'

Stung, Joel felt his eyes smart. So that was what she thought of him, was it?

'I'm a carpenter. I make beautiful things out of wood. Bespoke furniture... and memorial benches that people treasure, but you know that, don't you? I only cram in other jobs to keep a roof over my head and pay your maintenance,' he said, standing up and going over to the window so Leo wouldn't see his wet eyes.

The scene that met Joel's eyes wasn't particularly calming. The moonlit garden was beginning to resemble a cat speed-dating meet up and tonight Randall and Hopkirk were the ones having a romantic moment. They nuzzled each other enthusiastically and then the white cat lay on the floor, stretching out to its full length with a definite come-hither look. *You lucky sod*, Joel told it silently. *I wish I had your animal magnetism. Although, even if I did like Ingrid in that way... which I don't, we're just friends... I'd be punching above my weight. Or so my daughter reckons.*

Leo had come up behind him now. She cleared her throat. 'I'm sorry, Dad. That was out of order. I do like living here with you and I know you're a proper craftsman. I was just being a pig because I wanted you to try and get to know Baz. He's a nice person. He is, really. But can I still go to Ingrid's? I think it's best for us both.'

Joel bit his lip and didn't reply for a few seconds. Instead, he turned and pulled Leo into a hug. Kissing the top of her head, he said, 'Let's give it a whirl and see how it goes. I'll miss you though.'

'You too,' she said, hugging him back. 'I'm going to bed now.'

'And I'm going to lock the door, just in case Van Gogh decides to try his luck again.'

Leo rolled her eyes at him but had the grace to grin. As Joel made his weary way downstairs, he wondered how Ingrid would cope with his livewire of an offspring. If they were going to stand a chance of making this temporary solution work, he'd not only have to tread very carefully when selling the idea to Trina, he'd also need to have a private word with Ingrid about the Baz situation first. The thought of this forthcoming chat wasn't displeasing. On the contrary, it gave him a warm feeling that lasted even as he dropped off to sleep, oblivious to the howls of two cats having a fabulous time in the garden.

21

When Ingrid woke up on Thursday morning, there was an unfamiliar bubble of excitement in her stomach, and for a moment she couldn't think why. Then she remembered that Leo was meant to be moving in soon. Her initial misgivings were turning into a much more positive feeling. She hoped it was nothing to do with the fact that Joel would be more involved in her life from now on, but whatever the reason, these new developments were turning out to be a great distraction from the past. She lay on her back staring up at a strange, dampish mark on the ceiling that resembled a misshapen hammer. It reminded her of Tommy with his auctioneer's gavel, which he liked to bring down on the lectern with a loud bang and a flourish to seal a deal.

The vision of Tommy at work made Ingrid smile, and she realised that memories of her husband were gradually becoming more manageable. At a distance of a few months, she was less muddled by sadness and guilt and more able to see her marriage for what it had been. Tommy was unpredictable in many ways, but their home had been a safe place to be. Was safe a good or bad thing? Good in that Ingrid had thought she knew where she was with Tommy on a basic level, although at times he'd been difficult to live with. But then Ingrid guessed that living with her hadn't been exactly a walk in the park either, with her high-powered job and the constant pressure to prove herself. Putting those thoughts to one side, Ingrid realised with another leap of her senses that very soon Leo would be moving in. Everything was going to feel different with a houseguest around. The new normal was changing already.

Reaching for her phone, Ingrid sent a quick text to Joel to check the move was still going ahead, and tried not to fret when he didn't reply immediately. She'd had a shower and dressed in the colourful dungarees that Elsie loved and a red T-shirt before her phone pinged but when they eventually appeared, the words on the screen made her smile.

> Leo's looking forward to it. Will drop her off on Saturday morning, if that's OK?

> Sure. I'm assuming her mum is happy with the plan then?

> Yeah. Trina seems surprisingly okay with the idea, but she'd like to meet you. The only problem is that she's away on holiday (again!) today, but she says if I trust you to just go ahead, she'll contact you when she gets back. Can I talk to you first about a couple of things? I'm going over to the country park on Friday afternoon to check on an order for a bench at 3 p.m., any chance you could join me? I'll be by the café around half past three if that works for you?

Ingrid texted back before she'd had time to wonder what this might be about.

> Lovely idea. See you on Friday.

As soon as she'd pressed send, random worries started to bounce around her brain. She made tea, and with it a slice of toast lavishly spread with peanut butter but even this comforting breakfast didn't stem the flow of thoughts. Did Joel want to find out more about what happened all those years ago with Lennie? Maybe he'd changed his mind about leaving well alone. There was no point in second guessing the meeting though, and she couldn't deny that the idea of a chat with Joel was giving her a fizzy feeling.

With time on her hands and no prospect of distractions today, Ingrid went into the shop and tried to take an unbiased look at the progress so far. The partly repainted sign was propped up against one wall, and she could see that Leo had made great inroads into redesigning it. When she was living here, she would soon get it finished. The shelves were all clean and in place with a few choice items already artfully displayed here and there. The window was still masked to anyone looking in from outside by the pink cleaning fluid smeared over the glass, but it was almost ready. Winnie's drapes were making a huge difference, and all that was needed was one beautiful thing in the centre and some of the battery-powered white fairy lights which were still in their boxes, another purchase from the shopping trip with Leo.

Ingrid breathed in deeply, loving the smell of cleanliness and an underlying hint of lavender from the gauzy bags that still hung from the ceiling. Beryl had replaced the old, dried stuff with fresh sprigs from her garden, and the scent reminded Ingrid of her visits here as a child. She'd always enjoyed the family's trips to see Aunt Sylvia, even if one of her cousins had been impossible to like and the other too full of his own activities to bother with a gawky female cousin. The cluttered, busy shop had fascinated Ingrid then, and it still did now, especially in its new incarnation.

In the storeroom, heaps of boxes remained untouched, but some of the contents of others had been spread out on top of the full ones. These must be the items that Beryl and Anthea had particularly liked but had not yet found time to arrange. Ingrid picked up a large vase, holding it carefully in both hands. It was over 30 cm tall, and a very pleasing, rounded shape with a lip at the top. Mainly forest green with a range of mountains painted in greens and gold around the upper edge, its rich colours seemed to glow in the gloom of the storeroom. The rest of the vase was covered with ornate, oriental trees and figures that stood out from the background, all lavishly decorated in gold, scarlet and more greens.

'This baby must be worth a packet,' Ingrid remembered Tommy saying, as he'd unpacked one of his collections of spoils, but when they had researched the vase's history, it had turned out to be very run of the mill in terms of monetary value. Nevertheless, although Tommy had lost interest in his find at this point, Ingrid had always liked it.

Should I keep it? she asked herself now, but there was no saying where she was going to end up living, and it was unlikely that she'd be in a home big enough to accommodate this dramatic piece of pottery. She put it on one side, resolving that it must be the first beautiful thing to take pride of place in the window when Winnie was satisfied the setting was ready. Energised by her find, Ingrid carried on with her work, placing several more lovingly selected artefacts on the shelves and arranging them with care. This task was immensely satisfying, and kept her busy for several hours, interspersed with breaks for mugs of tea. It was after two o'clock before she realised she needed to eat, and so she hurriedly made herself a sandwich and settled upstairs to watch a programme about a couple who wanted to buy an apartment in Spain. Their demands were incredibly complicated, and Ingrid began to lose patience with the entitled way they dismissed every option shown to them by an increasingly tetchy presenter whose rictus grin was getting more and more strained.

Ingrid looked around her small domain. Would she swap it for a stunning home in a hot country with views of the sea? She realised with a shock that she wouldn't. She was feeling more and more contented in Sylvia's flat, and it would be good to have Leo to share it for a while. With the TV off, Ingrid got to her feet and made further inroads into preparing the guest bedroom. She found her spare duvet and its cover and added pillowcases patterned with sunflowers. With those on the bed the room immediately looked more welcoming. The wardrobe in here was still empty and so was the chest of drawers, so Leo would have plenty of room to store her belongings, and there was an easy chair in the corner and even a small table where homework could be done if Leo needed privacy.

Satisfied, Ingrid returned to the living room, beginning to really look forward to Leo's arrival. The next job was to contact Anthea, who had called earlier to make sure Ingrid had all the details she needed for tomorrow's hospital trip. As she'd hoped, there had been a cancellation and so in the morning Ingrid was going to have to give herself a mental slap and stop panicking about driving to Meadowthorpe Infirmary. That wasn't nearly such an enticing prospect.

22

Despite giving herself a serious pep talk, a creeping feeling of dread was making Ingrid feel distinctly queasy as she tidied the flat and got ready to go and collect Anthea the next morning. With hindsight, the large bowl of fruit and muesli might have been a mistake. Ingrid filled her water bottle, took a last look around the now immaculate living room and left the building.

Anthea's directions had been straightforward, and with the help of her satnav, even with the rush-hour traffic in full flow, Ingrid was early. She rang the doorbell of the imposing Georgian edifice, listening to the chimes echoing along the hallway. The house looked over-large for a person living alone. Ingrid was all too aware of how it was possible to rattle round in a place that didn't fit any more. Anthea came to the door looking tired but as glamorous as ever. Her linen dress almost swept the floor, and the flowing cardigan matched it in length. Both were in shades of amber, and the older lady wore slouchy beige suede boots and an exotic Aztec-style scarf patterned in rust, chocolate brown and cream. Her lipstick, an earthy shade with a touch of gloss, matched the whole ensemble.

'You look wonderful,' said Ingrid, feeling underdressed in her cropped cotton trousers and denim jacket. She made a sudden decision on how to take Anthea's mind off the forthcoming visit. 'I wonder if you'd agree to go through my clothes with me sometime and advise about what to keep? I gave a lot away when I moved here but I think I still need to be more selective. Leo's moving in with me for a while from tomorrow and I had planned to use the wardrobe in that room for the overspill of my things but now... well, I'd appreciate some help.'

Anthea looked delighted at the prospect, and this interesting topic carried the two of them through what might have been a silent drive, with Anthea on edge about her appointment and Ingrid still unsure of her driving skills. The older lady also wanted to know everything about the events that had led up to Leo leaving her mum's and then her dad's houses, and Ingrid found herself pouring out her worries about Baz and the possibility that he would clip Leo's wings if he could.

'She's got real potential as an artist, but that's going to need hard work if she wants to really develop herself and make a career of it,' Ingrid said, frowning as a man in a flashy black sports car cut her up as she approached the hospital entrance and screeched down the drive ahead of her.

'Concentrate on the car park now, darling,' said Anthea. 'Ignore Mr Flashy Car. He's obviously got something to prove.' She wiggled her little finger at Ingrid, almost causing her to crash into the first barrier. They were both giggling as they left the car and made their way, arm in arm, towards the main entrance, where two people wrapped in dressing gowns were smoking as if their lives depended on it. They were puffing away right beneath a large No Smoking sign. Ingrid couldn't help wishing she could join them instead of going inside, even though the only time she'd lit up a cigarette she'd been violently sick in a bush behind the school youth club.

Anthea breathed in sharply as they reached the bank of electronic check-in machines. 'I detest this place, and I hate those bloody things even more,' she said, in a voice so low, Ingrid could hardly make out the words. 'I can never make them work and then the woman on the desk looks at me as if I'm nothing but an ancient, daft biddy.'

'Well, it's a good job I came along too then,' said Ingrid. 'There's nothing daft about you and talking of ancient, I'm an old hand at this. I've got the equivalent of an A level in operating hospital screens. Come on, let's get this show on the road. The sooner it's over, the sooner we can go somewhere more fun and eat cake.'

Screens safely sorted, the two of them settled themselves on green plastic chairs in a room filled with morose-looking people either clutching letters or staring at the TV on the wall, which had the sound muted.

'At least we don't have to listen to that drivel, what do you say, darling?' said Anthea, pointing at the panel of women in a brightly lit studio who were discussing something to do with the male menopause, if the subtitles could be believed.

'I like catching up with daytime TV from time to time. It's... soothing,' admitted Ingrid. She'd never had the opportunity to watch this kind of programme when she was working, and if she and Tommy had now and again managed to be at home and both awake in the evening, he'd preferred a fast-paced thriller or an ancient comedy series or two that were so un-PC that Ingrid had wanted to hide her head under a cushion.

After what seemed like an age but, on checking her watch, Ingrid found was only ten minutes, Anthea's name was called by a youthful medic who looked even more nervous than his patient. Clutching Ingrid's hand in a vice-like grip, Anthea followed him to a side room where they were both pointed in the direction of yet more uncomfortable chairs.

'So, Mrs Kingston-Bottomly,' the man said. 'It's good to meet you. May I call you Anthea?'

'If you must,' said Anthea.

'And you are?' he said to Ingrid.

'She's a friend. A new one, but a friend in need all the same. Just get it over with. Am I dying, Doctor, or have I just got a dicky tummy?' said Anthea, glowering at him. 'Spit it out. Don't make a meal of it.'

The doctor exchanged glances with Ingrid, who was trying hard to brace herself on her friend's behalf. She couldn't read his expression. There was a short silence.

'I'm afraid it's not that simple, Mrs... Anthea,' he said slowly. 'Your condition isn't going to be easy to diagnose without more of an investigation. As I'm sure you already know, we need to run a few tests so that we can be absolutely certain the treatment we can offer is right for you.'

Anthea's shoulders sagged. She was still holding Ingrid's hand, but her fingers had loosened their tight hold. 'Yes, I discussed the prospect of tests with my own doctor, but I really don't want any messing about,' she said. 'Can't be doing with it. Needles, scans, machines that go bleep. It's all too much. If I've reached the end, I want to just get on with it.'

Ingrid opened her mouth to remonstrate, still not clear what – if anything – was wrong, but the doctor quelled her with a look. His eyes were full of compassion as he leaned forward in his chair to speak to Anthea.

'Nobody's predicting that you're near the end,' he said gently. 'There are a number of reasons why you might have been feeling so—'

'Shitty?' finished Anthea, with something of her old spark.

'Indeed. Let's take this to the next stage and see if we can make everything clearer. It's just going to involve a couple of blood tests which we can do today and an MRI scan and a couple of other things as soon as possible. Nothing intrusive, I promise.'

Anthea looked across at Ingrid, who nodded. 'I've always believed that knowledge is power,' Ingrid said. 'If there are decisions to be made, you need all the information you can get.'

The doctor beamed at Ingrid. 'My thoughts exactly. I'll examine you now, Anthea, just as soon as we can get a nurse to come in to be with us. And then can I go ahead and refer you for the tests?'

The silence was longer this time. Eventually Anthea stirred herself. 'If this young lady will agree to come along with me (which is beyond the call of duty, in my humble opinion, as we haven't known each other for long) then I'll fall in with your suggestions. Even though,' she added with sudden vehemence, 'I think you're probably flogging a dead horse, as my pa used to say when he wanted us girls to help in the stables.'

Back out in the car park after a long wait for Anthea to have samples of blood taken, Ingrid breathed in a cloud of cigarette from a new doorway posse and turned to give Anthea a hug. 'You're doing the right thing,' she said, her voice husky. 'Okay, we don't know each other very well... yet... but I don't see you as one of life's quitters.'

Anthea raised two fingers at the man in the black sports car who was now leaning an elbow on his open window and backing out of his parking space with way too much engine revving and cursing.

'He reminds me of one of my husbands. I might tell you

A New Lease of Life

about him sometime. His name was Ricardo, but I prefer to call him Dickhead these days. And you're quite right. I've never been a quitter and there's no reason for me to start now. Are you sure you don't mind coming with me next time and the times after, because it never ends quickly, this kind of thing, does it? I don't want anyone to know what's going on until there's something definite to tell, and anyway, you're the only one I want with me, Ingrid. Thank goodness you arrived when you did.'

The candour of this statement and heartfelt request was almost too much for Ingrid. She blinked hard and rummaged in her pocket for a tissue. Maybe there was a reason she'd washed up in Willowbrook. It wasn't only the shop that was in need of her attention. Leo, Anthea and possibly even Joel seemed to have been waiting for her. Ingrid only hoped she was up to the job in hand.

23

A few raindrops from a sudden shower still sparkled on the grass as Ingrid hurried across the green later that day. The thought of meeting Joel had kept her going through the less-than-cheerful drive home with Anthea and the time she'd spent reassuring her that there was no need to worry. It was a pointless exercise because of course Anthea was anxious. She diverted slightly to cross the brook via the little humpbacked bridge just for the fun of it and strode out past the pub, giving Ned the landlord a wave as he swept the front step.

'See you again soon?' he called, and Ingrid nodded, feeling as if she was already a small part of the fabric of the village. It wasn't what she'd expected or even wanted, but it felt good all the same.

The track that led to the country park smelt fresh and verdant, with a damp, peaty scent that made Ingrid's nose tingle with pleasure. The ancient oak trees that lined the path almost met over her head and she walked along luxuriating in their magnificence. Living and working for so long in a city, beautiful as York was, Ingrid had given herself no leisure time for walking in the countryside. Her drives in the Dales with Tommy hadn't filled her with this joy of being right inside the natural world, but this was perfection.

The water park areas were teeming with wildfowl this afternoon, and Ingrid stopped to take a couple of photos to send to... who? There was really nobody back in York who she wanted to update on her new life, and she'd never been one for living her life on Instagram, although actually, now might be a very good time to learn a few new social media tricks. Leo could probably take charge of that side of things. The shop would need publicity even if it was only going to be open in its current form for a short while.

Nearing the parking area, Ingrid hoped the Saga Louts weren't out in force today. The last thing she needed was a load of gossipy innuendos if she was spotted with Joel. Luckily, the courtyard outside the café was empty of all but a few children who looked as if they were on some kind of field trip. As she drew nearer, one of the group began to wave her clipboard madly. Ingrid recognised Elsie, her auburn pigtails bouncing as she jumped up and down on the spot.

'Hello, Mrs Ingrid Shop Lady, you've got your best dungarees on again. We're doing a project about autumn,' the little girl shouted. 'My dad's our group leader this time. He likes helping at school, don't you, Daddy?'

Sam gave Ingrid a lopsided grin as she stopped to say hello. 'I got roped in on my day off,' he said. 'One of the parent helpers went down with a bug.'

'It was my mum,' said one of the boys, who seemed to be doing his best to trip his partner up. 'She threw up all night. It was gross.'

The others all began to make vomiting noises, and Sam went into sheepdog mode to move them on. Just as he was leaving, he turned to say goodbye to Ingrid and spied Joel coming out of the café.

'Hey, mate,' he said. 'I thought you were working today.'

Ingrid thought Joel couldn't have looked more furtive if he tried. Not meeting Ingrid's eyes, he mumbled something about seeing a new customer. Sam glanced at Ingrid and raised his eyebrows, and she felt her cheeks growing warm. Surely there was no need for Joel to make this seem like an assignation. Sam was no fool, and he was obviously making assumptions.

They watched Sam doing a quick head count of his group before marching them away. 'We'll come and help you in the shop soon, Ingrid!' called Elsie as she left. 'I'll bring biscuits. Party Rings are my favourites. Leo says she'll show me how to paint like a proper artist.'

'Lovely, I'll look forward to it,' Ingrid answered. The courtyard felt very quiet when the children had moved on. She waited for Joel to take the lead, suddenly nervous again. If this was going to be about Lennie, she'd need very strong coffee, but he turned his back on the café and set off back towards the rows of benches lining the nearest lake.

'Let's go and sit down,' he said. 'I won't keep you long. I guess you're wanting to get on with more unpacking. I'd offer to help today but I've got to move straight on with designing a new commission and there's the last one to finish too.'

Only a couple of the benches were occupied this morning so there was plenty of choice. Joel chose the one with the best view. It was Frankie's bench, with the plaque that mentioned the sunshine girl.

'I like to come here,' Joel said, motioning for Ingrid to sit down. 'Frankie was Milo's sister. You met him in the café, didn't you? She was a great girl.'

'It seems as if everyone knows everyone around Willowbrook,' said Ingrid. 'Where I come from, I hardly ever saw my neighbours.'

'Why was that?'

Ingrid thought back to the small, select estate with its electronic gates and high walls. Tommy had adored living there simply for the kudos, but in the odd times when she'd been home alone and idle for any length of time, Ingrid had found the place more and more synthetic and oppressive.

'All busy with work, I suppose,' she said, not wanting to emphasise the relative grandeur of her former home. Then she remembered that Joel had already seen it when he came to pick up all her boxes.

Joel didn't comment further. He leaned back on the bench and regarded two swans who looked as if they were revving up for a fight. 'I wanted to talk to you about something,' he said. 'Just a word of warning, really. Leo's dodgy boyfriend is on the prowl.'

Ingrid tried not to look too closely at Joel as he recounted the events of the previous evening, but she couldn't help noticing the light shadow of stubble on his high cheekbones and the expressive way he gestured with his hands as he talked. Workmanlike hands, broad and pitted with various scars. He'd rolled up the sleeves of his faded denim shirt and his forearms looked strong and well-muscled too. She bit her lip and swallowed hard. What had got into her lately? Much as she'd cared about him, Tommy had never had this extreme physical effect on her. Nobody had, come to think of it. She suddenly longed to move nearer to Joel, to touch him... to...

'So anyway, I wanted you to be on your guard,' Joel finished, interrupting what was turning into the kind of fantasy that maybe should be kept for when Ingrid was alone... or stifled completely, if she had any sense.

'I'll make sure before I bring her tomorrow that Leo knows that neither you nor I will stand for any funny business from this Baz character,' Joel continued, oblivious to the raging thoughts Ingrid was battling. 'I really want her to stay on at school and go to sixth form when she's done her GCSEs but I think he'll have other ideas, if he's still around in the summer.'

'Does she say she loves him?' Ingrid asked, surprised that she could manage to make her voice sound relatively normal considering what had just been going on in her mind. 'I guess that's the crucial point you need to think about.'

'We didn't talk about the "L" word. She's just a kid.'

'Oh, no, she isn't, Joel. You can't let her think that's how you see her. Love can strike at any age.'

Ingrid's words, spoken without due thought, seemed to hover between them. Joel looked at the ground. He appeared to be fascinated by the sprinkling of daisies growing amongst the grass at his feet. 'Was it like that for you with your husband?' he asked eventually.

When Ingrid didn't reply, he got to his feet. 'I'm sorry, that was out of order,' he said. 'Let's go and get a coffee and some of Milo's fantastic cake. That's all of the serious talk out of the way.'

'I thought you were in a rush to get on with your work?'

'I can spare half an hour. I didn't have lunch, and you can't make a decent bench on an empty stomach.'

'I'll take your word for it,' Ingrid said, relieved that there was no need to answer his last question. She was beginning to think she might never have had the first idea about love.

24

On Saturday morning, Joel and Leo arrived laden with bags and boxes and made several trips up and down the stairs to the flat. Joel turned down the offer of coffee because his daughter was clearly desperate for him to leave her to settle in and unpack. This took the best part of the day, but by Sunday, Leo had persuaded Ingrid to have another trip out in the car, 'for practice'.

Ingrid wasn't at all keen on this idea to begin with. She had several boxes and bags ready to give to one of the charity shops but none of them would be open today and it seemed silly to drive around for no reason, but as soon as she was out of the little car park and on the road to Meadowthorpe, the budding confidence from the previous outing with Leo returned. They meandered around the lanes, eventually stopping at a country pub where they both ordered a large roast dinner.

'Everybody needs time off,' said Leo, leaning back in her chair and undoing the top button of her skinny jeans. 'That Yorkshire pudding was immense. It was nearly as big as my head. Mum doesn't cook on Sundays, she says she doesn't see why she should be slaving over a hot stove when she should be relaxing, and Dad's never tried a full roast dinner. Hey, maybe next week we'll do our own?'

Ingrid nodded doubtfully. It was a nice idea, but large Sunday lunches had never been part of her repertoire either. Tommy preferred to eat out if he wasn't working and she'd never argued. The tantalising aromas of a large joint of lamb or beef cooking slowly in the oven had always reminded her too much of her mum and dad and the cosy weekends of childhood, but this time in her life was turning out to be all about new beginnings, so why on earth not?

With Leo safely installed in the flat, life moved up a gear for Ingrid. On Monday, as her new housemate got ready for school, it was clear that the usual calm of the early mornings was now going to be shattered. Leo dashed from bedroom to bathroom to kitchen and back again, losing her shoes, finding her coursework, eating jam on toast and all the time talking at the top of her voice.

'I'm gonna love living here with you, Ings. Is it okay if I call you Ings? Ingrid just seems a bit stuffy,' she said over her shoulder as she finally headed for the stairs.

There was no time to answer before Leo clattered down to the shop. In the deep peace that followed her departure, Ingrid thought about the oddness of being known as *Ings*. Nobody had ever used that one before. Most of her workmates had either called her by her first name or referred to her as 'Boss'. Tommy had called her Ingers from the start, but then he'd had his own nicknames for everyone he knew well. It was kind of sweet that Leo wanted to start a new trend, but vaguely insulting that her given name was considered stuffy. Still, she told herself, fresh starts came in all sorts of forms, so maybe she would soon get used to being *Ings*. It was a small price to pay for a chance to find a solution to Leo and Joel's difficult situation.

The following morning took a different turn. Leo bounced into Ingrid's bedroom at six o'clock, coughed loudly to wake her up and told her it was time to put the kettle on and toast some crumpets, so Ingrid had better be ready for action.

'You don't need to get up, just put your dressing gown on and get back into bed,' said Leo. 'I'll be here again in five minutes for a planning meeting before school.'

Ingrid rubbed her eyes. 'I thought teenagers were supposed to like sleeping,' she said, yawning. 'I didn't think I'd see you for a couple of hours.'

Leo laughed. 'Lie-ins are for losers. I was meant to meet Baz before school and have a lift in, but his van needs a new something-or-other to stop it rattling so much, so that's not going to happen. I thought he might come and walk with me, but he says he's tired. I don't expect he'll get up until this afternoon, so I'm free.'

As the young girl left the room, Ingrid considered this statement, wondering why the irony of the comment about losers hadn't struck her new lodger. Baz was sounding less and less of a suitable mate for Leo, in her opinion. She decided to say nothing on the subject. A conversation about his shortcomings was never going to go down well. Not yet anyway.

By the time Leo was back with a tray containing mugs of strong tea and a plate heaped with hot, buttered crumpets, Ingrid had flung opened the curtains and opened the window wide. A fresh breeze wafted the curtains but even so, there was the definite promise of a fine day ahead.

'Good, you're already sorted,' said Leo, seeing that Ingrid had found her notebook and pen and was propped up against her pillows looking almost awake. Ingrid yawned again.

'I wasn't expecting this staff meeting, but it's always good to make an early start,' she said. 'Pass me my tea and you can get the proceedings underway. Shall I take the minutes as you seem to be in the chair?'

Leo giggled and made short work of her crumpets before licking the butter off her fingers and climbing onto the bed to sit cross-legged at the bottom end.

'Okay, this is the deal,' she said. 'My dad says he's free for a couple of hours tomorrow morning and so are the Saga Louts, I checked with Beryl, in fact you can have them all day. I can see you've been busy already working on your own and I can help with more sorting most days after school.'

'And your point is?' Ingrid was still feeling bleary. Her dreams had been punctuated with images of herself with her parents in tow, wading through a quagmire pursued by wild horses. Was it symbolic or had the hospital visit stirred up bad memories?

'Right, you're probably going to argue about this part, but I don't see why we shouldn't open up the shop for the first time a week on Saturday,' said Leo.

'But... no! I...'

Leo held up a hand. 'Just hear me out, Ings. The longer we leave it, the more you'll faff about trying to make everything perfect. We're nearly ready. A few more days arranging the shelves and we're good to go.'

'But how will people know about us? If we open the door to customers in less than a fortnight, there won't be anyone here.' Ingrid's head was whirling. This was all too much, too soon. She'd planned for a lot more time to get properly organised and the thought of starting her project on the back foot was unsettling to say the least, but Leo's eyes were shining, and she was holding out a piece of paper.

'I had double IT yesterday and my teacher's really cool. He let me work on a flyer for the shop as part of my coursework. I've added a bit that gives people 10 per cent off with their first purchase if they bring the flyer with them. Is that okay? Everyone loves a discount. My dad's got a colour printer so if I go round there on my way home after school, I can get a load of these ready. Me and Dad can go and pop them through as many letterboxes near here as we can manage between now and a week on Saturday while the rest of you get the shelves ready and Winnie finishes the window.'

'But... but...'

'I know what you're going to say, the sign isn't finished yet, but I can do the last bit of that at the weekend and then Dad can put it up for us... Also, I'm putting a post on the Willowbrook and district Facebook page and another on my own Instagram and Snapchat and I've told my mates to share the hell out of it from now until next weekend. We can open again the day after if we keep to Sunday trading hours, but we might not want to. Let's play that one by ear.'

Leo sat back and looked at Ingrid as if she was expecting to have to keep on selling her ideas, but the more the girl had talked, the more excited Ingrid found herself getting too. There was no good reason for waiting. She'd been sensible all her life so far. Maybe it was time to break out.

'Go on then,' she said, in the words of her favourite character from *The Detectorists* when his partner suggested heading for the pub.

'Really?'

'Yes, really. Let's do it!'

The day passed by in a blur once Leo had left for school. Fired up by the prospect of actually having the shop open, Ingrid spent the rest of Tuesday unpacking yet more boxes and deciding which parts of Tommy's collection were definitely not good enough for the shelves. She loaded the car with all her charity shop donations ready for delivery whenever Leo was free to direct her to the best drop-off place and by the time her new lodger returned laden with freshly printed flyers, Ingrid was very dusty, but more than a little pleased with her day's work.

'I can't wait to get these delivered,' Leo said, proudly displaying the results of her labours, which looked professional and eye-catching. 'Even Dad thought they looked good, and he hates getting junk mail through the door. He usually thinks they're tacky. Mine aren't though. I bet Baz'll help us deliver them.'

Ingrid doubted this but didn't want to be a wet blanket. 'They're fabulous,' she said. 'I can't believe you've got them done so quickly. Just give me ten minutes to tidy the shop floor so the ladies don't fall over my junk in the morning and then we'll go upstairs and cook something easy. I need to get my strength up for tomorrow if I'm going to have a full day with the Saga Louts and then film night on top of that.'

'I wish I wasn't at school,' said Leo. 'It feels like a total waste of time when I could be here helping.'

'Waste of time? When you've just produced that magnificent flyer there and you're learning how to design things like my sign? I need all the experts I can get around here!'

Leo tried her best to look nonchalant, but Ingrid could see she was pleased with the compliments. 'Oh, well, I guess you can manage without me till the weekend at a push,' she said. 'Just don't let them get their hands on all the best biscuits. I know exactly how many packets of Jammy Dodgers there are in that cupboard.'

A New Lease of Life

* * *

Ingrid felt as if she'd only just gone to bed when she heard loud knocking on the front door the next morning. She pulled on jeans and a sweatshirt and staggered down the stairs yawning, as Leo began her usual manic pin-balling around the flat as she got ready for school.

'I didn't know there were two seven-thirties in the day,' grumbled Anthea, as Ingrid opened the door to let the three ladies in. 'I don't normally have my breakfast until half past nine. It's tricky driving with your eyes closed.'

'Get out of it. You wouldn't want to be left out of all the fun, would you?' said Winnie. She set down a large picnic hamper and, without further ado, started rummaging in the stores for the fairy lights.

'Yes, give over moaning, Anthea. Leo's put a rocket under us with all this talk of opening a week on Saturday, and good for her, is what I say. There's no point in wasting time and life is for living! We may not be in the first flush of youth any more but we're not dead yet,' said Beryl, who had walked from her house dragging a wheeled suitcase behind her.

Anthea and Ingrid exchanged glances but neither commented, and Beryl was soon in her usual role of ruling the selection process of objects for display. 'What was this big vase doing in the middle of the floor?' she asked, bringing Ingrid's find into the main part of the shop.

'Oh, I left that out on purpose when I was tidying up. If Winnie agrees, I'd like it to be the first *one beautiful thing* for the window display,' Ingrid said, hoping to goodness there wasn't going to be an argument about it, because she'd set her heart on the vision in her mind. *It's my shop*, she reminded herself. *I need to make the important decisions around here.*

Winnie considered the vase with her head on one side. 'It's a bit Marmite,' she said eventually.

'How do you mean?' Ingrid wasn't sure how to take this comment. She felt protective about the vase now, as if she was the only one who appreciated its gaudy beauty.

'Well, you'd either love it or hate it. There's a certain charm about it though, and I think you're right. It's coming with me.'

With that, Winnie picked up the object in question and placed it right in the centre of her artful drapes, surrounded by the hundreds of twinkling white lights she'd just been testing. 'I'll get all this pink stuff cleaned off the window just before we actually open,' she said. 'It's best to keep our air of mystery for now.'

'That's great. What's in your suitcase, Beryl?' Ingrid asked, intrigued.

'A few prettifying bits and bobs. You'll see,' said Beryl. 'We'll get the shelves sorted and then we can do the finishing touches. Anthea's got a couple of extra things in her car too.'

By the time Winnie announced that it was lunchtime, Joel had arrived, apologising profusely for being late. 'I got caught up with work and didn't realise what time it was,' he said. 'Leo told me I might be needed today.'

Ingrid smiled at him and assured him there was nothing much for him to do, except take a load of flattened boxes and some crates to the recycling depot. 'But that'll do anytime,' she said.

'I'll do it now, and clear the decks in the yard,' Joel said. 'I don't like the thought of all that combustible stuff piled up out there.'

They watched him go, and Beryl grinned. 'He's looking out for you nicely, isn't he?' she said. 'Poor man. He needs someone to care about, what with his wife running off all those years ago and now his daughter preferring to live here with you.'

'He's not a poor man,' said Ingrid, flushing scarlet. 'And don't let him hear you say that. Joel's just being neighbourly. Nothing more, nothing less.'

Ingrid thought she heard Winnie mutter, 'Yeah, yeah,' under her breath but decided to ignore it. It was getting more and more difficult to look disinterested whenever Joel appeared. Best not to rise to the bait. 'Is it lunchtime yet?' she asked hopefully.

25

Ingrid's remark, dropped in mainly to divert Winnie, proved a popular one.

'I thought nobody would ever suggest food,' said Beryl. 'Let's get it ready and then Joel can join us. We don't want him to have an energy crisis. Who knows what you'll be needing him for later, Ingrid.'

There hadn't seemed to be anywhere to lay out the food before, but Anthea bustled out to her car and produced a folding garden table which she erected against a wall and draped with an ornate tapestry cloth. 'I know it won't look so pretty for now but I'm covering this with a plastic one,' she said. 'The other cloth is staying on after we've had lunch, ready for the shop opening, and I don't want it speckled with bits of food. We can use this table to set out our bargain basement objects. It'll make them look classier.'

She went back out while Winnie and Beryl set out the picnic and this time returned with a huge wooden standard lamp sporting a crimson fringed shade. 'This was my grandmother's,' she said, 'but it doesn't match my living room now. Can I put it in the corner?'

'You'd better say yes,' said Winnie. 'I had to have it poking in my ear all the way from home. I thought we were going to have to stick it out of the window.'

At five o'clock, Beryl, Winnie and Anthea downed tools and declared themselves done for the day. 'Truth be told, I'm knackered,' said Beryl. 'We'll see you round at my place at seven on the dot for film night, Ingrid.'

'And don't forget the dress code; dressy being the operative word,' said Anthea. She was looking less anxious now, Ingrid thought, but she'd made her excuses to go home for a shower and change rather than straight to Beryl's, and it was obvious that Anthea was in need of some alone time before being sociable again.

'You can drop me off at home, Anthea, and then pick me up on your way back. I'm bringing the food tonight, remember,' said Winnie. 'Don't go sneaking a crafty sandwich now, Ingrid. You'll be wanting an empty belly for what you're going to eat later. I was planning to cook at Beryl's, but I'd rather use my air fryer for some of it.'

'New-fangled nonsense,' said Beryl, with a sniff. 'What's wrong with a proper oven, that's what I want to know? They were good enough for our mothers and mine's good enough for me.'

Ingrid could almost see Anthea wilting at the thought of more tasks to fit in before she could relax. She made as if to shepherd Winnie out of the door, but her friend hadn't finished talking. 'We're having jerk chicken with rice and peas and corn on the cob tonight, ladies. That spatchcocked chicken's been marinating all day but I'm going to have to get a wiggle on to get it cooked in time.'

She fixed Beryl with a beady look and her friend chuckled. 'You're going to mention that pesky air fryer again, aren't you? So, so quick and efficient. Blah, blah, blah.'

Winnie smiled. 'You won't be grumbling about it when you see what comes out of it later, ducky. Grown men have been known to whimper when they eat my jerk chicken.'

Ingrid's stomach rumbled in readiness. The thought of home-cooked Jamaican food was tantalising. She felt a sharp pang of a different kind when she thought how Tommy wouldn't have appreciated the spices at all. He'd been a bangers and mash or cottage pie kind of guy, with a Sunday roast at a pub whenever they were both free at the weekend. Ingrid couldn't wait to try Winnie's signature dish, but it seemed like a betrayal to be looking forward to it so much. Widows surely weren't meant to be fantasising about their dinner. Shouldn't she still be pining for her husband and getting thinner by the day?

Sometimes the ghostly presence of Tommy faded away for a while but then reappeared so suddenly that it made her feel physically sick. However, despite the waves of melancholy that sometimes threatened to overwhelm her, Ingrid was actually enjoying being able to please herself in all sorts of ways. It was confusing and often disorientating to feel such a roller coaster of emotions. She sighed, once again plagued by guilt that she could still look forward to interesting food and a night of good company. Beryl glanced across enquiringly as she let herself out of the shop but didn't comment.

Ingrid watched them go, before sprinting up the stairs and having the fastest shower in recent memory. She wanted all the time she could spare to choose something decent to wear, and she was struggling to think what might be appropriate for an evening with three such ebullient ladies who definitely didn't

A New Lease of Life

approve of dressing down. Eventually she made her decision, when she was running out of options and the bedroom was strewn with her smarter clothes. The chosen dress was an old favourite and always made her feel more glamorous than usual but brought back some less than happy memories of nights out with Tommy and his gang. She found her best gold earrings and slipped her feet into strappy sandals. This was no time for looking back.

By the time Ingrid had strolled along Fiddler's Row to number five, she had managed to put any dismal thoughts behind her and was more than ready for a night of uncomplicated fun. As Beryl opened the scarlet front door, Ingrid held out the chilled bottle of prosecco that had been waiting in the fridge since the Tesco visit and beamed at her hostess, who was resplendent in an ankle-length frock of peach chiffon.

'You look amazing,' they said simultaneously.

'I told you there was no need to knock but I'm glad you took notice of the dress code for tonight,' said Beryl. 'I like your style. You should put on the glitz more often. If you hang out with us, we'll find you plenty of opportunities.'

Ingrid looked down at the full skirt of her vintage tea gown, black with large white spots. It had a stiff, black, net petticoat and felt a bit over the top as she walked down the village street, but as she entered the living room and spied Winnie through the kitchen door, dressed from head to foot in purple velvet, complete with matching head wrap, she knew she'd made the right choice.

Anthea stood up to greet Ingrid. She'd chosen a shift dress in turquoise linen for the occasion and had accessorised with several jangling gold bracelets and necklaces.

'Welcome to your first Saga Louts film night,' she said. 'Shall I open that bottle? We were waiting for you, to be polite, but I think these two are more than ready for some bubbles. I'm driving this time because I brought Winnie and the food.'

'I told you we could have got a taxi,' shouted Winnie. 'You can always leave the car here and fetch it tomorrow.'

'No, I'm happy to be on the fizzy water tonight,' Anthea said, exchanging glances with Ingrid. 'It'll do my liver good to have a break.'

Was that the problem? Ingrid couldn't believe that Anthea was the kind of woman to let her social drinking get out of control to the point of making her ill. Maybe she was just feeling under the weather. She certainly looked peaky, but the other two didn't seem to have noticed, so perhaps Ingrid was making the situation worse in her mind than it really was, and Anthea was just fretting about the forthcoming tests and results. Worry could have that effect. Ingrid mentally crossed her fingers that the next hospital visit would at least start the process of putting any fears to rest.

Beryl bustled around making sure her guests each had a small table for their glass and plates while Anthea poured drinks and Winnie dished up the aromatic chicken dish and its accompaniments into deep bowls. Ingrid made herself as useful as possible by passing round the rainbow-patterned paper napkins, but she could see that the ladies' routine was so well practised that help was unnecessary. Soon they were all seated.

'Ready for a bit of hunky Hugh Grant action, girls?' Beryl said, pressing *play* before they could answer, which was lucky because the others were already tucking into the fragrant food and had their mouths full. 'I hope you haven't got a thing about the "F" word, Ingrid,' she added, grinning, as the opening scene began.

26

The particular expletive that started the film had never been Ingrid's favourite, but in the hands of such masterly comic actors, she immediately changed her mind. The action played out as they ate, and Winnie preened herself as compliments flowed for her cooking skills. There was a short comfort break while dishes were cleared away and glasses topped up and the older ladies took turns to visit the bathroom while Ingrid gave herself a moment to drink some water. She was already feeling light-headed from the fizz, and she hadn't laughed so much in a long time. The agonising wedding speeches in the film brought back quite a few such occasions that she'd endured over the years, not least her own.

'What was your wedding like, Ingrid?' asked Beryl, her thoughts clearly going the same way. 'Mine was a riot.'

'That sounds fun,' said Ingrid.

'No, I mean *literally* a riot. Len's mates were rat-arsed before we even sat down to eat, and by the time the speeches started they were way out of line already. One of them shouted out a comment about my sister Glenda's ample bosoms. I think melons came into it somehow. Glenda was my maid of honour, and she was seven months pregnant at the time. My brother-in-law didn't appreciate it. He stood up, leapt over the table and smacked the man right under the chin. It all got a bit messy after that.'

'Oh, no! You must have been mortified,' said Ingrid, wincing as she imagined the scene.

'No, it was fine. I was more worried about the cake but luckily it was saved by another bridesmaid flinging herself across the room and catching it just as it was toppling, and we soon got the worst of the drunks ejected. After that it was dancing all the way.'

'Mine was quite tame compared to that,' said Ingrid, thinking back. 'Tommy's lecherous Uncle Vince tried to get off with one of my workmates, which didn't go down very well, but otherwise it was a good day.'

'Some men can never get the hang of *no means no*, can they?' Anthea said. 'I always found that a knee in the groin is very effective, but not everyone's in a position to do that, unfortunately. Self-defence classes are great, but we shouldn't have to go down that road.'

Ingrid shuddered. The recent conversation with Lennie was all too fresh in her mind. She hoped that now Joel had taken such powerful action on her behalf she might be able to forget the long-ago party, but it wouldn't be easy because the incident had lurked in the back of her mind for years. Ingrid realised that for a long time she'd been partly blaming herself for being vulnerable, but at last she was beginning to accept that the fault lay completely with the boy who had forced her to the ground and who, if he hadn't been interrupted, wouldn't have stopped for anyone.

A New Lease of Life

'Right, that's enough of the serious stuff, let's get this show on the road, shall we? There's a sad bit to come, so help yourself to tissues,' Beryl warned Ingrid.

The warmth of the room was making Ingrid sleepy now. She yawned, not taking much notice of Beryl's words, but her eyes opened wide when the penny dropped. The wildly extrovert man on the dance floor was going to... surely he couldn't be going to...? Ingrid caught her breath as he crashed to the ground. Images of Tommy doing exactly the same thing made her gasp. Didn't the ladies realise that this had happened to her? She couldn't remember if she'd told them how Tommy had died. She glanced around at the others, who were all sniffing into paper handkerchiefs and paying her no attention. They couldn't have known. They'd be mortified to be causing her any distress.

'This part always gets to me.' Winnie's voice was hoarse, and she gulped prosecco, covering her mouth and giving a ladylike burp afterwards. 'But it's a beautiful service. I want mine to be just as good. Mind you, I could do a great job of reading that poem out at *your* funerals, girls. There wouldn't be a dry eye in the house.'

'The cheek of it. I'm younger than you by a few months, and you know it,' said Beryl, pursing her lips.

'Absolutely. How rude. Who's to say which of us might go first?' Anthea chipped in, but only Ingrid noticed her increasingly sombre expression as they watched the poignant scene together. It was hard not to break down and sob, as the friends of the departed Gareth mourned him onscreen. Another life-and-soul-of-the-party, he'd been portrayed as a man so like Tommy in the way he effortlessly held centre stage without antagonising people or seeming egotistic. Always the first on the dance floor, Tommy was never shy of letting rip his favourite Elvis medley at karaoke nights (indeed, he'd been in the middle of a spirited rendition of 'Hound Dog' when his heart had suddenly stopped beating).

Ingrid remembered her husband's joyful presence with a melancholy dip of her spirits that she knew would take a long time to fade. She'd never felt she matched up to him, somehow. Tommy had married her on a whim, wanting to take care of her. Ingrid realised later that Tommy had expected when she'd recovered from the first traumatic grief of her parents' deaths, she would begin to emerge as a much more sociable partner. She hadn't. Working in hospitality had used up all Ingrid's efforts to sparkle, and when she was off duty, the last thing she wanted to do was to go out and party.

'The good thing about this film is there's plenty of bonking to balance the emotional stuff,' said Beryl, refilling everyone except Anthea's glasses. 'I mean, who could resist Hugh Grant, eh? Not me, that's for sure. Who's your favourite screen man, Ingrid? Do you like a smoothie or a bit of rough? Come on, be honest. You're with friends here.'

Ingrid laughed, and the tension of the funeral scene mercifully eased slightly. 'David Tennant, especially in *Good Omens*,' she said. It occurred to her that Joel had much the same kind of appeal, lean and hungry looking with smouldering eyes. *For goodness' sake, girl, get a grip*, she told herself. *You're just grateful because he came to your rescue with Lennie.* But the lingering image of the way Joel had looked at her on more than one occasion wouldn't go away. It was as if he'd been holding back from scooping her up in his arms, or was that merely wishful thinking?

'Oh yes, he's a cracker, that David Tennant,' said Winnie, her mind still on Ingrid's ideal man. 'He looks mean and moody but you can tell he likes a laugh. You've got to have a giggle when you're having sex. Me and my Ron used to raise the roof in more ways than one. I knew the moment I clapped eyes on him that he'd be dynamite in the bedroom.'

Ingrid blushed. She half-hoped the other two Saga Louts weren't going to join in with steamy reminiscences about their husbands but on the other hand, all this talk of overwhelming passion was strangely fascinating. She was beginning to wonder why she'd never felt an immediate attraction like this before. Tommy had been lovely – huge, loud, warm-hearted and ebullient. She liked him from the start. His loving bear hugs were legendary, and she'd greatly admired his exuberant character, but he hadn't given her goosebumps. Previous relationships had been tepid to say the least, and Ingrid had come to believe that she wasn't the kind of person to be bowled over by any man, or woman for that matter. So why was even the slightest thought of Joel making her tingle with anticipation? It was ridiculous.

With the funeral scene safely left behind, Ingrid determinedly put all thoughts of Tommy, Joel and any other distractions firmly from her mind and concentrated on the rest of the action. As the credits finally rolled, all four women leaned back in their seats and sighed with satisfaction.

'She didn't even notice it was still raining because he was such a good kisser,' said Beryl. 'I'm not surprised. I'd get my rain mac out in a jiffy if I thought Hugh was out there waiting for a smooch, wouldn't you?'

Winnie nodded. 'We chose this one because it's thirty years since it was made and it's still as good to this day, in my humble opinion. What do you think, Ingrid? And what were you doing all those years ago? I was loving that my kids had finally left the nest. They were good years, the last ones with my Ron. Not enough of 'em for my liking, but worth their weight in gold.'

Ingrid reached out and passed Winnie the tissues. She didn't want to revisit that time, but Beryl was already on the case. 'We were lucky to have found the ones we were meant to be with. It was a good time for us all,' she said, but Anthea shook her head.

'You two, with your rosy spectacles, saying everything was great. It's sickening. Well, it wasn't like that for me. Those were the years when I was stuck with Nigel, and he was...'

She ran out of words, and Beryl added helpfully, '...a right tit?'

Ingrid held her breath. Would Anthea be mortified to hear one of her husbands described in that way? But to her relief, the other woman laughed.

'He was, wasn't he, darling? I don't know why I put up with him for so long.'

'Oh yes, you do,' said Winnie. 'I haven't forgotten what you told me about the size of his—'

'Winnie!' Beryl cut in. 'Isn't it time we had pudding? I bought a tiramisu specially and it won't keep. Ingrid? You'll have some, won't you? I think you need feeding up a bit, dear.'

Ingrid got to her feet to help with the second course. This had been a very interesting evening, but she was more than ready for her bed now. She wondered how soon she could escape without being rude. She'd never experienced a group of women like this. No topic seemed to be out of bounds, and they were totally comfortable in each other's company.

Even so, when Anthea refused the tiramisu and said she was heading home, neither of the other two appeared to notice their friend's pallor and the droop of her shoulders. Maybe extreme familiarity made some things invisible. Ingrid couldn't help feeling that she was going to need to step up to the mark quite substantially here if Beryl and Winnie didn't twig soon that Anthea was struggling. Having helped both her parents through many hospital appointments, if the worst came to the worst, she was probably the one who was best qualified for this job. Ingrid sighed. That sad fact didn't make the prospect of future trips to the infirmary any easier. Not in the slightest.

27

Joel soon found that knowing Leo was staying with Ingrid was a mixed blessing. On the one hand it was wonderful that someone else was taking charge for a while, someone who Leo liked and respected, but he couldn't help feeling as if he was dodging his responsibilities in a big way.

Also, he really missed having his daughter around, even if the addition of Baz on the scene hadn't been a bonus. They'd kept in touch by WhatsApp since the last time he'd helped in the shop, but Joel was determined to give Leo and Ingrid a few days' space to get used to each other. It was hard not to call round to see how they were getting on, but work was consuming him at the moment, so he decided not to bother them until the weekend. By that time there would be only one more week before the shop opened so he was sure they'd be happy for him to pitch in and help then.

Joel's stomach rumbled as he finished brushing the last coat of preservative over the bench he'd been working on all afternoon and sat back on his heels and viewed his handiwork. It was one of Joel's most satisfying creations, made of seasoned oak sleepers, solid and functional. The brief had been to produce something beautiful but simple, and it had been a labour of love too. Harold and Penelope Henderson were treasured members of the Willowbrook community, and the loss of their only son had left them shattered. Their three daughters had commissioned and paid for the memorial to Gareth. The elderly couple were rarely seen out and about these days. It had been a while since they'd ventured further than the edge of their land but commissioning the bench had given them a new interest.

The pungent scent of the wood stain took Joel right back to the days when he and Gareth had built a treehouse in the Hendersons' sprawling garden, which ran all the way down to the river. Gareth had been happy with a few splinters and mismatched planks they'd foraged but even at twelve years old Joel had been a perfectionist and had begged some old tins of preservative and partly used sandpaper from Harold so that he could give their den a professional finish. It had been a work of art, and the Hendersons had mentioned it to him when they'd chatted earlier, saying their seven grandchildren were now getting just as much joy from the treehouse as had the previous generations of the family.

Thinking about their son now was also a strong reminder of how Gareth had teased Joel about his need to make everything he touched work out perfectly. Unfortunately, this train of thoughts led on to memories of Gareth's comments when Joel had announced that he was planning to ask Trina Page to marry him.

'She'll drive you mad, mate,' Gareth said, pressing another pint on Joel as they leaned against the bar in The Fox and Fiddle. 'That girl's even more anal than you are. Remember when we were at school, doing our Duke of Edinburgh's award and we went camping in Norfolk? She wouldn't take the tent her mum had bought her because it didn't have all the flash bits yours had got. She made you swap, didn't she? And hers leaked. You're a pushover when it comes to Trina 'I want it all' Page, always have been.'

Joel had ignored the warning. He hadn't wanted Gareth to be right because he was in love for the very first time. Or in lust, more likely. Trina had a shining smile, a curvy figure, masses of long brown hair, a steady office job and an apparent willingness to have lots of children. Okay, so she'd been a bit obsessive in her need to clean the house rigorously from top to bottom twice a week and hoover every day, but he'd been happy to share the chores, although Trina's perfectionism was easily equal to Joel's and this threatened to make even the act of putting an almost-empty mug down on a coaster on the smoked glass coffee table a reason for her to leap to her feet and rush to get it into the dishwasher.

However, actually having babies rather than talking about it as a future dream hadn't been something Trina was keen on when it came to the crunch. She'd put the deed off for years. Eventually, Olivia had been conceived and Trina had said she was pleased. She'd decorated the nursery exactly how she wanted it and Joel had lovingly made shelves and a cot and a changing table. It was only when Olivia was born that everything began to fall apart. Joel had ached to make Trina feel better when the postnatal depression took hold and had done his best to help, but the cracks that had been appearing for years in their marriage grew wider and wider. Trina had refused to see a doctor for months, and by the time Joel had persuaded her, even the swift and helpful treatment hadn't been enough to bring back any closeness between the two of them.

A New Lease of Life

Joel sighed, put the final touches to the bench and put his brush to soak, thinking that if Gareth hadn't had that freak diving accident in Thailand, he'd have been quite justified in saying, 'I told you so.' It was clear that Joel should have listened to his friend, but if he had there would have been no Olivia, or Leo, or whatever she decided to call herself next, and that was unthinkable. If only Trina was an easier person to have as a co-parent. Joel had a horrible feeling that they were sailing into more stormy waters now Baz was on the scene. He sincerely hoped the boy wasn't going to be a thorn in his daughter's side when she was absorbed in helping Ingrid with her project to clear the shop of its treasures.

Thinking of the shop made Joel long to be back there. Maybe Ingrid or Leo would be planning something for dinner by now. They must both be shattered. Perhaps he was over-thinking the need to keep out of their way. Should he go round and offer to knock up something easy and quick for them all? The doors to his workshop at the side of the house were standing open, and while he was still pondering this, he heard voices in the street and footsteps approaching.

'Yoo hoo, are you there, dear? It's only us,' called Beryl. 'Can we come in?'

Without waiting for a reply, she and Winnie made their entrance. Winnie was carrying her usual wicker basket and Beryl came close behind holding a wine bottle.

'We thought you might not have had time to think about food this early in the evening, and we wanted to talk to you,' said Winnie. 'So, we brought supper. That's what Anthea calls it, but then she's way posher than us. In my day, supper was a couple of cream crackers and a bit of cheese just before bedtime, with a mug of Horlicks if you were lucky. Anyway, it's only leftovers from earlier and some cans of soup.'

'Where *is* Anthea?' asked Joel. 'I thought you were all together at the shop.'

'She said she was too tired to come. That's one of the things we wanted to speak to you about,' said Beryl, heading for the kitchen door. 'But there's more. Quite a lot more, as it happens. I hope you didn't have plans for this evening?'

While Beryl heated up the soup and Winnie poured everyone a large glass of red wine – 'You're going to need this,' she said ominously – Joel laid the table in the kitchen and set out bowls and plates.

'We can talk while we eat,' he said, realising that the loud rumbling of his stomach was going to make conversation tricky otherwise.

'No, we can't. Let's sit down for a minute. You need to hear what we've got to say first, dear,' said Beryl. 'So, these are the things we want to discuss with you. I'll list them all at once and then you can pick which order you want to take them in, okay?'

Joel nodded and Beryl sat up straighter.

'Number one: Anthea's ill but we're not supposed to know it, although Ingrid does, for some reason. Anthea dropped a letter from the hospital out of her handbag and didn't notice. I picked it up and... well... I couldn't help seeing... anyway, more of that later.'

'Get on with it, girl,' said Winnie.

'That's what I'm doing. Number two: right now, your daughter is round at Baz Barker's flat, and his flaky mother and sister are out, we saw them going into the pub.'

She raised a hand before Joel could butt in and gabbled, 'Number three: we think you and Ingrid are just right for each other and you should ask her out.'

Dumbfounded, Joel stared at Beryl. 'I... what?' he spluttered, unsure where to begin but homing in on the scariest point. 'Leo's at Baz's flat, and she's *alone with him*?'

'Ah, I thought that'd be the priority. We know she's fifteen and so she thinks she's a grown-up already, but Baz's lot are toxic, and he's bone idle to boot. We thought you might want to give her a call? Just to kind of let her know that you know where she is... or something?'

Winnie was faltering by the end of the sentence. Joel reached into his pocket for his phone and pressed Leo's number. His heart was pounding alarmingly. She answered on the fourth ring.

'Hi Dad, what's up?' she said, sounding out of breath.

'Hello, love. Where are you? Are you eating at Ingrid's?' Joel asked disingenuously. 'Because if not, there's lots of great snacks here courtesy of Beryl and Winnie.'

'I'm... I'm not hungry. I'll have something later at the flat, thanks.'

Joel wondered what to do next. Leo had neatly avoided his first question, and he was all too aware how easy it would be to antagonise her. He could hear loud music playing in the background and someone with a deep voice singing along tunelessly.

'Sounds like you're having a party,' he said, trying to keep it light. 'Is everyone invited?'

Leo laughed. 'As if,' she said. 'I'll be going back to Ingrid's soon anyway.'

'Not if I can help it, babe,' the voice in the background called.

Leo didn't seem to hear the interruption. 'Could you text Ingrid and say I'll be back for dinner? My phone's about to die. Tell her I won't be too long.'

Joel ended the call, slightly reassured that his daughter was intending to be leaving Baz's place reasonably soon, even if not yet, and was thinking about food. 'Okay, I can't do anything else about Leo for the moment, but thanks for the heads up, ladies,' he said. He quickly fired off a text to Ingrid and turned back to his visitors.

'Let's move on to Anthea. How come Ingrid knows all this about your best buddy when you don't, and what kind of ill are we talking?'

'Now that's something we can discuss while we eat, because we can't do anything about it at the moment,' said Winnie.

Relieved and very hungry, Joel helped the ladies to serve the food. They settled down together and for a few minutes, the only sounds were of crusty bread being crunched and spoons clattering against bowls. Then Beryl took a sip of her wine and cleared her throat.

'So, the Anthea situation,' she said.

'What's wrong with her?' Joel asked, registering the anxiety in his own voice that matched Beryl's.

Winnie frowned. 'That's what we'd like to find out. The same day that Beryl saw the letter—'

'I didn't read it,' said Beryl hastily.

'You would have done if you'd had time.'

'I wouldn't. Well, I might have done, for her own good. I was worried she'd see me though. But soon after that I happened to hear Anthea talking on her phone the other day. She didn't think we were listening, but she was talking about an appointment, and she sounded stressed. Then I overheard her saying something to Ingrid about another lift to hospital, as if she'd already taken her there once.'

'Why's she cutting us out?' said Beryl, her voice almost a wail. 'We usually tell each other everything. We know all about her husbands. She's had quite a few. Three, was it, Winnie?'

A New Lease of Life

'Four,' said Winnie. 'And each one left her better off. There are no flies on our Anthea. Love 'em and leave 'em, that's her motto. She mainly just chose them for the bedroom action, I reckon. Didn't we all, dear?'

Joel's face was burning now, and he couldn't meet Winnie's eyes. He topped up all the wine glasses for something to do and tried not to think about the disturbing images Winnie's words had conjured up.

'Oh, bless the boy, he's blushing, Winnie,' said Beryl. 'The trouble with the youngsters of today is they think they invented hanky panky. We've had some fun in our time too, dear. Sad when it's over but great memories.'

'I'm forty-eight,' croaked Joel. 'I'm not exactly what you'd call a youngster.'

'We're getting away from the subject,' said Winnie. 'We're seriously worried about Anthea. What if...?'

She broke off and Beryl continued. 'There's no use beating about the bush, we think she's got cancer and she's keeping it quiet. It's horrible. So, we need to find out what's going on. We want to support her. We love her.'

Both ladies were struggling to keep the tears at bay. Beryl was the first one to pull herself together. She blew her nose and wiped her eyes. 'What are we going to do, Joel? She doesn't know we know there's anything going on, but she shouldn't be keeping something that scary from her very best friends, should she?'

'I'm sure she'll tell you when she's ready, if there's anything to tell. Maybe she doesn't know what's happening herself yet. Ingrid will take care of her. If she's taken on the job of hospital appointments, she must be prepared to support Anthea too. You'll just have to trust her to take over for a little while. She seems like a very kind person.'

'And that brings us neatly to my final point. Listen, Joel. You need to get together and get jiggy with the lovely Ingrid before somebody else snaps her up. It's time you stopped moping over Trina. She's not coming back.'

'Jiggy? Whaaat? And anyway, I don't want Trina back. That's over. It has been for a long time.'

'Hmm,' said Beryl, with a sniff. 'Just think about it, that's all we're saying. It'd be a shame to miss the boat.'

Joel's mind was whirling. Was Ingrid really in danger of being 'snapped up' and why did that thought bother him so much? What on earth was wrong with poor Anthea? Most worrying of all right now, exactly when was Leo going to be safely back at the shop?

'Is that it?' he asked. 'You're not going to spring anything else on me, are you?'

Beryl smiled. 'No, that's all for now. We'll finish eating and then get out of your hair. We've given you a lot to think about,' said Beryl. 'And while you're pondering, keep this one word in mind.' She tapped the side of her nose and winked. 'Jiggy,' she said.

28

The next full-on work party took place on Saturday which meant not only the Saga Louts and Leo were available but the whole team were free, including Joel, Sam and Elsie. Ingrid had been making slow progress on her own apart from a couple of hours of Leo's help after school, but Baz's presence still loomed. He hovered around outside or drove up and down in his van until Leo, with an apologetic look, slid outside to see him for a little while.

Ingrid's new curfew, agreed with Leo, meant the new lodger was tucked up in bed by ten o'clock every night and she did what she could in the shop in between some desultory homework and Baz but Ingrid was beginning to think the shop would never be ready to open, let alone in a week's time. The courtyard outside was full of empty crates and flattened cardboard and the resulting chaos of dust and packing materials made her sneeze so much that she thought the hay fever season had claimed another victim. Her spirits lifted considerably when she heard the rattle of the door at nine o'clock on

Saturday morning and watched the procession of her new friends making their way inside.

'We couldn't persuade Anthea to get up any earlier than this,' said Beryl. 'But we're here now and ready for action.'

Anthea was already in the corner, fiddling around with the standard lamp she'd donated the week before. 'Are you sure you want this?' she asked. 'I saw your face when we brought it in and I thought, "Uh oh, Ingrid thinks it's a monstrosity," but it fits there quite nicely, doesn't it? Gives a kind of vintage ambience?'

'It's perfect,' said Ingrid, who loved the lamp but by this time would have agreed to anything Anthea suggested, because she was looking so drained. The strain of waiting must be telling on the older lady. 'Sit down and have a cup of tea first, everyone. Let's make a plan of campaign before we start. Leo's got the kettle on already.'

'Are there biscuits?' asked Elsie, hopping on one leg and nearly demolishing a stack of books Ingrid had unearthed. 'Only Dad said there would be treats today if we worked hard.'

'You've only just had your breakfast!' Sam said. 'And you haven't actually done any work yet. Pace yourself, my love.'

By half past eleven, the team were on their second break and fuelled up and ready for whatever the rest of the day might bring. A choice of strong coffee or ice-cold fruit juice from Winnie's two flasks had helped, and Elsie's pink Party Rings were nothing but crumbs.

'Okay, that's the basic cleaning and tidying done,' said Ingrid, who was feeling much more optimistic now she could see the floor again.

'We can start on the finishing touches now,' Winnie said. 'I'm going to get rid of the pink stuff covering the window but cover my display with a sheet. That way passers-by can peep in but they won't get the full effect yet. We want to make them curious, don't we?'

'Great idea,' Ingrid said, watching as Winnie stood on a stool to clean the front window while Beryl foraged in her second suitcase of surprises to bring out a folded rug for the floor in front of the sofa and two large patchwork cushions. She added a shallow blue ceramic bowl next to the till and filled it with individually wrapped chocolates that gleamed in their multi-coloured foil wrappers. 'There!' she said. 'The place looks more homely now. Over to you, Joel. Time to get the ladder out?'

Joel took one look at the sign that Leo had just completed and said it was much too wet to hang today, so he'd call back tomorrow to put it in its rightful place over the window, if that was okay with Ingrid. She couldn't help smiling at the thought that he'd be back again so soon. The sign was stunning, painted in vibrant shades of crimson, green and gold. It would perfectly match the vase that was now shrouded in a large blue bedsheet. The whole effect was going to be dynamic.

Ingrid was eyeing up the sofa and thinking about settling down for a cup of tea, presuming the next part of the day would be more peaceful, but as Winnie made more and more of the glass clear and shining again, Ingrid's heart skipped several beats, because outside was a figure with dark hair and a solemn expression. Lennie? But her vision cleared, and her breathing soon settled to normal when she realised that this was no threatening cousin but a slim, nervous-looking woman staring in.

As their eyes met, the woman mouthed, 'Could you open the door, please?'

Ingrid had never been one for strange feelings of doom and suchlike. She'd always thought people who said they had premonitions were either deluded or overimaginative, but the shiver that shook her when she looked at the person outside was not exactly one of impending disaster. More a gut feeling that life was about to change.

'What part of *closed* don't people get?' Sam muttered, as he went to open the door a crack. 'We're still shut at the moment,' he said. 'We plan to open next weekend though. Could you come back then?'

'I'm not here to buy anything,' the woman outside said. 'I want to see the person who runs it. Mrs Copperfield?'

Ingrid stepped forward. 'That's me,' she said. 'How can I help?'

Sam stood back and Ingrid positioned herself in the doorway. She really didn't want anyone else coming inside today. Her feet hurt, her eyes were gritty with dust from all the packing materials, and she was longing for a shower and some mindless TV with her dinner on a tray and maybe a glass of chilled Pinot.

'I want to talk to you about something very important,' said the stranger, who on closer inspection appeared to be not much more than Leo's age. She was a beautiful girl, but with a fragile air about her; dark haired, with huge brown eyes that looked up at Ingrid with an odd sort of appeal in them. Pleading and yet oddly antagonistic.

'Could you give me an idea of what it's about?' Ingrid said, rubbing her aching back. 'It's been a long day and we're all very tired. I'm about to go up to my flat for the night.' She yawned, and the girl took a step forward.

'It really is urgent, and it's private,' she said. 'You'll want to hear what I've got to say.'

Sam was at Ingrid's side now, eyebrows raised. He put a protective arm around her shoulders. 'Look, I don't know who you are,' he said, quite gently. 'But I think you need to state your business before we decide if you should come in when we're obviously closed.'

'I don't mind you saying anything at all in front of these people,' Ingrid said, waving a hand at the others who were watching with interest. 'They're my friends.' A warm feeling flowed through her as she said these words. It was true. She trusted them all implicitly and yet such a very short time ago they'd all been strangers.

'Go on, then,' Ingrid said, when her visitor still didn't respond. 'What do you want to talk to me about?'

'It's... not going to be easy for you to accept this,' the girl said. 'I was going to ring or email, but in the end, I decided to come and tell you in person instead. You see... Tommy Copperfield was my father.'

29

A deathly silence met the girl's announcement as she stood in the shop doorway, feet planted slightly apart, and arms folded. It took a moment or two for Ingrid to take in what the girl had said, but the tension in her shoulders was clear and she looked as if she was bracing herself, as if for a battle.

'You're... my late husband's daughter. I see,' said Ingrid. *What a ridiculous thing to say*, she told herself. She didn't see at all. Of course she didn't. 'Well, in that case, you'd better come in.' She opened the door wide. 'It looks as if you and I need to talk. We can go upstairs. Will you excuse us, folks?'

The others nodded, albeit reluctantly. 'I'll be at home if you need me,' said Sam. 'Come on, Elsie.'

'But... I want to...'

'No buts. Bath and bedtime are calling, See you soon, Ingrid.'

'We'll be off too but all of us are handy,' Beryl added. 'Just ring.'

Joel nodded. 'I'll stay. Leo and I will have a final sweep up.'

Ingrid looked round at the circle of faces, all showing

concern. It was comforting to know her new friends were supporting her, but this was all so unexpected that she could hardly think straight.

She motioned for the girl to follow her upstairs and invited her to sit down. There was a short, uncomfortable silence. Then the girl cleared her throat. 'This must have come as a shock. I should have introduced myself when we were downstairs. I'm Uma. As far as I know, I'm Tommy Copperfield's only child. He promised he would always look after me, even if it was difficult for us. Even if he'd... gone before he could sort everything...'

'Gone?' echoed Ingrid. 'Was he expecting to go somewhere? To... to die?'

'No, I don't suppose so. And I wasn't expecting it to be this soon because he was still young really. I only found out he'd passed away last month and I've been searching for you ever since then. I already had your address in York but the people who live in your house now wouldn't give me the full details of your new place, only that you'd gone south to this village. I think the woman let that slip by mistake, to be honest.'

Ingrid leaned on the kitchen worktop and clasped her hands together to stop them shaking. It wasn't possible. Tommy couldn't have had a child. They'd talked about their lives before they met, and told each other everything about their respective pasts, good and bad. Or so she'd thought. How old must this girl be? Was her story actually true? And if it was, did that mean he'd fathered her when Ingrid and Tommy were already together?

'So, I decided to come and find you. We really need to talk,' the girl said.

Ingrid swallowed hard. She'd never in her life fainted but she guessed the whirling in her head might be what it felt like just before you suddenly fell to the floor and your eyes rolled up in your head, like in medical dramas or sitcoms. She held on to the handle of the kettle, as if it could stop her from sinking further. The familiar object steadied her, and the whirling gradually receded, leaving behind a vague sensation of nausea. She must try to keep everything as normal as possible. This was no time to collapse, although oblivion was tempting.

'I don't know what to say.' Ingrid's voice seemed to echo around her own head. Automatic hospitality kicked in, giving her something to cling to, at least for a moment or two. 'Tea? Coffee? Something herbal?' she asked, clicking the kettle on.

'Peppermint tea if you've got it, but are you sure you want to treat me like a guest? I don't expect you're pleased to see me,' said the visitor. 'Why would you be?'

'Let's have a hot drink and you can tell me more,' Ingrid said, beginning to take control of herself. She could do this. It was probably all a big mistake. Tommy couldn't have a daughter that she'd never heard about, it was impossible. Perhaps it was time to try for a more everyday kind of conversation to make the situation seem less crazy.

'Have you come a long way today, Uma?' Ingrid asked, surprised to find her voice quite steady now.

The girl shook her head. 'Not that far. I'm from Huddersfield originally.'

Ingrid put a hand up to her mouth. 'But that's where Tommy and I met.'

'I know. I was happy there, but my family all live in Leicester now. I'm okay with that, it's a decent place, but Mum and Dad... well, they need to leave.'

To Ingrid's horror, tears began to roll down Uma's cheeks and once she'd started crying, she seemed unable to stop.

Ingrid wished with all her might that she'd invited Beryl or even all of the Saga Louts to come up with her. They'd know what to do in this weird situation. She passed over a box of tissues and once she'd made their tea, sat down beside Uma on the sofa.

'Take a deep breath,' she said. 'And then start at the beginning. Don't leave anything out. I'm listening.'

It took a while of sobbing and gulping but eventually, Uma blew her nose one last time and reached for her mug. She took a gulp of the now-cooling peppermint tea and leaned back against the cushions.

Ingrid had never thought of herself as the motherly type, but there was something about Uma that was making her feel protective, even in the midst of this horrible situation. At least the girl's hands had stopped shaking now, and she drank her tea thirstily before putting down the empty mug.

'You look exhausted,' Ingrid said, feeling her own tiredness threatening to swamp her. 'There's no rush. Just tell me about yourself when you're ready.'

'Right. Here goes,' Uma said, lacing her fingers together. 'It's not a very nice story. Tommy Copperfield had a fling with my mother before she met my dad. They split up fairly quickly and he didn't know she was pregnant at the time. When Mum found out, she was terrified of what her father and mother would say. We're a devout Muslim family and my grandparents were very strict. She thought they would all disown her. My grandmother has died since then and Gramps has mellowed to some extent, but back then... well, it was a major crisis.'

Uma paused and took a few deep breaths. She steadied herself and carried on.

'My dad – his name's Rashid... actually, I don't know why I'm telling you that, but anyway – he'd been in love with my mum long before she met Tommy. They were childhood sweethearts. He offered to marry her as soon as he found out what had happened, and I was passed off as a premature baby. Everyone turned a blind eye. It was easier for them all.'

The bitterness in Uma's voice was palpable now. Ingrid winced. 'It sounds very traumatic. And still Tommy didn't know?'

'No. My dad wanted to bring me up as his own and my mum was very angry with Tommy. She felt as if he'd used her. My mum's called Maryam. I'm... I'm seventeen... if you were wondering.'

Her words were simultaneously a relief and a shock to Ingrid. At least Tommy hadn't been unfaithful to her, but on the other hand, he'd ditched Uma's mother seemingly without a backward glance. Ingrid's long-time affection and admiration for Tommy's ebullient character had already taken a battering when the level of his debts had been revealed. Now it appeared that he'd also been heartless in his treatment of Maryam.

'I expect you're wondering how I found out Tommy was my father when everyone had been so determined to keep it a secret,' Uma said.

Ingrid hadn't got that far in her thought process but now it was mentioned, how *had* Uma got to the point of confronting her in Willowbrook?

Uma stood up and began to pace the floor. She glanced down at Ingrid. 'My mum was very poorly about two years ago. She was in hospital and Dad asked me to bring some stuff from home for her... more nighties and so on. I wasn't snooping... I couldn't find what I was looking for, so I tried a different place, and I found a bundle of letters tucked away at the very back of her wardrobe.'

There was a silence. Uma was now standing by the window,

A New Lease of Life

looking out over the green. 'They were letters Mum had written to Tommy but had never sent. Heartbreaking letters. One even had a little photograph of me inside it. I... I went to the address she'd put on the envelopes. It was right in the centre of Huddersfield, not far from our old home.'

Ingrid's mind flew back to one of the most intense times in her life. Tommy had been based in that town when they'd first met, before Ingrid had moved to York to work. He'd seemed smitten from the moment he'd seen Ingrid behind the reception desk at the hotel where he'd been staying. It was a whirlwind time. He'd taken her out for dinner on her first available night off and after that, they'd been inseparable. The pieces of the puzzle were coming together. Her stomach clenched.

Uma was still talking, her voice husky now. 'Tommy had gone away from that flat years before... when he married you, I guess... but the people there weren't as cagey as the ones in your last house. They'd had the place ever since Tommy had left and they didn't mind telling me where he'd moved to. I followed the trail. It was kind of like a game at that point. I almost didn't believe it was real. My dad... I mean Rashid... he's always been amazing. I didn't want anyone else to take his place. I was just curious.'

Ingrid stood up too. She went to stand by Uma's side. The distress now seemed to be coming off the girl in waves, but she wasn't crying any more. They stood together, not touching. The top of Uma's head didn't come much higher than Ingrid's shoulder. 'Go on,' said Ingrid. 'You can't stop now.'

30

Uma rubbed her eyes and took a deep, steadying breath. Her once carefully applied eyeliner had smeared, and her mascara was in sad trickles down her cheeks.

'Well... when I found Tommy, everything changed. At first, he didn't want to believe me when I said he was my father, but it was soon obvious that it was true when I gave him crucial dates and all the information about Mum. He seemed more worried about you finding out than anything, but we arranged to meet just outside town the next day to talk properly.'

'Let's sit down again,' said Ingrid. 'I'll make more tea. The bathroom's just through that door if you want to freshen up. This is going to take a while.'

Uma nodded gratefully and picked her bag up from the floor before heading for the bathroom. Ingrid went back to the kettle and refilled it. She heard the sound of water running, and all too soon Uma was back out with her. They sat down on the sofa together again, the soothing aroma of the peppermint tea mingling with Uma's scent, newly sprayed. It was musky and heady, strangely at odds with the innocent look of the girl.

A New Lease of Life

Outside, the cries of children playing on the green reminded Ingrid that normal life was still going on out there. It was only here in her flat that everything had changed. 'Carry on with what you were telling me,' she said to Uma.

'Okay. Well, I met Tommy to talk and by that time he'd accepted that I was his daughter but of course, he hadn't said anything to you, so it was all very secretive. He wanted to go and see Mum to talk to her about everything, but I explained how ill she was, and he agreed to keep away. We arranged to meet again, and he went back to work.'

'And what did you do next?' To Ingrid, this whole affair was starting to have the air of a soap opera. In her mind's eye she saw the two of them huddled in the corner of a tearoom or pub somewhere away from the city centre, with Tommy muttering under his breath and glancing round furtively.

'I went home eventually and when he got back from the hospital that night, I confronted my dad. I was furious with my parents for keeping me in the dark. He admitted everything but Mum was still very sick. She'd just started her second bout of chemo. He begged me not to talk to her about Tommy and... I didn't.'

'But you carried on meeting him in secret?'

'I couldn't seem to help myself. He fascinated me. He was so big and boisterous, with that huge ginger beard and the loud laugh. I'm a lot like my mum but I'd always wondered why I didn't look quite like the rest of our family. My two younger brothers have slightly darker skin than me, and so do all my cousins. Now I can see why. We met twice more, always somewhere out of the way of prying eyes. I felt like his dirty secret, but I wanted Tommy to... to love me, I suppose.'

Uma struggled to regain her composure and Ingrid squeezed her hand. 'There's no hurry. Just carry on when you're ready.' She was still imagining the scene. Tommy would have been intrigued by this unexpected daughter but dreading Ingrid finding out, which somehow underlined how little he really knew his wife. After the initial shock, Ingrid was sure she'd have welcomed Uma. It was horribly sad that the girl had been kept in the shadows and made to feel unacceptable in Tommy's life.

'I was due to meet him again the month after he died,' Uma said huskily. 'I was surprised when he didn't get in touch as usual to arrange a place for us to see each other but I just thought his work must have got in the way. Eventually I began to investigate, and when I finally found out what had happened and where you were, I ended up joining a Facebook community page for Willowbrook village. It was only this week that I found it. That was when I saw your name mentioned.'

'My name? I don't use Facebook.' Light dawned. 'Oh, I see. You saw the publicity for the shop?'

'Yes. I already knew your name from Mum's letters. She'd found out that you were the one Tommy had chosen. Your new shop was being promoted. I came to find you as soon as I could. I don't want to make trouble for you, I really don't.'

Uma turned to look Ingrid full in the face. Her tense expression said clearly that she was at the end of her tether. Ingrid didn't blame her. This was a hideous situation.

'Okay, so you don't want to make trouble. I get that... I think. But Uma, in that case, why *are* you here?' Ingrid said, as gently as she could manage.

Uma swallowed hard. 'Tommy promised me more than once that he was going to make a new will. I'm not greedy, honestly I'm not. It's just that I need it so badly now.'

'You were hoping for some sort of inheritance?' Ingrid asked, although of course she knew the answer.

'Yes. I don't want it for me though. My parents need some help to make a new start somewhere different. Mum says she's recovered from the breast cancer, but she still seems very low, and my dad's job has just folded. He's got a bit of redundancy money coming to him but it's not enough. I wanted to help them to get some sort of business going, somewhere less busy where Mum can enjoy the countryside, where we can all start again.'

Helplessness threatened to overwhelm Ingrid. How could Tommy have left this poor girl in such a mess, having ignored her all through her growing-up years? But of course, he hadn't known she existed until fairly recently, had he? Even so, to treat Maryam like that by leaving her high and dry was unforgiveable. She looked more closely at Uma, so close to her on the sofa. The girl was poised and very pretty, even in her state of anxiety.

Also, there was something very familiar about her. She had Tommy's direct gaze, and a dimple in each cheek that reminded Ingrid strongly of her husband. There was very little doubt in her mind that all this was true, but ought she to suggest some sort of DNA test? She'd watched all the TV programmes about finding lost families and that often seemed to happen. She opened her mouth to suggest it, but the girl was wringing her hands together as if she was in a Victorian melodrama, and the strange thing was that her hands reminded Ingrid strongly of Tommy too. Her fingers were long and shapely, but her nails didn't seem to match her general elegance. They were unusually square and wide, just like his had been. She really must be Tommy's daughter.

'I hate to tell you this, Uma,' she said, 'but I didn't find out until after Tommy had died that he'd been running up serious debts for years.'

'Oh, no! You can't mean it.'

'I'm sorry. It was a shock to me too. I knew Tommy could be reckless, but I didn't realise he'd been making bad investments and spending way above his income. He kept it all to himself.'

'Then... there's no money? I don't believe you. You had that big house. Tommy was living it large.'

'Really, I'm telling you the truth. There is hardly any money left. I'm selling off his possessions in the shop and I'm going to make a new start myself. A caravan... or a houseboat... or something. It's all I'll be able to afford. And it's all I want anyway.'

The girl's eyes filled with tears again and her shoulders drooped. 'But... I need it so badly. What about Mum and Dad? They can't carry on like this.'

'I hear what you're saying, but as I say, after I'd paid everyone off, the sale of the house only left me with just enough to buy something very small and cheap to live in.'

In the long pause that followed, Ingrid began to feel something very like relief. She'd come through this unexpected trauma without losing the plot and she was still functioning. There was no large sum of money for Uma to argue about. The sooner she realised it, the easier this would be.

Just when Ingrid was starting to think she'd been wasting her time trying to explain her circumstances, Uma cleared her throat. 'I'm sorry I didn't believe you about the money and I'm sad you're in a mess too, but you can see why I thought you were loaded?'

They viewed each other with what felt to Ingrid like a new understanding. 'Absolutely,' she said. 'But Uma, I'm *so* not.'

'I didn't think it would be this easy to find you and persuade you to talk to me. It feels like we've got a lot more to say yet. Can I come back when the shop's open? I'd love my mum to see it, it's just her kind of thing.'

Ingrid groaned inwardly. This idea sounded way too intense when all she wanted was to get on with her new life, but the girl's eyes were pleading.

'I suppose you can if you really want to, but are you saying your mum knows you've come to find me?'

Uma looked at the floor. 'Erm... well... not yet, but I'm going to tell her as soon as I get back to Leicester. I hate secrets. It's got to be good to get bad stuff out in the open, isn't it?'

Ingrid didn't reply. In her opinion, some secrets were best left that way.

31

The following week went by in a blur of frantic, last-minute activity after the unsettling visit from Uma. She had taken Ingrid's contact details and promised to be in touch, but as time ticked on with no message, Ingrid began to tentatively hope that the situation wouldn't develop any further. Perhaps Uma's mother had been incensed at the idea of getting in touch and put her foot down to prevent further contact. The shop opening filled Ingrid's mind, and Leo was just as preoccupied. Her social media campaign seemed to be going well and Baz hadn't been seen around so much, although there was much messaging on Leo's part and heavy sighs when Baz often didn't respond for hours.

On Tuesday, Ingrid and Anthea were summoned to the hospital again and Anthea underwent several tests, but even though Ingrid tried her best to persuade her, Anthea still refused to talk to the other Saga Louts about her problem.

'They'll just make it all about them,' she said with unusual bitterness. 'It'll be all, "Oh, Anthea, what would we do without you if you pop your clogs?" and so on.'

A New Lease of Life

Ingrid doubted this. The love between the three ladies was much more selfless than that in her opinion, but there was no budging Anthea, so she held her peace, although she was certain Winnie and Beryl knew something was wrong. Their suspicious glances at Ingrid and Anthea when the three of them had a working morning in the shop on Wednesday gave them away. It made Ingrid's heart ache to think there was a rift between them, but all she could do was follow Anthea's lead and put up with the agonising wait for the test results, trusting that, either way, the other two would need to be told what had been going on at that point. Ingrid fervently hoped that all this secrecy wouldn't harm the Saga Louts' close friendship. It was too precious for that.

Thursday morning started badly. Firstly, Leo used all the hot water and then dashed off to school early, saying she was going to call in and see Baz on her way because 'He's gone silent on me again.' Ingrid, who was inwardly seething as they said a hasty goodbye, had to make do with a quick wash and then found that her lodger had also taken the last of the milk to make herself a large hot chocolate. The not-quite-empty mug had been knocked over in Leo's rush to leave, and now a sticky brown trickle was working its way along the living room floor.

Muttering all the expletives she could muster, Ingrid cleaned up the mess and made herself a black coffee. At least there was some bread left for toast, although the butter had been left out of the fridge overnight after Leo had created a late-night gourmet snack of a cheese toasty with Marmite. Ingrid wiped up the greasy smears left behind and wondered if Joel's delight in his daughter moving in with her had less to do with his ex-wife's temperament and more of a relief from chaos.

Down in the shop, however, Ingrid's mood lifted. The

shelves had now been filled with all sorts of objects, and she began to walk around the place, picking up the occasional cup or vase or paperweight and holding them up to the light. A delicate gold-patterned urn with slender handles was particularly pleasing with its swirling pattern of leaves, and an ornate fire screen propped against a wall was appealing too, covered in exquisite Japanese ladies with jet-black hair and vibrantly coloured kimonos.

Ingrid couldn't wait to see what the first wave of customers would snap up. The bargain basement table still needed Beryl and Winnie's attention when they unpacked more boxes, but she couldn't be sure if they'd have time to do that today, although they had both texted to say they'd be at this morning's final team meeting before the big day. It had been planned for ten o'clock, and it seemed that everybody bar one could make it.

Leo was furious to be missing the action because of school, but Ingrid had promised to take copious notes and fill her in later. Elsie's school had a teacher-training day and Sam and Joel had both made sure they were free. Ingrid hoped she wasn't putting too much pressure on them all. This teamwork business was a delicate balance of making her new friends feel appreciated but not taking them for granted when they all had other lives to lead.

At half past eight, Ingrid made the sudden decision to walk round to the other village shop to replenish the milk supplies. She was too restless to start any more sorting before the meeting and anyway, a fresh stock of pink biscuits would be needed if Elsie was going to join them. She was sure Beryl and Winnie would bring supplies for lunch again but there was no harm in adding to the feast, and the shop often had an early delivery of crisp, golden baguettes and pastries.

A New Lease of Life

Slipping on a coat, because the April morning was still cool, Ingrid set off briskly on the route that would take her past Beryl's nearby cottage and then along the road towards Joel's house. She already felt very much at home in the village, which hadn't been part of the plan and made her a little edgy but was in some ways welcome after all the years with hardly any neighbourly contact. Willowbrook was looking at its best in the weak morning sunshine. Hanging baskets were beginning to blossom outside many of the houses and many of the streets were tree-lined and tidy, with only the odd overgrown front garden showing that not all the villagers were willing or able to live up to the high standards set by their neighbours.

Ingrid passed the church, admiring the solid edifice with its squat, square tower. She'd been intending to go to a Sunday service as soon as she was organised. It seemed like the next step to being partly integrated into the community. As the days went by, Ingrid was feeling more and more certain that even if the concentrated sociability of village life wasn't for her, somewhere near Willowbrook with the opportunity of joining in events when she wanted to would be an ideal compromise.

She carried on past rows of semi-detached 1930s-style houses and through a small park until she came to Joel's street. Ingrid couldn't decide if she was hoping to see him or not, because if Joel *was* around, he might think she'd started stalking him, but there was no sign of anyone. She was just telling herself that it was a good job he was otherwise engaged today when Joel popped his head out of an upstairs window and called her name.

'I was just getting ready to come to the meeting but I'm too early,' he said. 'Wait there, I'm coming down.'

Joel soon appeared wearing a battered donkey jacket and faded jeans. 'How are you doing?' he asked.

'Fine, thanks,' said Ingrid, who was trying not to let Joel see how pleased she was to see him. 'I'm off to get milk for the troops.'

'Don't tell me, the cuckoo in the nest drank it all. Did she by any chance have a very long shower too?'

Ingrid bit her lip. She hadn't meant to drop Leo in it, but the girl's dad clearly knew all her ways. 'It's okay,' she said. 'I needed some fresh air. It's good to have a break before we start again.'

'There's still quite a lot to do, but you've got all of us to help now. Hey, why don't you have five minutes here first? There's plenty of time.'

'Yes, there is, thanks to my team. I know you've got plenty of work waiting but I really appreciate you making time this morning to come and help with the run-down to opening day.'

Joel shrugged. 'It's fine. Anyone would do the same.'

'Oh, come off it, don't try and play your generous nature down. You're one of the good guys.'

'Is that how you see me? Generous? A good guy?' Joel asked, sounding genuinely surprised.

'Of course I do. Look how you've helped me out so far and we only met last week. Your daughter obviously adores you and even the Saga Louts are smitten.'

'And what about you?'

Ingrid could see that Joel hadn't meant this last outburst. He'd turned away from her and was pretending to watch a robin hopping around on a nearby hawthorn branch. 'What about me?' she echoed.

'Well, yes. You've given me a glowing report from Leo and the ladies but what's your honest opinion apart from the *generous and good guy* bit? I wouldn't normally ask anyone a question like that; I'm not fishing for compliments. I'd just really like to know, because my ex-wife messaged me this morning to say that in her view, I'm an absolute waste of time as a father, just as I was a husband.'

'Ouch. What did you do to promote that tongue lashing?'

'Do? Nothing, as far as I know. She's often angry. I think she's mainly sore this time because Trevor the Tosser forgot her birthday again.'

'And that's your fault?' Ingrid felt as if she was opening a huge can of worms here, but the distress on Joel's face tore at her heart. On impulse, she reached out and took hold of his hand. His fingers entwined with hers as if he'd been waiting for her to make the first move. Ingrid held her breath. This wasn't what she'd meant to do at all, but now Joel's warm palm was against hers, and her heart was racing.

Joel looked at her and smiled. 'I haven't sat and held hands with anyone for years,' he said. 'This is like being a teenager again. Do you do this often? Comfort the distressed, I mean? You're very good at it.'

Ingrid swallowed hard. Here she was, dry-mouthed and almost hyperventilating with sudden lust and Joel thought she was merely trying to make him feel better. Now it was going to be hard to pull away without him noticing her embarrassment. Before she could say anything, Joel let go of her hand.

'Thanks for being so understanding, but I think we'd better get a move on if we're not going to be late for your meeting. You've still got to get milk, haven't you?'

Ingrid stood up, watching him go back up the drive and wishing she had the power to teleport back to the safety of the shop. Or better still, to rewind time so that she hadn't had this unsettling moment.

She'd totally mismanaged that situation. Or had she? Did she really want Joel to think of her as anything but a friend?

But the memory of the warmth of his hand was still making Ingrid jittery. If just touching him like that had this effect, what would it be like to kiss him, to hold him close, to be held tightly in return?

Taking several deep, calming breaths, Ingrid gave herself a stern talking to. *You're recently widowed, you're probably starved of any sort of bodily contact and you're not in a position to think lewd thoughts about a man who looks unnervingly sexy and also much in need of a cuddle. Pull yourself together, girl*, she said firmly to the ridiculously shaky inner Ingrid, who didn't seem to be listening very hard.

'See you soon,' called Joel from the door of his workshop. 'I won't be late.'

Ingrid raised a hand in reply and headed for the shop. It took several minutes for her heart to stop pounding. Very shortly she'd need to face Joel at the meeting and act as if nothing had happened. And it hadn't really... had it? A few minutes sitting on a wall. A bit of friendly hand-holding. A chat with a man who clearly had a lot of baggage. *Nothing to see here*, she told herself. *Get on with the job in hand and stop acting like a lovesick schoolgirl.*

32

The shop meeting didn't take long, because everyone was keen to get on with the final preparations. Ingrid was half expecting them to start questioning her about Uma's bombshell, but since that day, they all seemed to have adopted a tactful silence and were studiously avoiding the subject. If Uma didn't make contact again, there would be no need to ever refer to the surprise visit. Ingrid was starting to believe that this might be the case.

After a brief discussion, it was agreed that on Saturday morning, the whole team would be ready for the opening time of 10 a.m.

'There's no point in making it any earlier,' said Winnie firmly. 'Nobody round here gets up at the crack of dawn at weekends.'

'I do, don't I, Dad?' said Elsie. 'I'm s'posed to wait until seven o'clock before I wake him up,' she told the others. 'But it's not very easy. I get hungry.'

'I used to make my boys a sandwich and drink on a tray and pop it just inside their bedroom for when they woke up,' said

Winnie helpfully. 'On a Saturday the rule was that they had to stay put until they heard me making a cup of tea. And it was never before nine o'clock. Usually much later if we were lucky.' She winked at Beryl who nodded in agreement.

'You have to have rules,' she told Sam, who was beginning to look defensive. 'Children like rules really.'

'I don't. Rules are for suckers. Leo told me that,' Elsie said to Joel. 'And she knows a lot of good stuff.'

'Hmm. Or thinks she does,' Joel muttered. Ingrid remembered that Leo had promised to come straight back from school today. She hoped Joel wouldn't bring up the subject of rules. She and Leo had had quite a few discussions about guidelines for cohabiting and also regarding her relationship with Baz. It was a delicate balance between being Leo's friend and her landlady/temporary guardian. There was no need to rock the boat at this point, but she couldn't tell him that.

The rest of the day passed relatively peacefully, although the tension was mounting between Anthea and her two friends. They edged around each other with none of their usual banter, and once Ingrid spotted Winnie and Beryl whispering in a corner while Anthea was in the loo. Eventually, she decided enough was enough. Everyone looked jaded and Elsie made it clear that she was bored with all the small jobs that Sam had found to occupy her. As the clock that Beryl had hung on the wall in the shop struck half past three, Ingrid shooed them away with grateful thanks.

'See you Saturday,' they chorused as they left, and Ingrid went up to the flat to fetch the new card reader Leo had said was essential. When she came back downstairs, she found Joel still there, looking shifty.

'I thought you'd gone home,' Ingrid said. 'You've done more than enough today.'

Joel didn't seem to want to meet her eyes, and his cheeks looked flushed. Even so, the sight of him caused alarming flutters in Ingrid's chest, and she decided she'd need to give herself another firm talking to as soon as he'd gone.

'Is everything okay?' Ingrid asked. 'Did you want to talk to me about something?'

'I'm going to level the shop sign, because I've realised it's tilted slightly to the left, but yes, I did want to talk to you. I've had a bit of a weird interlude with Winnie and Beryl and it's been on my mind,' Joel said. 'They're worried about Anthea being ill and not telling them. They think you know something about it, and they're hurt that she hasn't told them too. Very hurt, in fact.'

Now Ingrid was avoiding looking at Joel instead of the other way round. He waited. Ingrid felt herself squirming. It was just as she'd thought. Now what? But if the other two already knew there was a problem, it couldn't hurt to tell Joel about it. Secrets were corrosive within friendships, she'd always thought, and she could always square it with Anthea later. While Joel organised his tools for the sign hanging job, Ingrid filled him in on the basics of the hospital visit.

'So Anthea's got some sort of problem and she's had tests,' Ingrid finished. 'I guess that's when the results come back, she's going to tell the others. She's very much keeping things on a need-to-know basis.'

By common consent, they moved outside the shop. Joel fetched the stepladder from the storeroom and got busy making sure the fixings for the sign were level and secure. He didn't answer for a moment, but then looked down at Ingrid from his lofty perch and said, 'Also they told me Leo had been at Baz's flat. Alone with him.'

'I know. She told me. But she always comes back here for

dinner, so that's okay, isn't it? Do you want to eat with us later tonight?'

'No, but thanks for the offer. Beryl's picnics are epic. I ate too much, and I really have got to go and get on with some work.'

Ingrid smiled. It was comforting to think that she'd landed in this place where wonderful if slightly wacky ladies appeared regularly with food parcels.

'Was there anything else? You still look worried,' Ingrid asked.

The uncomfortable look was back again, and Joel acted as if he hadn't heard the question. How odd. Ingrid was about to probe further when there was a roaring and clunking and Baz's battered old van pulled up alongside the shop. Joel muttered under his breath, knocked the final nail into the surround for the sign and came down the steps, wiping his hands on his jeans.

'Baz,' he said, nodding an acknowledgement to the younger man as he shuffled around from the driver's side. Leo was also getting out, but she was holding a wriggling bundle tightly in her arms.

'What the...?' Joel stared as she put a very small dog down on the pavement and made sure its lead was secure.

'Hi Dad,' she said. 'We went to your house but when you weren't in I guessed you'd still be here.' She pointed at the little animal, which was relieving itself up against a nearby lamppost. 'This is Gerald, and what he really needs is a new home. Long story. I said you'd take him in for now. You've always wanted a dog, haven't you? He's house trained, and everything...' Her voice tailed away as she registered Joel's expression of horror.

Before he could reply, a voice from just inside the shop said,

A New Lease of Life

'Oh my life, it's a dachshund! How sweet is he? I used to have one, but he died years ago. I still miss him.'

'Beryl? Where have you been hiding? I thought you'd left with the others,' said Ingrid, thinking back frantically. Had Beryl overheard her telling Joel about Anthea's troubles? And why had she been lurking around anyway?

'I nipped back into the storeroom to look for a few more things for the bargain table and then I got distracted. Sorry if I made you jump.'

Beryl came out into the street, her eyes on the dog. Gerald looked up at her, his own eyes dark and mournful. 'He's absolutely gorgeous. Is he yours?' Beryl asked Leo.

'Not yet,' Leo said, smiling at her dad.

Ingrid met Joel's gaze properly at last and they both raised their eyes heavenwards. This might cause an extra hiccup in Joel's life but the whys and wherefores of Gerald's arrival or final destination weren't her problem. Now all she needed to worry about was how to tell Anthea that her hospital visit was no longer a closely guarded secret, and to find out if Beryl had overheard her conversation with Joel. A headache was forming behind Ingrid's eyes. This wasn't the simple life she'd expected when she decided to come to a peaceful country village.

'Let's go inside and have a nice cup of tea, Leo,' Ingrid said, channelling her beloved late mother's favourite words. 'We can talk about Gerald, and you can tell me about your day at school. Did the IT teacher approve of your new poster design for the shop?'

'School's a waste of time. I dunno why you bother,' said Baz, speaking for the first time since his arrival. All eyes except Gerald's swivelled to look at him, but he didn't seem fazed.

Leo shrugged. 'You're probably right, babe, but I've got double art tomorrow so there's no way I'm bunking off.'

'There's no way you're bunking off any day,' growled Joel.

Ingrid cringed inwardly. If she'd been nearer, she'd have kicked him to tell him not to comment. Baz was clearly after a reaction. Confrontation was only going to make things more volatile, in her opinion, but now Beryl was stepping in.

'Education is really important,' she told Baz earnestly. 'I think you youngsters all need to get as much of it as you can. I just wish I'd had longer at school. I thought it was a waste of time too, but I was wrong. What is it you do?'

'I'm an artist,' Baz said. 'But I'm not interested in the formal education crap and no way I'm wasting years at uni. The school of—'

'*The school of life*? I expect you're going to quote the tired old phrase that came from some loser or other,' said Beryl, smiling sweetly at Baz. 'I've heard that one before. And it's a load of old bollocks, if you'll pardon my French. Learning is the key to a happy life.'

'Really? And who are you to say that?' Baz asked, sticking his bottom lip out like a sulky toddler.

'I'm the daughter of a man who worked hard all his life but probably never reached his full potential and a woman who would have loved to have gone to university but didn't get the chance,' said Beryl, staring him down. 'Now, are you going to take this beautiful boy inside and give him some dinner? And I don't mean you,' she said to Baz as she scooped Gerald up and passed him to Leo.

Leo gave Baz an inscrutable look but went into the shop. After a moment, Baz opened the passenger door and pulled out a large bag. 'Stuff for the dog,' he muttered. 'Food, dog bed, toys and all that crap.' He turned on his heel and got back in his van, chugging away in a cloud of fumes. Ingrid, Beryl and Joel were left standing on the pavement watching him go.

'Right. Well, that was an interesting, if confusing few minutes,' said Ingrid. 'It looks as if I've got an extra dinner guest but I'm assuming you'll keep the dog, Joel?'

Joel looked at Ingrid and Beryl who were both standing with their arms folded and identical forbidding expressions. 'Do I have a choice? My daughter might never speak to me again if I make Gerald homeless,' he said.

'Get away with you, you love dogs. I've seen you making a fuss of that Jack Russell that lives next door to your house. It'll be company for you now Leo's not there,' said Beryl. 'You can come back and fetch Gerald and his collection of belongings later, can't you? I hope there's something useful in there.' She gave the bag that Baz had jettisoned a shove with her foot. 'Anyway folks, I'm off. And if you two were wondering, yes, I did hear what you were saying about Anthea.'

With that, Beryl turned on her heel and stomped off down Fiddler's Row.

Ingrid and Joel watched her go and then turned to face each other. 'Oh, bugger,' said Ingrid.

'My thoughts exactly. So, I'll come back shortly for the new member of my family and his luggage, shall I? I need to get the van if I'm taking Gerald and his belongings and all my tools. Look, try not to fret about what Beryl overheard. You didn't know she was there, and she already knew most of it. She'll be on the phone to Winnie before I'm even back home so they can have a team talk. It's probably a good thing to get all this out in the open.'

'You might be right. I hope so.'

Ingrid could feel her shoulders drooping. Joel leaned forward and pulled her into a hug. 'You worry too much about everyone,' he murmured into her hair.

Just as suddenly, the hug ended, and he too was striding

away. As she watched him go, Ingrid wrapped her arms around herself, unconsciously trying to recreate the warm, safe, enticing feeling of Joel holding her close. After a moment, she turned back towards the shop. Time to meet yet another new challenge. First a teenager in her space and now a dog. Whatever next?

33

Gerald soon found he didn't like Ingrid's flat and made his feelings very clear. Above the little dog's piteous howls, Ingrid tried to make sense of the situation.

'Why is he here with you anyway?' she said, struggling to make herself heard above the din.

'Why are any of us here?' said Leo, picking Gerald up. 'Dogs have as much right to a place on this planet as we do, you know.'

Ingrid shot her an exasperated look but tried hard to keep her temper. The dog was quiet now, nestled in Leo's arms. If he'd been a cat, he would have purred. 'Yes, I do understand that we must love all living creatures,' she said through gritted teeth. 'But why is this particular one here with us? Can you please explain?'

Leo smiled nervously. 'Well, he was given to Baz's mum as a surprise present.' She paused as if trying to find the right words to go on. Ingrid frowned.

'A box of chocolates always goes down well for a gift, in my book, or a bunch of flowers. Why would anyone give a person a dog for a surprise?'

'Gerald is Baz's grandpa's dog, and he's moved to Spain to run a beach bar. There was nobody else to have Gerald, but he hates the stairs at Baz's flat and he won't go in the lift. I think it's because it smells of wee, although dogs usually like that kind of thing, don't they? Baz's grandpa lived in a bungalow with a garden and the dog had a flap in the kitchen door so that he could come and go whenever he liked. He was howling because he doesn't like your stairs, I guess.'

Gerald gave a small whimper as if to agree that his previous home had been far superior to that in which he now found himself.

'But there's still a cat flap from when we had Tiger, and Gerald can have the run of the garden if he comes to stay at Dad's place,' said Leo. 'I'll carry on trying to find somewhere permanent, honest I will.'

'It's really good of your dad to agree to step in,' said Ingrid. 'But why isn't Baz sorting out the problem? It's surely not up to you to fix it.'

'They don't like dogs, none of that family do. His mum and his sister say they're allergic, but I don't believe them. Baz said he was going to take poor Gerald to the RSPCA. We can't let him do that. You know we can't.'

The little dog whimpered again. He really was very sweet, Ingrid thought. His eyes resembled liquid velvet and he looked as if he was smiling. His left ear pointed up quirkily and the other down, giving him a rakish air. Leo stroked his smooth, dark brown coat. Someone had obviously taken good care of Gerald up to now. He was sleek and glossy, and he gazed at her with such a piteous look that Ingrid suddenly knew without a doubt that she'd have agreed to take him in if Joel hadn't seemed amenable.

'I'd have him myself if I wasn't in a first-floor flat but maybe I can help your dad walk him?' she said.

Privately, Ingrid didn't think that Gerald's short legs would be up to much of a walk but the idea of strolls with Joel was a definite bonus. The warmth of his hug was still lingering, and she was beginning to think that all this denial of her growing feelings for him was pointless.

'Is that Dad back already?' Leo had heard the roar of the van but seemed unwilling to disturb Gerald even to look out of the window.

Ingrid went to open it and called down, 'We didn't think you'd be here yet.'

'I decided to fetch the bag of dog kit and my tools then come back on foot for Gerald,' Joel called back. 'That way he can have a walk back with me. See you very soon.'

Ingrid closed the window and turned to Leo. 'Your dad doesn't seem at all fazed about fostering a dog now. He was smiling,' she said.

'I knew he'd come round quickly. He's never stroppy for long. That's one of his good points. Mum's a different matter, she's an Olympic-style sulker. She texted me to say Trevor forgot her birthday. He'll be sorry,' said Leo, with a grin.

Feeling sorry for Joel that he still had to deal with his ex-wife's moods wasn't something Ingrid wanted to get into. That was his business. More important was to make sure the new arrival wouldn't start howling again. She wondered aloud if they should feed Gerald. With no experience of a small dog's eating habits, she was unsure what to do next.

'Baz says Gerald usually has a little meal morning and night and Dad's taken all the food and dishes, so we'll just need to wait. Do you want to hold him while I start the dinner?' asked Leo, without much enthusiasm.

'No, it's fine, I'll sort the food. The jacket potatoes have been in the oven for ages. You're doing a great job there. Comforting hugs must be a family talent,' Ingrid said.

As soon as the words left her mouth, she regretted them, but Leo was far too busy cuddling Gerald to notice. Ingrid went over to the sink and began to scrub potatoes. She would need to think before she spoke in future. This situation was feeling more and more like a minefield by the minute.

34

Having dropped the van off, Joel jogged round to the shop as fast as he could, reluctant to park Gerald on Ingrid for any longer than necessary. Not only that, he was still buzzing from the way she'd felt in his arms but wanted to make sure he hadn't offended her with the sudden hug. He was painfully aware of the boundaries he'd imposed on himself. Someone so recently bereaved, and with the Lennie experience in her past into the bargain, surely wouldn't appreciate being grabbed like that. Although she hadn't resisted. In fact, she'd melted against him as if she needed to be held as much as he needed to hold her.

'Are you ready to hand Gerald over?' Joel said to Leo as he entered the flat. 'I'd better get off home and settle my new tenant in as soon as possible. Do you fancy coming along in case he won't walk on the lead for me? It looks as if you're his chosen person.'

Leo looked from Ingrid to her dad and back. 'I was going to have a jacket potato,' she said sadly. 'But I do want to come with you and see Gerald organised.'

'Don't worry, I'll make you a food parcel, Beryl style,' said Ingrid. 'You can come back later when he's safely tucked up in his bed.'

'Thanks so much, Ingrid,' said Leo. 'I won't be too long, I promise.'

'Okay. Your beloved isn't going to turn up again though, is he?' Ingrid asked.

'Nah. He'll be at one of his mates' houses by now. He's harmless anyway. He *is*,' she stressed, when she noticed Joel's dubious look.

Joel and Leo watched as Ingrid bustled around the kitchen, grating a mountain of cheese and packing up Leo's potato along with a container of beans. It gave Joel a comforting feeling to have someone other than himself fussing over his daughter. Trina had never been one for that kind of approach to mothering. Her view was that everyone, however small, should stand on their own two feet. He reflected sourly that Trina herself was probably being more cosseted now with Trevor than Leo had ever been, apart from the lack of birthday cards, but there was no point in dwelling on his ex-wife's character when here in front of him was a confident woman who could stand on her own two feet and fight her own battles but also instinctively knew how to make life cosier for those around her.

With a horrified lurch of the heart, Joel realised that in the short time he'd known her, Ingrid had already got seriously under his skin. He'd liked her right from the first time they met, but this stronger attraction didn't sit well with him. It wasn't right at all. He must try his very best not to let her see what he was thinking. Ingrid was still grieving for her husband. If she ever sensed that Joel was seriously interested in getting to know her better, she'd be bound to run for the hills.

A New Lease of Life

Ingrid smiled at Leo and Joel as she gave the girl the food box wrapped in a tea towel. Joel didn't think there was any difference at all in the friendly way she looked at him and his daughter. It simply wasn't possible that she could be experiencing the rush of sheer passion that was making Joel want to wrap her in his arms again. He cleared his throat.

'Goodnight,' he said briskly. 'Shall I see you soon, Ingrid?'

'Well, it's only two days till the grand opening of The Treasure Trove so yes, you definitely will.'

'Great. If you decide you need any help tomorrow, I could swing by when I finish work?'

Swing by? What prat said that these days, or ever? Leo was looking at Joel oddly and he cringed, but Ingrid didn't seem fazed.

'No, it's fine. Tomorrow is just for last-minute tweaks. I hope you get on well with your new friend. Good luck.'

Leo passed Gerald over to Joel and the little dog licked his nose. Joel grinned. 'I think we're going to get along just fine,' he said.

As he walked home with Leo, Joel could feel the tension coming from her. They'd always had a close bond and now, although he could tell she was immensely pleased with him for giving Gerald a place to stay, Joel assumed... and hoped... that Leo wasn't at all happy about the way Baz had acted when it came to getting the dog out of his way. He'd been brusque and thoughtless. Perhaps she was seeing Baz in a new light today, which was no bad thing, but he hated to think she was going to be more and more distressed as she realised what her boyfriend was really like.

Gerald trotted along on his lead, head in the air, and Joel reflected that while he would probably cope quite well with a dog in the house, dealing with this giddy attraction for Ingrid wasn't going to be so easy. When he saw her on Saturday, he'd need to make sure he was sociable and helpful, but no more. It would be easy to frighten her off when she must be still dealing with her own emotional turmoil and deep feelings of loss. But later... maybe, just maybe there would be a chance for him. He looked down at Gerald and the dog wagged his tail, tongue lolling happily. At least a third of the party was contented. *One out of three ain't bad*, he told himself firmly, paraphrasing Meatloaf. For now, that would have to do.

35

Friday morning found Joel in his workshop with Gerald. The little dog had made himself completely at home but he was insisting on following Joel wherever he went, whether it be kitchen, bedroom, bathroom or – his favourite place so far – the workroom. There were lots of interesting smells here to investigate, and he was currently chasing a fascinating curl of wood shaving around the floor, yelping happily.

Joel leaned against the wall and watched him. He'd not realised how much he'd missed having a dog. As a child, his family had been mad keen on Collies, and his parents still owned three. The dogs made a big fuss of Joel whenever he visited but he'd never had the urge to make the effort it would need to persuade Trina to adopt one of their own. Since she left, Joel's work had taken up all of his time and energy, and although he'd have loved a puppy, it didn't seem fair when he'd have to leave it behind in the house for hours at a time.

Gerald, on the other hand, was extremely portable. He loved scampering along on his short legs when they went for a walk but after their early-morning stroll, Joel had needed to make a quick trip to deliver a quote and the dog had been equally happy curled up in the van. He was the perfect pet for a busy person.

However, although the new arrival had settled in with no problems, and hopefully Leo would soon see that Baz was a bad bet for her, Joel's mind was still in turmoil. Seeming to sense his distress, Gerald sidled up to him and sat on his hind legs with both paws held out, as if offering support. Joel bent to stroke him, furious with himself for feeling so discombobulated. This was painful. His whole body was longing for Ingrid. He'd so nearly kissed her a couple of times now but managed to stop himself just in time. What was she doing to him? Joel had had a few brief interludes of seeing different women since the split with Trina, but none of them had anything like this effect on him and each time he'd kept things low key and ducked out as gracefully as possible before anyone got attached to him. Nobody had been hurt. He'd always blamed himself for not being ready for a new relationship and from the start had never given anyone cause to think otherwise.

Now, after only a few days, Joel's carefully preserved independence was being shaken to the core. It wasn't only the thought of Ingrid's emotions being in a vulnerable state that had held him back this morning. He knew in his heart that his self-confidence still hadn't recovered from the sudden ending of his marriage, however long ago it seemed, and the thought of leaving himself wide open to being hurt again was terrifying. Joel had a very strong feeling that if he let himself really fall for Ingrid, there would be no turning back.

In the quiet of his workroom, listening to the contented snuffling of his new companion and breathing in the familiar scents of sawdust and varnish, Joel considered his options. He could keep on hoping that in time Ingrid would give some sign

A New Lease of Life

that she was ready to start again, and then he could make it subtly clear that he was her man. Alternatively, he could give up all chances of ever taking further steps and content himself with a good solid friendship. He supposed both depended on whether Ingrid planned to stay around Willowbrook. If she finished her project and took off again, there was no point in even thinking about it all.

As Joel pondered, his phone rang, and he saw Sam's name on the screen. Glad of the distraction, he answered. 'Hi, mate, are you okay?'

'Hiya. Do you still need me to help move that bench this morning? Only, I'm free but Elsie's off school again. They put two training days together this time so I'd have to bring her along.'

'Sure, the more the merrier. Elsie can meet Gerald,' said Joel, looking down at the little dog, who was now lying with his nose tucked into his paws by Joel's feet and dozing peacefully.

'Who?'

'I'll explain when you get here. We'll have a coffee first, yeah?'

Ten minutes later, Sam appeared holding Elsie by the hand. She was carrying a glittery purple backpack and wearing sparkly wellies.

'You look ready for an adventure,' Joel said. 'Are you going into the rainforest, exploring?'

'No, silly Uncle Joel,' said Elsie. 'We've done about the rainforests and jungles at school. They're a long way away.'

At that moment Elsie spotted Gerald. He'd been having a wander around Joel's rather overgrown garden which at the moment definitely held some similarities to a jungle.

'Who's this?' she squealed, running towards the dog and dropping to her knees. 'He's lovely. Is he yours, Uncle Joel?'

'Just for now. This is Gerald. He needs a new home. I guess I'm his foster dad,' said Joel.

'We could...' began Elsie, but Sam held up a hand.

'Don't even think about it, sweetie. You know the rules of our flat. The landlord doesn't allow any pets bigger than a goldfish. He's not an animal lover. Or a people lover, actually,' Sam added under his breath to Joel.

Elsie was now rummaging in her backpack, and soon produced a tennis ball. 'Can I play with him in the garden? I expect you need coffee. Grown-ups always do. My teacher makes us go outside even in the rain so she can have coffee and biscuits with the others. I wonder if my mummy likes coffee?'

Sam ruffled her curls. 'I don't know the answer to that one, but you're absolutely right, we do need hot drinks to keep us going. I'll give you a shout when we're ready to load the bench, okay?'

Elsie pottered off happily with Gerald at her heels, and Joel led the way into the kitchen.

'Elsie doesn't often mention Lara, does she?' he asked.

'No, but I think now she's a bit older she's thinking about her more. I knew it'd happen eventually and I'll deal with it somehow, but it's a tricky one.'

They drank their coffee in silence, and Joel thought about Elsie's relentlessly extrovert mother. She'd been a teenage fling for Sam, who had realised fairly soon afterwards that he was gay. Lara had left the area with her raucous, semi-feral parents when Elsie was just a small baby, saying that Sam would be much better at bringing their daughter up. He'd proved this to be true, although Joel knew it had been a struggle at times. Now Sam was in a relationship with Luka, who was the son of Milo at the Willowbrook Country Park Café. It was a long-distance affair at the moment because Luka was at uni.

'How are things going with the toy boy?' asked Joel. He'd always jokingly referred to Luka as that, and Sam had never minded, but now he frowned.

'It's not funny,' he said. 'The age gap thing isn't easy. I'm twenty-four and he's nineteen. It's only a small age gap, I guess, but it seems a lot when he's doing all the crazy *away from home for the first time* stuff and I'm still here, being sensible and boring.'

'You could never be boring,' said Joel. 'I can see the problem though. A gap can be tricky, but only if you let it be.'

'Ah, I can tell you've given this some thought. You see, I think in your situation, age-wise the perfect set-up would be if the bloke was a bit younger than the lady and both of you had already experienced life and relationships but were ready for something completely new.'

Joel looked at Sam with suspicion, but his friend gazed back, innocent and guileless.

'And your point is?' he asked.

'My point is, are you getting anywhere with the lovely Ingrid?'

'Who says I'm trying to get anywhere? She's only just lost her husband, Sam. Have a bit of respect.'

Sam laughed. 'Your face is giving you away, mate. Take my advice, never play poker. Okay, I'm backing off. Let's get this show on the road. That bench won't move itself.'

They finished their coffee and went out into the garden, where Elsie was still throwing her ball for Gerald. His ears were starting to droop, and he was panting. When he saw Joel, he scampered towards the kitchen.

'Gerald's done a wee in the long grass but only because I told him to, so I think he likes me quite a lot,' said Elsie. 'Can we take him with us in the van?'

'No, not this time, sweetheart. I would do normally but he's had a busy morning already. I expect he's ready for a good long drink and a nap now,' said Joel. 'He'll be better off here. I won't be too long. You can follow him into the kitchen and settle him down with a chew if you like. There's a packet of them on the table.'

They loaded the bench onto the van and set off, with Elsie strapped in between Joel and Sam, singing a song about ten in a bed that Joel remembered from his own childhood. The song got louder and louder and lasted until they reached the parking area by the café but mercifully ended at that point, just as Joel was thinking his ears must be bleeding.

'Oh, look, there's Aunty Kate's next-door neighbour and her friend!' shouted Elsie, pointing to the door of the café where Beryl and Winnie were standing. 'They don't look very happy though,' she added.

Joel parked in the courtyard and the three went over to say hello to the ladies. 'Is everything okay?' Joel asked them. 'Elsie noticed that you didn't look as cheerful as usual.'

'It's Anthea,' said Beryl. 'She's in hospital. I rang her this morning to see how she was and she didn't answer for ages but then she messaged to say she'd had to call an ambulance in the night because she was having such bad stomach pains. She's still on a trolley in A&E. They've done some tests.'

Winnie and Beryl both looked devastated. Joel reflected with a pang that he'd never, until now, seen the two of them without smiles on their faces. 'Do you want me to give you a lift over to the hospital when we've unloaded the Hendersons' bench?' he said. 'It's no problem.'

Sam shook his head. 'You'd be better to wait until Anthea's been sent to a ward, I reckon,' he said. 'You won't be able to talk to her in a corridor. You'll just be in the way. Let's keep in touch

A New Lease of Life

with her for now and make a plan later. We can still all go to the shop when we're free. Anthea'll want all the gossip as soon as she feels more like herself.'

Beryl nodded thoughtfully. 'You're probably right. Look, let's have a cup of tea and a bun while we're here. Elsie can come in with us. Maybe Anthea will text again soon. Come on, let's see if we can get the table by the window.'

Joel and Sam soon had the bench unloaded and stashed it away in one of the old stable blocks until such time as the Henderson family were ready to have it installed in its permanent place in a wooded area near the smallest lake.

'I wonder if Beryl and Winnie have let Ingrid know that Anthea's so unwell,' Joel said, doing his best to sound casual as he and Sam walked back to the café.

Sam grinned. 'Well, I expect someone else had better tell her if they haven't done it,' he said. 'I wonder who could do that job for them? Hmm. Ingrid will need to be told as soon as possible, won't she?'

'Well, yes,' Joel blustered. 'Ingrid took Anthea to the hospital the other day and she was the only one who knew Anthea had been having tests. I don't know why you're looking at me like that, Sam. I'm only trying to help.'

His friend was laughing now, and Joel punched him none too gently on the arm. 'Shut up. You're making things worse. I'm already all mixed up about her. I don't need you to embarrass me, I can do that for myself.'

Sam gestured to a seat outside the café. 'Let's have a minute before we get sucked into the world of Elsie again. Tell me what the real problem is here.'

Joel leaned back on the wrought-iron seat. Its metal framework dug into his back, but he hardly registered the discomfort, preoccupied as he was with the need to put into words the thoughts that had been bugging him ever since he realised his feelings for Ingrid were escalating into something a lot more than just friendly. A party of ramblers was heading for the café, chattering and laughing, and when they were safely inside, Joel noticed that the air was full of birdsong. A warm breeze lifted Sam's golden curls as his friend stretched out his long legs and prepared to wait for an answer. There was no escaping this.

'How are you with soppy, romantic stuff, mate?' Joel asked eventually, when the silence between them was making him edgy.

'More relaxed about it than your average twenty-something bloke, I'd say,' Sam replied. 'I watch the odd romcom and I'm partial to a good schmaltzy love song. "Islands in the Stream" is mine and Luka's favourite. We do that one together at karaoke nights at the pub whenever we get the chance. How about you?'

Joel watched two sparrows fighting over a crust of bread that someone had thrown out of the café window. He cleared his throat. 'I hate to admit this, because I've not got what you'd call a good success rate with relationships as you know, and it's going to sound really cheesy. But... I've got a horrible feeling that I've gone and fallen in love.'

36

On the afternoon before the grand shop opening, Ingrid stood in the flat with the Saga Louts in front of her, minus Anthea of course. Ingrid had been horrified to receive a brief message earlier from Beryl to tell her that Anthea was in hospital and no visitors were allowed yet. She and Winnie had said they'd call in at the shop sometime later to give a further update, and here they were, tension in every bone of their bodies.

'Oh, we both know now that you took her to hospital for her appointments so don't look so guilty,' said Winnie. 'But nobody expected it to turn out like this. She had hideous stomach pains, apparently, and the ambulance was there within minutes. It was a blue light dash. She asked us to pass the message on to you because she's trying to save her phone battery until we can bring her a charger.'

'My goodness, that's even worse than I imagined! Can we go and see her? What's happening? Do they know what the problem is?' Ingrid said, trying not to mind that Anthea hadn't called herself. Of course she'd need her phone to last out and these two were her oldest friends, but even so, it stung a little.

'She's still in A&E on a trolley. They've done a few tests and she's waiting for a bed on a ward. We might be able to go later if she gives us the okay,' said Beryl.

'Should I call the hospital, do you think? There might be some news by now.'

'They won't usually tell you anything unless you're a close relation, Ingrid. We'll just need to be patient. For now, we thought we'd all be best to keep busy so we've come to see if you could do with any help.'

Ingrid set the two ladies to work adding a few more oddments to the bargain table, more to keep them busy than because it was necessary. She was just about to pack them off home with the promise of taking them to the infirmary if Anthea phoned to say visitors were allowed after all when there was a rattle at the door, and they all turned to see a young woman with multi-coloured dreadlocks standing outside.

'Oh, gawd, not another of your Tommy's daughters, is it?' Winnie said with a cackle. 'He must have put himself about a bit if so. Mind you, this one's got great hair.'

Ingrid didn't reply to this dig. She picked up one of Leo's flyers and went to open the door, trying not to feel edgy. It was probably just an early customer sussing out the action.

'Hello there. We're not open until tomorrow but I can give you this to claim a discount on your first purchase,' she said.

'Hi. I know you're not open yet, but I wanted a word before that, if possible? I'm Candy,' said the woman, smiling broadly. 'I saw the shop advertised on the Willowbrook Facebook page and I wondered if you'd be up for an interview on local radio? I host a live music and chat show that airs on Monday and Saturday evenings. I could fit you in this coming Monday night if you're free? You could give a shout-out to the shop?'

'Say yes!' shouted Beryl from behind Ingrid, where she'd been shamelessly eavesdropping. 'It'll be great for business.'

'Yes, you go girl!' Winnie added, coming up to stand at Ingrid's shoulder. 'This is Candy Channing. I always listen in to your shows, honey, especially the phone-ins. I bet you see my phone number popping up every single show. I love your reggae hour on Saturdays. You should see me boogying in the kitchen.' She gave an enthusiastic wiggle to demonstrate, nearly knocking Ingrid over.

Ingrid smiled. 'You'd better come in. My PR team seem to be in favour of this idea but I've got to say I'm not so sure.'

Candy was in the shop almost before she'd been invited, looking round with interest and sizing Ingrid up into the bargain. 'I love the idea of this place,' she said. 'I wish my parents would do something similar. They're still in Jamaica but they're moving over here soon to be near me and my sister. It's giving us a horrible feeling they're going to be bringing everything they've collected over the years with them.'

Beryl and Winnie gave Ingrid thumbs-up signs as Candy wandered around the shop. 'Don't be a wimp, dear,' whispered Beryl. 'We need all the publicity we can get.'

Ingrid was beginning to feel backed into a corner but with her friends' eyes on her, she found she couldn't say no. 'I've never done anything like this before, but I'll give it a go,' she said to Candy as the other woman finished her circuit of the room. 'Presentations to colleagues are one thing, but live radio? You're very brave to even be asking me.'

'I've got a good idea of who will and who won't come over well,' said Candy. 'You've got a sophisticated air about you. It's that Joanna Lumley look. I mean when she's being herself, not in Ab Fab mode,' she added hastily. 'You don't look the sort to get smashed on bolly, get lippy on your teeth and chain smoke.

Can I take a few photos of you and your shop for our web page? Then I can do a bit of promo before you arrive. If you give me your number, I'll text you the details of where to come and what time, okay?'

This all seemed very impetuous and informal to Ingrid, who, if she'd ever given it any thought, had imagined the world of radio to be as full of important advance schedules as TV, but she did as she was asked and hoped she wasn't setting herself up for a fall. There wasn't much to talk about yet, and if no customers appeared tomorrow, the whole project could end up as a huge flop.

'Don't look so worried,' said Candy. 'You've obviously got great back-up here.' She grinned at Beryl and Winnie, who beamed back delightedly. 'And whoever's sorting your social media promo knows what they're doing. It pulled me in, didn't it?'

'You're not the only one it dredged up,' said Winnie, then put a hand over her mouth as Ingrid shot her a look. 'Sorry. Ignore me, Candy. I talk too much.'

'That sounds intriguing. Maybe there's more to discuss on the show than I expected? My listeners love a good story,' Candy said. 'Are you up for it, Ingrid? Add a bit of colour?'

'Not a chance. It's a sensitive subject.'

'Even better. Ah well, I can see from the look on your face that one's not happening, but you've got lots to talk about anyway. I'll see you on Monday. Good luck tomorrow, girls.'

They watched Candy go and Ingrid locked the door behind her. 'That was... unexpected,' she said, unsure whether she was excited about having such great publicity offered for free, or just terrified.

'It's brilliant,' Beryl said, clapping her hands. 'And even if poor Anthea's still in hospital on Monday we can let her know about the radio show and she can listen in. I guess it's not likely we'll get the okay to visit tonight so I'm off home. Coming, Winnie? Where's young Leo?'

'She's called to tell me that she's visiting her dad and Gerald,' Ingrid said, with some relief. 'I'm going to take advantage of her being out for a while to have a long shower and use up loads of hot water. See you in the morning.'

Both ladies hugged Ingrid, and she realised with a shock how much she was coming to rely on their warmth and friendship and how much she longed to see Anthea back home and well again.

'I should be thanking you more often for all you do,' she said, with tears in her eyes.

'Oh, give over,' Winnie replied. 'We don't go in for that mushy stuff, do we, Beryl?'

'No, let's have none of it. Happy to help a friend in need. See you.'

The remaining two thirds of the Saga Louts made a quick exit and Ingrid went slowly up to the flat, lost in thought. *A friend in need*, she said to herself as she stepped into the blissfully hot shower. *I suppose I am. But I never would have imagined so many people would already think of themselves as my friend.*

The happy bubble lasted until, dripping wet on the bathmat, she heard someone yelling her name accompanied by a loud banging on the door and guessed that Leo must have forgotten her key. As she hurried downstairs wrapped in a large bath towel and muttering vague oaths under her breath, Ingrid reflected that some of her new friends were turning out to be a little more high maintenance than others.

37

Ingrid was up before dawn the next day, too excited to sleep any more. Leo emerged shortly afterwards and polished off three rounds of toast and jam while Ingrid was still on her first cup of tea.

'This is going to be immense,' Leo said, spraying crumbs across the table. 'I can't wait to open the door to customers for the first time.'

'Don't talk with your mouth full,' said Ingrid automatically, then cringed at the words because she sounded just like her own mother who had a habit of ignoring important comments and going for the trivial response instead.

Luckily Leo didn't seem offended. 'Soz, Ings,' she said. 'But you've got to admit it's awesome.'

'But... what if nobody turns up?' Ingrid said. 'We're all going to be stuck here like lemons with nothing to do. It'll be horrible.'

'Don't be so negative. I'm no lemon and neither are you. Come on, let's get dressed and go down to the shop. I want to make sure everything's perfect and you need to hang up that curtain over the door so nobody can see in before ten o'clock.'

The rest of the team were all assembled in plenty of time. Ingrid had the card reader ready and waiting next to an antique till that really fitted in with the ambience. Winnie was armed with a handful of dusters because yesterday she'd applied one more coat of the pink window cleaner so that there could be a grand unveiling this morning. As the hour of reckoning approached, Ingrid went to stand by Winnie and her eyes opened wide in amazement. Outside was a queue of people, all peering at Winnie as she rubbed and polished the smears away.

'Oh, my life!' she gasped. 'We've got customers.'

'Well, of course we have, duh!' said Leo. 'I didn't do all this prep work for nothing. Let's go!'

The clock on the wall struck ten, and the whole team cheered as Ingrid opened the door with a flourish. The first set of customers made their way in, looking around with keen interest. They parted ways and milled around the shelves, picking objects up, examining them, often putting them down again but sometimes holding on to the ones they liked best.

Beryl's eyes were sparkling. She gestured to the sight of an elderly couple who'd settled themselves on the navy sofa bed and were watching the proceedings as if they were in the front row at the theatre. As Ingrid watched, the man seized one of Beryl's cushions and tucked it in behind his tiny wife and she nodded her thanks, twinkling up at him. Hand in hand and feet placed neatly side by side, they observed the goings-on with benevolent smiles.

'Look,' Beryl hissed. 'The Hendersons are here.'

'Is that significant?' Ingrid whispered back.

'Yes! They live in one of those big houses on the edge of

Willowbrook Country Park near the river and they're the nearest thing we've got to local gentry. If you get their seal of approval, you're as good as made.'

Ingrid walked over to the sofa and smiled down at the two onlookers. 'Hello, I'm Ingrid Copperfield,' she said.

'We know who you are,' said the man, doffing his trilby. 'I'm Harold Henderson and this is my good lady, Penelope. We just wanted to see what you were up to, my dear. I was saying to Penelope that we should do something similar with our excess of memorabilia.'

'But where to begin? That's the problem,' said his wife, who was elfin and dainty with wispy white curls. 'We've lived in that house since we were first married, and I must confess to being rather a magpie.'

'That's the understatement of the year,' said her husband. 'And yes, I admit to being almost as bad myself.'

'The old coach house is stuffed with crates full of all sorts of random objects, isn't it, dear? And most of them are yours.'

Harold nodded. 'We were hoping you could advise us on how to tackle the job, as you've clearly been in the same position yourself. I don't suppose you'd come over to join us for a spot of afternoon tea after you shut up shop one day? We have a wonderful lady who comes in to help us with some cleaning and cooking and she makes the most delicious scones. Have you the time to spare?'

'You had me at scones,' said Ingrid, her stomach rumbling in anticipation.

'I beg your pardon?' Harold, a worried frown puckering his already lined forehead. Penelope patted his hand.

'It's one of those things young people say these days, dear,' she said. 'I keep up with the trends by watching reality TV,' she told Ingrid, confidingly. 'But Harry only really likes documentaries about wildlife, so he doesn't understand the lingo. Do come and see us. I've got a thing somewhere with our telephone number on it...'

She rummaged in her bag and produced a thick, gilt-edged card, just as Joel joined them.

'Hello, you two,' he said, crouching down on his haunches so that he could talk to them more easily, because the shop was really filling up now and space was getting limited.

'I'd better go and help Leo,' said Ingrid. 'Lovely to meet you both.'

She wove her way through the groups of chattering customers to where Beryl and Leo were manning the till. Because they were hoping that there would be a fairly quick turnover of stock once people found out about the shop, they'd decided to keep pricing simple, so rather than labelling each item, Anthea had come up with the plan of colour coding them with stickers. There were five prices and Leo had printed out notices that were spaced around the shop so that nobody was in any doubt about payment, although if a number of items were being bought, they made it clear that the total was sometimes negotiable. 'It's called a *bundle*,' said Beryl, rather smugly. 'We do it at the car boot sales sometimes.'

Sam had seemed to be everywhere Ingrid looked this morning, troubleshooting if necessary and generally keeping an eye on the proceedings. She watched as he went over to the sofa to help the elderly couple out of their low seats. Elsie skipped around them, singing a nursery rhyme about Old King Cole. 'That's who you remind me of,' she said to Harold. 'He was a merry old soul. Have you got a pipe and drum?'

Penelope laughed heartily, tears trickling down her papery cheeks. 'He has got an ancient briar pipe, as it happens,' she said. 'And a very smelly thing it is too. But if Harry's the king, that must make me the queen,' she said, when she'd recovered.

'You do look a bit like the lady on my Aunty Kate's tea towel, the one with the dogs with the short legs,' Elsie said. 'I think that queen's deaded though,' she added sadly.

'Yes, God rest her soul,' said Penelope. 'A wonderful woman and an example to us all.'

'Why, do you like little fat dogs too?' asked Elsie.

'Well, I do, as it happens, but that wasn't quite what I meant. Anyway, being any sort of queen is a bonus for me.'

'I'll be your princess then,' said Elsie. 'I'm not going to wear a frilly frock though, okay? No way.'

Sam ushered his daughter away at that point, with apologies, but Ingrid could see that Penelope Henderson was beaming and seemed loath to let them go.

The two on the desk were managing wonderfully, but Ingrid could see that although Beryl was thoroughly enjoying herself, she was starting to flag.

'I'll take over here,' she said to the older lady. 'Would you be able to go see the Hendersons out? They seem like the sort of people we want to encourage.'

Beryl bustled away importantly, and Ingrid moved into the space she'd vacated.

'Nice one, Ings,' said Leo out of the corner of her mouth. 'I could tell she was drooping but she hates anyone suggesting she's anything but super-fit.'

Ingrid was too busy for a while to answer, because the queue of customers was getting longer. Winnie was now frantically unpacking more items and making snap decisions on which stickers they should have, and Sam and Elsie had taken charge of the cash-only £1 bargain basement. Elsie was loving every minute of playing shops.

'We've got lots of lovely money,' she shouted to Ingrid. 'You'll be able to go shopping now. Can you get some more of the pink biscuits with holes in next time?'

'This is amazing, Leo,' said Ingrid, when they had a brief breathing space. 'I can't believe you got this many people in on the very first day. How did you do it? You told me about the social media thing but even so, this is crazy.'

'I know. I was surprised how many of my mates shared it, and I've sent Baz out with another load of flyers now. He wasn't impressed with the idea, but we've all got to muck in with this or it'll never get properly off the ground.'

A cross-faced woman appeared in front of them at this point holding two china mugs and a vase. 'This is chipped,' she said, plonking the vase in front of Leo on the counter. 'You shouldn't sell damaged goods.'

Leo frowned back and folded her arms. Ingrid strongly suspected that she was about to let fly with an acerbic comment that might not be appreciated, so she stepped in. 'If you're buying the mugs, you can have the vase for nothing, if you like,' she said. 'We must have missed the chip when we were setting out the shelves. I do apologise.'

'Oh. Well, in that case... I will.' Mollified, the woman nodded approvingly as Leo rather grudgingly swathed her goods in some of the yards of bubble wrap and brown paper Ingrid had ordered online and passed them over. She rolled her eyes at Ingrid as the woman pushed her way out of the shop.

'You're too soft, Ings,' she said. 'I'd have told her to piss off. She was just rude.'

Ingrid laughed. 'Years of working in the hospitality trade has given me a thick skin,' she said. 'The customer is always right. She went away happy. Happyish anyway.'

'Hmm. Oh, here's Baz. He must have finished that paper drop. D'you mind if I go now? I think he's getting restless.'

Ingrid turned, just as the peculiarly individual scent of Leo's boyfriend assaulted her nose.

'Coming, or what?' he growled.

'Yes, just on my way.' Leo looked unusually flustered and Ingrid mentally cursed the boy for taking her usual chutzpah away.

'Thanks for doing the delivering, Baz. Those flyers have been worth their weight in gold today,' she said, going for flattery as opposed to the much sharper approach she'd have liked to use.

He shrugged, looking down at the heap of discarded flyers that Leo had impaled on an old-fashioned spiked block as she'd received them. 'S'nothing,' he mumbled. 'Come on, babe. I'm gagging for some chips and a beer. We can go back to mine, Mum's out for the day.'

Leo shot an anxious glance at Ingrid but picked up her hoodie and followed him out of the shop. Ingrid saw Joel stand up and make as if to go after them, but seeming to sense her watching him, he turned and met her gaze. She shook her head slightly. He mouthed *talk later, got to work*, and went out of the shop via the storeroom.

The next hour was easier, as the flow of customers turned to a trickle and then only a handful remained, chatting idly.

'We're closing in five minutes,' Ingrid announced to anyone who was listening. 'We need to restock. Thank you all for coming. We hope to see you again soon.'

Maybe this place was going to turn out to be more than just a shop. The village already had a community hall, but it was right on the other side of Willowbrook. She wondered what the rules were about serving hot drinks. Ingrid had noticed earlier

A New Lease of Life

that without mentioning it to anyone else, Beryl had somehow managed to find matching teacups and saucers to make the Hendersons a drink but that couldn't happen normally. She'd probably need all sorts of health and safety checks. It was one thing giving the Hendersons an unofficial cup of tea but another setting up a kind of tea bar.

Ingrid made a mental note to research catering rules and started the difficult task of herding the remaining few people out without offending them. She closed the door with a huge sigh of relief, dropping the latch and turning the OPEN sign to face the opposite way. The first day of trading had gone swimmingly, and better still there had been no sign of Uma or her mother.

'Three cheers for The Boss,' Sam shouted, and the Treasure Team erupted in whoops of joy. Ingrid couldn't speak for a moment. Hearing her old tongue-in-cheek title had taken her right back to her hotel days, but this was so much better.

'There's prosecco in the fridge, and Leo's been back for long enough to get the glasses ready,' said Beryl. 'Get the tray, dear. Let's celebrate. And while we're raising a glass to our Ingrid, let's spare a thought for the missing team member.'

Joel popped the cork on a chilled bottle of fizz and Leo carefully filled five champagne flutes, pouring two extra ones of apple juice for herself and Elsie. 'To Ingrid and to Anthea,' the others all chorused. Ingrid, still lost for words, lifted her own glass in a toast.

'So, are we opening again tomorrow for a few hours?' Joel asked.

'You bet we are,' said Ingrid, finding her voice at last. 'There's no stopping us now.'

38

When Joel arrived at The Treasure Trove on Sunday morning, he was surprised to find his daughter was already down in the shop. She was talking animatedly into her phone at the same time as arranging a random selection of vintage kitchen utensils. Some of these looked more like medieval torture aids to Joel, but he presumed they'd been designed to mince and chop meat rather than persuade prisoners in dungeons to spill secrets. He coughed loudly and gave Leo one of his best stern looks.

'Don't look at me like that, Dad, I'm allowed to speak to Baz, aren't I?' she said after she'd ended the call. 'I was just making sure he was awake because he promised to help today but I reckon he was asleep again before I'd even finished talking. Where's Gerald?'

'I dropped him off with Sam and Elsie for a quick walk but they'll be here soon. Honestly, that dog is having a better social life than I've had for years. Did Baz ask how he was getting on?'

'Who?'

'*Gerald*. Who did you think I meant? He's really still Baz's responsibility. I'd have thought he'd have at least wanted to make sure his grandpa's pet was okay.'

Leo shrugged and carried on with her shelf arrangement. Joel gritted his teeth and tried not to imagine all the things he'd like to say to Baz right now.

'Is Ingrid okay?' Joel asked eventually, when no further comment from his daughter was forthcoming. He checked round to see if she was in the shop.

'Yes, she's fine. She's a tough cookie. She's just on the phone to the hospital trying to get some up-to-date info, because Anthea's given the nurses permission to talk to her or Beryl or Winnie, I think. Anthea hasn't got any kids or brothers and sisters. Sad, innit? It sounds as if she's had to have an emergency operation. Gall bladder, or something. It was about to burst, Beryl said. Yuk.'

'Can Ingrid visit yet?'

'Well, she might be able to go soon, but I think she's putting it off because she's still not keen on driving that car and she hates the hospital car park. It's really hard to get a space at visiting time.'

'Poor Anthea. I could give Ingrid a lift to see her later if she wants me to, I guess,' Joel said, trying and failing to sound casual. His daughter fixed him with a beady stare but didn't comment.

Ingrid entered the shop at this point, to Joel's relief. She smiled at him but looked anxious and preoccupied. 'Anthea's doing okay, but she's still very poorly and quite woozy,' she said. 'So they've moved her into a side room so that she can get a bit more peace and quiet and they don't want her agitated. That kind of suggests she's been a bit...' Ingrid paused tactfully, and Joel filled in the gap.

'Stroppy?'

'Well, possibly. The problem's going to be what happens when she's discharged. I told the nurse there were plenty of us to help with keeping an eye on her at home, but they say she'll need someone there all the time for a little while.'

Beryl had now also come in with Winnie and caught most of the conversation. 'Hospitals usually don't want you hanging around for long taking up their beds so if they're keeping her, she must be still really shaky. You know what they'll recommend, don't you?' she said. 'They'll want her to go into respite care when they let her out, even if it's only for a little while. If it was me or Winnie we'd jump at the chance. All that bingo, hot meals sorted, great cake, a bit of a singsong in the evenings. We'd love it.'

Winnie nodded. 'But Anthea wouldn't handle that. She'd go mad.'

'I know. The nurse said as much. They did suggest it but just the mention of respite sent Anthea's blood pressure rocketing sky high. So anyway, I said she could come here. Just for a week or so, that's all she'll need... I think,' Ingrid added doubtfully.

'Hmm. Are you sure? It'll be a lot of work for you and a big responsibility. It might be better to have a couple of weeks in a nursing home or similar first?'

Ingrid didn't reply to Winnie's suggestion, but headed back upstairs with the others to have a team talk about what she should say on the radio on Monday.

Joel was about to follow them when he heard the sounds of Elsie's chatter before he saw her and opened the front door, preparing to fill his friend in on what had been happening during the morning so far. Elsie bounced up and down impatiently, pigtails bobbing.

'Can I go upstairs and play with Gerald? He's had his walk

and he wants to watch a Disney film with me now,' she said hopefully.

Sam said she could if she didn't get in Ingrid's way while she was busy. He watched his daughter skip away and then gazed around the shop as if he'd been dropped into an alternative universe as Joel told him the latest news.

'What is it with this place?' he said. 'Nothing much ever happens in Willowbrook and then Ingrid appears, opens a quirky shop in what seems like the blink of an eye, causes family upheavals with Trina for you and Leo, moves her new lodger in, finds an unknown stepdaughter, offers to take in and nurse the woman who's probably going to be the trickiest convalescent ever and then you...' He prodded Joel in the chest for extra emphasis, '*you* then have to go and fall for her, big time.'

'Erm... yes, that does sound quite a lot to pull in. But hey, it's not going to be boring while Ingrid's still around, is it?'

Sam glanced across at Joel and narrowed his eyes when he registered the false jollity of this statement. 'You think she won't be here long then, is that what you're worried about?'

'Not a clue, mate. She said from the start that she only intended this to be short term. Who knows what she'll do next?'

Joel's spirits sank as he let this thought settle. If he was going to get anywhere with Ingrid, he'd need to at least let her know how much of an impact she'd had on his life already, but if he rushed into it while she was still in the earlier stages of grieving, he'd do more damage than good. It was a difficult one.

Never had Joel felt so helpless. With Trina, he was young and inexperienced enough to have jumped into a serious relationship without much thought for where it was going, and since his marriage had imploded, he'd been very cagey about getting involved. Nobody since Trina had had any effect on his heart at all. Now, just the thought of Ingrid was making Joel shiver, as unsure as a teenage boy at a school disco waiting hopefully for the last dance.

The two men made their way up to the flat, where they found the others seated in a circle, some on the sofa and the others on chairs. Elsie was kneeling on the rug in the centre, opening the packet of Party Rings that Ingrid had provided, with Gerald in close attendance.

'Does anyone else like the pink ones?' she asked. 'Only, they're my favourite but Dad says I have to share.'

Everyone else shook their heads and Elsie settled down cross-legged with a sigh of pleasure. She had a sketchbook and pencil case and was soon happily munching and drawing at the same time. Beryl began to dish out mugs of tea and coffee.

'Grab a cuppa while you can, lads. If we're as busy as yesterday we won't have much time for a brew later,' she said to Sam and Joel. 'We've given Ingrid some tips about how to give the shop the biggest shout-out ever on the radio tomorrow.'

Ingrid smiled. 'The most important thing I want to tell anybody listening is how amazing you all are and how I couldn't have done this without you, at least not so quickly and not nearly so well. I only had a vague idea of what I'd taken on, but this team has lifted The Treasure Trove to a whole new level.'

Elsie put her felt-tip down and clapped her hands together with a whoop. The others all joined in the applause and Ingrid's eyes shone with pride as she looked at them all. Joel felt his heart squeeze. This tenderness he felt for her was getting almost unbearable. He wanted to jump up and lead Ingrid from the room, far away from the gathering so he could hold her tightly and tell her how much she was working her

A New Lease of Life

way into his soul. She met his gaze and looked away quickly. Had he given himself away already? But Ingrid was off again, outlining her next plans.

'Leo's upping the social media output with the help of her friends and we'll carry on unpacking as we go along. The most urgent job now is for me to clear the third bedroom ready for Anthea, whenever she's discharged from hospital.'

Beryl and Winnie exchanged glances. 'Are you sure you know what you're doing, dear?' asked Beryl. 'Anthea's one of my best friends but much as I love the old— I mean, fond as I am of her, I could no more live with her than bungee jump from the church tower wearing only a leopard-skin thong.'

'Same here,' said Winnie. 'Anthea's got a heart of gold, but she hides it well. Ingrid, you should think about this long and hard. She's used to having staff. It's not just the cleaner that calls twice a week. She's got another lady who pops round regularly to batch cook for the freezer and prep salads and cakes, and a gardener too. There's also a regular slot at Queenie's – you know where I mean, the beauty salon on the other side of the village. Hair, nails, massage... you name it, Anthea has it. You'll end up being a skivvy.'

'What's a skivvy?' asked Elsie with interest. 'Is it like a divvy? Dad calls me that sometimes.'

The others all began to discuss the Anthea issue, and Elsie's question was swamped by a whole range of helpful and not so helpful suggestions. Eventually, Leo raised a hand.

'Listen guys,' she said. 'It's not just Ings living here, there's me too. I can help. And if Anthea starts being a bit of a b—' She flicked a glance at Elsie, who was listening avidly. 'If she gets too demanding, I'll tell her to wind her neck in, okay?'

Elsie stood up and made a great show of trying to wind her own neck into an impossible position.

Joel cleared his throat. 'Look, I don't want to be a wet blanket, but you need to wait until you've talked to the staff who've been looking after Anthea before you make plans to move her in right away. They might say she's going to need extra care. That happened with my gran,' he said. 'And she quite enjoyed it in the end.'

'He's right, you know, dear,' said Beryl. 'It's really kind of you to make the offer when you've hardly known any of us for five minutes but let's just wait and see. Maybe Anthea can come here later, when she's got a bit of her old oomph back and can manage the stairs. Anyway, let's see where you'll put her if she does get to move in eventually.' Winnie and Beryl headed for the bedroom earmarked for the third Saga Lout while Leo collected the mugs. Sam and his daughter made a sharp exit, with Elsie protesting all the way down the stairs and out of the shop. Only Ingrid and Joel were left. When he'd moved the chairs back into place, Joel sat down next to his hostess on the sofa. She looked exhausted. The violet shadows under her eyes that he'd noticed when they first met were back and she yawned widely and stretched her arms out, almost clipping his ear.

'Oops, sorry,' she said. 'I didn't sleep very well last night. I think I was worrying about the radio show.'

Joel took a deep breath. 'I'll make a suggestion about what you should do,' he said. 'Have some early nights. You need them. Get the radio show out of the way. How about on Tuesday or Wednesday evening, if you get the okay to see Anthea by then, I'll order in pizza for Leo and she can chill out and watch *Love Island*, or something? Then you'll be free to come out with me for dinner. We can call into Meadowthorpe Hospital and visit Anthea first if necessary.'

Ingrid raised her eyebrows. 'Are you sure? I'd probably nod off, like last time.'

'No, you wouldn't. We can go somewhere relaxing and quiet. There's a little Italian restaurant that'd be easy to call at on the way back from the hospital. You can start with an espresso to wake you up and if you like we'll just have one course and some ice cream so you can be in bed by ten o'clock.'

Joel had a sudden glorious vision of Ingrid coming back to his house after dinner and being gently guided upstairs to his own bed. Even if she fell asleep before he got round to anything serious, she'd be there, snug and warm in his arms. He gave himself a mental slap as he waited for her to respond, not holding out much hope for a *yes*.

'Actually, that sounds like heaven,' Ingrid said, causing Joel to sit up straighter and beam all over his face. 'It might be possible if Anthea's well enough. If so, I can be ready for... say... six-ish when the shop's closed and I've had time to get changed. Would that be soon enough to visit Anthea and then eat?'

'It'd be absolutely perfect,' said Joel. 'I...'

But before he could tell Ingrid how happy he was to be taking her out, she held up a hand. 'This is a bit difficult,' she said in a low voice, 'but I should probably get it off my chest now though, so we know where we stand. I know how you still feel about your ex-wife because Leo's told me. I don't want it to be awkward for us in any way. We're friends. I'll never get the wrong end of the stick if we go out together, it'll be just for fun. You don't need to worry.'

Ingrid got up from the sofa and went to see what Winnie and Beryl were up to. Joel waited until she was out of sight and put his head in his hands.

'What's up, Dad?' Leo asked, coming back into the living

area. 'Are you coming down with a lurgy, or something? You look kind of funny.'

Joel looked up and attempted a smile. 'No, I'm just a bit tired,' he said. 'Do you fancy a pizza here on Tuesday or Wednesday? My treat. You can have the TV to yourself because I'm probably taking Ingrid to see Anthea if we get the all-clear to visit and we'll need to eat somewhere while we're out.'

As Leo made it clear that this was the Best Idea Ever, Joel got to his feet, trying not to frown when he looked at his daughter. Despair threatened to overwhelm him. The wrong end of the stick? Ingrid couldn't have been more wrong if she'd had a whole bundle of sticks to grab. Why had Leo gone and said that to her?

There was only one thing for it. He'd have to find some other way of showing Ingrid how he felt without frightening her off. A tempting idea began to form in his mind, sparked from a memory of how a much younger Joel had made his first fumbling attempts at courtship. Times had changed since then. He'd need Sam's help, and he'd have to get a move on, but could it work? There was only one way to find out.

39

By the next morning, Ingrid was beginning to think that Candy Channing had forgotten all about her. She was vacillating between relief at not having to put herself through the ordeal of the show when she wasn't at her sparkling best and disappointment that a free plug for the shop wasn't going to happen when an email appeared on her phone.

> Hi Ingrid. Looking forward to chatting with you later today. Please be at the radio station at 5 p.m., half an hour before we go on air so we can get you signed in and comfortable. I hope you don't mind but I got in touch with those two wonderful older ladies and I asked them to come along too. Can you bring them? What a pair of characters! Our listeners will love them.
> All the best, Candy

The show's programme of events and the address of the radio station followed with clear directions. There was no escaping it, but the thought of the loose cannons that would be

Beryl and Winnie live on air was somewhat alarming. As Ingrid typed a reply, the front door rattled, and Ingrid's two partners in crime arrived, Beryl on foot from up the road and Winnie in a taxi. They had told Ingrid the day before that they'd cancelled all their other social engagements this week so that they could be available to help in the shop, for which she was very grateful. Both were dressed up to the nines this morning. Beryl was resplendent in a mauve two piece with purple court shoes and a feathery fascinator that reminded Ingrid of part of a squashed pigeon and Winnie was decked out in a tropical-print dress that reached her ankles and a matching head wrap. Ingrid wondered if they'd quite grasped the idea that the radio listeners wouldn't be able to see them, but Winnie forestalled any comments by explaining that Candy had promised to take more publicity photos for the radio station's website.

'We don't want to let the side down,' she said. 'A lot of our friends are tuning in tonight and most of them are Super-Silver-Surfers like us. We've very computer savvy, me and Beryl. We've even thought about going on that Tinder thing, but we don't think any of the old geezers on there could keep up with us, to be honest. Young blood, that's what we need.'

'We're aiming to be leopards, Ingrid, that's what we want to be now,' said Beryl.

'You're aiming to be... what?'

'Cougars. She means cougars. How many times have I told you, Beryl? She told Candy we were going to be cheetahs. The poor woman was really confused.'

Ingrid tried not to giggle. She looked down at her own choice of more casual clothes and decided to run upstairs and change as soon as the shop shut at four o'clock. She could put on her favourite mid-season uniform of long flowery dress, denim jacket and white pumps. Her hair was in a chignon today and she'd already added silver hooped earrings and a necklace with ornate turquoise and silver beads.

The day went smoothly, although the customer count had now dwindled drastically.

'Mondays are quiet everywhere,' said Winnie soothingly. 'Now we'll all have a quick tidy up in here and then off you pop and get ready, Ingrid. Oh, here's young Leo. I hear you're minding the place tonight.'

Leo grinned. 'And Dad says I can't invite Baz round. Not that I would, obvs,' she added hastily when all three ladies frowned at her.

'You'll do,' said Beryl with an approving nod as Ingrid emerged from the flat after a very fast revamp. 'I didn't want to rain on your parade, dear, but those dungarees... they're fine for a walk to the café but we need to think of our public today.' She pulled out a jewelled powder compact and touched up her lipstick. 'We're ready when you are.'

Ingrid was happy to leave there and then. She wanted to be on the way plenty early enough to give herself time to get lost, find her way again and then park in a spot near enough for them not to have to make a mad dash to the recording studio. Soon, Beryl and Winnie were strapped into the Range Rover and Ingrid, feeling surer of herself every time she did this, was inching out of her parking space and heading towards the town.

At first sight, their destination was disappointing. It was a modern, mainly glass box on the edge of an industrial estate. From the outside, the best thing about it was probably the generous car park. However, once they'd been buzzed in through the door, the general excitement of live radio soon distracted her from the mundane window dressing. They were met in reception by Vincent, a dapper man who Ingrid guessed to be in his early sixties but had a combover and black hair dye job that must have made him feel a decade younger at least. The receptionist was fearsome and hadn't been told to expect the three visitors, but Vincent smoothed her feathers with easy charm and led them to a waiting area where they were plied with instant coffee and shortbread biscuits.

'Well, isn't this exciting, ladies?' he said. 'Have any of you been radio stars before?'

None of them had, which pleased Vincent very much. He clapped his hands together and began to explain what would happen next, but he was only just getting into the swing of his monologue when Candy breezed through the door, dressed in a workmanlike denim boilersuit.

'My dungarees would have been fine, you see,' whispered Ingrid to Beryl, who gave her the sort of look that said, *In your dreams, sweetheart*.

'Are we ready to entertain the listeners?' Candy asked, gesturing for them to follow her down a long corridor.

Ingrid, Beryl and Winnie trotted after her, with Vincent bringing up the rear. 'I was just telling them about...' he began, but Candy was already leading her party into a small studio with three swivel chairs on one side of the console and various huge microphones suspended in front of them.

'My show's on after the break,' she said. 'So, we've got plenty of time for a practice. I'm going to talk to Ingrid first about how she came up with the idea for the shop and why she chose Willowbrook. Then I'll move over to you two, and you can tell me what impact The Treasure Trove has had on the village and how you both feel about it, okay?'

They all nodded, suddenly speechless. Candy carried on talking, pouring out a soothing stream of reassurance as she put them through their paces. It seemed like no time at all when she sent them into the waiting area with Vincent and got ready to begin. Ingrid was dry-mouthed now, wishing she'd never agreed to take up this mad invitation, but Beryl and Winnie fizzed with excitement, unable to sit still and glaring at Vincent when he shushed them.

Candy's introduction to her show was brief, as she invited her listeners to ring in with any suitable record requests, and her first tune was soon playing. Ingrid had no idea what it was, but Beryl and Winnie were already on their feet and dancing around the small waiting room. Vincent rolled his eyes at Ingrid. 'Wasn't expecting this, to be honest. They must be closet Bruno Mars fans,' he said.

Ingrid heard the chorus begin and realised it was a song about treasure, although she still didn't like it much. When it seemed to have gone on forever, Vincent, who was wearing a discreet earpiece, motioned for the three guests to follow him into the studio. Candy waved to them as they sat down, and Vincent gave them each a set of headphones. As the music faded, the presenter pointed to her visitors, put a finger to her lips and then began to speak.

'Well, hello everyone. I'm very excited to be here with you today to welcome my first guests, who are Ingrid, Beryl and Winnie, all residents of the beautiful village of Willowbrook. The reason for their visit is an interesting one. Ingrid recently relocated from Yorkshire with the aim of opening a pop-up shop in Willowbrook. Now, this in itself isn't all that unusual, but Ingrid's is a shop with a difference. It's called The Treasure Trove, and I'll let her explain a bit more about it herself. Over to you, Ingrid. What made you decide to come to this area, and why open this particular shop?'

For a moment Ingrid thought the butterflies in her stomach were going to stop her speaking at all, but an encouraging nod from Candy and a pat on the leg from Beryl roused her from her frozen state. She swallowed hard.

'In a nutshell, my husband died suddenly a few months back, leaving me with a lot of debts and a big house crammed full of his assorted memorabilia. At the same time, my aunt, Sylvia, was leaving the village shop she had run for many years, and struggling with the decision of whether to sell it or rent it out. It was a light bulb moment for me. Sylvia agreed to let me have the shop for a short while to see if I could shift at least some of Tommy's accumulated "treasures".'

Candy gave Ingrid a thumbs-up sign, and she began to relax. This wasn't so bad after all. The next couple of questions went smoothly, giving Ingrid plenty of time to say how happy she was to have such a brilliant team of volunteers working alongside her, and then came a break for some music.

'A listener from Willowbrook who wants to remain anonymous has asked me to play this song,' Candy said, smiling at her guests. 'I'm saying no more.'

The first bars of the tune didn't mean anything to Ingrid, but then she recognised The Three Degrees, singing 'When Will I See You Again?'

Beryl and Winnie nudged each other and giggled as Candy whispered, 'So come on, spill the beans, who's got the admirer?'

The song ended, and Candy grinned. 'That was The Three Degrees, and my three are here looking puzzled. I sense a mystery fan, but which of you fabulous ladies has set someone's heart on fire? I have to tell you all that these girls are looking stunning. If you take a look at our website after the show, we'll have added some photos to show you just how gorgeous they all are.'

Beryl and Winnie preened themselves and smirked. 'It

A New Lease of Life

could be any of us,' Beryl said. 'We're all widows and we can get quite merry, if you know what I mean.'

'Yes, Beryl and me have always had our fair share of admirers at the Super-Silver-Surfers club and in the pub,' said Winnie. 'Our friend Anthea too. Oh, she might be listening from the hospital. If she is, we miss you, Anthea! Come home soon.'

'But what if the song's dedicated to Ingrid?' suggested Candy, mischievously. 'Have you been around here long enough to attract that kind of attention, Ingrid?'

Ingrid very much wanted to think it might have been Joel. He was the only male who had shown what she'd convinced herself was a slight interest, but in all honesty, she couldn't imagine him going to the trouble of choosing a song and then ringing up a local radio station to request it.

Candy was moving on now, saying that they just had a couple more minutes before these lovely ladies would have to leave the studio. She asked Beryl and Winnie how they saw their role at The Treasure Trove. They both began talking at once but then Beryl nodded to Winnie to continue.

'We're mainly looking after our new friend, Ingrid,' she said. 'It's interesting to see what people will buy too. I wouldn't give most of it house room, but you just never know, do you?'

Beryl chipped in. 'It's a lovely idea, and the customers are having a great time browsing. But like Winnie says, we want to make sure Ingrid's okay. Losing your partner is a massive shock, however it happens. We're keeping an eye on her, that's all.'

Ingrid couldn't speak. Tears filled her eyes, and she reached a hand out to each of them as they perched either side of her on the high chairs. Candy seemed almost as touched as Ingrid was. She reached for a tissue as she moved swiftly on to the next song, thanking them for coming and reminding the three to let Vincent take their photographs before they left the building.

As they posed for several informal photographs, arms linked and laughing at Vincent's impression of a flamboyant paparazzo, Ingrid's mood lifted. She had friends now. The Saga Louts, Sam and Elsie, Leo and Joel. At the thought of the last person on her mental list, her mind jumped forward to the next evening, when they'd be alone again. She pushed the thought away as she made sure her charges were safely strapped into the car. Left to themselves they were far too excited to think about such trivial details.

The journey home passed without incident, and Ingrid began to feel as if she was really getting the hang of this driving lark. Maybe tomorrow would be a straightforward continuation of the shop being more organised and gaining more customers, now the ordeal of the radio show was over. Ingrid was ready for some peace for a change.

40

Joel sat at his kitchen table, finishing off the design for a new project as he listened to the radio. When he heard his requested song playing, he wanted to stand up and punch the air but then told himself that Ingrid probably wouldn't think that it was from him or specifically for her. Why would she? A much less subtle method was needed before the message would be clear, and he still wasn't sure if it was right to make a move so soon after Tommy's death. Was there some sort of unwritten etiquette in place here? He was well aware that after a bereavement or divorce some people never, ever felt ready for a new relationship and were either perfectly contented to live a single life or too emotionally battered to ever love again. It was very early days for Ingrid, in any case.

Picking up his phone, he texted Sam for help. This was too difficult to mull over alone.

> Are you free, by any chance? Fancy a coffee at mine? I've got jam doughnuts… I need your advice and wise words.

The reply came back almost instantly.

> Wise words? You're kidding, aren't you? I'm up for the doughnuts though, Elsie's having a sleepover at Kate's tonight. See you in 5.

Joel filled the kettle, nervousness at the thought of sharing his hopes making him clumsy. He'd already stubbed his toe on the fridge, spilt some milk and almost dropped his favourite mug by the time Sam arrived. Gerald sniffed out the sweet scent of doughnuts and begged prettily but Joel hardened his heart, warning Sam not to give in either. They settled opposite each other with brimming mugs of coffee and a doughnut each, but Joel's appetite had suddenly disappeared. He watched Sam demolish his cake in four bites and felt slightly sick.

'What's up, mate?' Sam said. 'I've never known you to take this long to eat a doughnut. Is something wrong with Leo? Is it the Baz situation?'

Guilt stabbed Joel in the stomach. He hadn't even thought about Leo and Baz today. 'I think she's okay,' he said. 'She seems to be on an even keel at the moment, which is sometimes all you can aim for with a teen. No, it was something else I wanted to run past you.'

Sam waited. 'Go on then,' he said eventually, when it was clear Joel's words had dried up.

Joel took a gulp of coffee. 'I want to make a mix tape,' he said.

'A what?'

'You know what I mean, don't you? A compilation of songs to show someone how you feel about them?'

'Yes, I know what that is, but a tape? Are you a messenger

dropped in from the dark ages? Cassette tapes went out years and years ago. I've never even seen one in real life.'

Joel sighed. 'It was just a figure of speech. We used to use cassettes back when I was at school and trying to impress someone but now it should be much simpler. How would I go about it?'

'Spotify's the best way,' said Sam. 'I did something like this when I was first trying to get somewhere with Luka. I made him a playlist of all my favourite tracks.'

'And did it work?'

Sam shook his head. 'Nah, it was useless. He's five years younger than me, remember. That's a long time in musical terms. My choices weren't old enough to be vintage classics but already too dated to mean much to him. I'm guessing... this mix is destined for the lovely Ingrid?'

Joel's silence gave Sam his answer. After a moment, the younger man said, 'Do you want to get started now? I can help.'

'But is it a good idea, or is it too much like stalking, do you think? What if she isn't interested in me in that way or if it's just too soon?'

'There's only one way to find out,' said Sam, getting out his phone. 'Let's do it!'

Once Sam had set Joel up with the app he needed and given him some brief instructions on how to operate it, he set off to make the most of his evening of freedom by having a drink with Milo. Joel watched his friend go with mixed feelings. He wanted to get this thing absolutely right and then send it to Ingrid safely, but he was in no way sure he could do it alone. If Leo was here, she'd know what to do, but... oh, that would be a really bad idea.

On the other hand, his choice of music was going to be so

personal and potentially embarrassing that it was probably better to do this by himself and stop being such a technophobe. Like most people, Joel was well up to speed with the necessary skills to email and bank online, but he'd never been a fan of social media, and he avoided Facebook like the plague. TikTok was also a closed book to him, although he'd grudgingly let Leo set him up with an Instagram account to showcase his carpentry.

'You're forty-eight, Dad, not a hundred and eight. I don't know why you're making such a fuss about this,' Leo had said, as she clicked and swiped so fast on Joel's phone that he hadn't a hope of following the process. She'd tried hard to get her message across that the real world wasn't centred on the peaceful, sawdust-centred oasis of his workroom. Sociable and friendly when necessary, Joel was at heart a natural loner, which was one of the many reasons his marriage had crumbled. Trina had wanted to go out and party whenever they could get a babysitter, whereas Joel had been happy to stay at home listening out for his daughter and watching something relaxing on TV with a can of beer and some salted peanuts by his side.

It was time for Gerald's evening walk. With that done, Joel sat back down with his mug refilled and ate his doughnut for inspiration and sustenance. Bearing in mind Sam's comments about age difference and musical tastes, he thought long and hard about which songs would get his message across but not be purely chosen from his growing-up years or significant moments since then.

An hour later, he'd narrowed his selection down to ten wonderful songs with inner meanings that he hoped would be obvious. They ranged from hits remembered from tapes his parents had played constantly in the car on family holidays to tunes that had made him happy through the following years.

All had significant lyrics. Joel told himself proudly that he might be a bit of a slouch when it came to keeping up with some trends, but he'd never let his love for music become stuck in one particular era or type. The radio was constantly playing as he worked and he listened to a wide variety of radio stations, widening his knowledge of new and old bands with a healthy input of classical music too.

Soon, gaining confidence and completely absorbed in his task, Joel began to add the final choices to his very first Spotify playlist, being careful to get the order right. It wasn't easy because it turned out there were a huge number of love songs that could put across what he wanted to say to Ingrid, and also the app's algorithm kept suggesting more that he'd forgotten. Eventually, as satisfied as he'd ever be with the result, he took his phone out to the workshop and pressed play as he hunted around for the right wood for his next job. Listening carefully, he tried to imagine how Ingrid would feel as she did the same. When the last track ended, Joel rummaged for a notepad and pen and wrote down the titles and artists to see if the message was clear even without playing the tracks, mentally adding his own comments to each one.

Let Your Love Flow – The Bellamy Brothers

Starting cheerfully with the main message. Don't want to go straight in with the emotional stuff and spook her.

You've Got a Friend – James Taylor

A bit of reassurance here, and even though I want to be a lot more than her friend, I want her to know that I've got her back and will never let her down. Friends first and foremost.

A Good Heart – Feargal Sharkey

A reminder, if it's necessary, that I know we're both vulnerable people and need to be careful with each other's hearts.

I Get the Sweetest Feeling – Jackie Wilson

Moving on to the main message now. This is definitely how I feel when I see her. She makes every day brighter.

Here I Am (Come and Take Me) – Al Green

Too obvious? Hey, there's no point in beating about the bush any more, is there? Leaving myself wide open to rejection but 'faint heart never won fair lady', and all that stuff.

Here Comes the Sun – The Beatles

No mix tape should be complete without a Beatles classic. Too many love songs to choose from, so this is all about hope for the future.

Make You Feel My Love – Adele

Gentle and poignant now. Cards on the table. This is what I really want to say.

Come Away with Me – Norah Jones

I wish. Too much, too soon? But the words are so good...

Handle With Care – Traveling Wilburys

Final reminder that I know we've both been hurt in different ways but we should be able to move on together and make each other happy again.

When Will I See You Again – The Three Degrees

Just to leave Ingrid in no doubt who requested the song and that every time I say goodbye to her, I can't wait to see her again. Yes, it was me! I was the one who rang in. Now, when can I see you?

The titles alone definitely spelt his meaning out, Joel surmised. Might Ingrid panic at such an overt show of emotion? As Sam said, there was only one way to find out. All he needed to do now was decide when to send her the playlist, and that part... well, that part was going to take some nerve.

41

An eerie sense of déjà vu crept over Ingrid as she let herself into the shop. There stood Uma with Leo by her side. This time, however, there was another woman standing beside the previous visitor and she was so like Uma that she could only be her mother.

'I thought it was Dad trying to get in, so I came downstairs,' Leo said. 'But... it wasn't.'

'We decided to come to Willowbrook on the spur of the moment, and we managed to get a room at a travel inn place near the lake,' said Uma. 'I wanted to wait until tomorrow and message you first but—'

'But I couldn't wait, I'm afraid. I'm Maryam,' said the older woman.

Maryam stepped forward and held out a hand for Ingrid to shake. She was even more stunning than her daughter, if that was possible, with long chestnut-coloured hair in a plait down her back and large brown eyes.

'Hello Ingrid,' she said. 'I'm so sorry to drop in on you with no warning like this, but I thought if I didn't bite the bullet and come now, I'd never do it.'

Ingrid did her best to look welcoming, although she was longing for nothing more than to flop on the sofa and hear what Leo had thought of the broadcast. She pushed aside her qualms that the shock of finding this woman here had triggered, smiled at the visitor and offered her a cup of tea upstairs. Maryam didn't look confrontational but she was obviously very tense. Best to get this over with.

'Do you want me to come too, Mum?' asked Uma, her eyes wide with anxiety.

'Oh no... no I don't,' said Maryam quickly. 'We've got a lot to talk about, but we should do it on our own, I think. Perhaps...' She left the sentence unfinished, looking at Leo with appeal in her eyes.

'Hey, why don't I show you what we've got for sale in the shop,' Leo said to Uma, stepping up to the mark with a speed that impressed Ingrid. 'There's a kitchen down here too. We can have a Coke and chill for a bit.'

Uma didn't look convinced. She watched as Ingrid ushered her mother towards the stairs. 'Shout if you need me!' she called.

Maryam didn't reply. When they were safely in the flat with the door closed, she turned to Ingrid. 'I really am sorry not to give you more warning that I was on my way,' she said. 'But Uma told me all about this place and about you when she got back to Leicester and she's stirred up feelings that I've been burying for way too long. It's time for the truth.'

This sounded alarming. Ingrid offered tea and set about preparing a hospitality tray to be proud of, with an earthenware teapot she'd liberated from one of the boxes, china cups and saucers patterned with violets and a matching milk jug. There was even an embroidered tray cloth that had been tucked away in a drawer.

'This looks lovely,' said Maryam, her hands twisting together in her lap as she watched Ingrid moving around the kitchen area. 'I'm not sure you'll feel like spoiling me when you hear what I've come to say.'

Ingrid didn't reply for a moment. She busied herself pouring tea and making Maryam comfortable, and then sat back. 'Go ahead, I'm ready for whatever it is,' she said, with more bravery than she felt.

Maryam took a delicate sip of her tea and glanced around the room. 'You've got a very cosy home up here,' she said. 'Uma has told me how calmly you welcomed her the other day, which makes it even harder to say my piece.'

Ingrid waited. The silence lengthened. After another few tense moments, Maryam said, 'You see, Tommy came to see me after Uma discovered him, and it wasn't just the once. I imagine you didn't know that. And neither does my husband, of course.'

'I... I... no. I didn't know anything about you or Uma until she arrived at the shop.'

'So, it wasn't the case that you tried to block him from seeing her and refused to even meet her?'

Ingrid shook her head, blinking sudden tears from her eyes. 'No, absolutely not. He told you that, presumably?' Her husband's betrayal reared its head again, but this was worse. 'And you say he came to see you too?'

'He did, but Uma didn't know that. As far as she was concerned, it was a part of my past that I'd hidden, and it must never be spoken about. Also, my husband Rashid is very protective. He would have been horrified to think Tommy had approached me again after so long, and even more angry that I'd agreed to see him at all.'

There were so many questions battling for first place in Ingrid's mind that she had to give herself a moment to process all this. Then she said softly, 'How many times did you see him? Uma said she'd only known he was her father for a couple of years, since your illness.'

Maryam stood up and went over to the window, wrapping her arms around herself. 'It was four occasions in all,' she said eventually. 'He would arrange to be at a motorway services not far from my home in Leicester. It was never for more than an hour and he seemed on edge for most of the time we were together, but he insisted that we keep meeting. He... he said he'd never stopped loving me.'

The brutal words sliced through Ingrid's fragile composure. She gasped, the sound escaping as suddenly as if she'd been punched in the solar plexus. 'And you felt the same?' she managed to ask.

'I thought I did to begin with, but only very briefly. He was my first great love, you know. He broke my heart, and it took me months to get over him leaving. But by the last time we met, I'd had time to think properly about everything that happened, and I realised that I didn't love him. Maybe I never had. There's a special magic in meeting an old lover after a long time apart. But I soon realised that these few rather seedy liaisons with Tommy were just an exciting interlude in my life and the real gold I had was Rashid and Uma. Tommy didn't take it well when I said I wasn't going to see him any more. We never... I mean... I'm happily married. I believe in faithfulness.'

'You didn't sleep with him again?' Ingrid didn't know if this was a comfort or not. She guessed Tommy would have wanted to, and to meet at a motorway services where there was usually a Travelodge or similar available was a telltale sign.

'No, I did not. To tell the absolute truth, I think I was mainly curious to see what sort of man he'd become. And it was very romantic the first couple of times. He brought flowers. Of course I couldn't take them home with me, but I appreciated the gesture. I gave them to an elderly lady I know who never had any visitors, so they weren't wasted. Rashid isn't romantic. Not a bit. But he's a loyal, loving husband and father. I know I'm lucky. Tommy was... fun, exciting... but not very reliable, I think.'

She stopped speaking, seeming to realise she'd gone too far. Indeed, Ingrid felt bruised and battered. It had been hard enough to think that Tommy hadn't trusted her enough to know that she'd have welcomed his daughter. Now it looked as if her own supposedly loyal husband hadn't been that way at all.

'Why do you want to tell me all this?' she asked Maryam, genuinely bewildered. 'Is it some sort of revenge? Did you think I'd stolen him from you?'

Maryam came back to sit opposite Ingrid and met her gaze. 'Not at all. I'm not a vindictive person, but you'll have to take my word for that. I have given the whole sad situation a lot of thought,' she said. 'In the end I decided that if it was me, I'd want to have a full picture of what my man had been like before I moved on.'

'But I can't challenge him about it now,' Ingrid said huskily, as the ache in her throat grew, threatening to choke her. 'I'm just going to be stuck with a whole heap of anger. Wouldn't it have been better for me to have stayed in the dark about Tommy's other life?'

'Would you really want that?'

The question hung in the air. Ingrid shivered. No, actually she wouldn't. Painful as all this was, at least now she knew exactly what Tommy had been like. It was gradually dawning on her that perhaps it wasn't her fault that she hadn't had the overwhelming, passionate love for him that she'd seen other couples share. Maybe it was because he just wasn't that loveable. Entertaining, charismatic, attractive in a colourful, exuberant way but not someone who would open his heart to you and treat your own heart with care in return.

'I don't know if this would be helpful,' said Maryam. 'But when my grandfather died, a counsellor told me to write him a letter. We'd had a very... tricky relationship. I put all my angst down on paper, and then burned it. Write to Tommy and tell him how he's made you feel. It can't do any harm.'

She got up from the low sofa in one graceful movement. 'I'm leaving now. I'll spend the night with Uma in our accommodation and we'll go home tomorrow. Here's my mobile number.' She handed Ingrid a folded piece of paper. 'If you want to ask me anything else, feel free. Rashid is away tonight, trying to find a job. I hope he can find something. We really need a new start, but that's not your problem. I'm sorry, it's just that it's on my mind.'

Ingrid stood up to see Maryam out. Her head was spinning. She needed time to process all this, and then she was meant to be going with Joel to visit Anthea and afterwards for dinner. She heard the buzz of new conversation as Maryam joined Uma and Leo and wondered vaguely what excuse Uma's mother would give for her need to speak to Ingrid alone. Would she let her daughter know exactly what kind of man Tommy had been or would she allow Uma's memories of him to be undamaged? A groan escaped Ingrid's lips. Life was getting way too complicated, and she was tired of being buffeted from one crisis to another. Visiting Anthea with Joel might turn out to be even more unsettling. Maybe she should cancel him and go to see Anthea alone, once she'd double-checked with the hospital staff that a short visit would be allowed.

Even as the thought crossed her mind, Ingrid knew she wouldn't do that. To see Joel would make the day worthwhile. She didn't want to examine her reasons for feeling like this, so she took Maryam's advice and rummaged in a drawer for some notepaper and a pen.

Dear Tommy, she wrote, before she could change her mind.

I've missed you in a lot of ways since you left me so suddenly but now, I'm done. You were great fun for most of the time, but it turns out you not only ran up some hideous debts, but you cheated on me (and probably would have gone the whole hog if Maryam had let you), deceived me and lied about me to those nice, gentle people. I have met someone who I know I could fall for in a big way but he seems to still be emotionally entangled with his ex. So, Tommy Copperfield, I'm going to carry on alone, and have the best kind of life that I can. I'm not sorry I met and married you, we had some great times, but enough is enough. I'm selling your junk, I'm going to find somewhere lovely to live, somewhere just for me and I'm never going to look back over my shoulder again.

With affection, and probably more love than you ever deserved,

Ingers x

Ingrid heard Leo go out into the street to see the visitors off. Before Leo had a chance to come back inside, she picked up the matches she'd been using to light her candles with in the evenings, ran down the stairs and let herself out into the yard behind the shop. There, she set fire to her letter and watched the smoke curl upwards and the flames consume the sheet of paper.

'Goodbye, Tommy,' she whispered. 'This seems much more permanent than your funeral ever was. It's over.'

42

A heavy shower of early-evening rain had made the pavements shine by the time Joel picked Ingrid up in his van the next evening, once she'd at last been given the green light to visit Anthea. He'd given the elderly vehicle a wash in her honour and removed the evidence of several weeks of snacks from the floor, but he still wished he had a less workmanlike mode of transport to take her to the hospital and out for dinner in. He jumped down to open the passenger door when Ingrid emerged from the back of the shop wearing a long, black raincoat, and she gave him a grateful look.

'I'm so glad to see you,' she said. 'Sorry to appear dressed as the Grim Reaper but stupidly I got rid of most of my more useful coats when I moved, and I've only got this one of Tommy's. He was wider than me, so it'll flap a bit too. Not a great look.'

'Looks fine to me. Mine's ridiculously short compared to that one though. When we go into the hospital, people will think you're taking your small boy to have his tonsils out, or something.'

Joel closed his eyes and wished he hadn't spoken. Would she think he was referring to their age difference? Ingrid didn't seem fazed by this image. She yawned and rubbed her eyes. 'Whatever. *What people think* is the least of my worries.'

'Why? The radio show was great. What's gone wrong?'

'Let's save it for later. Can we have some music instead?' Ingrid put on her seatbelt and looked hopefully at the radio.

Joel was tempted to go straight in there with his playlist which was primed and ready on his phone but resisted the urge and leaned forward to flick a switch on the dashboard instead. Soon they were bowling along the back roads into town and Ingrid was humming along to a romantic Eric Clapton track that Joel was now wishing he'd included on his list.

'Do you like this one?' he asked, as the van splashed through a huge puddle and rocked over an equally large pothole.

'I love the tune,' Ingrid said. 'But come on, Joel, he's taking the mick, isn't he?'

'How do you mean? He's telling her she looks wonderful tonight. That's good, isn't it?'

Ingrid laughed, somewhat bitterly. 'Oh yes, he can talk the talk but all he actually wants to do is to party, get drunk and then for her to drive him home and put him to bed. He needs a chauffeur and a nanny, not a lover.'

Joel negotiated another pothole and switched the wipers on to combat the driving rain that had started again. He wondered if Ingrid was going to be this cynical about his playlist choices. He really hoped not. Had her softer side been soured by something that had happened in her marriage? Perhaps she just wasn't the romantic kind, in which case he'd wasted a lot of time and effort on trying to show his true feelings. He sighed.

'What's up? Did you have a bad day too?' she asked.

'No, it was mostly good. I've started a new commission and tomorrow the Hendersons have asked me to site their bench for them and join them when they have a short dedication of it. The vicar's coming to say a few words. Her name's the Rev Bev. She's the right person for the job. She does—'

'A good funeral. So I hear,' said Ingrid. 'Beryl's very impressed with her, but then I guess as you get older, you get to be more of a connoisseur of such things. Anyway, on a lighter note, I spoke to Anthea earlier, they brought the phone over to her. She thinks she might be allowed out tomorrow so I'm going to have to finish getting her room ready in the morning before I open the shop.'

Joel wondered how to slow this whole process down without offending Ingrid. It was incredibly kind of her to offer to have Anthea to stay but he couldn't help feeling it was too soon. 'Erm... aren't you jumping the gun a bit? What if the doctors think she needs more specialist care to get back on her feet?'

Ingrid frowned at him. 'Do you really think they will?'

'I wouldn't be at all surprised. Might be best to have a word with someone as soon as we get there.'

Ingrid didn't answer but she was clearly giving the matter serious thought by the preoccupied look on her face. They drove in silence for a while, as a segue of Beatles songs followed the unfortunate Mr Clapton. Joel wondered if he'd be doomed forever to wish he'd picked better tracks for Ingrid. The one she was currently singing along to was called 'I Will' and perfectly summed up his hopes for their future. Never mind, if his new tactic was successful and won her over, he could make her plenty more mixes, and if not, well... Joel's mind shied away from the alternative as he drove into the hospital car park. *That way madness lies*, he told himself.

Anthea was out of bed and sitting in a lurid pink wipe-clean armchair when they arrived. She stood up when Ingrid and Joel approached but tottered slightly.

'Thanks for coming,' she said as she eased herself back into her seat. 'Pull up a couple of chairs. I can't wait for you to bust me out of this crazy joint.'

A passing nurse pulled a face at Anthea and she chortled. 'I didn't mean anything bad about you, darling,' she said. 'The staff are all angels.' She lowered her voice and gestured with her head to the other inhabitants of the side ward. 'It's the rest of them.'

'Could I have a quick word?' Ingrid said to the nurse, making to follow her to the central nurses' station. 'Back in a minute,' she said to Anthea.

Joel fetched chairs, then glanced around at the other inhabitants of the ward and smiled nervously. He was met with three blank gazes.

'Lavinia over there must be ninety if she's a day and she spends the night calling for her mother, the woman in the corner who only answers to the name "Mrs Prendergast" reckons she needs the toilet every five minutes and as for my neighbour, Gertie, she tried to get in bed with me last night and then stole my shortbread biscuits. I want to go home.'

Joel chatted inconsequentially about shop matters and village gossip until, after what seemed a very long ten minutes, he saw Ingrid coming back.

Ingrid sat down and cleared her throat. 'I suppose the nurses have mentioned to you that I'd love it if you'd come and stay with me while you recuperate?' she asked. 'Just for a short time,' she added when she noticed Anthea's ferocious stare.

'They did say something about that, but I'll be fine at home. There's no need for you to bother yourself. I'm quite capable of—'

The same nurse came back as Anthea spoke. 'Oh no you're not, and you know it,' she said. 'Don't forget you nearly went headfirst into the shower cubicle this morning and you're not fit to cook for yourself yet. We only want you to be safe. I think you should be saying thank you for the invitation rather than arguing, but before that happens, your friend here and I have discussed with the doctor what you need next.'

'You see what I have to put up with?' said Anthea. 'Bullies, all of them.' But she reached out and grasped the nurse's hand as she spoke. 'I'm sorry, Ingrid. I'm being ungrateful. It's just that I've always been independent. Husbands and lovers come and go but I can rely on my own company. Can you fetch me tomorrow?'

'Well, that's the thing. The lovely staff here are really worried that I won't be able to manage the transition while you get your strength back, so they've found a room for you in the residential part of Cedar Grove, just for—'

'Hang on a minute!' burst out Anthea. 'That's a last resort for *old people*. Isn't it where your aunt Sylvia's got a place? I don't want to—'

'Let's just talk about this calmly,' said the nurse, exchanging glances with Ingrid. 'It's only for a very short while and then you'll be able to move in with your kind friend until you can go home. We like to do these things in stages, you see.'

After another few protests, Anthea finally gave in, but without enthusiasm.

Ingrid followed the nurse back to the reception desk to make the arrangements if Anthea should be deemed well enough to leave in the morning. Joel edged closer to Anthea and said, 'You'll like Cedar Grove, it's a friendly place. My gran was there for a while.'

'Yes, I remember. She died.' Anthea grimaced. 'Is that supposed to be an encouraging recommendation?'

Joel laughed. 'Sorry, that didn't sound too good, did it? But my gran was a hundred and two when she went, after all, and it'll be better for Ingrid not to be responsible for this first bit of convalescence, especially while she's trying to get the shop going. When you're ready, you'll still be able to have a great time at Ingrid's, you know. It's all happening there.'

'What do you mean?'

Joel tapped the side of his nose and gave her his best mysterious look. 'I'll leave it to Ingrid to fill you in, but there have been *developments*, and I don't even know the whole story myself yet. You definitely won't be bored.'

Anthea was looking a lot more cheerful by the time Ingrid returned, and the rest of the visit passed peacefully with only one sticky moment when Gertie wandered along and sat on Joel's knee.

'You're a nice bit of stuff,' she said, with a toothless grin. 'Is he yours?'

This question was directed at Ingrid, who blushed and shook her head.

'Well, can I have him then?' said Gertie, hopefully. It was a while before two nurses were able to persuade her back to bed and by that time Joel was starting to check his watch.

'I'm taking Ingrid out for dinner, so we'll need to head off now,' he said to Anthea.

'An excellent idea and about time too,' she answered, but to his relief, didn't elaborate on this statement.

Soon, the van was chugging back along the road towards Willowbrook. The rain had stopped now, and the clouds were clearing at last. Joel took a right turn and pulled into a small car park beside a long, low building. There was a green and white striped canopy over the front of the restaurant and olive trees in pots either side of the door. The sign proclaimed this to be Concetto's.

'I love this place,' said Joel as he helped Ingrid down from the van. 'I usually come with Leo, and sometimes with Sam if he can get a sitter,' he added, in case Ingrid got the impression he was always wining and dining other women. 'She's a big fan of Concetto's pizzas.'

As he opened the door, the mingled aromas of garlic and herbs made Joel's stomach rumble in anticipation. He hoped Ingrid was hungry. She was sniffing the air rapturously now, which was a good sign.

'I'm ravenous,' she said. 'And I feel wide awake again. I think I've been worrying about how much care Anthea will need but she looked better than I expected. I'll have to keep her amused but that's easy enough with everything that's been going on.'

'Let's order and you can tell me the next instalment,' said Joel as they were ushered to their corner table by a waiter.

For a while, Ingrid and Joel were kept occupied by choosing their food and chatting to the owner, who burst out of the kitchen to hug Joel and, after being introduced to Ingrid, kissed her on both cheeks. Eventually they were left in peace with a basket of bread, a jug of iced water and a small flagon of red wine for Ingrid.

'I wish you didn't have to drive,' said Ingrid, as he filled her glass.

Joel thought it was probably just as well he wasn't drinking. At least this way he wouldn't accidentally let slip all kinds of embarrassing declarations. They settled down to wait for their starters, Joel having happily abandoned his original plan of a quick main course and home.

'Right, fill me in on what's been going on at The Treasure Trove,' he said, leaning back and preparing to listen.

Ingrid was only part way through telling him about Maryam's visit when they were presented with a sharing platter of delicious-looking cured meats, olives and other antipasti. They were finishing their main courses when she finally ended her story.

Joel drained his water glass and wished very much he'd decided to get a taxi. 'That's some story,' he said. 'You certainly don't lead a dull life.'

'I dream of having a dull life,' Ingrid said. Her cheeks were flushed now, and as he watched, she released her hair from its clip and ran her fingers through it, leaning back in her chair. It was the first time Joel had seen Ingrid looking anything less than groomed and ready for the day. He thought she looked absolutely adorable, as if she was about ready to tumble into bed. His bed. He tried hard to pull himself together.

'Have you got room for pudding?' he asked.

'Just coffee, I think. I'll be asleep before you get me home otherwise.'

They ordered, and Ingrid excused herself to go to the cloakroom. Joel felt his phone vibrate in his pocket. It was Sam.

> Did you do the deed? If not, why not? Send that playlist NOW.

Joel stuffed the phone back in his pocket as Ingrid returned. 'I... I've got something to send to you. Have you by any chance got Spotify on your phone?' he said.

'Well, if you'd asked me that a couple of weeks ago, I'd have said no, but Leo's been educating me on her music, so now I have. I made my first playlist the other day,' she said proudly.

'Great.' The moment had come, and Joel's heart was racing.

'Go on then,' Ingrid said. 'Are you going to send me one of yours? I hope you're not in competition with your daughter to change my tastes. Is it ancient prog rock? Please say it isn't.'

'Let's have our coffee and then I'll take you home and send it over later. That way you can give it a listen when you get up tomorrow.'

'Okay. Music to have a shower to, in that case? Or a soundtrack to munching cornflakes?'

Joel didn't reply. Suddenly this all seemed like a very bad idea.

43

Lulled by the wine and a certain amount of relief that Anthea's visit was going to be postponed until she was more mobile, Ingrid slept deeply after her outing with Joel and woke later than usual. Leo was almost ready for school when Ingrid emerged from the shower and had left the usual trail of destruction behind her. Dashing around the flat, simultaneously tidying and nagging Leo to help her and trying to find something ironed to wear, Ingrid didn't think about Joel's promise to send her a playlist until her houseguest was safely out of the way and peace descended at last.

'Where did I put my phone?' she muttered to herself, rummaging under sofa cushions and beneath her duvet in her haste to find it, but although she searched everywhere she could think of, it wasn't to be found. What she did discover, to her alarm, was Leo's phone nestling among the toast crumbs on the kitchen worktop.

'For goodness' sake!' she yelled at it, pointlessly.

Sitting down at the table, Ingrid stared at the offending

object. Leo's phone was locked and Ingrid had no idea what the code was to get into it.

This mix-up had happened once before due to the fact that their handsets were very similar but that time the mistake was discovered fairly quickly when Leo had started fretting because Baz hadn't been in touch. Luckily, at this moment Ingrid heard the now familiar rat-a-tat-tat at the front door, as Beryl and Winnie announced their presence. One if not both of them would have a phone with them.

'Hello, dear,' said Beryl, bustling into the shop followed by Winnie. 'We've brought supplies. Can't have you providing bed and board for poor Anthea on your own. I've made a fruit cake and sausage rolls and Winnie's brought a goat curry and all sorts of other spicy stuff.'

'That's wonderful, thank you so much. I'll freeze them. She's not coming here just yet, she's going to have some respite first but more importantly, have you got a phone?' Ingrid gabbled, glancing at the clock. 'I was supposed to ring the hospital to say I'd meet her at Cedar Grove. She'll be fretting. It was hard enough persuading her that the change of plan was a good idea.'

'Of course I've got a phone, I'm not a dinosaur,' said Beryl. 'It's one of the latest iPhones, I'll have you know. My niece helped me to choose it. It can—'

'I'm sure it can do lots of things, but can I borrow it, please? Leo's accidentally taken mine again. I really want to see Anthea settled in.'

Beryl fished her phone out of her bag, unlocked it and handed it over. Ingrid ran back upstairs, found the hospital number and five minutes later she was grabbing her bag and telling the others she'd hopefully be back as quickly as possible.

A New Lease of Life

'No rush, love,' said Winnie, settling herself comfortably on a stool behind the counter. 'We'll open up for you.'

'You guys have been here more than me lately. I promise I'll make it up to you as soon as I can,' Ingrid said, leaving the two of them protesting that they were loving being in the shop as she left through the storeroom.

Ingrid reached Cedar Grove just as the hospital transfer ambulance was pulling out of the car park. She checked out Anthea's new accommodation, arranged her clothes in the wardrobe and then found the lady herself seated in a very pleasant lounge, waiting for her room to be ready.

'I want to talk to you,' Anthea said, pulling Ingrid down to sit beside her. 'You really didn't need to come here this morning. I know you're busy, but I'm glad you did.'

Ingrid obeyed, but perched on the edge of the sofa ready to make a getaway, feeling guilty about leaving the others to man the shop.

Anthea looked at Ingrid with her head on one side. 'So, what are you going to do about that nice young Joel?' she said.

That was a tricky one. 'Do?' said Ingrid, hedging for time.

'Yes. You must be able to tell he likes you. Are you still hung up on that husband of yours? Is that the problem?'

Ingrid decided that shop or no shop, she'd need to put Anthea straight about the developments with Uma and Maryam. She made herself more comfortable and launched into the tale. Anthea was satisfyingly agog, and interrupted several times with questions but eventually Ingrid reached the point where Maryam went away to spend the night with her daughter.

'I don't suppose I'll ever see her again,' she said. 'But it cleared the air, and now I'm beginning to understand that marriage with Tommy was just a chapter. I can leave it behind now. There were good parts and not so great times. He wasn't honest with me about his past and he went behind my back to meet Maryam but it's over.'

'That's wonderful news. And Joel's free too.'

'But he isn't, is he? He's still in love with his ex-wife.'

Anthea burst out laughing, making herself cough and hold her side. When she'd calmed down, she said, 'Who told you that?'

'Erm... Leo did.'

'That girl's impossible. She never gives up.' Anthea raised her eyes to the ceiling and tutted loudly. 'She's been convinced her mother was coming home ever since the two of them left Joel. Trina's got no intention of ever being Joel's wife again and even if she had, he'd never have her back. He's moved on, and Leo needs to do the same. He might have regretted Trina leaving just to begin with but that was years ago.'

The wave of relief that Ingrid was experiencing took her breath away for a moment. 'Are you sure, Anthea?' she asked, when she could speak.

'Certain. I've known Joel since he was a little boy; so have Beryl and Winnie. He can't hide anything from us. And what we want now is to see him happily settled with a woman who'll care about him properly. That's you, Ingrid.'

'But he's never said anything...'

As she spoke, Ingrid suddenly remembered the playlist. She slapped herself on her forehead and groaned. 'Oh yes, he has,' she said. 'Or at least I think he's trying to tell me something important and I've got no idea what it is. Damn and blast houseguests. Not you, Anthea,' she added hastily when she saw the look of horror on Anthea's face. 'You're going to be more than welcome when you arrive. It's Leo. She's taken my phone

A New Lease of Life

with her by mistake and now I can't see what music playlist he's sent me.'

Anthea was silent for a few seconds and then she said, 'Spotify?'

'Yes! How did you know? Do you use it too?'

The older lady looked mildly outraged. 'Of course I do. We're bang up to date, us Super-Silver-Surfers,' she said. 'We're always sending each other compilations. You can find any music you like these days. It's marvellous. My friend Maurice,' she batted her eyelashes and made an attempt to look coy, '... well, you wouldn't believe the songs he's sent me. It's enough to make you choke on your Battenberg.'

Ingrid laughed. 'I bet it is. I'll have to go now and make sure the others are okay,' she said. 'But as soon as I get hold of my phone, I'll find out once and for all how Joel feels about me.'

'Don't forget to keep me posted,' Anthea said. 'And now if you don't mind, I think I'll get them to take me to my new room and have a little nap. All this excitement's quite worn me out.'

44

Typically, as often happens when you're waiting desperately for something, random delays come along to make the wait even longer and more agonising. This was the case for Ingrid as she clock-watched and paced the floor of the shop, which was now closed. Where was Leo? She was usually back long before this and there was no way of checking where the girl had got to since their phones were in totally the wrong places.

Finally, at half past six, Ingrid heard the back door open, and Leo emerged through the storeroom doorway into the shop. Even before she saw her, it was blatantly obvious that Leo was crying. She was making piteous whimpering noises and tears were flowing down her cheeks, dripping off her chin. Without a word she flung herself into Ingrid's outstretched arms.

'He hates me!' she wailed, when she finally managed. 'It's over. Baz has dumped me.'

'Really?' asked Ingrid, trying to muster sympathy when her gut feeling was one of delight. She wondered how soon she could reasonably ask for her phone back, but it clearly wasn't yet as Leo resumed her sobs, louder now.

'He said... he said I didn't care about him because I never answered his messages. I realised I had the wrong phone as soon as I got to school but the horrible history teacher confiscated it even before my first lesson. He said I was using it in assembly, the git. I was just trying to think of a way to swap back without leaving the school. Then I got a detention for arguing with him about it, so that made me even later.'

'And you saw Baz after that?'

'Yes, he was really nasty to me. He called me a liar.'

Ingrid had the feeling she was walking into a minefield. 'And you're upset that it's over or that he was horrible?' she said, playing for time.

Leo didn't answer.

'Look, I've made dinner and it's ready. Come and have some of my special chicken and vegetable soup. You'll feel better when you've had something to eat.'

Leo looked mutinous. 'I can't eat. I'm too upset,' she said, but she followed Ingrid up the stairs and sat at the table.

Ingrid served the soup and Leo started to eat with enthusiasm. Relieved that the brief hunger strike was over, Ingrid handed Leo the TV controls.

'I'm just going downstairs...' began Ingrid, but Leo wasn't listening, already absorbed in an old episode of *Friends*. 'Can I have my phone back now please?' she said more loudly. Ingrid placed Leo's phone on the table and, still eating happily, Leo reached into her pocket and passed Ingrid her own phone.

In the shop, Ingrid sat down out of view of the street and clicked on the app she needed. Immediately she was presented with a playlist entitled *Just For You*. She pressed play and the first song rang out. 'Let Your Love Flow'. Ingrid had always loved this one and the joyful music was just what she needed to lift her mood, but as the list played on, the lump in her throat grew bigger and bigger until she was crying nearly as hard as Leo had been earlier.

'He loves me,' she whispered to herself, wiping her eyes. 'He really loves me. He thinks I'm the one for him.'

When the final song told her that, yes, it had been Joel who'd phoned in to the radio station to say he wondered when he'd see her again, she knew it was time to call him, but now seemed like totally the wrong moment. She had Joel's daughter upstairs who was not only traumatised by the break-up of her own relationship but who'd made it clear that she wouldn't approve of her beloved dad drawing a firm line under his relationship with her mother.

As she pondered, her phone's screen lit up with Joel's name, and taking a deep breath, she answered the call, trying hard not to let on that she'd been crying.

'Hi Joel.'

'Hello, are you okay? You sound kind of... gaspy.'

'I'm fine. My phone was in your daughter's bag all day. Long story. I've only just managed to listen to your playlist, and it's made me a bit emotional.'

'Ah. Emotional in a good way... or not?'

'Definitely a good way.'

'Right. Well, that's a start. I've been on tenterhooks all day thinking you didn't like it, and all because of Leo.'

'But sorted now. It's beautiful, Joel. Such lovely choices. I'd like to say thank you properly.'

'You can do that right now. I'm outside your back door.'

Ingrid dropped her phone as if it was made of molten metal and turned, just as Joel entered the shop. He came to the door of the storeroom and beckoned her in. As if on autopilot, Ingrid moved towards him and as soon as he was near enough, he reached out and pulled her close. Held tightly in his arms, Ingrid breathed in the mingled scents of sawdust, shampoo and healthy, clean man. He smelt wonderful and he felt even better, as he pressed her to him and bent to kiss her. The kiss went on for so long that Ingrid's head was spinning, her whole body feeling as if it was melting into Joel's.

At last they came up for air and both started to speak at the same time.

'So are you—?'

'Does this mean—?'

They laughed. 'You first,' said Joel.

'Thanks. So, are you really over Trina? Completely over her, I mean?'

Joel stroked Ingrid's face and kissed her again, long and hard. 'Yes,' he said. 'And have been for years. Does that answer your question?'

She nodded. 'Now your turn.'

'Does this mean, you and me... are we... together now?'

'I've never felt more together with anybody in my whole life,' Ingrid answered truthfully, following Joel's example and using another kiss to convince him.

They were still entwined and had no plans to do anything else for some time when the storeroom door opened, and a small voice said, 'I heard you come in and guessed you might be doing this. It's a bit yukky, to be honest, Dad.'

Ingrid pushed Joel away with both hands and felt her face flaming. 'Oh Leo, I'm sorry, I—'

'Well, I'm not sorry, and neither should you be,' said Joel firmly. 'It's time for some honesty. I love Ingrid and I'm pretty sure she feels the same about me, unless she's a very good actor. I hope you'll be pleased for us when you get used to the idea. It's not going to change the way you and me are, Leo. We'll just need to adjust a bit. There's more than enough love to go round.'

Leo didn't reply for a moment. Then she shrugged. 'Okay... I suppose. Do we all have to live together now though?'

Joel looked at Ingrid and she shook her head. 'Of course we don't. It's much too soon to think about anything like that. We're fine as we are for now,' she said. 'When I've finished with the shop, I'm going to buy somewhere just for me. Somewhere very near to here, if I can. That's as far as my plans go. The way things are going, I think by Christmas I'll be ready to move. After that, who knows? But wherever I am, you'll always be my favourite houseguest.'

'Would you both like to go out for dinner?' Joel asked. 'I'm suddenly starving.'

'To celebrate, you mean?' There was an edge to Leo's voice and Ingrid was alarmed to see the mutinous look return to her face. She smiled at her in what she hoped was a reassuring way. 'Let's just stay here. Joel and I can have the rest of the chicken soup and we can open a bottle of wine. There's a cheesecake in the fridge, Leo. We might help you eat it.'

So that was how Ingrid marked her first evening's partnership with Joel. There was nothing in the least romantic about it on the surface, but Ingrid felt more alive and buzzing than she had for years. Or ever, if she was completely honest. The soup was a resounding success, and the three of them dug out Sylvia's old Monopoly set and played a fiercely competitive game before Joel got up to clear the kitchen.

'I've got to kiss you again before I go home or I'll explode,' Joel whispered to Ingrid as they washed up together. 'Come and see me out.'

Leo watched them go and rolled her eyes at them,

mumbling, 'Yuk,' and 'Get a room,' but Ingrid didn't care a jot. All she could think about was being in Joel's arms again. They barely made it to the back door before the kissing began. It was definitely more X-rated this time, and it was some time before they came up for air.

'When will I see you again?' Joel said, his voice muffled as he kissed his way down Ingrid's neck, making her shiver with longing. 'Hey, that sounds like the cue for a song.'

Ingrid tried to prise her body away from his, but it was impossible to leave the warmth of his arms just yet. 'The short answer is, as soon as possible,' she said. 'I'm not playing games. Except Monopoly, of course, which incidentally, you won by ganging up on me with Leo.'

'As if.' Joel finally loosened his hold on Ingrid and placed his hands on her shoulders. 'I'm weaning myself away from you bit by bit now, but it's not easy. I'll message you when I get home,' he said. 'And probably in the morning too. Let me know if it gets too much. It's such a novelty knowing that you feel the same way. You don't mind, do you?' he added anxiously. 'I don't want to crowd you.'

'Not one bit. So long as I've got the right phone, I'm your woman to text. Now off you go, or I'll have your daughter breathing down my neck. We're going to need to tread carefully there.'

Joel kissed Ingrid once more before finally leaving, a less lingering one this time but somehow, even more loving. She heard the van trundle away and wondered how she was going to sleep with this crazy, fizzing sensation inside her.

'Are you ever coming back upstairs, Ings?' called Leo. 'I've found an old Cluedo set in the sideboard. Are you up for another game?'

Ingrid climbed the stairs slowly, thinking how much her

life had changed since Joel and Sam had dropped her here, straight into a most exciting village where she could find friends, a wonderful second chance at love and hopefully a permanent home.

'Yes I am, but I'll win this time. Onwards and upwards!' Ingrid shouted back. And actually, she reflected happily, those words summed up this new life quite perfectly.

45

EIGHT MONTHS LATER – CHRISTMAS

The shop felt strange and slightly eerie in its almost-empty state, and Ingrid's voice echoed as she called to Leo and Uma who were upstairs in the flat. Uma had become quite a regular visitor in the last few months, fascinated by the treasures in the shop and keen to help whenever she had free time. Leo seemed equally happy to have made a new friend, and the two were now busy getting the food ready together and dog-sitting Gerald, who was now a permanent fixture in Joel's life, and making sure he wasn't anywhere near the sausage rolls.

'Hey, girls. We've only got an hour before they all arrive,' Ingrid shouted. 'Will we manage it?'

'You bet your life we will,' shouted back Leo. 'The cavalry are on their way. Dad messaged to say he's stopped off to get more bubbly and the Saga Louts are just coming down from Beryl's.'

Right on cue, Beryl, Anthea and Winnie appeared at the front door laden with bags, and Sam and Elsie followed them in. Sam was carrying a large artificial Christmas tree under one arm and Elsie had a carrier bag that jingled intriguingly.

'Action stations, troops,' said Beryl, as Anthea quickly erected a folding table and Winnie began to unpack enough party nibbles to feed most of the residents of Willowbrook.

'I hope there's enough,' Sam said doubtfully. 'If only you hadn't invited so many people, we could have done pizzas and kept it simple.'

'Pizzas? Are you kidding? I wanted the shop to go out with a bang, not with a soggy Margherita. We're going to do our Ingrid proud tonight,' said Winnie, waving to Joel as he staggered in with a crate of prosecco.

Ingrid looked around the room as she unboxed champagne flutes onto the table that had previously held the bargain offers. Most of the shelves had been moved back to the wall and the ladies had provided a fine selection of garden chairs for the more infirm visitors to perch on. The navy sofa with its cushions and throws was still in place, and as she watched, Ingrid saw exactly why her Treasure Team had made the previous months so special. They worked seamlessly together, making the shop into the perfect place for a Christmas party.

Leo and Uma were now bringing trays of hot mince pies and sausage rolls and various dishes of salad down from the flat and Elsie was absorbed in adding string after string of silver bells to the tree. Sam had already twined coloured lights around it, and by the time Elsie was satisfied with her work, he was ready to switch them on. The empty shelves had twinkling white lights draped around them, and the effect was magical.

'You're all amazing,' Ingrid said, turning off most of the main lights to appreciate the beauty of the scene. 'The guests of honour should be here soon and then the rest of the people we invited. This is going to be a fabulous swansong and welcome at the same time. Let's have some festive music to get us in the mood.'

A New Lease of Life

The sound of Elton John filled the room as he asked them all to step into Christmas. Joel had made sure the prosecco was handy for the glasses, and he was standing beside Ingrid observing the proceedings too. She felt him slip an arm around her and give her a squeeze. They were avoiding overt shows of affection when other people were around, partly because they both found that kind of thing tacky and partly because Leo was sometimes still prickly if she caught them holding hands. Joel noticed his daughter watching them, but he left his arm where it was.

'She'll get used to it,' he said when Ingrid made as if to move away. 'It's a good job she likes you so much.'

Ingrid was about to reply when the shop door opened and three people came in together. The procession was regally led by Sylvia Nightingale and behind her, looking nervous, came Maryam and her husband, who was now known to them all as Rashid. The two of them had visited together the previous month for the first time. Ingrid wasn't sure how Maryam had squared her wish to make contact again with Rashid but Uma seemed to have had a big hand in it, and they looked delighted to be at the party, if a little daunted.

'Here we are,' announced Sylvia. 'I hope we're not late. Is the fizz open yet?'

Leo came forward to say hello to the new arrivals and presented Uma's family with chilled glasses of orange juice, while Joel made sure Sylvia had prosecco. 'It might make her crack her face with a smile, for once,' muttered Joel under his breath to Ingrid. 'She always gives me her best mean glare.'

'Oh, leave the poor woman alone,' said Ingrid, grinning. 'She's finally made the right decision about her shop, or that's what I think anyway. Cut her some slack.'

Within half an hour, the shop was as full as it could

possibly be, and the villagers who'd been invited to this event, plus a few more who'd invited themselves, were making determined inroads into the drinks and looking hopefully at the tables of food. Ingrid reached for the brass bell that she'd previously kept on the counter to signify closing time and gave it a shake. The hubbub of conversation paused, and she jumped in quickly.

'I think you all know why we're throwing this party,' she said. 'But I'm going to ask my Aunt Sylvia to say a few words just to formalise the event.'

Sylvia stood up, looking rather pink in the cheeks. She took a final swig from her glass and held it out to Joel for a refill. 'This stuff's going down very nicely,' she said, with a genteel burp. 'Of course, it's a shame you didn't run to real champagne, but it was a nice touch to have a little get-together.'

She looked round at the assembled company. 'I just want to say that although not everyone thought my niece's idea of opening The Treasure Trove was a good one...'

'Bloody Lennie,' mumbled Joel, and Ingrid nudged him sharply. She was glad her cousin hadn't gate-crashed the party as she'd had a feeling he might, thinking there'd be safety in numbers and not wanting to miss the action. The haunting memory of what happened between them was fading now, but the last thing she needed was an encounter with Lennie.

'...I must say,' continued Sylvia, with only a slight slurring of her words, 'I must say that in the end it proved to be a big success and had the bonus result of introducing us to the Habeeb family, who are going to reinstate my little shop as a proper general store. Maryam, Rashid, Uma and her brothers will be moving in after Christmas and hope to have the place up and running very soon.'

The Habeebs looked embarrassed but pleased as everyone clapped. Sylvia was on a roll now.

'I was undecided as to whether I should just sell the shop and flat. My boys both thought that was the best option...'

Joel snorted at this, but Ingrid shushed him.

'But having listened to local opinion, it seems that there's still very much a need for a friendly, local store and I'm very happy to say that the Habeebs have agreed to rent the old place from me for a year to see if they can make it pay. I'll pass you over to Maryam and Rashid now, who are going to say a few words.'

Ingrid watched as the couple, both dressed smartly and giving off an aura of shy friendliness, stood together in front of the crowd.

'We won't keep you long, because I'm sure you're keen to get to the important part of the evening – the food,' said Rashid, generating a number of cheers. 'We just want to say how happy we are to be making a fresh start in your beautiful village. We hope to stock everything you need, but if it's not on the shelves when you come in, please ask and we'll do our utmost to provide it next time.'

Maryam nodded her agreement. 'The success of any village store these days is based on a joint effort, in our opinion,' she said, smiling around. 'Supermarkets are cheaper, but they're not so handy and they don't give you that personal touch. You need to use us or lose us, as they say, and we aim to provide a wonderful service to keep you doing just that. It's a team effort, just as I know The Treasure Trove has been. So, let's raise our glasses to new beginnings and new friends. Cheers!'

Maryam raised her glass of orange juice and everyone else followed suit. Joel began to circle the room refilling glasses as the Saga Louts made sure all the food was uncovered. Taking the chance of some fresh air, Ingrid slipped out of the back door and into the courtyard. She leaned against the wall gazing at the stars and wondering why a wave of butterflies in her stomach was making her feel as if she was on the brink of something alarming.

Five minutes later, she heard footsteps and Kate came to stand beside her. In the last months, Ingrid had visited the café in the country park as often as she could and she and Kate had become friends, but they had never yet discussed anything too serious. Now, Kate's expression was thoughtful.

'I guessed from the look on your face that you're having a few second thoughts about what comes next, but I think you're doing the right thing renting a log cabin on the country park for a while before you decide whether to settle here for good,' she said. 'You can have space to be on your own with Joel there too. Now his daughter's back living with him, you'll not be wanting to spend all your time at his.'

Ingrid turned to face Kate. 'I've had the feeling for a few weeks now that you were wanting to give me some advice, but you were holding back for some reason,' she said. 'Is that true?'

'Well, yes. I was worried that you were going to leap straight into living with Joel. After my marriage fell apart, or imploded would be a more accurate description, I met Milo and I think everyone who knew me was secretly fantasising about us having this perfect romantic life in a cottage with a dog and a cat, and also with his son thinking I was marvellous and all that sort of thing.'

'And that's not what you wanted?'

Kate shook her head. 'I like us living in our own spaces,' she said. 'I'm in Fiddler's Row and Milo's over the café. We do share a dog and the cat now, but they live with Milo. His son Luka's

A New Lease of Life

getting used to me more and more too. All I wanted to say was that I think you'll like living by yourself, even if it's just for a while. And I'm going back in now because I can see Joel approaching. Don't tell him I was sticking my nose in, okay?'

Kate gave Ingrid a brief hug and then grinned at Joel as he came out into the courtyard.

'Is it going well in there?' Kate asked him.

'It sure is. The food and the fizz have nearly all disappeared. It's been a great party, and it's good for everyone to have met the Habeebs too. The shop's going to have a whole new lease of life with them in charge.'

Kate left and went inside. Joel came towards Ingrid and held out his arms.

'Well done for tonight. It's all gone really smoothly,' he said, pulling her close. The thing with Joel's spectacular kisses, Ingrid reflected, was that they put every other thought right out of your head. This one was particularly scorching, and Ingrid's whole body responded as if it was on fire. As Joel released her reluctantly, she finally remembered something important.

'I made you a playlist,' she said, somewhat breathlessly. 'And I've already sent it, so whenever you're ready...'

Joel didn't answer, but his face said it all. His eyes shone and he began to kiss her again, but she pushed him away gently.

'I just wanted you to know how much you've meant to me since I came here. To begin with when I left York, the next part seemed pretty scary but I think I was trying to rush into it. The shop's been great, but it was only ever meant to be a stepping stone. I thought I'd be ready to buy somewhere permanent by now but we're still finding out about each other, and we need our own space to do that.'

Joel didn't answer, and Ingrid began to think she'd upset

him, but after a moment she realised he was thinking about her previous announcement.

'You made me a playlist!' he said. 'That's so cool. I can't wait to hear it. Let's start to shoo all these people back to their own homes and then you can have a peaceful night in the flat before we move you out tomorrow and I'll go home and have a listen to your choices. I'll come round with the van and Sam in the morning and we can start on the next chapter.'

With one last kiss, Joel went back inside, and Ingrid took a final look up at the starry December night sky. 'I've loved this interlude,' she said aloud. 'But now it's time to move on. I won't forget you, Tommy, and the good times we had. You didn't mean to leave but somehow you managed to nudge me towards a whole new set of family and friends. The Saga Louts, Uma, Maryam and Rashid, Sam and Elsie, Kate and Milo, lovely Leo and best of all, Joel. The future is out there waiting, and it's Christmas Day next week.'

'Are you talking to yourself?' Leo's voice cut into her reverie and Ingrid turned, embarrassed.

'Don't worry, I already know you're bonkers. Nice bonkers though,' Leo added, coming over to give Ingrid a hug. 'I've got news. Mum and Trev have booked a last-minute package holiday to Tenerife over Christmas. You know what that means, don't you?'

'You mean you can...?' Ingrid was suddenly too happy to speak. What a great Christmas present.

'Yes, I can be with you and Dad and Anthea instead of trying to split myself in two. I'm glad she's coming for Christmas too. Beryl's staying with her niece for a couple of days over Christmas and Winnie's going to her eldest son's house so it'll be just us four.'

'Perfect,' said Ingrid. 'Let's go and find your dad. Oh, but I guess you've told him already.'

'I have, but he's gone somewhere now. He was fiddling around with his phone as he went. I thought I heard music. I'm not sure what he's up to. Come on, let's go inside, it's freezing out here.'

Ingrid smiled to herself as she followed Leo into the shop.

'So, *do* you know why Dad dashed off like that?' Leo asked, over her shoulder.

'I think I might,' said Ingrid. 'Anyway, let's talk festive food. I'm assuming you're not expecting pizza or chilli on the big day?'

They sat down together and waited as the shop gradually emptied. Leo leaned against Ingrid and began to list all of the things she'd like to eat on Christmas Day. There was still no sign of Joel, but that was nothing to worry about. Ingrid was sure he'd be somewhere quiet, listening to his brand-new playlist, and one thing was certain. Wherever he was, Joel would be smiling.

'Are we having turkey?' Leo asked. 'And cranberry sauce and chestnut stuffing and pigs in blankets, and—'

'All of those things and more,' said Ingrid. 'The log cabin's got a great little kitchen.'

'I can help to get everything ready, and we'll set Dad to work with the washing up,' said Leo. 'We'll be right in the middle of the country park so we can have a walk and feed the ducks if we're too full afterwards. And then we'll play Monopoly and later on we'll eat lots of cheese and biscuits. I expect Anthea will want to watch *The Sound of Music* at some point, but that's okay. I can handle it.'

'You can handle anything you put your mind to, Leo, and so

can I,' said Ingrid. 'Let's go and see if the visitors have left us any mince pies. I was too busy to eat earlier.'

She got up and held out a hand to pull Leo to her feet and the girl gave her a quick hug. 'This is going to be the best Christmas ever, so long as you and Dad don't go and get all soppy on us,' Leo said. 'You don't want to embarrass Anthea, do you?'

'Embarrassing anyone is the last thing on my mind,' said Ingrid, making a mental note to tell Joel to ditch the mistletoe he'd planned to hang over the door to the cabin. There would be plenty of time for mistletoe when they were alone. For now, this was perfection.

As she and Leo walked into the shop together, Ingrid saw Beryl over by the CD player fiddling with the buttons.

'I just wanted to play this one more time. It's my favourite,' she said.

The opening bars of 'White Christmas' took Ingrid right back to winter evenings watching the old film with her mum and dad. For a few moments she was overcome with regret that these two beloved people would never meet Joel, Leo and all the others, but then she smiled as Winnie and Beryl joined hands with Anthea to warble along with Frank Sinatra. Joel came back in just as they reached the final verse and joined in with gusto, and Sam and Elsie swung each other around in their own version of a waltz.

Leo nudged Ingrid. 'I wonder if it's too late for us both to get plane tickets to Tenerife?' she muttered.

Ingrid laughed. 'You know you wouldn't change these treasures for the world,' she said. 'And neither would I. We're in exactly the right place. Now, where are those mince pies?'

* * *

MORE FROM CELIA ANDERSON

Another laugh-out-loud story of fun and friendship from Celia Anderson, *Life Begins at 50!,* is available to order now here:
www.mybook.to/Life50BackAd

INGRID'S PLAYLIST

'Don't Stop' – Fleetwood Mac
'The Right Place' – Eddi Reader
'My Love' – Wings
'Sweet Surrender' – Bread
'I'd Really Love to See You Tonight' – England Dan & John Ford Coley
'I'll Have to Say I Love You in a Song' – Jim Croce
'I Will' – The Beatles
'Crazy For You' – Madonna
'Truly Madly Deeply' – Savage Garden
'The Right Thing to Do' – Carly Simon

ACKNOWLEDGEMENTS

It was so good to be back in the village of Willowbrook to write the next one in this series after *Life Begins at 50!* and even better to know that there's going to be at least one more story set there. Although the books feature some of the same characters, each has its own newcomers and their lives are interlinked. 'No man is an island', so the quote goes, but some are harder to reach than others.

The strong links between my friends, family and new neighbours have been immensely important to me this year. The support of the kind and generous people both around me and in the Midlands town of my birth has been so very much appreciated as I settle into this lovely seaside location, a single person for the first time in many, many years. I wanted to celebrate life's various connections in Ingrid's story, and although Tommy is nothing like either of my two dear departed husbands (I know, I've probably been careless there...) the crippling, mind-blowing grief of suddenly being without your life partner is the same the world over.

It has to be said that the chief inspiration from Ingrid's story came from the giant task of downsizing when Ray and I moved 200 miles into a much smaller house. The distribution of decades of tat and treasures alike was both gruelling and liberating. It certainly clears the mind when there's only limited time to decide which items can go and which you simply can't part with. I still can't find the hoover attachments (not much sadness there) and I wish I'd kept a few more plastic boxes. Oddly, after I'd thrown most of them away, their missing lids surfaced. Hey ho. At least my dad's desk made it here, although my fine collection of hundreds of different sized envelopes had to be jettisoned. It was very satisfying to do it all again via Ingrid. She's much too classy for Tupperware.

One of the biggest changes as far as my story-creating goes is the lack of a live-in muse to bounce ideas off, sometimes in the middle of the night. My lovely agent Laura Macdougall is always willing to help when needed (although strangely, she's never offered that support in the small hours) and I have had the enormous benefit of being edited by the amazing Francesca Best at Boldwood, who at times seems to understand what I'm trying to say even before I've written it! Also, thanks go to the whole Boldwood team, as well as Cecily Blench the copyeditor, Rachel Lawston the cover designer and Candida Bradford the proofreader. Your hard work, creativity and advice has been very much appreciated.

To be in cuddling distance of my grandchildren with another baby girl on the way and to be able to laugh and cry with their lovely parents has been my saving grace in the last months. Thank you so much, Laura, Hakan and Ida and Hannah, Mark and Levi. And as always, thanks to Ray for making our lives so much more fun. When the champagne corks pop, when the candles are lit, when fresh flowers are in the vases, when the Christmas decorations come down from the loft, he'll be with us. Onwards and upwards. Some connections are too strong to lose.

ABOUT THE AUTHOR

Celia Anderson is a top ten bestselling author of women's fiction. She writes uplifting golden years fiction for Boldwood.

Sign up to Celia Anderson's newsletter and get a FREE short story!

Follow Celia on social media:

- facebook.com/CeliaAndersonAuthor
- instagram.com/cejanderson
- x.com/CeliaAnderson1
- goodreads.com/CeliaAnderson

ALSO BY CELIA ANDERSON

Life Begins at 50!

A New Lease of Life

BECOME A MEMBER OF THE SHELF CARE CLUB

The home of Boldwood's book club reads.

Find uplifting reads, sunny escapes, cosy romances, family dramas and more!

Sign up to the newsletter
https://bit.ly/theshelfcareclub